'The Lady Anne'

Gloria Berneville-Claye

Published in 2009 by New Generation Publishing

A CIP catalogue record for this title is available
from the British Library.

The Lady Anne

Douglas crouched down in the ditch next to the dirt road, his feet were in water and his uniform splattered in mud. He could hear the thud of the guns in the distance, evidence that things on the ground were changing rapidly. He screened out the gun noise and listened intently for sounds that might render immediate danger to him. He heard a rustle in the undergrowth behind him, he swung round, rifle at the ready, his eyes trying to penetrate through the curtain of green. Nothing – it must have been an animal scurrying to hide itself – just as he was doing. It was then that he heard the faint rumble which grew steadily louder, the clanking of the caterpillar tracks and the roar of the engine. Douglas sank lower into his position, he knew what it was and he wanted to avoid it at all costs.

Everything was chaotic in these last few days of war. The German forces were in full blown retreat, some in utter panic, discarding their uniforms as they fled, others trudging along in despair, all the fight gone out of them. But Douglas had a great respect for the German soldier. He had seen them as a fighting machine at first hand, a disciplined force under the right leadership. Douglas had, in fact, been monitoring just such an officer in the last few days. He was in charge of a Panzer Division, young for such a command, but the German army now had young boys and old men within its ranks. This officer had rallied his men, made sure they were fed, ordered the jettisoning of all obsolete equipment after repairing what could be salvaged. Douglas felt a slight pang of sympathy for him as he relayed the tanks' position back to his headquarters, but he hadn't hung around to witness the results brought about by the transmission of his information. He had scarpered from the area as fast as his long legs would carry him.

Douglas himself was one of the youngest officers in the S.A.S. and his team had been behind enemy lines for the last week or so, harrying the German retreat. He had ordered his group to split up in these final days and make their way back to their own lines any way they could. They were all highly trained in survival tactics and stood more chance alone than as a group. They were all in German uniform and spoke the language fluently, but if captured, they stood every

3

chance of being shot as spies. So now they were all scattered, Douglas had no idea who had survived, been injured, captured or worse.

The noise was getting nearer. Douglas parted the greenery just a smidgeon, he could see the tank commander, he looked bone weary, facing the way they had come, as was the tank's gun. Infantry limped along behind and there were stretcher cases on every level surface. Douglas covered his face as the tank trundled past as clouds of exhaust shot out of its side. He rolled over smothering a cough and touched something cold and hard, it was a discarded German helmet. It was imperative that Douglas ditched his own German uniform. His priority was to steal some civilian clothes and to make contact with his own unit. Douglas pushed off through the scrub. He wanted distance between him and the road, where there was one tank there was likely to be another. The wood thinned out after half an hour of scrambling through mud, ditches and being scratched by brambles. In front of him in the distance were farm buildings. The farmhouse looked to be in ruins, still smouldering, the outbuildings appeared to be intact – relatively! Douglas decided it was too dangerous to cover open ground in daylight, he would watch and stay put until dusk. He woke with a start. Clouds were scudding across a half moon hung low in the sky. There was no sign of life in the farm buildings, no lights to be seen anywhere. Douglas crawled forwards on his belly, nothing happened. He levered himself into a half crouch and ran hell for leather to the wall of the first building, he half expected the betraying bark of a farm dog but all was silent. He steadied his breathing, gingerly looked around the corner, the whole place looked deserted. He made for the barn door which was hanging half off its hinges and darted inside. He fell headlong over something soft on the floor. He immediately rolled over into a corner, springing to his feet, revolver in hand, but there was no sound and nothing moved. Douglas's eyes quickly became accustomed to the gloom and made out the shape he had fallen over. It was an old man. There was congealed blood on his head, by the look on his face he had died in agony. Douglas had seen too much bloodshed to feel any sympathy. He assessed the man's physique, thinner and smaller than himself, but the old man's clothes, old and ragged as they were, hung off him. Douglas quickly stripped the body, dumping his own uniform, wrist watch, and everything German, including the supposed photograph of his German family, a pretty wife and two children, which had been taken from a German prisoner, under the straw and donned the farm labourer's clothes. Not too bad, if a little short in the leg, but beggars can't be choosers in this hellhole. He kept the suicide pill of cyanide potassium he had been issued with for the time being – you never know in these uncertain times. He decided to hunker down for the rest of the night. The presence of the old man's body didn't phase him at all, and he slumbered until day break. Heaven knew where the front line was now.

Douglas awoke with pangs of hunger gnawing in his belly, he checked out the farmhouse–nothing. He decided to retrace his steps to the dirt road through the woods and was back in position by midmorning. The sound of heavy guns was now very faint and had moved on considerably since yesterday. It was not long before Douglas heard traffic noises, not a tank this time, something considerably lighter, but to which side did it belong? He squinted up the track, he could see the dust that the transport was kicking up but he couldn't make out the markings. They're jeeps – they're allies – they're Canadians! Douglas sprang out onto the road waving his arms furiously above his head; he didn't relish the idea of some trigger happy soldier raking the ditch with automatic gunfire. A jeep veered off into the side just missing him and a sergeant jumped nimbly out of the front seat. 'What the hell do you think you're doing fella? Want to get yourself killed?'

'No,' replied Douglas in an upper-crust English accent, 'I was rather hoping to cadge a lift actually old man.'

The sergeant gawped at him open mouthed, 'Who the hell are you?' he demanded. Douglas rattled off his rank and number. The sergeant levelled his rifle at his belly, 'Hands up over your head,' he commanded, 'you don't look anything like a Captain to me.' He squinted at him, taking in his dishevelled appearance. 'You a deserter then?'

Another soldier shouted down from the jeep, 'Careful Sarge, some of these Germans speak the lingo pretty well.'

'Yeh.' growled the sergeant, 'turn round and spread-eagle on the floor.' He prodded Douglas viciously in the chest. Douglas repeated his rank and number adding he was a serving S.A.S. Officer in the British Army.

'And I'm related to the King of England buddy.' replied the

sergeant, frisking Douglas for weapons. He found none. Douglas had thrown his German revolver far into the woods and dumped the suicide pill as soon as he had identified that the jeeps belonged to allied soldiers. The sergeant indicated that Douglas should stand up, he did so. The sergeant pushed him roughly towards the last jeep in the line. 'Get into the back between these two.' And to the two soldiers he said, 'secure his wrists and don't take any crap from the sucker, he'll probably claim to be Monty's right hand man.'

Douglas was indeed planning to try and pull off such a stunt but thought better of it. This hard-bitten sergeant wasn't going to be fooled by his cultivated upper crust accent, instead he repeated his rank and number again and added, 'There's a code word that will identify me.'

'What is it?' barked the sergeant.

'Boudicca.'

'What the hell is that?'

'She was a Queen of England.'

'No Queen I've ever heard of.' Then to his men, 'Take him back to H.Q. let them sort it out. We've wasted enough time here.' And he swung back into the front seat of his jeep and roared away. Douglas glanced sideways at his two guards, they were young recruits and Douglas guessed, correctly, fresh to the theatre of war. They were jumpy, but as long as he didn't make any sudden moves he judged he would be alright. Douglas relaxed, he was dying for food but even more pressing was the need for a cigarette, he would just have to wait.

Back at H.Q. tents and feeding stations had been hastily erected together with a first aid post. The walking wounded were queuing up for attention. Stretcher cases were taken straight inside the tents, German as well as the Allies. Douglas scanned the faces of the wounded men, he didn't recognize any of his group amongst them, but they could be anywhere. Captured German prisoners were being herded into makeshift compounds which were surrounded by barbed wire and armed guards. Douglas was dragged out of the back of the jeep. A British Officer strolled up and pointed to Douglas. 'Who's he then?' he enquired of the Canadian rookies. They told him the story of Douglas's capture, expecting him to be thrown into the compound with the other prisoners. The British Officer glanced across at Douglas who was just about to open his mouth, but before he could utter a word the British Officer said, 'Keep him over there near the compound and keep your eye on him, his story might be true, we have had such covert operations ongoing, but I haven't time to sort it out right now, he'll keep for a while.' He abruptly turned on his heel and disappeared into one of the tents. The two Canadians looked at each other in surprise and at Douglas with renewed interest.

'Any chance of a fag?'

The tallest of the two soldiers brought out a packet of American cigarettes, he lit two, handing one to Douglas. 'You really S.A.S.?' Douglas took a deep drag on the cigarette, relishing the burning smoke as he drew it down into his lungs, then he slowly exhaled. He looked straight into the young fresh face, smiled and tapped the side of his nose and sank down onto an upturned crate, his back against the wire of the compound and closed his eyes. He could hear the scuffling of German boots behind him. He heard one of the captives say, 'Sorry Sir.'

He was quickly reprimanded by a different voice, an authoritative voice, one used to giving commands and to being obeyed. 'Shut up Schulz, you don't know who's listening.' he hissed. Douglas slowly turned his head, but gave no sign of understanding the spoken German, and, out of the corner of his eye, he saw a German soldier with his head down, slowly moving away from another man, a man in an ordinary soldier's uniform, but given space by those around him. Douglas couldn't see this man's face but he was intrigued.

Just at that moment the British Officer appeared gesticulating for him to come forward. Douglas followed him into the tent and was invited to tell his story again. The Officer listened intently and asked Douglas who he was to report to. Douglas replied, 'You don't need to know that, just check my code word, it's Boudicca.' The Officer reached down for his brief case, he withdrew a sheaf of papers, leafed through them and withdrew a small booklet. He scrolled down the list, looked back up at Douglas, picked up a field telephone and spoke quickly and concisely to someone at the other end.

'So, you've got our Captain Coulter, you can keep him for the time being, he may be of some help to you.'

The Officer looked speculatively at Douglas. 'I expect you'll appreciate a change of clothes, a shower and a hot meal Captain Coulter?'

'Yes, I would, I'd certainly appreciate something to eat, I'm famished, but there's something odd going on in the prisoner's compound. What do you intend doing with them?'

'They're due for interrogation and then we'll send them down the line. But what do you mean - something odd!' Douglas told him what he had overheard and what he suspected.

'But if that's the case, how do you propose we suss him out? His men will protect him.'

'Shove me back outside again with a flea in my ear, I'll loiter by the gates. Bring them out for interrogation in small groups, I'll see what I can pick up, but first give me some grub.' Douglas was duly pushed out of the tent and told to be on his way; otherwise he would be put into the compound with the other prisoners. Douglas made himself scarce, but gradually sidled back to the compound gates and squatted down pretending sleep. The prisoners were taken out a few at a time. Douglas made sure he got a good look at each miserable face. On the fifth selection, he was sure he had seen one particular face quite recently. He got to his feet and shambled after them, keeping at a discreet distance. The other prisoners were trying not to show deference to one of their own but there were tell tale signs to a keen observer, and Douglas was a very keen observer. The prisoner in question was also a keen observer and he glanced back in Douglas's direction. Their eyes met for a brief second, the prisoner had brilliant piercing blue eyes. Douglas was sure. He had been watching this man through his binoculars only a couple of days ago. He had been in charge of a Panzer Division, a strange position for an ordinary soldier to occupy. Douglas loitered by the tent opening where the initial questioning was taking place. An official translator was present as was a medical orderly. Name, rank and number were the only information forthcoming. This information was duly recorded and the prisoners moved out, but one particular prisoner was detained. Douglas had made sure the British Officer in charge of the interrogation had seen the pre-arranged signal; he had dropped his cigarette into the dirt and stamped it out with his left foot, a sign which singled out the Panzer Commander.

Douglas, now back in uniform, was being driven back to his unit. He was eager to be re-united with his group. They would undergo a session of debriefing, then be given a period of rest and recuperation.

Events were moving rapidly now, everyone expected the war to be over in a matter of days. On the 27th March, Field Marshall Walter

Model disbanded his army group and walked into the forest and shot himself. On the same day the allies crossed the Rhine. By April the 11th the Americans were only fifty miles from Berlin. The Soviets were poised at the river Elbe. On April 16th the Soviets commenced the deadly bombardment on Berlin which caused massive destruction and devastation to the city. Thousands of the inhabitants were killed and many more were wounded and would later die of their injuries. Hospitals were no longer operating. All systems in the City were failing. The Goebells family had joined Hitler in the bunker beneath the Berlin streets. On April the 25th the Americans and the Soviets met up at Torgau. There were scenes of dancing and jubilation amongst the soldiers of both armies. Hitler was dead. He had committed suicide on the 30th of April. His body together with that of his recently married wife, Eva Brun, were doused in petrol and burned beyond recognition. Germany was in turmoil. Eisenhower's insistence that the end of the war could only be concluded by the unconditional surrender of the Germans had resulted in chaos between the German High Command. It fell to General Joedel to negotiate the end of hostilities which he did in Rheims on the 6th of May. On the 8th of May General Joedel signed the unconditional surrender with the allies, but significantly, not with the Russians, which gave them the perfect excuse to overrun Berlin raping and looting with impunity as they went. They marched many of the German prisoners of war as well as the captured Russian prisoners to camps in Russia and Siberia, their futures uncertain. Eisenhower had made the decision, which many of his staff disagreed with, that the Soviets could take Berlin. The Russians immediately turned their backs on the promises made at Yalta and set up a puppet Soviet style government in Berlin. The big land grab was under way. Refugees were everywhere. Violence and famine stalked the streets of Berlin. People with grey faces hid in cellars and bombed out houses, only coming out in a desperate search for food and fuel. Apathy and hopelessness and a pervading fear of the Russians were everywhere.

CHAPTER 2

The noise assaulted Douglas's ears and it was bone chillingly cold with his back pressed against the metal frame. He was being buffeted against his fellow passengers, their kit piled in the centre of the fuselage. The Dakota D.C. 3 was descending through the morning mist towards Northolt Aerodrome. He looked out of the port hole and saw the newly laid tarmac rushing up to meet them. Then the bang as they hit the ground, the plane rose again before coming down with another thud. Not a text book landing he didn't think, but they were on the ground and slowing down. They came to a standstill near to a group of officers who were there to meet them. The men grabbed their kit and formed an orderly line to disembark. They saluted the welcoming committee and made for the Aerodrome buildings. There was excited chatter amongst the men; all were pleased to be back home in Britain. Some were due for demob, some for redeployment. Others, like Douglas, had been given a week's leave with orders to report to their respective headquarters when it would be decided what to do with them. Some of Douglas's platoon were going out on the razzle-dazzle in London before heading home. Others couldn't wait to see their families and were heading straight off.

Douglas hadn't been invited to join his men, but it didn't worry him. He wasn't the most popular Officer; there was just something about Captain Coulter. His men didn't doubt his courage under fire, or his ability to make swift decisions in times of stress and danger. No, his unpopularity stemmed from his behaviour in company, particularly in the company of the ladies. They soon realized that no-one's girlfriend, sister or wife was off limits to Captain Coulter. He charmed them all regardless of the consequences. He seemed to have a strange fascination for them. He was undoubtedly handsome, tall, well built with dark brilliantined hair swept back in the fashion of the day, and had a thin pencil moustache to finish things off. He looked like a film star, David Niven or Errol Flynn and the ladies flocked to him.

Douglas had the precious rail pass safely in the top pocket of his jacket and he made his way to the railway station as soon as they had been given clearance. He settled himself into a corner seat in a first class compartment and the train chugged out of the station. The third class was overflowing but here in first there was more room to stretch out and the rhythmic movement of the train soon lulled Douglas to sleep.

His parents had retired to run a little country pub in the West Country, The Star Inn. His father had been a career soldier like himself. He had distinguished himself in battle and had been awarded the M.B.E. He had retired with Officer Rank and a small pension. He knew his father would be pleased to see him but he wasn't given to great shows of emotion. His mother on the other hand would be over the moon and puffed up with pride. Her soldier son as she always referred to him, home for a whole week, a week, to pamper and fuss over him as she had always done since he was a little boy. From the day he was born he had been the apple of his mother's eye, he could do no wrong in her eyes. She had tried to mollycoddle him, but his desire for adventure and mischief proved too strong for her. He was always in the thick of the rugby scrum, he adored sport of any kind; he had a very combative nature.

Douglas awoke with a start, it was the guard, 'Sir, this is where you change trains.' Douglas smiled and slipped a half crown into the man's hand. He collected his bags and changed to the little country train which would stop at every tiny station on the line. Never mind, he would reach his destination before dark. The whistle blew and the train threw great clouds of white smoke into the air as it pulled out of the station. This was the train that catered for the middle class matrons who had been out shopping for the day, but these days there were fewer of them. The clerks and bank managers and country solicitors all used this train so there was plenty of activity at each stop.

Eventually Douglas reached his destination. He had spotted the little Austin car his mother tootled around in, so she was here to meet him as he knew she would be. It was a warm late spring evening and he spotted his mother waiting on the platform. She was wearing a full skirted summer dress with bright flowers dotted all over it, and a little mink jacket to top it off. She wasn't wearing the jacket because it was cold; it was more of a statement to those who saw her, that she could afford a mink jacket. Douglas disembarked, a tall figure, immaculate in his uniform, easily spotted amongst the dark suited battalions of office workers. His mother was waving a white handkerchief, but she stayed where she was at the entrance to the station. She wanted as many people as possible to witness the tearful reunion of her hero soldier son and his doting mother. She clung to his arm as they made their way to the little car. Douglas drove, his mother beside him, chided him not to drive too fast. They reached The Star Inn, where, at the sound of the car's engine, his father came out to greet them. He shook Douglas's hand firmly and patted his arm. He wasn't overtly demonstrative, but he looked into his son's face and asked quietly how he was. Douglas was aware what his father alluded to, he had also been in the front line in battle. He reassured him, 'I'm fine father.' His father nodded and retrieved his bags from the boot of the little car.

'Take them up to his room Stephen, I want to show my son off to our regulars.' And she took Douglas by the arm and marched him into the pub.

Marianne Coulter was still a good looking woman, but now past her best. She had always had pretentions above her current station but her aspirations in life had been sadly dashed. She was an unashamed social climber. As a young woman she had been the centre of attention in her limited circle, flighty and full of fun. She lived with her parents in the army town of Aldershot so there were always plenty of young men on hand to dance attendance on the young Marianne. They spent what money they had on her and she was always the belle of the ball at the frequent dances held at the army camp. Her attention was drawn to a handsome young soldier, Stephen Coulter. He was sporting new shiny corporal stripes on his arm. He was more serious than most of her conquests but he presented a challenge to her. She set about being noticed by him. She was gay and amusing and cast flirtatious looks in his direction. She danced all night and made sure he saw how many partners she had to choose from. Marianne knew jealousy was a powerful emotion. Quite a few of her admirers had come to blows over her. Marianne was a tease! Stephen was captivated from the start. Marianne thought that Stephen, who unlike the others, was a much more serious young man, was going places. If she could hang onto his coat tails he would propel her into the social circle she so aspired to join. After a whirlwind courtship, they were married.

It was soon apparent that this young couple were not ideally suited. She wanted to be out partying every night, he enjoyed reading books. She also enjoyed spending money, so the Coulters were nearly always short of funds which created tension in the household. Stephen Coulter soon tired of Marianne's pouting when she couldn't get her own way. What had seemed so alluring had grown cold very quickly. Stephen was very aware he was a great disappointment to his wife. He had achieved promotion to Colour Sergeant but had then hit a ceiling. What Marianne never realized was that she was the drag on Stephen's coat tails that held him back. She simply was not considered to be suitable material to be an Officer's wife. Stephen however, who was of the old school, had a granite sense of moral duty. He had sworn an oath for better or worse, in sickness and in health. Unfortunately it had turned out to be 'for worse' but Stephen had made his bed and he must lay on it. For years the couple made each other miserable but then, suddenly, out of the blue, Marianne was pregnant.

The birth of Douglas Coulter changed Marianne's life. She had someone to focus all her attention on. This little someone didn't judge her; he cooed and smiled at her. She was able to mould him into the type of person she was, to instil her values into him. To his shame, Stephen was relieved when Douglas came along, the constant pressure of his wife's nagging was lifted somewhat. As time went by, he became more and more distant from the two of them. But one thing though, he had insisted upon, and that was he was determined to teach his son to ride a pony. It had always been a solace to him to go out in the early morning and ride hell for leather on the back of a good horse. One could temporarily forget one's troubles with the wind blowing through your hair and the thrumming of a horse's hooves in your ears. Douglas was plonked onto the back of a pony when he was only three years old. He loved it from the outset and his father taught him well, despite Marianne's constant hand wringing for her precious son's safety. As Douglas grew up and showed an interest in a career in the Army, Stephen encouraged him; he thought the discipline enforced during his training might iron out the kinks and flaws in his character. What it did was to increase his desire for danger and adventure.

Stephen returned to his position behind the bar, he glanced over to where mother and son were holding court at the end of the bar. He noticed that a bottle of his best champagne had been opened and the little group were toasting the return of the warrior son. Marianne was glued to Douglas's side and hung on his every word. She was loud and demonstrative, she looked up, saw Stephen watching them. 'Stephen, bring us some more champagne, this is a special night.' Stephen knew from experience that all the next seven nights were going to be special

13

nights. He didn't begrudge his son his celebrations, he knew from his contacts in the war office that Douglas had acquitted himself well in the theatre of war. They had also hinted that Douglas was being considered for a sensitive appointment. He did as he was told. It was quite a night at The Star Inn; the drinking went on until the early hours of the morning. At least a dozen bottles of champagne had been consumed as well as numerous shorts. At last the party broke up and Stephen was able to secure his pub.

Next morning Douglas woke late, his head was a little fuzzy from the intake of so much champagne, but he had time to recover, nothing arduous was expected of him in the next few days. His eyes squinted against the sun streaming in through the bedroom window. He knew his mother would be alert to any noises coming from his room, when she heard them she would appear with his breakfast. He hoisted himself up on his elbow, plumped up his pillows and leaned back. Ten minutes later his mother appeared with his breakfast on a tray, farm cured bacon, two fried eggs which had been collected that morning and plenty of field mushrooms. She had also brought up the morning paper that no one else was allowed to read until he had finished with it. He gave her a big beaming smile, 'Aren't I a lucky boy to have such a mother as you.' He was rewarded by a quick kiss on the forehead.

'You just relax son, you deserve all the attention I can give you after all you've been through.'

Douglas finally showed himself in the bar during the lunchtime session. He was wearing full uniform, his Sam Browne shone and his shoes had been polished to perfection by his mother. If Stephen Coulter thought he was going to get some help in running the pub, he was to be sadly disappointed. After consuming a 'hair of the dog' as Douglas put it, he asked his mother if he could borrow her car.

'Of course darling, but don't drive too fast will you, our local bobby is a bit fierce when it comes to speeding.' She gave him the keys, and he kissed her on the cheek, waved cheerily to his father and was gone. He didn't appear again until after ten o'clock, just before closing time. But he took his place in the corner beside his mother and regaled her with his exploits of the day. He told her he had met up with some friends. They had motored to the coast and had had a meal out at a friendly little place at a village he couldn't remember the name of. Most of it was true, except the 'friends' were an attractive young woman who had been in the bar the previous night. Her husband had been ordered to Palestine to deal with the troubles there.

The locals flocked around Douglas, firstly because he was a welcome diversion from the monotony of their lives, and secondly, because there was a prospect of a free drink. Douglas was very generous with his father's hospitality. He had a slate, which his father knew, from previous experience, would never be wiped clean, except by him. As the week went on, it was noticeable that the clientele of 'The Star Inn' had changed somewhat. There were more single ladies, and married ones for that matter, whose husbands were occupied elsewhere, in evidence. But none of them could dislodge his mother from his side. She was like the Queen Bee holding court. Each day Douglas borrowed his mother's car and 'entertained' a different young woman. It was too dangerous, Douglas reasoned, to see the same girl twice in a small place like this; they might have 'expectations'. He was also careful not to show too much attention to any one of them at the public bar, he didn't want tantrums of jealousy. His mother took him aside one night and told him to be careful of the local female brigade, 'Not one of them is worth your attention my darling.'

'Don't worry mother,' he said with a smile, 'I'm always careful, very careful.' She patted his arm. His leave sped by and Douglas's mother drove him to the station early in the morning. The commuters were much in evidence and Marianne Coulter clung to her son, wiping away the odd tear that she so gallantly tried to stem, with a white lace handkerchief. Marianne liked an audience. The train arrived, the other passengers made for third class. Douglas strolled to the first class compartment, gave his mother a final hug, promising to come home again as soon as he could, he got in and slammed the door shut behind him. He hung out of the window as the train pulled out, waving to his distraught mother. When she was out of sight, he settled down in the corner seat, put his long legs up on the other side and closed his eyes.

Douglas had been ordered to report to Headquarters and he strode up the steps two at a time. The soldier on guard duty asked to see his pass and moved aside to let him through, giving him a smart salute as he did so. In the foyer, there was a pretty young corporal behind the desk wrestling with a number of files and an old typewriter. Douglas showed her his pass and one of his most winning smiles.

'Captain Coulter,' she consulted a list in front of her. 'Room twenty two, second floor then turn right, third on the left.' Douglas tapped his cap with his swagger stick and rewarded her with another smile, and made for the stairs. He turned round, she was watching him. She blushed and quickly looked down at the papers in front of her. Douglas was satisfied. He reached room twenty two, and knocked lightly on the door. It was immediately opened by an adjutant. The occupants of the room all turned around as he entered. They each had a sherry glass in their hand. His Commanding Officer, Brigadier Forsythe came forward a pace or two towards him. Douglas stood to attention and saluted. 'Yes, yes, at ease Captain Coulter, you know Wing commander Latimer I believe.'

'Yes sir.' The Wing Commander nodded in Douglas's direction.

'This is Captain Waverley.' The Captain, wearing a naval uniform acknowledged him, but gave him a sceptical look. The third person present was wearing civvies. From the cut of his suit Douglas deduced he was not English, another give away was the crew cut. The man was regarding him very carefully, weighing him up. Brigadier Forsythe introduced him, 'This is Colonel Mason.' He stepped forward and shook Douglas's hand, looking deep into his eyes, he had a firm handshake but he didn't say anything.

'Pleased to meet you Sir.' said Douglas politely.

'Colonel Mason is with the Allied Military Government in Berlin, General Eisenhower appointed the Colonel himself, his particular expertise is in reconstruction and I don't need to tell you Captain what a mess Berlin is in at present.'

'No Sir.'

'I want you to be our Liaison Officer with our American cousins, in that capacity you will be working with Colonel Mason.'

'Yes Sir.' Douglas noted the phrase, working with, not under the command of, it was very significant.

'You can pick up your orders at the desk, but in the meantime you have a forty eight hour pass. You haven't time to go home though; you must be on the flight to Berlin with Colonel Mason on Friday. The flight leaves at ten hundred hours.'

'Yes Sir, thank you Sir.' Douglas saluted. But the Brigadier hadn't quite done with him.

'There's just one other matter Captain Coulter, you are to report to the parade ground tomorrow morning at nine hundred hours sharp.

General North is presenting you and some of your colleagues with the Military Cross. Congratulations Captain.'

Douglas's eyes widened in surprise: 'Thank you Sir.'

Brigadier Forsythe smiled, 'Enjoy your leave Captain.'

Douglas was a controversial choice for this sensitive appointment. It hadn't been unanimous but Brigadier Forsythe thought he was the right man for the job. He was an accomplished linguist, was a bit of a renegade and took short cuts. He was no respecter of red tape or rank, but he had a nose for things people were trying to hide and could get to the nub of a problem quickly. He could think on his feet which was a great attribute and he wasn't afraid to act accordingly.

The Wing Commander whispered in the Brigadier's ear, 'It's an interesting appointment Freddie.' The Brigadier nodded.

Douglas walked slowly down the stairs; he approached the desk where the pretty corporal had a folder containing his orders waiting for him.

'I have your orders here Captain.'

He held out his hand making sure he brushed her hand ever so lightly, and whispered in her ear, 'And I have an order for you, meet me this evening at twenty hundred hours outside the Cafe Royale.' She blushed bright red. He winked at her as he turned away. Outside he went into the nearest chemist and bought a packet of 'johnnies.' He thought of the boy-scout's motto, 'Be prepared.' and smiled, you never know your luck.

Douglas was waiting on the tarmac to board the U.S. transport plane. He had read and thoroughly digested his orders, as always, it was what was to be read between the lines of the carefully worded document that was interesting. He had been transferred to the intelligence branch as the intelligence liaison Officer in the combined services. He was to be working in the detailed Interrogation Centre which was charged with flushing out the truth from the numerous intelligence operatives, spies and pathological liars that were awash in Berlin right now. The journey back to Berlin was much more comfortable than the journey out had been. Douglas decided he must always try to travel with Senior Officers in future.

Walking through the devastated streets of Berlin, Douglas had to concede it was not a pretty sight, if this was the aftermath of war, Douglas was glad he was on the winning side. There was hardly a building standing, old women and children were picking through the rubble to salvage anything that might be useful, saleable or swopable. Fights broke out over the smallest thing, there was no such thing as ladies and children first here. It was the one who was the most powerful who came away with the goodies. Berlin was a boiling cauldron of refugees of all nationalities, many from Eastern Europe who had been deported to the camps and others from all over Europe who had been used as slave labour. The Red Cross and other volunteer agencies were completely overwhelmed by people wanting handouts, desperately wanting to find relatives or to find out what had happened to them, and most of all by people trying to go home. The dislocation in Europe was unprecedented. Naturally, there were others who took advantage of this chaos. The black marketers, thieves and hustlers were having a field day. There were prostitutes of both sexes plying their trade. Spies and counter spies, wheeler dealers, smugglers, middle men and arms dealers, all making huge profits. The city was an international clearing house where information was bought and sold, where people were pitted against each other or co-operating in a thin veneer of friendship to gain an advantage for themselves. It was against this backdrop that the Allied Military Government was endeavouring to bring about a semblance of order and reconstruction. To be a member of that organization was to weald unlimited influence and power and Douglas was part of it.

Douglas himself, was quite a complex character, his vices were as extreme as his virtues. His mother had had an early influence on him. She had instilled in him the love of money and the desire to move in the highest social circles. But he was a very different character to her. He was intelligent, cool and self possessed, yet subject to mercurial mood changes. He was also full of laughter and mischief and able to talk on almost any subject. He was a man to whom the presence of danger was essential, a hard character full of dash and verve. And above all else, he was irresistible to women. A pretty face would always claim Douglas's attention.

The interrogation centre where Douglas worked was located on the outskirts of Berlin. The sessions were held in large hangers with desks along one end. A yellow line had been drawn ten yards in front, and behind which, the queues of prisoners awaiting their turn to be processed snaked out to the back of the hanger. The interrogations were being conducted by the Americans. Douglas was the liaison Officer for British Intelligence and in that capacity had access to all the files and the information collated at these sessions. He was strolling slowly behind the interrogators with his swagger stick under his arm. He was watching the proceedings and listening to snatches of conversations, ready to be called on in cases of difficulty in interpretation. The files for each prisoner containing any known history were piled on the left hand side of the desk. When the interrogation was completed they were placed on the right hand side of the desk together with the questionnaire, the comments of the interrogator and his recommendations for further action and follow up procedures as necessary. These could include immediate imprisonment pending trial for war crimes or recommended for release as appropriate. They were then collected at regular intervals by the clerks for vetting by a senior Officer, Douglas being one of them. Each prisoner was given a different coloured docket which he had to hand to the guard on duty as he left the hanger. The Americans were particularly on the look out for scientists who had been involved in the rocket development site at Peenemunde, also in advanced fuel systems, radar guidance, advanced weapon systems and most definitely those involved with the development of the atomic bomb. These people were to be immediately transported to the United States and offered immunity and protection with a new identity if necessary, but only if they agreed to work for the U.S.A. All this information on the activities of the Americans was compiled by Douglas and sent back in his reports to his superiors in London.

Douglas strolled back the way he had come and looked along the lines of those prisoners still waiting to be questioned. He noticed one prisoner in particular, he was now wearing the correct uniform for his rank although it was stained and a little ragged. It was the Panzer Commander he had picked out at the British compound a couple of months ago. He wondered why he had ended up here to be questioned by the Americans. He saw a flicker of recognition in the man's eyes. On impulse, Douglas decided to conduct the interrogation of this particular prisoner himself. He approached the desk and tapped the interrogator on duty on the shoulder. 'I'll take over from you for an hour or so, you can take a break.' The interrogator didn't need asking twice, he was dying for a cigarette.

'O.K. Sir, thank you.' He knew Douglas was an experienced operator and linguist. 'I'll go get myself some chow.'

'No need to hurry.' Douglas sat at the desk and pulled the relevant folder over and opened it. There were two photographs, face full frontal and a side view. He looked smarter than he appeared now. He needed a hair cut! His name was Dieter von Rheinhart, born into an aristocratic family whose estates were near Bremen. He was the second son. He had volunteered for the Waffen S.S. at the outbreak of hostilities. His elder brother had been killed in the first months on the Russian front. He was known to be fluent in Italian and Dutch, possibly English as well but he hadn't been heard using it. In these circumstances it was a good idea to keep quiet about it if possible thought Douglas. That's how you can pick up snippets of information. He read on, there was no known connection to the Gestapo or to the concentration camps. He had been awarded the Iron Cross in 1944. Douglas looked up from the file. The man's hair was wiry and almost white in colour. His eyes a bright blue, he was a little taller than Douglas but only by an inch or two. He could definitely do with a hair cut. Douglas gestured for him to come forward and sit opposite him. They stared at each other for a while. Neither showing any discomfort. Douglas started the interview. He conducted it in German. Dieter von Rheinhart gave clear and concise answers. He showed a little surprise when Douglas didn't pursue a particular line of questioning that he might have done. The interrogation lasted just over twenty minutes. Douglas wrote his conclusions and recommendation in clear handwriting in English at the bottom of the sheet. He sat back, leaving the file open in the middle of the desk. He knew Dieter could see it even if it was upside down. He saw the flicker of understanding in his eyes. Douglas wrote out a white docket to give Dieter. As he handed it to him he said in a very low voice in Dutch, 'When I finish here, I like to go to unwind at the Rattskellar. Do you know where it is?' Dieter responded with an almost imperceptible nod. 'I'm usually there by eighteen hundred hours.' And he waved him away.

He took the next file and motioned the soldier to come forward. He conducted another three interviews, the last one was suspected of being a guard at Auschwitz/Birkenau concentration camp. Of course he denied it. The horrors perpetrated in these camps was now public knowledge in the military as well as in the Civilian population so anyone being found to have any connection to them, however tenuous, could expect no mercy. And so it was with Douglas, he gave the man a red docket. The original interrogator returned and took over from Douglas. He had done four cases for him; he looked at the recommendations of each. Two white dockets, one pink and a red. He looked at the red docket closely and nodded in agreement.

Douglas, still in uniform, was sitting at a table in the Rattskellar. He had ordered his usual coffee and cognac, it was real coffee not the terrible ersatz stuff the population of Berlin were now forced to drink. He was leaning back with his long legs stretched out in front of him. He was suddenly aware of somebody standing behind him. He looked round, already on his guard. It was Dieter von Rheinhart, he was also still in uniform. He must have entered by another door because Douglas was facing the entrance to the main street. Douglas asked him to sit and gestured for the waiter who speedily responded. The Allies were the masters here now! 'Two coffees and two cognacs.' The waiter returned and put a coffee and a cognac in front of each Officer. If he thought it strange to see a British Officer and a German Officer at the same table he had more sense than to show it. These were strange times in Berlin, and it was none of his business. The scrabble was on for the almighty American Dollar and it was the British Officer who had the dollars in his pocket. Douglas was the first one to break the ice, 'I didn't really expect to see you.'

'Really, then why did you tell me you would be here?'

Douglas chuckled but didn't answer. Dieter took a sip of his coffee, he savoured it, real coffee, he hadn't tasted one in months. 'Why did you recommend me for release today?'

Douglas considered this question for a moment before replying. 'Because you were a good officer, I saw you in the forest, you looked after your men and they respected you.'

'Are you telling me you tried to kill me, and now you want to save me? Why?'

'I wanted to kill you because you were the enemy, it was my duty. You don't seem to me to be the enemy any more.'

'But you also exposed me at the British camp.'

'I wondered if you'd sussed me out. What did I do wrong? It's a case of professional pride you understand.'

Dieter took a sip of his cognac, he let it burn down his throat.

21

'You weren't subservient enough for a German farm labourer.' Douglas laughed out loud. The waiter looked up.

'What are you going to do now?'

'I'm going home, home to Bremen.' He finished his coffee and tossed back the last of the cognac.

'Another?'

'No, no thank you. It's probably not a good idea for me to stay too long in your company I think. You are responsible for my release. They may think I have bribed you.'

Douglas laughed again. He liked this German Officer. He stood up and offered Dieter his hand. Dieter took it. 'Well, good luck. If you ever need a subservient farm labourer, I'm usually to be found here around this time.' Dieter smiled, he clicked his heels, saluted, turned and left. Douglas sat down again, waved to the waiter and ordered another cognac.

CHAPTER 3

Dieter made his way home to Bremen. He was now in civvies. He stood outside the ruins of the Gatehouse. The large iron gates guarding the entrance to the drive had long since gone, taken for the war effort along with any other railings and metal work that could be found. He slowly walked up the tree lined driveway. Those trees that had stood for hundreds of years were now blasted and twisted stumps. Some had been hacked away for firewood or for timbers for the local people to rebuild their ruined homes. He reached the bend in the drive. He should have had a lovely view of the house from here. Instead he looked upon a pile of stones. A wall or two were still standing like broken jagged teeth against the skyline.

Dieter sat down on the grass. He thought of his life here before the war. He had had a privileged upbringing. His brother and he had had private tutors, they had been taught French, Italian and English. For a very short time Dieter and his brother had been sent to an English Public School to perfect the language, they both hated it and returned to Germany after only one term. They had travelled extensively with and without their parents. There were flunkeys to wait on them at every turn. They rode out nearly every day and swam in the lake. Their parents gave extravagant parties and thought nothing of it. The best champagne and food was available at all times. His mother wore the latest Paris fashions and had the most exquisite jewellery made for her by the finest craftsman in Amsterdam.

Dieter and his family had observed the rise of fascism from a lofty distance. They had little time for the posturing brown shirts. He regarded anti-Semitism as vulgar and Hitler as an upstart. And then the war came and above all else his family were patriots. Things went on as normal for quite a while at home, except of course both Dieter and his brother had immediately volunteered for the Military, they were both destined to go there anyway, it was just a little sooner than expected, particularly for Dieter being the youngest. Things went well for quite a while, then gradually all the able bodied retainers were recruited into the army, then the family cars were commandeered for the war effort. That was when the gates disappeared as well. All the valuable paintings, antiques, silver and the best china were stored up in the attics. These things had surrounded Dieter all his life; he had just taken them all for granted as his right. Eventually all the staff was laid off. The last one remaining was his father's chauffeur who helped look after the old man. Dieter's mother was quite a bit younger than her husband but it was a love match, unusual for those times. It was quite awhile before news filtered through that his brother had been killed on the Russian front. His parents were devastated and never really recovered. Conditions were so bad out there that it was a wonder anyone survived at all. It was a disaster of monstrous proportions for the German Army and a turning point in the war. Then one day, after a bombing raid on Bremen, a stray American bomber flew low over the house. It had been raked by anti-aircraft fire and left a trail of fuel and flames from its rear. The crew unloaded the last of their payroll on the house. It was a direct hit, he was sure his mother and father wouldn't have known anything about it, at least he hoped that was the case. The only one to survive was the chauffeur who had been in the stables at the time the bombs hit. The plane had crashed into the lake killing all on board. Dieter got to his feet, there was nothing to be gained here. There was no sign of any livestock, horses and cattle long gone. The stables had fared a little better than the house, but every thing of value had been destroyed or looted. Dieter couldn't blame the locals, they needed roofs over their heads but so did he.

One evening Douglas was relaxing in the Rattskellar after a taxing day at the interrogation centre with his usual cup of coffee and cognac chaser, out of the corner of his eye he spotted a German workman loitering outside in the street. Under his cap Douglas could just see a wisp of blond hair. The man looked undecided; then he suddenly made his mind up and headed for the Rattskellar. As soon as Douglas saw his eyes he knew who it was. Dieter had lost weight, he looked hungry, but then who didn't in Berlin in these times. His cheeks were a little sunken and his clothes were shabby but the eyes were as bright as ever. Dieter entered the cafe and looked around. Douglas wasn't hard to spot. Douglas pushed a chair back as a sign Dieter should join him. He called the waiter over and ordered a coffee and cognac for Dieter. Neither of them had broken the ice as yet, Dieter put his hands around the mug of coffee as if warming them. He savoured the aroma but didn't drink it. 'I need help to find somewhere to stay.' he said simply.

'How was Bremen?' Douglas asked.

'Much the same as here.'

'And your home?'

'Flattened.'

If Dieter thought he would illicit sympathy from Douglas he was mistaken.

'You were on the losing side.'

'Yes.' Dieter couldn't resist the coffee any longer. He took a sip, then another.

Douglas sat back and studied him, 'I can probably help, but what would I get in return?'

Dieter's mouth tightened, but he controlled his emotions. He didn't want to antagonize Douglas. He needed a favour from him. 'I was never a lover of the Nazi regime-----.'

Douglas cut in, 'Any supporters of the Nazi regime are very hard to find these days.'

Dieter looked at the floor. He had to acknowledge the truth of that statement.

'I am not a spy. I won't do anything or say anything to harm my country. But I need to eat, I know plenty of secrets about people I do not consider to be patriots.'

It was Douglas's turn to look at the floor, 'I can probably help, come back in two or three days, I will have sorted something out by then.' Douglas didn't want to seem too eager to help Dieter; he needed to stay in control. It wouldn't hurt Dieter to have to wait a little while longer. Dieter had finished his coffee and he downed the cognac in one go which made him catch his breath a little. Douglas knew Dieter had hated having to come to him, he must be desperate indeed.

Dieter was desperate. He had been staying with his father's chauffeur in a poky little room in the centre of Berlin. There was only one bed which Dieter insisted the old man should have. Dieter was sleeping on the hard cold floor. All the facilities of the once proud house were now shared between three families. There was hardly any food to go round and Dieter felt terrible about having to deprive the loyal old man of his meagre rations. He had decided to move out and try to fend for himself. Trouble was, there was no accommodation to be found and, there were no jobs to be had. Dieter had been used to a life of luxury and wealth, the reality of life in Berlin and his home town of Bremen was a chilling shock to the system. Douglas was Dieter's last resort, he had swallowed his pride to come and see him. Douglas watched him cross the road and disappear down the street. When he was sure he was out of sight Douglas got up and left the cafe. He had got things to do - strings to pull.

A week later, Douglas was wondering if he had overplayed his hand. There had been no sign of Dieter. Berlin was a dangerous place, especially on the streets at night. Douglas speculated that anything could have happened to him - he could be laying in an alleyway with his throat cut. He wasn't though; he was shambling in through the back entrance of the cafe. Douglas had just decided to leave when he caught sight of him in the mirror on the wall. Douglas sat down again and ordered two coffees and croissants; he didn't order cognacs for them. Douglas reasoned that if Dieter really had been living on the streets, a cognac on an empty stomach wouldn't do him any good at all. He looked thinner and dirtier and hungrier than before. Douglas pushed his croissant over on to Dieter's plate. Dieter fell upon them ravenously, but he sipped at the coffee. The blue eyes were as fierce as ever. When Dieter had swallowed the last crumbs of the croissants Douglas said, 'I think I have found just the place for you. I want you to leave before me and wait on the corner of Wallstrasse and Grunstrasse. Do you know where I mean?'

'Yes,' replied Dieter, 'I know this town backwards now.'

Douglas had to smile. 'I will be about ten minutes behind you.' He paused, 'Would you like a refill before you go?'

'No. I don't want to be seen around here too often.' Dieter got up to go, but as an afterthought he turned around and said, 'but thank you.' Douglas watched him walk in the opposite direction to the one he had indicated, he would get there, by a circuitous route, but Douglas was certain he would get there. Douglas stayed where he was until he was sure no-one had followed Dieter. Then he himself left walking in the opposite direction to the one which Dieter had taken. This ruse wouldn't fool an accomplished foot soldier, but one on his own would find it difficult to follow divergent paths. As Douglas neared his destination, Dieter was nowhere to be seen. Douglas didn't slow down and Dieter materialized out of nowhere at his side. Douglas ducked down an alleyway halfway down the street. The apartment he had found was on the ground floor in the old Jewish quarter, the area was extremely rundown but most of the buildings amazingly, were still standing. The beauty of this place from Douglas's point of view was that it had a back door leading onto another alleyway, so the occupant or visitors could come and go undetected – hopefully! Douglas opened the stout heavy wooden door. A musty smell assailed his nostrils. It was a one bed-roomed apartment. In the bedroom was an old iron bedstead, a relatively new mattress with some coarse army blankets on it. In the other room were two old scuffed leather armchairs in front of a decrepit electric fire. It would at least warm the place providing there was an electricity supply; cuts were all too frequent a hazard. The small cooker ran on bottled gas. Douglas had provided matches, a supply of candles and a torch with a spare battery. In a corner was a small wooden table with two rickety dining chairs. To complete the furnishings there was a wall cupboard. Dieter opened the doors to reveal tins of army rations, bits of crockery and a packet of real coffee, sugar and powdered milk. A small bottle of cognac and two glasses nestled in one corner. Dieter turned round and looked questioningly at Douglas.

'I like something reasonable to drink when I come visiting.' Douglas placed the keys to the place on the table, 'I'll be back tomorrow; I've organized some translation work for you to do. The Military Government are churning out leaflets and orders for the civilian population by the score, our people can't keep up. If you do a satisfactory job, I'll give you a work permit and that'll enable you to apply for a ration book. At least it will keep the wolf from the door.' Dieter turned round and was just about to say something. Douglas held up his hand, 'Don't,' he said, and with a twinkle in his eye, 'I might change my mind.' Dieter cracked a smile, he held out his hand to Douglas, who took it. Douglas threw Dieter a smart salute and left. Dieter immediately turned to the cupboard, quickly selected a few tins and had his first warm meal in days.

Douglas was as good as his word, he brought a couple of day's work to start with and when these proved to be satisfactorily dealt with, he brought more. Gradually they built up a rapport between them. They would sometimes sit companionably together on an evening enjoying a glass of cognac. Douglas kept Dieter supplied with cognac as alcohol was prohibitively expensive on the black market. Douglas had sussed out his own supplies of drink and American cigarettes and had a nice little sideline going with a corrupt American sergeant. Dollars were a very handy commodity just then in Germany. Dieter was looking more prosperous these days, he had put on a little weight and had ditched his workman's clothes. However, Douglas was not ready to be seen out in public with him yet.

On one of these little evening sessions, Douglas broached the subject of his work at the interrogation centre. There was a protracted case going on. Douglas's sixth sense told him all was not as it seemed with this individual, but he had been unable to trip the fellow up. The American's were all for releasing the prisoner. Douglas asked Dieter if he had ever come across his name. Dieter was quiet for a while and then he admitted he had. 'Would you consider him to be a patriot Dieter?'

'No,' he said emphatically, 'No, I would not.' Both Douglas and Dieter were painfully aware of what had gone on in the name of the German State and in Dieter's eyes it had shamed his beloved Country.

'To bring him to book Dieter, I need to know what he was involved in.' Dieter told him. After the first time, Dieter found it easier to off load some of the guilty secrets he knew. Douglas never pressed him if he was reluctant to divulge anything.

Douglas was supplying London with a wealth of good quality information. It was a feather in his cap that he had unmasked a major war criminal right under the noses of the Americans. His boss, Brigadier Forsythe felt vindicated in his controversial choice of his liaison Officer. Douglas's relationship with Colonel Mason was another matter however. Mason didn't trust Douglas one inch. Douglas was living way beyond the means of a mere Army Captain. He didn't know if Douglas had independent means or not, but he strongly suspected Douglas of being involved in smuggling rackets, particularly cigarettes, which in some quarters were being used as currency. If so, he wouldn't be the first, many of the Colonel's own countrymen were up to their crooked little necks in the trade. What was much more worrying to Colonel Mason was that he suspected Douglas of accepting bribes. Being part of the Allied Military Government bestowed a lot of privileges and power on the individual. With this power went responsibility, in the wrong hands it could easily be misused. The Government was responsible for licensing businesses and overseeing construction work. The temptation to give and accept favours was ever present and it needed a strong and moral disposition to resist. Colonel Mason judged Douglas to be the kind of man who would fall at the first hurdle. But he was clever and manipulative, his section in London were pleased with his work and were prepared to overlook any minor infringement of the rules. Catching Captain Douglas Coulter out would be a difficult task indeed.

Dieter was doing more and more work for Douglas. He was also finding things out about himself. He sorely missed his position of authority in this new Germany. He missed the comforts that wealth had always afforded him. He missed the fact that there had always been someone there to do his bidding. He missed wearing decent clothes, riding horses and the many other country pursuits of the aristocracy. He had also discerned a desire in Douglas to aspire to the same lofty heights in society that he himself had been born into. They were spending more and more time together. Dieter genuinely liked Douglas; he liked his sense of adventure and his recklessness. He liked the way he flouted authority with seeming impunity. The difference between them, thought Dieter, was that he wondered if Douglas knew who he was. Dieter definitely knew who he was. Dieter had been brought up strictly, to always do the 'right thing'. Dieter was finding out that always 'doing the right thing' didn't always get you to where you wanted to be.

Douglas started to involve Dieter in his little schemes and scams. Dieter could go to places and get to people he couldn't. He also knew things about people that Douglas didn't. They started to make real money. Douglas had got himself a cosy little pied a terre in the centre of Berlin where he could entertain. It wasn't so easy for Dieter, being one of the vanquished. One evening when they were having a drink together at Dieter's squalid apartment, Dieter asked Douglas, 'Would you bring a woman back here?'

Douglas looked at him over the rim of his glass and laughed out loud, 'Point taken Dieter.' And within a couple of days Dieter was re-housed into somewhere much more palatial in a much better district.

One of the things Dieter knew was the whereabouts of the special Reich Marks issued by the Nazis for use by the German Armed Forces. One Military Reich Mark was worth ten German Reich Marks. Between them, Douglas and Dieter devised a way of introducing them into the black economy in small numbers so as to avoid suspicion. He also knew that the Nazis had forged plenty of ordinary German Reich Marks which had been used to pay off foreign agents and foreign

29

companies which supplied the German Army with munitions, raw materials and fuel. Large amounts of counterfeit English ten pound notes had also been printed in a special section of the Sachsenhausen concentration camp under the direction of an S.S. Officer called Bernhart Kruger. It was known as the devil's workshop. The prisoners, printers, engravers and the master forgers who worked in that section were given special privileges. They had better food, a bed each and bedclothes. But not one of them doubted that when the time was right they would all be killed to keep the secret. The original idea had been to flood Britain with these notes and in that way to ruin the British economy. The scheme was never implemented because it was thought, rightly as it happened, that the British had been tipped off about it. Near the end of the war, the majority of these notes had been transported to Austria, put in large wooden crates and dropped in deep water in Lake Toplitz – but not all. The prisoners involved in this operation were driven to a deep mine shaft, the intention was to kill them, but the prisoners resisted and the guards ran off. The Allies were very close by and the guards decided they wouldn't have had time to cover up their crime. The plates for the forgeries of the British currency and for the printing of one hundred dollar bills had been hidden. Dieter had an idea where they may have been taken to, he also knew of a prisoner who had survived the death camps who might know others who knew the secret.

CHAPTER 4

Things were happening rapidly in Berlin now. There were four sectors of the city operated by each of the Allies, the three sectors run by the Americans, British and French mainly co-operated with each other but not the Soviets. The Marshall Plan for the reconstruction of Western Europe began in July 1947, it was offered to the Russians but they declined to participate. Inflation of the German economy was also becoming a problem and to make matters worse the winters of 1946 and1947 were the worst in Europe in living memory. Food and fuel were still in short supply, rationing was still enforced vigorously, electricity cuts were the norm. Everyone who could be was out on the streets and in the countryside scavenging for wood. Furniture was being used as fuel. The population burned anything they could lay their hands on that would burn. Hundreds froze to death. Life was very very tough in all the sectors of Berlin.

Hyper-inflation of the Reich Mark was now a very serious problem, the black market was totally out of control. American cigarettes were being used as currency quite openly. It was decided that something drastic had to be done. In great secrecy plans were drawn up to replace the old currency with a new Deutsche Mark. The exchange rate was agreed as one for one for wages and rents, but any surplus including savings was to be at the rate of one for ten. The introduction of this new currency would effectively put a stop to the barter and black market trade overnight. The news of these plans alarmed Douglas, there was still a stack of the Military Reich Marks to be unloaded and the flow of his illicit income would be seriously affected. Douglas arranged with Dieter to flood the markets with the Military notes for dollars at a very favourable rate. It meant taking a loss, but not nearly as bad as waiting for the introduction of the new currency. The sudden appearance of these Military Reich Marks didn't go unnoticed. It was brought to the attention of Colonel Mason. This operation had been a closely guarded secret, there were only a few military personnel in the know and Douglas was one of them. The leaking of the date for the issue of the new notes had to be an inside job, and Colonel Mason suspected Douglas as the source, but he knew he wouldn't be able to prove it. Deception came naturally to Douglas; he was a very slippery character to nail down.

31

The new currency was introduced on 21st June 1948 to a stunned population. But it had an unforeseen consequence. The Russians had been advised of this imminent reform, just days before it happened. They were greatly alarmed, considering it a western threat to undermine the stability of the sector controlled by them. On the 12th June, they closed the autobahn ostensibly for repairs. On the 21st June they stopped all barge traffic reaching Berlin and then on the 24th June all rail traffic was suspended. They had effectively isolated the City of Berlin. The reserves held at this time by the Western Allies, was thirty five days of food and forty five days of coal for a population of over two million. The Western powers had failed to negotiate a pact with the Soviets guaranteeing these ground passage rights. Fortunately the air routes had been secured. Three twenty mile wide corridors provided access to Berlin. The American and British forces were now greatly outnumbered by the Soviets. The Western Allies had seriously scaled back their armies post war, the Soviets hadn't. The Allies decided to stay and bluff it out, their prestige was at stake. General Lucius Clay was in charge of the U.S. occupation zone, he estimated the blockade would only last a few weeks. He reasoned the Soviets wouldn't want to start a third world war–they might invite a nuclear response. Only the Americans had the atomic bomb and the means to deliver it. The duplicity of Ffoukes, a communist living in America, had not yet been unearthed, but it would be some time yet before the Russians had the capability of building a bomb.

Fortunately for the Allies, the British were already airlifting supplies to their troops in the British sector. They had calculated the amount of supplies it would take to keep the city functioning. A total of 1534 tons of food was needed per day and 3475 tons of coal and gasoline. The population would have to make sacrifices. The meagre rations were cut again and again. Starvation stalked the City once more. The people would go cold and hungry; they were also terrified that the Allies would abandon them to the mercy of the Soviets. They still remembered the butchery they had suffered when the Soviets marched into the City virtually unopposed at the end of the war.

The first aircraft flew in on the 26th June; the operation was called 'Vittles and Plainfare'. The Americans used the Rhein Main airbase, Weisbaden and Tempelhof. The British used R.A.F. Gatow. At first, the French refused to participate but as time went by they also joined in. They built a new airport in their sector using thousands of female labourers who worked day and night. The logistics of the operation were immense. The aircrews were drawn from all over the Commonwealth, Australia, Canada, New Zealand and South Africa. The Combined Airlift Task force was based at Tempelhof. The local people were used as labour to unload the planes and to effect repairs to the runways. The incentive was an additional supply of rations. On August 10th the Soviets started harassing the aircraft. Soviet fighters were buzzing the planes as they attempted to land. That winter was a bleak one indeed. An extra 6000 tons of coal was required. More ground crew were needed so ex Luftwaffe personnel were drafted in to help. To speed up the turnaround, the crews stayed in their aeroplanes and young women rushed out with refreshments and drinks. Another problem to be faced was the weather, in November and December of 1948 fog shrouded Berlin for weeks leaving only one week's supply of coal. Fortunately, in January, the weather improved and by April of 1949 it was apparent to the Soviets that the airlift was a success. On the 12th of May the blockade was lifted. The Russians had been humiliated. But flights continued to build up a surplus of supplies, It was by now, quite apparent to all, that the Soviets were not to be trusted. The airlift officially ended on the 30th September 1949. In total there were 101 fatalities, seventeen American planes and eight British planes crashed in an operation lasting seventeen months.

CHAPTER 5

Douglas, now Major Douglas Coulter, was seriously running out of funds, his rate of spending far outstripped his income. There had been little opportunity during the airlift to replenish his savings. Dieter had also suffered the same plight. But Dieter had a plan. His mother had used a jeweller, a master craftsman based in Amsterdam to make her some exquisite pieces of jewellery. He was a Dutch Jew and had been deported to the Auschwitz/Birkenau concentration camp. Against all the odds he had survived and Dieter knew he was back in business. He also knew he had been involved in a little diamond smuggling before the war. Dieter wondered if he would be tempted to resume the activity in these times of severe privations. He thought it worth a try. He mentioned his idea to Douglas. Douglas was very enthusiastic, but it would need a great deal of thought and meticulous planning. The first course of action was to contact the jeweller. This was left to Dieter and he was successful in arousing the man's interest.

Leon Weinbakker had at first been left alone by the Nazis, but it wasn't to last. One night during a terrible disturbance in the street below, Leon Weinbakker was yanked out of his bed and thrown into the back of a truck along with the other unfortunate residents earmarked for deportation. The journey to the Polish camp was terrible and many did not survive. Once there, they were segregated, the able bodied men were separated from the rest of the prisoners. They were destined for manual labour, to work until they dropped. The women and children were marched away. The remainder were questioned about their previous employment. It seemed certain tradesmen were required, and luckily for Leon he was one of them.

When the prisoners arrived at the camp, all their belongings were stripped from them. It was well known by the Nazis that the Jews carried their wealth with them. Gold coins and jewellery were the favourites, it was easier to flee with these items hidden about the person or sewn into their clothes. Leon was set to work in what was called the reception hut. All the clothes and baggage was meticulously searched for anything valuable. The items were sorted, the gold and jewellery kept to one side. The German clerks kept records of all that was found. It was Leon's job under strict supervision of course, to then sort out the good pieces from the mediocre, to decide what pieces should be kept and which melted down for the gold, and the stones recycled. The High Ranking German Officer's were not averse to a little pilfering however and Leon made pieces of jewellery for their wives and mistresses. Leon knew that he owed his life to his expertise.

Each night he was taken back to the huts. His living conditions were the same as the other inmates but he got extra rations during the day to keep him going. Leon wasn't oblivious to the suffering he saw there, but Leon was determined to survive at all costs and he turned his mind away from the deprivations suffered by his fellow prisoners. Many showed a marked antagonism to him but it didn't worry him, they were much weaker than he was and most of them didn't last long anyway. There were new faces every week and he was protected by the sonder commandos by order of the Germans.

As time went by Leon was regarded like a piece of worn furniture by the guards. But Leon kept his eyes open, he noticed that the clerks recording the pieces of jewellery brought into the hut, only put into the ledger the type of jewellery they had recovered, a gold and diamond bracelet, a platinum and ruby brooch, a pearl necklace for example. They didn't record the number of diamonds, rubies or pearls. The floor of the hut was made of rough hewn wooden planks, they didn't fit too well in places and there were a few gaps in the flooring. Leon saw his chance, if he survived this terrible place, and he had every intention of doing so, he wanted something out of it. So when pieces were due to be broken up into their component parts, and the clerk's attention was elsewhere, Leon endeavoured to drop one or two of the best stones between the cracks in the planking. Because some of the pieces were small, the clerks didn't consider them worth saving, but some of these items were of the highest quality. Over time there was a considerable fortune sitting under the floorboards. How Leon was going to retrieve the jewels he didn't know, but his chance would come, he was sure of it. He couldn't risk carrying anything out on his person; he was searched far too rigorously by the guards.

Douglas had worked out a scheme for getting the two of them to Amsterdam. He had been grooming a sergeant who worked on the transports in the car pool. He had been assiduously supplying him with nylons and American cigarettes for just such a venture as this. Douglas was a resourceful man and he was due some leave. He asked the sergeant if he could supply him with a vehicle that wasn't logged out to him. He spun him a yarn about a girlfriend who had got herself into a spot of bother. 'I need to sort it out.' he told him. He knew he would be sympathetic because the nylons were for the sergeant's German girl friend.

'It just so happens that a car has just come in for servicing Sir and I haven't written up my log books yet. Providing its back in the pool by Monday morning nobody will be any the wiser.'

'Petrol?' enquired Douglas.

'There are a couple of jerry cans over there Sir, by the petrol pump. I'm needed at the other end of the garage for a moment or two. I won't be a jiffy Sir.' Douglas filled the cans and put them in an obscure corner. Now he had to act fast. He had secured a British Corporal's uniform and the necessary documentation for Dieter who was to act as his driver. He raced up to his quarters and collected the uniform placing it in his overnight bag. Now he sauntered down to the car pool, placed the jerry cans in the boot, and got into the driver's seat, the keys were in the glove compartment. He drove out of the car pool and stopped at the gates, nonchalantly chatting to the guards as they opened them. They saluted as he drove away. Douglas drove to Dieter's apartment and Dieter quickly changed into the uniform. He looked every inch a soldier, and so he should, he had been one for years. Douglas got into the back of the car and Dieter drove them to the first check point. It was the first test, but they were through on the nod. They drove to the border of Germany and Holland, making sure they drove within the speed limits. The last thing they wanted was to be picked up by a stray patrol. At the border Douglas showed his and Dieter's papers. He appeared totally unconcerned and after a quick scrutiny they were through.

Dieter drove to the outskirts of Amsterdam. He told Douglas it would be best if he went to see Leon on his own, he could be a tricky character he told him. Douglas agreed but added if Leon went for the scheme, he definitely wanted to meet him, 'Faceless people can do you a lot of damage.'

Dieter turned into the street in question. He parked on the other side of the road and entered the door opposite. After about twenty minutes he appeared at the doorway and beckoned to Douglas to join him. It was a dingy stairwell with steep stone steps, their boots echoed eerily as they mounted the stairs. Leon wanted to know if he was

36

having visitors, he had been surprised once before.

The apartment was on the third floor. On entering, it appeared that there was no-one at home. It smelt of damp and had that uncared for feel about it. There was a small fire burning in the grate, but there was no feeling of warmth emanating from it. There was an old battered leather sofa which had seen better days placed against a wall. There were two leather arm chairs of the same vintage as the sofa placed near the fire with a table between them. One had an indentation in the cushion, noting it out to be the preferred chair. It was facing the door and window. A small thin dark man emerged from the other room. He had greasy hair and small black darting eyes. He was wearing a black shiny suit with a grubby white shirt that was frayed at the collar and cuffs. Douglas could just see the first numbers in blue ink of the tattoo which denoted him to be a holocaust survivor. The irony of the situation was not lost on Douglas. Here was a German S.S. Tank Commander and a man who had suffered terribly at the hands of the German race doing business together. The little man had summed up Douglas in an instant. 'Herr von Rheinhart has told me about your proposition, it sounds interesting. It just so happens that I have some merchandise that a fellow merchant in London may be able to make use of. I understand you are due to fly there within a day or so.'

'That's right,' agreed Douglas.

'I suggest a trial run.' He produced a small leather pouch and placed a black velvet cloth on the table. He emptied the contents of the pouch on the velvet. There were about a seven or eight small diamonds.

Douglas frowned, 'Is that all of them? Surely there should be more.'

'These stones are of the finest quality.' The old man shot back.

Dieter intervened between the two of them, 'Leon knows his business Douglas.'

'It is Menheer Warner to you, Menheer Leonard Warner.' He looked fiercely at Dieter. There was a new order in Germany now and Leonard wasn't going to be patronized any longer, especially by the race that had caused him so much suffering.

When the war was over and the Americans only a short distance from Auschwitz, the prison guards had fled. It was then that Leon had taken the opportunity to retrieve the stones. He hid them in his prison garb. No one was going to search him now. He had made his way back to Amsterdam and found this apartment. He paid for it in diamonds. Now he needed a way to move them on. His fellow Jews had paid a high price for him to have these stones. He needed to convert them into money and it looked as though providence had provided Major Douglas Coulter has a means of doing just that.

Douglas wanted to know if they had agreed a split. 'We have,' said Leonard, 'it's sixty, forty in my favour.'

'What!' exploded Douglas.

'Sixty, forty.' repeated the Jew. 'Take it or leave it.'

'I'm the one who's risking my liberty here, fifty-fifty. Take it or leave it!' challenged Douglas.

Leonard Warner looked venomous. 'You are the ones that came to me remember, you need me and my diamonds.'

'And you need me to transport them.' retorted Douglas. It was stalemate. The silence in the place was electric. After five minutes or so, Douglas picked up his cap and made for the door. He was half way through before Leonard blinked.

'I agree.' His face was set like thunder, he wouldn't forget this. Without another word, Douglas picked up the black velvet cloth, wrapped it around the diamonds, placed them in the leather pouch and put it into his brief case. He walked out of the apartment, down the stairs and went straight to the car. Dieter was only a few minutes behind him.

They drove back into Germany and stopped off at a respectable road side hotel for a few hours sleep. They arrived back at Allied Headquarters just before lunch the following day. The sergeant wouldn't be on duty until later when he would see to the documentation. Douglas showed his pass to the guards who knew him and Dieter drove straight through to the carpool. As luck would have it, Colonel Mason was late for a luncheon appointment and he had decided to drive himself rather than take a driver. He was just leaving when Dieter drove past. Colonel Mason recognized Douglas sitting in the back and was extremely puzzled. Douglas was supposed to be on leave, he should have been back in Britain by now. He had been booked on a flight to London yesterday. What was he doing here? He would be up to no good that was for sure. The Colonel had also got a good look at the corporal driving him; he knew the face but couldn't immediately place him. The Colonel looked in his mirror and noted down the car number plate. He would get to the bottom of this the minute he returned. Douglas had also spotted the Colonel. He swore under his breath, he knew he had been rumbled but the first priority was to get Dieter out of the place. He took him up to his quarters where Dieter changed into Douglas's civvies; fortunately they were of a similar build. The corporal's uniform was packed away to be disposed of later. Douglas himself took Dieter to the gate. He explained to the guards Dieter had been doing a job for him, it was accepted without question. Douglas had made a point of always being chatty and befriending those on guard duty. He wasn't too worried about Colonel Mason. The sergeant would cover for him and he could always use the same yarn about the girl friend. The worst that could happen in Douglas's estimation was that he might get his knuckles wrapped. He flew to London that afternoon.

As soon as Colonel Mason returned from his appointment he returned his car to the pool. The one Douglas had used was still where Dieter had parked it. The sergeant had just come on duty. He hadn't had time to wind the clock back or to do anything else about it as yet. The Colonel strolled over to the car and took a note of the mileage. The Sergeant spotted him out of the corner of his eye and was apprehensive. The Colonel called him over.

The Sergeant stood to attention and saluted. 'Yes Sir.'

'Bring your log book with you Sergeant.'

'Yes Sir.' The sergeant knew what was coming.

'Tell me about this car Sergeant.'

'It's in for servicing Sir.'

'When was it brought in Sergeant?'

'I haven't booked it in for servicing yet Sir.' he said, looking down at his log book.

The Colonel held out his hand for the book. The Sergeant reluctantly handed it over. 'This car was brought in over two days ago Sergeant, why haven't you logged it?'

'I must have forgotten Sir.'

'I saw the car being driven in here just two hours ago Sergeant with Major Coulter as the passenger, he had an army driver with him and judging by the discrepancy in the mileage he has been on quite a journey.' The Sergeant knew the game was up. The Colonel was relentless in pursuing matters he thought were wrong, especially if it involved Major Coulter. 'Do you have an explanation Sergeant?'

'Yes Sir. Major Coulter asked me to bend the rules a little Sir. He told me he had a delicate matter involving a young lady to sort out Sir.'

'Did he really, and how did he get the petrol to go and sort out this delicate matter Sergeant?'

'I don't know Sir; I was at the other end of the garage Sir.'

The Colonel opened the boot of the car. The petrol cans, clearly marked as Army property, were still inside the boot. 'You are relieved of duty Sergeant; I want you in my office right away.'

'Yes Sir.' The Sergeant's shoulders slumped; this was going to mean his stripes and all for a few nylons and cigarettes.

Colonel Mason didn't waste any time. He got the whole sorry story out of the Sergeant including all the 'presents' he had received. He signed the full statement and he was right – he lost his stripes. Colonel Mason was jubilant. I've got the bastard he thought; at long last I've got the bastard. Mason turned his mind to the army driver, he knew that face and then it dawned on him who he was. It was being in uniform that had thrown him for a while. He was the German civilian that Coulter spent quite a lot of time with, probably Coulter's informant. So where had he got the uniform from? Colonel Mason made enquiries of the guards on duty at the gate that afternoon. Yes, Major Coulter had personally escorted a German civilian from Headquarters, and no he didn't have a package with him. So, thought Colonel Mason, that uniform is still here. He ordered Douglas's quarters to be searched. The uniform was soon found. It didn't belong to anyone on the base, so it had been specially made outside. Mason phoned London and spoke to Brigadier Forsythe. 'I'm afraid your man Coulter has been very naughty,' he told him.

Forsythe listened to the list of charges against Douglas: Procuring an army vehicle for his own use whilst on leave, the theft of army petrol, bribing an American Army Sergeant, bringing a German civilian onto the base and providing him with a Corporal's uniform. Mason also told him he suspected Douglas of involvement in the distribution of Military Reich Marks just before the currency changeover, but he couldn't prove that one.

Forsythe agreed; they couldn't sweep this little lot under the carpet. Action would have to be taken. It was a shame he thought, Douglas had been very effective as his Liaison Officer, but these were very serious charges and Mason had a signed statement. He wasn't going to let it go. The Brigadier reluctantly agreed a court martial was the only way forward. But he was adamant he didn't want a custodial sentence for Douglas, a dishonourable discharge was punishment enough. Forsythe pondered Douglas's fall from grace, a man could enter the war as one person and come out the other end as a completely different person. The adjustment from an army of fighting men to an army of peacemakers was always going to be a difficult one. Brigadier Forsythe shrugged and returned to studying the file in front of him.

Mason wasn't a naturally vindictive man, but Douglas Coulter had been a thorn in his side for long enough, he wanted him out of the military. So he settled for that.

Douglas grabbed a taxi at the airport. He was still in full uniform, the diamonds safely contained in his brief case, plainly marked H.M. Government. Wearing the uniform helped going through customs and getting taxis. He made his way to Hatton Gardens and paid the taxi off with a generous tip. He found the address he was looking for, an anonymous door in an anonymous street. There was a brass name plaque on the wall with an intercom. Douglas had also spotted a discreet camera pointing down at the entrance. He rang the bell.

A baritone voice answered. 'What is your name please? And state your business.' Douglas answered with his name and rank and told the disembodied voice that he had just arrived from Amsterdam. 'Please remove your cap Major.' Douglas did so. So they wanted a good look at him. He heard the door unlock and the voice said, 'Please come to the second floor, first door on your right, you will see my name on it.' Then the intercom clicked off. When Douglas arrived outside the door he tapped gently on it. It was opened immediately by a young woman very smartly but soberly dressed. She stood aside to let him pass into an anteroom, there were antique chairs against one wall with a coffee table in front of them. Expensive magazines were strewn across the coffee table's polished surface.

'Mr Liebthal will see you now Major.' said the young woman and she opened the door into a large office. This room was in complete contrast to Leonard Warner's apartment in Amsterdam. There was an opulent carpet on the polished wooden floor. Show cases stood against the walls, and a huge mahogany desk dominated one corner. Behind the desk sat a large man with a corpulent figure. He was going bald but his black hair was slicked straight back from the high domed forehead. By the empty fireplace were placed two antique library chairs with a table between them. The big man rose and indicated that Douglas should take the right hand chair. Douglas did so, his briefcase on his knee. Mr Liebthal sat opposite.

'Would you care for a drink Major Coulter?'

'Yes please, I think a whiskey and soda would slide down nicely.' The big man just raised an eyebrow at his secretary who dealt very efficiently with the request. She glided over and placed a heavy cut glass whiskey tumbler in front of Douglas and discreetly withdrew to the other room.

'Are you not going to join me?' asked Douglas.

'No,' responded Mr Liebthal, 'I don't drink when I am conducting business.'

'Well I do.' replied Douglas and took a sip of his whiskey.

'My counterpart in Amsterdam tells me you are carrying something that may interest me Major.' Douglas opened his briefcase and pulled out the leather pouch. He took out the black velvet and opened it on the table. The diamonds glittered as they caught the light. The London diamond merchant leant forward, he placed a glass in his right eye which he had retrieved from his waist coat pocket, and very carefully picked up each stone in turn with a pair of tweezers. He turned them this way and that and gave a grunt of satisfaction. He opened a drawer in the table and took out a brown envelope and placed it in front of Douglas. 'I think our business is concluded Major.'

Douglas slipped the envelope into his brief case. They both rose at the same time, Mr Liebthal turned towards his desk.

'There is just one other matter to settle however.' said Douglas. The diamond merchant turned round slowly to face him.

'And what is that Major?'

'The question of my expenses.'

The two men locked eyes, neither of them moving. Then Mr Liebthal went to his desk and opened a drawer, he drew out a wad of notes and counted them out on his desk. He turned and handed them to Douglas without a word. Douglas took them and put them straight into his jacket pocket. He held out his hand to Mr Liebthal, the diamond merchant didn't take it. Miraculously the secretary was immediately on hand to show him out. Douglas left Hatton Gardens with a jaunty step.

He was in London, on leave with money in his pocket, there was only one thing to do with that, and that was to spend it. He booked into a Central London Hotel, rang a favourite girl friend and thoroughly enjoyed his evening. He left for the West Country the following day.

His mother was overjoyed to see him. She thought he was still in Berlin. He told her he had been on War Office business in London, very hush hush, and had been given some unexpected leave and of course he couldn't wait to come home to see her, but it was only for a few days. He looked up his old girl friends and had a good time, spending the rest of his money in the process. Still, easy come, easy go, there was plenty more where that came from he thought. On the last day, Douglas was in his room packing when his mother tapped on his door. She entered with a parcel in her hand. 'I was going to post this to you son, but as you're here, you may as well take it with you.' And she placed it on his bedside table.

'I hope it's got one of your fruit cakes in it mother, they're the only thing that keeps me going out there,' he smiled at her, 'and they remind me of home,'

'You always were partial to my fruit cakes Douglas.' She left preening herself and with a little tear in her eye. Douglas finished his packing and was just about to put the parcel into his bag. He hesitated, he looked at the label. His mother had completed the customs form and it was clearly marked for H.M. Forces, Army of Occupation in Germany. He made a sudden decision. He carefully undid the brown wrapping paper, inside amongst other things was the fruit cake wrapped in grease proof paper. He carefully inserted the brown envelope containing the diamond money between the layers of grease proof paper underneath the cake and wrapped the parcel up again. On careful inspection, it didn't look as if it had been tampered with. He placed it back on his bedside table. His mother drove him to the station and walked with him onto the platform. Just as he was about to board the train, he told his mother he had forgotten to pack the parcel, would she be a dear and forward it to him as soon as she could, he hadn't had a slice of her cake in days.

'Of course I will.' She said fondly, 'come home again as soon as you can. I do miss you so.' She stretched up and pecked his cheek.

The flight back to Berlin was uneventful. Douglas collected his briefcase and his greatcoat and waited to disembark. The flight had been full with service people and civilians. Dieter was waiting at the airport to meet him. He was up on the viewing deck. He watched as the passengers streamed off the plane, he saw Douglas who looked up and gave Dieter the thumbs up sign. Dieter made his way slowly down to the arrivals entrance. He stood back waiting for Douglas to appear. Slowly people started coming through, then they came in a steady stream, but there was no sign of Douglas. The crowds were starting to thin out, still Douglas didn't appear. Dieter had a funny feeling in the pit of his stomach. He moved further away but kept his eyes firmly on the entrance. At last Douglas appeared, he was flanked by two military policemen in white helmets. He was ashen faced. Dieter watched as they marched Douglas to a waiting police vehicle, they all got in the back. Douglas was sitting between the two white helmeted policemen as the driver slowly pulled away. Dieter knew exactly what this could mean for Douglas, he doubted even Douglas's silver tongue could talk his way out of this one. Dieter went back to his apartment. He poured himself a drink and sank into an armchair. Such a shame he thought, just as things seemed to be going so well. Another lucrative side line cut off. Then he thought of Leonard, what was he going to tell him. He would have to try his best and appease him but that wasn't going to be so easy: no money, and no diamonds.

The court martial was a foregone conclusion. It was properly constituted, the President of the Court was a Brigadier and he sat with four other Senior Officers. Douglas was properly represented. The charges were read out and Douglas was asked how he pleaded. It had been made crystal clear to Douglas that if he tried to fight this case, he stood every chance of getting a custodial sentence, the evidence was very damning. The hearing was over in about ten minutes and Douglas had received a dishonourable discharge from His Majesty's Army. He was led away in disgrace. He was allowed back to his quarters, he was stripped of his rank and his beloved uniform but he wasn't left alone again while he was on army premises. He changed into civvies and packed the rest of his belongings. His mother's parcel had been delivered and was on the table. Douglas picked it up, it hadn't been opened. He slipped it into his suitcase with a smile, 'My mother's fruitcake.' he said to the policeman chaperone.

Douglas made his way to his little love nest in the City centre. He sat down and opened a full bottle of cognac. He didn't stop drinking until it was empty. Next morning feeling a little the worse for wear, Douglas called on Dieter. Dieter had had no means of knowing what was going on, he had been sitting at home for days waiting for news. He hadn't dared to approach any of the usual crowd for fear of compromising the situation, but he had expected the worst.

'You look like shit!' he said to Douglas as he entered the apartment.

'And I don't feel much better.' grimaced Douglas. 'Mind you, I could use a coffee.'

Dieter set about making a pot, 'Leonard is spitting blood,' he told Douglas over his shoulder.

'Is he? Leonard's an old woman.' Dieter turned around and gave Douglas a questioning look. He had placed a brown paper parcel on the coffee table.

'Would you like a piece of fruit cake with your coffee?'

'No thank you, I don't really like fruit cake.'

'Really, my mother made this especially for me, I think you might like this one. I'm definitely going to have a piece.'

Dieter turned right round to look at Douglas, 'Are you sure you're feeling alright?'

'I will be in a minute.' He was busy undoing the parcel; he took out the fruit cake, turned it upside down and extracted a brown envelope from between the waxed paper. He placed it triumphantly on the table. 'This should make Leonard feel a bit better.' He extracted the money and fanned it over the table.

Dieter laughed out loud, 'You should be in the circus.' He brought the coffee over to the table. 'Shame we won't be able to perform this trick again though.'

'Of course we will.'

'But how? You're bound to get searched and caught, customs are as keen as mustard about the currency restrictions, you know that.'

'They don't search military personnel though.'

'But you're not-----' the words died on his lips. He had followed Douglas's thinking.

'People look at the uniform not at the face, although in my case, I'm so handsome they may look at both.' he said tongue in cheek.

Dieter sat down and sipped his coffee, 'I think I will have a piece of your mother's cake after all. Then this afternoon I have to go out. I have to track down some important people, wait for me; I don't know what time I'll be back.' When Dieter had gone, Douglas leaned back in his chair. He put his feet up on the table and threaded his hands behind his head, his face like thunder, he was furious. He was furious at the way the army had treated him. He thought, I'll get my own back, I'll not let the buggers get away with this, I'll show them! I'll show the whole bloody lot of them!

Dieter returned late in the evening, he had had a satisfactory day. He had been on the trail of the best forger in Berlin, the one responsible for the counterfeit money produced by the Nazis. The man had agreed, at a hefty price, to provide forged passports and any other documentation Douglas might require for his frequent journeys between Amsterdam and London. Dieter knew they would be the best money could buy and would fool the most eagle eyed customs man. Dieter slumped down in the armchair opposite Douglas.

Douglas poured him out a drink, 'Busy day?'

'Yes, my feet are killing me,' he smiled at Douglas over the rim of his glass, 'It's your turn tomorrow, you have an appointment with your tailor, you're to be measured for your uniforms, you decide which service and the rank. Oh and you need some mug shots, then we'll see just how handsome you are.' Douglas was measured for uniforms for all three armed services, The Army, Royal Air Force and the Senior Service. A Major, a Wing Commander, and a Lieutenant Commander, all the uniforms were the real thing, after all, his tailor had been making uniforms for Officers for years.

Douglas explained to Dieter, 'I need a rank that conveys authority, if it's too grand people fall over themselves saluting you and you get noticed.' Within a few weeks Douglas's wardrobe sported Military uniforms, a number of Savil Row suites, silk shirts and all the paraphernalia that would declare him to be an English Gentleman. He also had passports backing up all these personalities.

Douglas and Dieter had been to Amsterdam to see Leonard, he needed placating, he thought he had lost his diamonds and lost the money to boot. But Douglas reassured him that the trip to Covent Gardens had gone smoothly and he had a trick or two up his sleeve for concealing the diamonds. Bringing currency back posed a much more difficult problem. There was only so much Douglas would be able to carry, that was one thing the Customs people were very keen on, no matter who you were. It was decided by far the safest thing was to bank the money in Britain and transfer it to a bank in Zurich. The account needed all three signatures. It seemed nobody trusted anybody these days. Douglas did a few more successful drops. He also received his expenses which entertained him in London. The bank balance started to grow. Douglas was getting tired of traipsing to Amsterdam. He decided it would be easier to buy an apartment there as they were relatively cheap at the moment. In addition Berlin was full of back biting and back stabbers. His face was too well known there and he didn't have the protection of the Military machine anymore. He asked Dieter to come with him to Amsterdam, but Dieter declined. 'I have other dreams,' he told Douglas, 'I want to rebuild my estate, it will be quite an undertaking, but it's what I want to do. I have made a start already, the Gatehouse is habitable. The stables are my next priority. You must come and stay with me Douglas, when I have horses, we can ride out together.'

CHAPTER 6

As soon as Douglas was settled into his apartment in Amsterdam, he took a walk along the main canal bank. There were other people out that evening but not many. He looked into the murky water, there were eddies of rubbish collecting in pockets that the slow moving water couldn't shift. He walked on slowly and pulled out a pack of American cigarettes removing one. He stopped and cupped his hands to light it and drew the smoke deeply into his lungs. In the shadows there was evidence of the other side of Amsterdam society. The odd derelict that slept in shop doorways, some of them discharged soldiers still haunted by the sights they had seen during the war, unable to come to terms with their current circumstances. There were plenty of the dispossessed and bereaved who had gravitated to the city looking for answers and work. He turned and threw the remains of the cigarette into the gutter, behind him he heard the scraping of boots on the cobbles as the race was on to retrieve it. He returned to his apartment.

He decided to pay a visit to Dieter who was comfortably ensconced in the Gatehouse at Bremen. He had completed the stables and was on the look out for some horse flesh. They spent a pleasant few days touring around looking at likely animals. Both rode well and were good judges of horses. They visited the local races where horses regularly changed hands. Douglas couldn't resist the betting ring and came away with extra cash in his pocket. They bought a mare and two hunters.

That evening Douglas said to Dieter, 'You know, we could make a killing at these country race meetings. I don't know about you, but I could always use some extra cash.' Douglas was a profligate spender and Dieter's renovations were acting like a sponge on his resources. 'The stallion out there is a damned good horse and I reckon I can win or lose at will on that creature.'

'How exactly is it going to work?' Dieter wanted to know.

'Easy, you place the bets, I do the riding. I'll tip you the wink if I'm going to win, or come a close second.'

Dieter had to laugh, 'You're a very resourceful man my friend.'

'I wasn't born with a silver spoon in my mouth Dieter.'

'I was and it's been taken away from me, and you know what, I

48

resent it.'

They clinked glasses, 'To the races.'

At the next meet, Douglas was on the back of the stallion, he was a very accomplished horseman. He wanted to ride to win to shorten the odds on his mount, he made sure though that it wasn't a runaway win. He also rode out on the mare at the same meeting, this time he made sure he lost, but only just. Dieter had placed the bets and they came out well on the winning side. It was decided they should regularly go to these meetings at different courses. Douglas would win by fair means or foul if that is what he wanted. He was adept at the use of the whip on his own mount or on his opponent's if need be, sometimes on the opposing jockey as well. There was always a lot of argy-bargy at these race meetings and Douglas was expert at bumping his opponent's horse at just the right moment to put it off its stride. He made sure he was never spotted by the officials but a lot of muttering went on in the changing rooms about the foreign rider. They made reasonable amounts of money but it was never enough for Douglas. He saw money as the way to advance himself socially and to ingratiate himself at the very top of society. Dieter, who had been born into that society, needed money because he had grandiose plans to rebuild his estate.

They decided to widen their net of operations. Both men had always enjoyed a game of cards and had a talent for it. Lots of Dieter's friends were gambling men, for some it was an addiction they couldn't resist, but games were hard to find. Gambling parties were the answer. Dieter would find the venues and the players. Douglas would set the scene and set up the game. Dieter knew who had money and who hadn't, he knew who the inveterate gamblers were and knew they would travel to join in a good game. People were sick of the post war gloom and craved some excitement. The venues were carefully chosen. Dieter rented rooms in the best and swankiest hotels and in the grandest country houses and mansions. Douglas organized the lavish hospitality, he had innate good taste. He was looking for a seductive atmosphere of luxury and amusement. You had to understand the psychology of gambling and exploit it to its fullest extent. These punters were looking for a party with plenty of free drinks and lots of laughter, they wanted a fun time, and Douglas was determined to give it to them and at the same time relieve them of their money. Douglas, when he chose to be, could be a charming and plausible host, he had panache and an infectious magnetism. He was full of jokes and bonhomie but he was also without scruple, ruthless and mercenary and an opportunist. These people were ripe for the plucking and plucked they would be. The house take was five per cent of every wager, the odd croupier bent the rules in favour of the house, but generally the games were clean. As an area became saturated or got too hot with the local police, they would have to move on but the parties became very popular with a coterie of fanatic gamblers who would travel anywhere to get their kicks. This was obviously an area where there was money to be made, but the blueprint wasn't right. It became more and more difficult to find the right venues and it was expensive setting up each new place. The answer was a permanent location, but that wasn't going to be easy to find.

Douglas returned to Amsterdam, Leonard had a collection he wanted taking to London. Douglas decided to use a newly acquired identity; he was going to travel as the Honourable Webster St. Aubyn McCloud, a minor Scottish nobleman. It appealed to his fantasist nature. He had always had the ability to impersonate and was a great mimic, a heady and dangerous combination, but Douglas was amazed at the condescension shown to him. One day, he thought, I'll move higher up the social scale, the more danger involved in being discovered, the more Douglas enjoyed the game. His trip was successful and Douglas returned to Amsterdam to ponder the problem of a venue for the card games. He took a stroll down the canal banks. The water was sluggish with an oily sheen on the surface; it was a very dirty brown colour. Lots of litter had washed up on to the banks. People were using the canals as dust bins. He could see old bike frames and small boats in various degrees of disintegration, and a little further along, an old river boat partly under water. He reached the river boat, and leant against the railings looking down at it. He lit a cigarette, and watched the smoke curl lazily into the air. He could just see the name plate of the old boat which was partly obscured by the filthy water. 'The Lady Anne', well she didn't look too much like a lady now. He started to wonder about her past history, she looked like one of the many pleasure boats that had plied up and down these canals for the delight of the many tourists who used to flock here. He wondered what would happen to her, she would probably be broken up, he thought. The authorities were making louder and louder noises about cleaning up the canals, and about time too, they were a disgrace. Douglas returned to his apartment, he had 'expense' money in his pocket, so he took one of his many young ladies out for dinner. Next morning Douglas again found himself staring down at 'The Lady Anne', he wondered who her last owner had been and what had happened to him. It seemed unlikely he would come and reclaim her. He walked further along the bank and decided to call in and have lunch at a little restaurant which had recently opened called the De Kelderhof. He had a pleasant leisurely lunch; he sat for a while over his coffee, cognac and cigarette. He thought again about 'The Lady Anne' and decided he would go and have another look. On further inspection she wasn't as bad as she had at first appeared. She looked as though she had had three decks. She was down in the water by the head but not completely submerged, she was obviously resting on the mud. A fantastic idea occurred to him, but he dismissed it as being unrealistic. He turned and walked slowly away, then back again. No, it was a ridiculous idea he decided and returned to his apartment. That evening his thoughts kept returning to 'The Lady Anne', perhaps it wasn't such a far fetched idea after all. He decided the only thing to do was to research the idea further. He needed to check with the authorities what plans they had for the disposal of the wrecks in the canals. He would do that first thing in the morning, but for now, he needed diverting.

Next morning Douglas turned up at the appropriate department dealing with the proposed clean up of the City's waterways. He was directed to a middle aged man who seemed overwhelmed at the enormity of the task allotted to him. Douglas asked what was to happen to all the boats that had been abandoned on the canals. The man told him that the first task was to try and find the various owners. If they could be traced they were asked to make the boats sea worthy or remove them. Naturally he told Douglas most of the owners denied the boats belonged to them. That meant the city authorities were responsible for the cost of moving them and there was only so much money allocated for the task. The clean up would take place, but it would take time. Douglas specifically asked him about 'The Lady Anne.' The man pulled a folder towards him and opened it. 'The owner was killed during the war,' he told Douglas, 'so far we have been unable to trace any beneficiaries and it's most unlikely that we will.'

'So,' Douglas asked, 'if someone were to come along and offer to take her off your hands, there would be no difficulty in claiming ownership?' The man looked at him as though he had lost his senses.

'If someone were to come along and make such an offer, we would be delighted. We would supply that person with a certificate of ownership and provide indemnity against a claimant turning up in the future. There's a time limit for claimants to come forward and for 'The Lady Anne' the time limit has nearly expired.' He looked expectantly at Douglas, but Douglas merely thanked him for his time and information and left.

Douglas went straight back to look again at the partly submerged boat, it could work he thought; it really could. He would have to do a feasibility study, but first he would have to win Dieter over to the idea. He arranged to go and see him. Dieter was very sceptical, the idea as a river boat doubling up as a casino didn't appeal to him. But Douglas got to work on him, his very enthusiasm was infectious and he gradually wore Dieter down.

'O.K. Do a feasibility study and we'll discuss it again, I think finance is going to be the problem though.' That was all Douglas needed to hear and he went straight back to Amsterdam. This sort of project was just up Douglas's street, he loved solving the unsolvable.

Douglas toured around the boat yards and the repair yards. They had plenty of work on and it was debatable that 'The Lady Anne' could be salvaged. They weren't interested. Douglas wasn't easily deterred but he met with the same response the following day. It was on the third day on trying a small repair yard, that the elderly owner told him he remembered 'The Lady Anne'. She was a fine old boat he told Douglas, proud as they come. She took hundreds of happy tourists up and down these canals. He had fond memories of her. When Douglas told him he was interested in renovating her, bringing her back to her old glory days. The old man's eyes became dreamy. Douglas asked if he would be prepared to undertake such a task. After a few moments thought, the old man agreed, he said it would be a labour of love for him. Douglas arranged to meet him at 'The Lady Anne' the next day. Douglas was elated.

The old man was as good as his word, he promised to supply Douglas with his costings within a week or so and if they were acceptable he would book 'The Lady Anne' into his schedule of work at the repair yard.

As soon as the costings were available, Douglas shot off to see Dieter again. He had done some drawings so Dieter could see his vision of how 'The Lady Anne' would look once she was renovated. Dieter was impressed but on examining the bottom line he said gloomily.

'I can't raise this amount Douglas, I've already made commitments here and it will be a while before the estate starts bringing any money in. I'm afraid the best I could manage would be a third. What about you? Could you manage the rest?'

Douglas gave a hollow laugh, 'Not with my rate of spend, it would mean going without the company of the fairer sex for years. I'd never manage that.' Dieter shook his head with a smile and shrugged his shoulders. 'I'm determined to get this project off the ground Dieter, well I mean in the water. I know this is the right way forward, once the venture is up and running the money will roll in.'

'I agree, having thought about it, I'm much more enthusiastic now than I was. The only suggestion I can make, and you won't like it I know, is we need a third partner.'

'You mean my little grasping friend Leonard don't you?' Dieter nodded. 'All he ever does is sit in that grubby little room while we earn money for him.'

'But the point is Douglas, unlike you and me, Leonard doesn't spend it.'

Douglas leaned back in his chair, 'You'll have to go and sweet talk him Dieter, he wouldn't even get out of his chair for me.'

'Give me all the papers then, including the drawings, Leonard likes money, he won't go for anything less than a third share though, even though all he does for it is sit in that grubby little room.'

Dieter managed the impossible, he roped Leonard into the scheme, and he was right, a third share was the minimum price he would accept.

On his return to Amsterdam Douglas set about sourcing all the materials he would need to bring his vision of 'The Lady Anne' to fruition. He was careful to keep his true intentions for the boat a secret from the owner of the boat yard. He had made the vessel watertight and pumped out the ingress of water. She was floating, securely tied up to the canal bank, drying out and waiting to be towed to the repair yard where work would start in earnest. The old man had made 'The Lady Anne' a priority and his work force was ready to start.

It was a slightly breezy spring evening and Douglas decided to take a walk along the canal bank. There were other people out and about this evening, taking advantage of the waterside cafes which had recently sprung up here and there, a welcome sign of individual entrepreneurship. There were young couples walking hand in hand, people walking their dogs, and people like him just out for a leisurely stroll. Douglas walked slowly on, he lit a cigarette and slowly exhaled, the blue haze streamed out behind him. In the distance he could see the outline of 'The Lady Anne', he quickened his pace slightly. As he drew level with her his eyes raked over the hull once more, the murky water slopped against her sides. He turned away and decided to go to the little restaurant he favoured. It was handy and warm inside, and the proprietor did his best with the produce on hand. When he left the restaurant a couple of hours later, it was dark and it had started to drizzle. The cobbles glistened in the street lights as he retraced his steps and found himself once more by 'The Lady Anne'. He put his foot on the rails and peered over at her, he stayed there for a while mulling things over in his mind, then he straightened up and started to turn round. Just as he did so a figure bumped into his shoulder, there was no apology forthcoming. Douglas just caught a glimpse of a pale face and long blond hair, the woman was wearing a white mackintosh tied tightly around the waist. He watched as she walked purposefully along the bank, his intuition made him keep watching her but she stopped about two hundred yards away from him and looked at the canal the way he had been doing. He lost interest and looked away. The moon was shining on the surface of the murky oily water highlighting the rubbish as it lapped against the canal side. It was then that he heard the slight splash. He knew immediately what had happened. He looked to where he had last seen the figure of the woman; she was no longer in sight. He ran to the spot and looked over into the canal. He could just see a white mackintosh as it floated slowly away. Without thinking Douglas struggled out of his coat and kicked off his shoes. He dived into the mucky water and struck out strongly towards the billowing coat. He grabbed it and turned her over. The eyes were closed in the pale face; there was no sign of life. He pulled her to the bank and dragged them both half out of the water. Amazingly there was no-one else in sight, they either hadn't noticed or just went about their own business. He put her into the recovery position and pumped at her

54

lungs, after a few minutes of exertion Douglas was rewarded by a slight cough and water dribbled out of the side of her mouth. He worked on her for a bit longer, the cough got stronger and there was movement in her limbs. Douglas looked around him, there was no-one around. Douglas considered his options, he could call the authorities, but attempted suicide was a crime and Douglas didn't want the police focusing on him. He could just get up and walk away or ---. Douglas decided on the or. By now he was shivering, he collected his things and got the girl to her feet. Fortunately his apartment wasn't far away and he pushed and half dragged the girl there. What people thought as they made their way there he didn't know, their hair was plastered against their mud streaked faces and their clothes dripped water everywhere. Once inside, the priority was to get out of their wet clothes, he stripped the girl expertly and shoved her into the shower. She showed no resistance. He dug out warm clothing for them both, scooped up all the towels he could find, pulled her out of the shower and gave her plenty of towels then quickly cleaned himself up. The warm shower helped. Next was food, he warmed up some soup, sat her down at the table and made her eat. Douglas had seen this reaction before, she was in total shock. He knew it would be pointless to question her now, what she needed was sleep. He found a pair of his old pyjamas and once again stripped her and bundled her into them. Not a bad figure, he thought but young and skinny. It occurred to him that there weren't many fat people to be seen in Amsterdam these days. The soup had helped; she seemed a little more animated now. Douglas steered her towards the spare bedroom, he told her she was safe now and the best thing for her was sleep.

'You haven't called the police have you?' It was the first thing she had said since he had pulled her from the canal.

Douglas wondered what her story was. There were so many stories these days. 'No, I haven't.' Immediately she seemed relieved, but she was still shivering. 'We'll see what's for the best in the morning.' Douglas was beginning to wonder what his impulsive actions had got him into, the last thing he wanted were complications in his life. 'Go to bed and get some rest.'

She turned towards the bedroom and then back at him, 'Please don't leave me alone.' She looked absolutely desolate. Her shivering was out of control, 'Please,' she whispered, tears welling over and slowly rolling down her face.

Douglas sighed; he was none too warm himself. 'O.K. it's a double bed, we can have half each.' Anything he thought to get her to go to sleep. He sorted out another pair of pyjamas, he had better wear some tonight; normally he went to sleep in the buff. She got into the bed and rolled up into a ball pulling the covers up over her. He got into the other side and stretched out, he felt her cold hand touch his shoulder; it seemed as if she must have contact with another human being. Amazingly she fell asleep in no time. The irony of the situation was not lost on Douglas. At any other time he would have used all his considerable charm and persuasion to lure a member of the opposite sex into his bed, but on this occasion he wished she was anywhere but in his bed. He drifted off into sleep and woke some time later with a start. It was still dark, the events of last night still fresh in his mind. He turned towards the girl. She had rolled over towards him seeking his warmth in her sleep and thrown her arm across him. He could feel her breath against his cheek. She still felt very cold; he was worried she had hypothermia. He certainly didn't want an invalid on his hands. He moved a little nearer to her, sharing his body heat, she didn't stir. He closed his eyes but lay awake a long time. Suddenly he felt a slight movement next to him; he looked across at her. Her eyes were open staring straight into his face. She buried her head into his shoulder and shuddered. She pressed herself closer to him and to his horror he felt his manhood twitch. She was aware of his response and she held on to him very tightly. She pulled him on to her and manoeuvred urgently. It seemed she was in desperate need of this basic form of human contact. She gasped as he entered her, but clung on tighter still. It seemed as if she wanted to suck the very life force out of him. Spent, he rolled away from her, but she snuggled into his side, he could feel the wet salty tears on her cheek as her breathing slowly subsided. Gradually her breathing became regular and he realized with a shock that she had fallen asleep again. Douglas marvelled at the resilience of the human spirit and slept himself.

Next morning he woke up to find the sun streaming in through the window. The girl was still fast asleep, her tousled blond hair spread over the pillow. He quietly slipped out of bed, went back to his own room and got dressed. He padded into the kitchen to make breakfast. Fresh coffee, rolls with real butter and his favourite apricot compote.

He heard the bedroom door open behind him; she emerged wearing his pyjamas and dressing gown. He indicated that she should sit at the breakfast table, he sat opposite her. She wolfed down the food and her eyes lit up at the taste of real coffee. When she had finished, he sat back. She spoke first, 'You haven't called the police have you?'

'No, why would I want to do that? It was an accident wasn't it? The stones on the canal side are very slippy, especially after rain.'

'Yes,' she agreed, 'I was very clumsy. I wasn't watching where I put my feet.'

'You're not hurt are you?'

'No.'

'Where do you live?'

A long pause ensued, 'Nowhere.'

'You must be from somewhere.'

'I used to live in Eindhoven.'

'What about your family.' Douglas knew this was a loaded question in these times. He saw the tears well in her eyes.

She somehow sensed he didn't respond well to tears, she controlled them. 'My parents are dead.' Douglas didn't press the point. 'I don't know where my brother is. He left to join the partisans. I haven't heard anything from him since, he's probably dead too.' They sat in silence for a while. She looked too young to have been on the streets fending for herself. 'May I have another cup of coffee?' Douglas smiled; a spark of life! He poured another cup for her. She sipped it very slowly, savouring every drop.

'Someone must have taken you in.' he pressed.

Eventually she responded, 'My Aunt Bertha.'

Getting information out of her was like getting blood from a stone, but Douglas had been trained in interrogation techniques. You couldn't rush these things. 'Why did you leave?'

Another pause, 'Aunt Bertha said Uncle Wilhelm was becoming too fond of me. It was best that I left.' Douglas sensed an underlying story here, but he changed direction. 'So you came to Amsterdam?'

'Yes.'

'Looking for work?'

'Yes,' then defiantly, 'but there is no work ----only.' And she trailed off.

Douglas knew what the 'only' referred to. 'You haven't been

living on the streets?'

'No, I was lucky, I found an attic room, but I've run out of money now,' panic was in her voice, 'I already owe a month's rent, and Geerhaart said if I didn't----' she broke of again wringing her hands, 'and I can't, I haven't got the money.'

It wasn't quite what Douglas had thought, 'If you didn't what?'

She looked him straight in the face, 'That if I didn't pay the arrears by Thursday, I would have to leave, but I've got nowhere to go.' she said plaintively. Douglas sat back trying not to smile, relieved that the situation wasn't as bad as he had expected. 'And this Geerhaart is going to throw you out.'

'Yes, but you can't blame him really. He was badly wounded during the war and he can't work anymore. He relies on his rents to live off.'

'Come on,' said Douglas, 'get dressed, we'll go and see this Geerhaart of yours.'

'I can't, I can't find my clothes. I had to put this on.' She fingered the dressing gown, 'And anyway, what good would that do, I still can't pay him.'

'Maybe not, but I can.'

She looked at him wide eyed. 'Why would you want to do that?'

He didn't answer, but thought, to get you out of my apartment for one thing. 'Right! first things first! I threw your clothes into the wash bag. You can't wear those, they're filthy. You look to be a size ten to me. I'll nip out and get you something to wear. I won't be long.'

'But I can't pay you back either.' They were both thinking of last night, the desperate act of sex, but neither of them said anything.

He got up to leave, 'Make yourself some more coffee if you want, everything you need is in the cupboard there.' He closed and locked the door behind him. He was away for about half an hour. He bought a few undies, a skirt and blouse from the local market, and from a nearby shop, a decent dress. When he returned to his apartment and put the key in the door, he heard a scurrying noise. He quickly went in, she looked guilty. She had the remnants of crumbs and jam on her lips. 'Here, try these on.' He handed her the bag, she went into the bedroom and came out wearing the skirt and blouse. She had combed her hair and twisted it into a chignon. Her hair was a white platinum blond and natural he noticed. He was keen to get her out of his apartment now, he

58

didn't want any complications. 'Where does Geerhaart live?' She told him. He knew where it was. They went into the street; it was a fine spring morning. She tried to keep pace with him but kept having to break into a run at his side. He slowed down a little. They soon arrived at the street where she lodged.

The house was a typical four storey terrace of the type to be found all over Amsterdam, that is, those that were still standing. Douglas knocked on the heavy door; the green paint was peeling away badly. After a while he knocked again, this time he could hear shuffling behind the door, the sound of a leg dragging on a solid floor. The door opened a crack and a middle aged man with receding hair peered out. 'What do you want?' he asked. Douglas suddenly realized he hadn't asked the girl what her name was.

She stepped forward, 'It's Greta.'

He opened the door wider, 'Your things are still in your room, have you come for them?' Douglas could now see he leant heavily on a crutch. One leg had been badly broken and was bent and was now shorter than the other one.

Douglas intervened, 'No, we haven't come for that; I've come to pay the arrears.' Geerhaart's eyes widened in surprise, he had thought Greta was a good girl fallen on hard times, and now here she was with a foreigner in tow offering to pay her rent. Well, well, better not to judge. 'How much is it?' asked Douglas.

'It's ten gilders a month.'

Douglas pulled out a wad of notes from his pocket, 'Here's the arrears and one month in advance.' That should give her time to find some work and hopefully that would be the end of his involvement with her. However, he had a sudden desire to see what he was paying for. He stepped into the gloomy hallway, Greta followed him. The floor was tiled, but most of them were broken. On the right was a doorway, the door was slightly ajar. That must be where Geerhaart lived. Douglas couldn't see him being able to climb the stairs so often in his condition. The wooden stairs were right at the end of the hallway, uncarpeted and rising very steeply with sharp turns. He climbed them two at a time, he heard Greta coming up behind him.

'My room is right at the top on the forth floor.'

'That's where attics usually are.' he answered tartly then regretted it. She went quiet, he reflected that it was only last night she had tried to end her life. The wooden door confronting him had only a token amount of paint on it. The room was stuffy with a low sloping ceiling. The rickety bed had a flocked mattress on it that dipped in the middle where lots of bodies had lain. There was a wooden table and one chair. A primus stove for heating food, no other obvious sign of heating. It must have been bitterly cold in there in winter thought Douglas. An old cupboard stood against the wall, he looked inside. There was a bag of rice, less than half full, a small jar of the deadly ersatz coffee and some powdered milk. No sign of any sugar, the coffee must have tasted awful. He turned round to face her.

'It was the best I could find and the only one I could afford.' she said defensively.

'You're going to need some supplies.' He quickly made up his mind. 'First we're going out to lunch, then to the market.' She didn't argue with this strange man who had pulled her out of the canal, she was past that now. She couldn't decide on his nationality, British she thought, definitely not American - Americans never tried to learn a foreign language. He spoke Dutch fluently with only a trace of a foreign accent. Their footsteps echoed as they went down the stairs, bringing Geerhaart to his door but he said nothing. She followed him out onto the street. He took her to the de Kelderhof restaurant. The owner was surprised to see him back so soon. He didn't recognize the woman he was with, she certainly didn't look his type. The women he usually brought here were attractive certainly, but a little loud and flashy. They sat in an inconspicuous corner. Douglas ordered the set menu. When it came, Greta tried hard to restrain herself but it was obvious she was hungry. He wondered how long she had been surviving on just rice. When the plates had been cleared away, Douglas ordered her a coffee and something stronger for himself. Hardly any conversation had passed between them during the meal. He studied her face, a little colour had returned to her cheeks, she was perhaps older than he had at first thought, and prettier. She didn't look too bad at all in the clothes he had bought. He must try and resurrect her mackintosh. It was, he was sure, the only coat she possessed. He attracted the owner's attention and asked for the bill. He paid it and left a substantial tip. They headed for the market where Douglas bought enough provisions to last for a few weeks then went back to the attic room. Douglas unloaded the food onto the table, there were tins, powdered egg and milk and some sugar amongst other things. When she wasn't looking he slipped a ten gilder note under the tins. 'I have to go now,' he told her, 'will you be alright?'

'Yes,' she said, 'I don't know how to--------'

'Then don't.' he said brusquely. At the door he turned back, 'No more walks in the rain?'

'No,' she paused. 'I haven't got a mackintosh.'

He put his hand to his forehead; it was still in his wash bag. He hoped it was salvageable, if so, he would drop it off. She could hear his footsteps echoing down the stairs and heard the door close behind him. She stood on the chair to look out of the pokey little window, but she couldn't see down onto the street. She sighed and started to put the groceries away.

Douglas went straight back to his apartment, it was now getting quite late in the afternoon. He must sort out the spare bedroom and see if the mackintosh could be sponged down. It was obvious she would need a coat and it would save him buying her one. First he tackled the wash bag; he gingerly lifted out the clothes, they were streaked with filth and mud and were very smelly. He decided to throw them away. The mackintosh wasn't as bad as he expected, he could do something with that or the woman who came to clean for him could. Next on the agenda was the spare room. His pyjamas and dressing gown were neatly folded as were the towels. He shoved them all in the wash bag for collection on Thursday morning. The bed was the next thing to be tackled. He threw back the sheets and stopped in his tracks. There was blood where she had been laying, his mind shot back to the frantic sex. He groaned out loud, the woman must have been a virgin, he remembered now the cry of pain when he entered her and the strength of her arms as she held on tight. Pragmatic as ever, Douglas thought, well, she isn't a virgin now, and he chuckled, Uncle Wilhelm didn't get his oats then.

Douglas felt slightly disoriented from the events of the day. He decided he needed a diversion. He rang one of his many lady friends up to ask her out to dinner. He was quite put out when she told him she already had an engagement that evening. He tried another number, but the telephone just rang and rang. He gave up. He was feeling quite peckish but couldn't be bothered to make anything for himself, so he decided to go back to the De Kelderhof. It was nearby and the service was quick. When he arrived, quite a few of the tables were already taken. The owner, who was surprised to see him twice in one day, ushered him into a window seat on a table for two and took his order. After a few minutes he brought Douglas an aperitif. His meal was a little late in arriving and he was served by the owner himself which was strange. In the evenings he was usually in the kitchen cooking. Gradually the restaurant started to empty. Douglas sat with his coffee and a glass of cognac. He noticed that there had only been one waiter on the tables all evening apart from the patrone himself. When he was ready he called for his bill. The owner brought it 'A little short handed this evening?'

'I do apologize sir; one of my regular staff didn't turn up.'

'Not very reliable, eh.'

The little man smiled, 'Usually, but no, not tonight.'

Douglas had had a brain wave, 'I think I can help you there. You remember the young lady that was with me this lunchtime.'

The little man was wary, 'Yes sir, I remember.'

'Well, she's looking for a job. I'll bring her round tomorrow. Shall we say three thirty, after you have finished with lunches.' Without waiting for an answer Douglas rose: he paid his bill and left a huge tip. The owner realized that he would have to offer the girl a job if he wanted to keep Douglas's custom. And he did, he was a regular customer and brought quite a bit of business with him and he was an excellent tipper. He reasoned he could always get rid of the girl in a few weeks if she was no good.

Next morning after breakfast, Douglas decided he had better go round to see Greta and give her the good news. So, with her mackintosh over his arm he set out for Geerhaart's house. The Green door was closed and he knocked on it loudly, there was no response, he knocked again, Greta's room was way up at the top of the house, it must be difficult to hear the door. He knocked louder still. He heard the dragging of a leg and the door opened just a fraction. When Geerhaart saw him he said, 'Oh, it's you back again, well she's not in.'

Douglas immediately thought the worst, 'When did she go out?'

'Quite early this morning, I heard the door close.' Douglas immediately relaxed. Suicides don't go and do the deed in the morning; they usually attempt it in the very early hours when the libido is low. Geerhaart closed the door on Douglas leaving him standing in the street with Greta's coat over his arm. He was just about to leave when Greta came around the corner. She was wearing the skirt and blouse he had bought for her. She saw him, but didn't quicken her pace.

She slowly walked up to him. 'Thank you for bringing my coat back.' She held out her hand to take it from him.

'I want to talk to you Greta, and not out here on the street.' She reluctantly opened the door and they climbed the stairs to her attic room. 'I've had a word with the owner of the De Kelderhof and he has agreed to give you a job.' Greta's face lit up at this news. 'Have you had any waitressing experience?' She nodded her head. 'Good, I'll call for you at three o'clock this afternoon.' He turned to go then added, 'Oh, and wear the dress I bought you.' Her face blanched. 'What's the matter?' She looked down at the floor, nervously clenching and unclenching her hands. 'What is it?' he asked again.

'I can't.' she whispered.

'What do you mean, you can't?'

Still looking at the floor she repeated quietly, 'I can't because I've sold it.'

'What did you say?'

'I've sold it.' she mumbled.

'You've done what?' Douglas was angry now, really angry.

She lifted her head in defiance, 'I sold it because I needed some shoes.'

Douglas opened his mouth to speak but closed it again. He looked down at her feet. She was wearing a pair of stout black shoes. He took a minute or two to simmer down then added, 'Well, I suppose I can understand that. You'll just have to come as you are, you look reasonably presentable.' She flushed at his rudeness. 'That is, apart from the bare legs. I'll bring a pair of stockings with me.' And then as an afterthought, 'I suppose you have something to hold them up with?'

'Yes, I have.' She held her head high. Douglas turned on his heels and left.

Promptly at three Douglas knocked on the green door, he heard the sound of footsteps on the stairs and Greta opened the door. Her hair was done up in a chignon, and he noticed her nails were scrubbed clean. He delved into his coat pocket and brought out two pairs of nylons. He gave them to her, 'Go put those on, I'll wait here.' She took them from him and ran back up the stairs. He called after her, 'And don't sell the second pair.'

She stopped on the second flight and peered over the rails at him, 'No, I won't.' He noted the slight smile on her face. They arrived at the restaurant dead on three thirty.

The owner opened the door to them. He explained the duties expected of her and the hours he wanted her to work. He told her he wouldn't pay the full hourly rate until she had proved herself. If all this was satisfactory she could start in the evening the following day. She agreed to the terms laid down. 'Just one more thing,' he said, 'you will need a black skirt and a white blouse and apron. I don't supply a uniform.' The owner looked stubborn.

Douglas sighed, here we go again he thought, but it was a price worth paying to finally get her off his hands. They went back to the market and Douglas bought two of everything she needed, one for the laundry and one for wearing he explained. He handed her the parcel and said, 'Now scoot, before I change my mind.' She shyly kissed him on the cheek and walked away. He watched her go; she turned round once and then was gone. Douglas walked slowly back along the canal bank, stopped and stared down at 'The Lady Anne' for a few moments, she was due to be moved to the repair yard the following morning. Then he continued thoughtfully past the spot where he had yanked Greta out of the water only a couple of nights ago.

CHAPTER 7

Douglas decided he was in need of some rest and recuperation or at least a change of scene. He rang Dieter and arranged to spend a few days with him. Dieter had acquired another couple of horses and was keen to hear what Douglas thought of them. Douglas asked him to arrange a couple of races for him; he needed to feel some adrenalin coursing through his veins. Strangely for some reason, Douglas had decided not to tell Dieter about his recent adventure, it just felt wrong.

The first morning in Bremen, the two of them were out early exercising the new occupants of the stables. Dieter was on the chestnut mare, Douglas astride a black stallion. They could both run like the wind. Douglas asked Dieter if he had managed to organize a race for him. Dieter told him he had entered him into two races in a couple of day's time.

'Good,' said Douglas, 'we can have some fun with these two and win ourselves some money at the same time. Let's swap mounts; I'd like to get of feel of the mare before I race her.' Dieter obliged and they galloped back to the stables at quite a lick. Dieter was ahead by a length or so. They went into breakfast and discussed the tactics to be employed at the race meeting. The stallion was the better looking of the two horses so the likelyhood was that the odds would be shorter on him. 'I'll win on the mare, she's faster than she looks, and I'll come a close second on the stallion. I'll leave the betting to you.'

On the day of the race meeting, they loaded up the two horses. Douglas went to get ready for the race and Dieter went to saddle up his horses. He ran his hands over the stallion. He was really pleased with his purchase and intended to breed from him. Douglas arrived as Dieter was adjusting the saddle on the mare, he jacked Douglas up onto her back and he cantered out to the start. It was a windy afternoon threatening rain but conditions weren't too bad. There were nine runners in the field and Douglas jumped off to a reasonable start. He kept the mare going at an even pace alternating between third and fourth place. As the winning post loomed he brought her up to the second spot and with a kick in her ribs and a judicious slap from his whip she nudged in front by a head. It was a masterly piece of horsemanship, the odds had been very favourable and Dieter had placed a substantial bet on the nose right at the last minute. The stallion was entered into the last race and he was joint favourite. By now the rain had started and the wind had got up a little. Douglas cantered down to the start. This time he jumped straight into the lead. Horse and rider were as one. They were flying justifying his place as joint favourite. On the half way mark they were three lengths ahead of the rest of the field. Dieter began to wonder if Douglas had remembered the race plan, a lot of money rested on the horse coming in second. The field were thundering down the course, the rain had intensified. Douglas was slowly being reeled back but he looked a certain winner. The second horse was now only half a length away when suddenly Douglas's mount put his lead leg into a dip in the track. He buckled at the knee. The speed was such that Douglas stood no chance and he was catapulted over the horse's head and landed with a thud near the rails. He instinctively curled into a ball so he was less of a target as the stallion went head over heels in front of him, sliding on his back for quite a long way before coming to rest. The rest of the pack missed Douglas but the stallion received another thud as he tried to regain his feet and he was bowled over again. Douglas was badly winded and stayed where he was for a few minutes. When he tried to regain his feet, a sharp pain shot through his right leg which made him wince. He had badly twisted his ankle and something else was wrong. He sank down onto the ground and waited for the course medic. Worse was to follow, the stallion was trying to stand but couldn't, he was whinnying pitiably, it was obvious he had broken his leg. The poor thing had to be put down. Dieter was distraught. He loved his horses. The race meeting had been a disaster. The horse he hoped to breed from was dead. Douglas was injured and they had lost money, the insurance from the horse wasn't enough to cover his value.

Douglas had damaged the ligaments in his leg, he had a pot on it and he would be incapacitated for at least a month. Dieter had to drive him back to Amsterdam and had to stay until Douglas had mastered the crutches he had been given. At least he could get around his apartment without too much trouble. Dieter had to divide his time between Bremen and Amsterdam. Douglas was able to co-ordinate quite a lot of things by telephone but Dieter had to do the running around. The diamond runs were also on hold for the time being, but Douglas thought at least some future trips should be undertaken by a man on crutches, they were an ideal hiding place for the contraband stones. Leonard was now dealing in diamonds smuggled in from Africa, blood diamonds as they were commonly called. His supply culled from his own race had now run out. Douglas was still taking in a few counterfeit ten pound notes, but he couldn't do it in large quantities. Currency restrictions were still in place and would be for some years to come.

The pot was taken off Douglas's leg; he still had to use a walking stick though for a few days. Dieter was down until he was fully mobile. They decided to have lunch at the De Kelderhof. Douglas had been once or twice since getting Greta a job there, but he hadn't taken any of his lady friends there since. The meal was up to the usual standard, Greta had served them. They were having a coffee and cognac, Douglas was smoking a cigarette. Greta was clearing away the other tables and Dieter remarked, 'The waitress is a pretty girl, pity she doesn't smile though.'

Douglas immediately felt protective, 'Hands off Dieter, anyway, perhaps she hasn't got much to smile about.' Dieter was mildly surprised by Douglas's reaction but said nothing. Douglas hadn't related Greta's story to Dieter, somehow it seemed an invasion of her privacy. Douglas glanced at Greta as she worked, yes, he thought, she has lost that pasty look and she's put some weight on, but I suppose that's one of the perks of working in a restaurant. They paid the bill and left a hefty tip, then made their way to the repair yard to sort out some minor details with the owner. The work was coming on in leaps and bounds. The engines had been removed and were being overhauled, the generators were to be replaced as more power would be needed when she was up and running. The three new decks were in place. Plates and stringers had been replaced as necessary and frames strengthened. She would soon be moved to the fitting out yard when Douglas's work would start in earnest. Dieter returned to Germany, and Douglas returned to full mobility, much to his relief. He had been deprived of female company long enough while he had been incapacitated and he had every intention of making up for the shortfall.

The day came for 'The Lady Anne' to be put back into the water. Dieter drove down to witness the event, even Leonard Warner turned up to watch. She went in sideways making quite a splash. She wobbled from port to starboard then gradually stabilized. A big cheer went up from the workers in the yard and the owner beamed from ear to ear. Douglas had provided bottles of vintage champagne and everybody had a glass and drank a toast to 'The Lady Anne'. The next day she was towed to the fitting out yard.

No expense was to be spared in fitting out 'The Lady Anne'. The third deck was where the serious business was to be conducted out of the sight of prying eyes. The portholes had blinds fitted showing scenes from the Moulin Rouge. The carpet was a deep plush blue with soft furnishings to match. There was a discreet bar situated in one corner stocked with spirits and every liqueur you could think off. The glasses were cut crystal and sparkled in the subdued lighting. The card tables had plenty of room between them enabling people to move around freely, the chairs were antiques but comfortable. They wanted people to be able to sit in them for hours on end. The lighting was soft but each table was adequately illuminated. Gambling was the name of the game on this deck. The second deck was given over to rest areas and sumptuously fitted out cabins, the main one being the owner's cabin. It was envisaged that either Dieter or Douglas would want to stay there on occasions to entertain friends and host their own private card games with selected clients. The top deck was the legitimate front of 'The Lady Anne'. It was to be a five star restaurant, the concession had already been given to a first rate chef. He would be responsible for the waiting staff and the bar on that deck. He was renowned for his food. He only used first rate ingredients ordered daily. Success was assured. There was no other venue quite like it on the waterfront and he was already fully booked before he even opened. Douglas had personally interviewed the people he required for his domain. He had a head croupier and a team of others working under him. The bar staff were professionals and he had interviewed the hostesses whose job it was to serve drinks and food to the players when requested. They were all good looking girls with good figures but they were not there to distract the guests from their card game; that had been made quite clear to them. If a player left the table for a rest, he could request a hostess to accompany him but Douglas had made it quite plain, it was up to each individual hostess how she fulfilled that aspect of her job. There was to be no coercion from the management side and if a client overstepped the mark he would be asked to leave and wouldn't be invited back.

The big day arrived, the lights were turned on at the restaurant and the great and the good of Amsterdam turned out to sample the gastronomic delights of this newest edition to the night life of the City.

The specially invited guests were shown down to the third deck through a discreetly curtained door and this venture too was a great success. Dieter had arrived that afternoon and he was ensconced in the owner's cabin. Douglas and he cracked a bottle of vintage champagne between them before they went to join their guests on the third deck. Dieter stayed for a full week, there was just the odd fault here and there to iron out. One croupier wasn't quite up to the job and had to be replaced, but, all in all, the opening went like clockwork. Douglas was to be in charge of the day to day running of the boat and Dieter returned to his horses. The take from the gaming had been increased to ten percent of every wager because of the enormous capital outlay involved in getting the boat up and running, but the punters didn't seem to mind. These people were hard and fast gamblers and they had money.

CHAPTER 8

Douglas had been so busy of late he hadn't been to the De Kelderhof in weeks, but now things were running smoothly at ' The Lady Anne' he decided to go and have lunch there. He chose a table in the corner and waited for his order to be taken, he couldn't see Greta but perhaps she was in the kitchen, or perhaps it was her day off. The owner came to take his order, he seemed somewhat evasive, but thought Douglas, perhaps it's because I haven't been for such a long time. His meal appeared brought by a waiter Douglas hadn't seen before. Afterwards Douglas ordered a coffee and his usual cognac and settled down to enjoy a cigarette. His bill was brought by the new waiter. Strange thought Douglas, it was always the proprietor who had brought it before when he would enquire if everything had been to his liking. The waiter came to collect the bill. Douglas kept his hand on it as he enquired when Greta was next on duty. He informed Douglas that there were only waiters employed at the De Kelderhof now. Douglas kept his hand on the bill and asked to see the owner. After a few minutes the owner appeared wiping his hands on a towel. He came across to Douglas's table but was reluctant to look him in the eye. Douglas asked him what had happened to Greta. He hopped from one foot to another, eventually he told Douglas he had had to let her go. 'But why?' asked Douglas, 'has she let you down?'

'The job was getting too much for her,' he said limply, 'it was too tiring.'

'What are you talking about?' demanded Douglas, 'you told me she was highly satisfactory, that you were very pleased with her work.'

The man went bright red. 'I had to ask her to go, she was starting to show, it wasn't good for business.' Douglas was stunned. He sat down again with a bump taking his hand off the bill. The owner quietly removed it. Douglas knew exactly what the owner meant. Greta was pregnant. He didn't have to do any calculating to know whose child it was. Douglas lit another cigarette. He noticed his hand trembled slightly. So much for the boasts he had made to his mother, he was the one who was careful, very, very careful and he had been caught out with one night of unprotected sex with a virgin! Douglas sat there for a full five minutes recovering from the shock and considering his options. He didn't really have any options he decided, he would have to go and see her. He got up slowly and left the restaurant, the owner had been watching from the kitchens. He was relieved when Douglas left, he thought it a shame to lose a good customer but he hadn't been around much of late anyway.

Douglas slowly made his way to where Greta lived, he had no idea what he was going to do or say. Then a thought struck him, maybe she had moved, maybe she had gone back to her family. That was no get out, he would only have to go and find her. He knocked on the door; the green paint was in a worst state than ever. He heard no clattering of feet down the stairs. He knocked again, this time he heard the dragging of feet on the broken tiles. Geerhaart opened the door a crack.

'Oh, it's you' he sneered, 'we haven't seen you in quite a while have we?'

'Is Greta in?'

'Yes, she's in.' He sighed, 'where would you expect her to be in her condition? And what are you going to do about it? Did you think I would have thrown her out? Plenty would in my place.' Douglas pushed past Geerhaart and climbed the stairs two at a time. He rapped on Greta's door, there was no reply.

'Open the door Greta; I know you're in there.'

'Go away, I don't want to see you, I don't want to see anyone.'

'Don't be foolish Greta. Open the door.'

'No!'

Douglas put both hands up against the frame and kicked against the lock with his foot. The wood splintered and the door swung slowly open on its hinges. She was sitting in an old fireside chair. Her white hair was in a tangle around her face and her eyes were red and swollen.

'Please go away,' she whispered.

'Why didn't you tell me?' She didn't respond, just looked down at her clasped hands resting in her lap. Douglas could definitely see the bump. 'If you had told me early enough I could have done something about it.'

She looked up defiantly, 'That's why I didn't tell you,' and then added in a whisper, 'anyway you weren't around.' It was stuffy in the attic. Douglas loosened his tie and turned slightly away from her resting his hand against the wall.

'What about your family? Will they help?'

'No, I haven't told Aunt Bertha, she would never get over the

71

shame.' She started to cry very softly. 'Geerhaart says I can stay here, he has been very kind to me.' Then all of a sudden she cried out. 'Why did you have to interfere? Why couldn't you have left me alone? If you had I wouldn't be in this mess.'

'If I had, you wouldn't be alive now.' he shouted back, 'you wouldn't be alive to have my baby.' His outburst had shocked him. He had turned to look at her in his anger. God, my baby he thought, she's carrying my baby. He walked over to her, kneeled in front of her and gently wiped her eyes. 'This isn't doing us any good.' He looked around the dingy room, 'and I'm not having my child born into a place like this.' Greta stared into his eyes. 'You'll have to move in with me until I can think of something better.' She went bright red, then pale. Douglas had made up his mind; he might as well act on it. 'Come on, get your things together, anything you need we can get later.' Greta got shakily to her feet. Douglas looked around for a bag, he opened the cupboard doors and stuffed her few possessions into the bag.

'But I can't go just like that, Geerhaart------'

'I'll deal with Geerhaart, Come on, we haven't got all day.'

'Geerhaart has been good to me; I won't have you treat him badly.' Douglas smiled at her spark of resistance, but took her by the elbow and manoeuvred her towards the stairs. She shook his arm away, 'I can manage the stairs on my own.' Douglas went down ahead of her.

Geerhaart was out in the hallway, concern showing in his face. 'Are you alright Greta? Do you want me to throw him out?'

Douglas peeled off some notes from a wad he had taken out of his pocket. 'She's going to be fine Geerhaart.' It was the first time Douglas had used his name, 'this will cover the repairs to the door upstairs and this is a couple of months rent.' Geerhart's jaw dropped a mile.

When Greta drew level with him, she put her hand on his arm. 'I'll be alright Geerhaart, I'll come back and see you soon.'

Greta had been staying in Douglas's apartment for a couple of weeks. Douglas was on the telephone to Dieter, he wasn't sure how to break the news to him but Dieter sensing something in his tone of voice asked him.

'Have you been a naughty boy Douglas?'

'It's a little more serious than that Dieter, you remember the waitress at the De Kelderhof? Can you come down and be my best man?'

Dieter whistled in disbelief but told Douglas to expect him in a couple of days. Later when they were in the owner's cabin on 'The Lady Anne' Dieter ventured, 'Are you sure about this Douglas?'

'No, not really, but I'm thirty two now. I don't see any of my girlfriends as wife material, do you?' Dieter just looked at him with raised eyebrows, 'I'm not going to let it interfere with my lifestyle, but I feel responsible for them.'

'What about your trips to London?'

'I've got every excuse to travel to London, after all I've got family there.'

'And if she wants to meet your family?'

'Well, she can't. I'm going to start as I mean to go on, she must understand that.'

The wedding was a brief affair, there were only half a dozen guests, Dieter was the best man and Greta had insisted on Geerhaart being present. They had a wedding breakfast at the De Kelderhof and then it was back to Douglas's apartment and back to business on 'The Lady Anne' by the evening. Now money was coming in Dieter had shown Douglas the plans he had for rebuilding his old home. 'I know it's going to take years,' he told Douglas, 'but I'm determined to do it.' And he left with a gleam in his eye. Douglas was at 'The Lady Anne' until the early hours each morning, then he went home and slept late until the afternoon. This arrangement suited both Douglas and Greta. She liked to go for a little walk in the morning; she was quite used to spending time on her own. They had a light brunch together when Douglas woke up and then he would disappear into his study to do his paperwork. Greta had seen a midwife at Douglas's insistence and they had been reassured that everything was progressing normally. Greta was quite large by now but she had a glow about her.

Early one morning when Douglas returned to the apartment, he heard a low groan coming from the bedroom. He raced through to find Greta on the floor on her knees. 'How long have you been like this?'

'It's only just started but it hurts.'

'I'm told it does, but let's get you onto the bed, you'll be more comfortable there.'

'Will you ring the midwife?'

'Are you sure? My mother told me she was in labour for days

73

when she had me.'

'Please.' winced Greta, 'the pain is very severe.'

'O.K. if it'll put your mind at rest.' So Douglas went into the hallway and telephoned the midwife. The phone rang for a minute or two then a very slurred voice asked who it was. Douglas told her his wife had started with labour pains.

'It's a first baby isn't it?' asked the voice.

'Yes.' agreed Douglas.

'She'll be hours yet, just make her comfortable and ring me back at a more civilized time in the morning.' The phone went dead.

Douglas returned to the bedroom to find Greta sitting up, legs splayed apart, her waters had broken. Douglas had a quick look and saw the baby's crown. He dashed straight back to the telephone. When the receiver was picked up he shouted, 'Get here straight away, my baby's being born right now.' He dashed into the bathroom and collected every towel he could find. Greta was moaning through gritted teeth. Douglas didn't have time to think, the baby's head was out, black hair plastered against its skull and blood smears down the side of its screwed up face. Greta gave a great heave, Douglas put out his hands and the child slithered into them. Douglas wiped the baby as best he could, he wiped around the nose and mouth. He saw the baby's chest give a great heave as it took its first breath and it let out a loud yell. Douglas wrapped it in a huge towel then quickly unwrapped it again, he checked the vital bits, it was a boy. He had a son! He did what he could for Greta and placed the child next to her. He heard the doorbell and he shot down the hall to let the midwife in. His first words to her were, 'It's a boy, I've got a son!' And he led her to the bedroom. Douglas went to the bathroom to clean himself up, he peeped into the bedroom, the midwife was still busy with Greta so he went to the living room and poured himself a large glass of whiskey.

Douglas's routine changed with the birth of his son, for the first few weeks when the child was still waking up through the night, Douglas made sure he was home before midnight. Dieter filled the breach at 'The Lady Anne' when he could. He seemed just as delighted with the birth of Douglas's son as Douglas was himself. He asked what they were going to call the boy.

'This little chap,' Douglas said, holding the child aloft, 'is called Jan Coulter, Jan, meet your Uncle Dieter.' He handed the little bundle over to Dieter, who held him in the crook of his arm like a rugby ball.

'I can't say he looks like you Douglas, he hasn't got a moustache for one thing. His name surprises me though, why Jan?'

'Must humour the little woman,' smiled Douglas, 'she insisted. Jan was her brother's name but I put my foot down at Jan Geerhaart though.'

As Jan started to make himself understood with baby noises, Douglas insisted than only English must be spoken in the apartment. Greta knew some English but Douglas made no allowances for her. She must become fluent as well. Douglas had plans for this little boy. He told Dieter he was going to be educated in the English Public School System.

'Poor Jan.' was Dieter's response.

'Why do you say that?'

'Have you had any experience of English Public Schools?'

'Well no,'

'I have, and I couldn't escape quickly enough.'

'I'm determined that Jan will have every advantage in life. You can't get anywhere without going to the right school in my country Dieter.' Dieter didn't respond. He knew how touchy Douglas was about the class system into which he himself had been born. As Jan grew from a baby to a toddler, he started to make more demands on his parent's time. There was more disruption in the household and Douglas couldn't get the rest he needed. He started to sleep on 'The Lady Anne' and returned to the apartment in the afternoon. It meant he got to see much more of his son who was now as blond as his mother. Douglas was able to play and join in the child's games with him and he was there at bedtime to read him his bedtime stories. A bond was developing between father and son.

Douglas returned to the boat before the evening session began to make sure everything was running smoothly. The restaurant had proved a huge success and was fully booked nearly every night, it was the 'in' place to go and be seen in Amsterdam. To those in the know, the third deck of the 'The Lady Anne' was just as popular and money was rolling in for the partners. Dieter and Douglas spent their share as soon as they got it. No-body knew what Leonard did with his share. Dieter was a regular visitor, both at the boat and at Douglas's apartment. Whether it was seeing Douglas's family regularly that prompted Dieter is questionable, but he told Douglas he thought he would have to grasp the matrimonial nettle himself soon. 'I need an heir, I must keep the family name going, I'm the last one, but it's not something I'm looking forward to.' he told him.

'Have you got anybody in mind?'

'Unfortunately, yes.'

'Anyone I know?'

'I doubt it. Her name is Grafen Christa von Rotenburg.'

'She sounds very grand.'

'Her family have known my family for ever, her land buts onto my estate, so it makes sense to join them together.' He paused, 'my elder brother would have been in line for the honour had he lived. The second son can usually marry for love. My mother would have arranged the match had she survived.'

'You don't sound very enthusiastic Dieter'

'No, she looks like a horse.'

'But you like horses.' laughed Douglas.

'Yes, I do, but not in my bed.'

The invitation to Dieter's wedding arrived a few weeks later. Dieter had warned Douglas he would have to bring Greta. His wife to be would not accept a mistress no matter how beautiful and charming the mistress might be. Greta was delighted at the thought of attending a society wedding. It was the first time that Douglas had asked her to accompany him on such an occasion. Dieter had asked Douglas to be his best man. Douglas was very flattered to be so honoured; Dieter had some very influential friends. Douglas went with Greta to choose her clothes for such a grand occasion. He was very particular, he also had very good taste in such matters and she was happy to leave the final decision to him. They travelled to Bremen a couple of days before the ceremony. Dieter had booked them into a hotel. He was still living in the Gatehouse, but after his marriage his farm manager was due to move in. The rebuilding of the main house was still in the early stages so the wedding was to be conducted from the Bride's family home, which would become Dieter's home until his own house was ready. When Douglas and Greta were introduced to Grafen Christa von Rotenburg, Douglas had to agree with Dieter's description of her. The poor lady had a very long morose face and a very long aquiline nose. Her face was transformed however when she laughed. She took to

Greta immediately and thought Jan adorable the moment she saw him. She whisked them through to her apartments to view her wedding dress and to see the wedding presents which would be put on display in the main hall in due course. Dieter took Douglas through to a room that was designated to become his study. He poured them both a drink.

'Well. My friend, you asked me a question before I got married. I'm going to ask you the same thing. Are you sure about this?'

Dieter chuckled, he couldn't help himself. 'I will give you the same answer. No, I'm not sure, but in my case, I need an heir. This marriage will never be a grand passion, but we have shared interests, she likes horses and dogs. She's a country woman at heart so I think we'll rub along.'

The wedding was quite a grand affair. Christa's relations were there in force. Many of them had skipped the country to far flung estates before the war started but had now returned to West Germany. Some had had estates in East Germany which were now lost to them. Most hadn't expected Christa to marry even though she was a very wealthy woman in her own right, especially to the handsome Dieter von Rheinhart, but then again he had been ruined by the war. Their sort must stick together. Society in Germany had undergone a revolution. The old families had lost nearly all of their influence in the new post war Germany.

CHAPTER 9

'The Lady Anne' was running like a dream. It was a few months after Dieter's wedding. Dieter was due down to spend a few days on the boat; he told Douglas he needed a break. They were in the owner's cabin, Dieter looked glum.

'I know what you need, why don't we go out on the town. Let's go find some playmates. 'The Lady Anne' will look after herself for one night.'

Dieter brightened up, 'I suppose you have somewhere in mind?'

'I do indeed and I also have some playmates in mind.'

'It might be just the tonic the doctor ordered, the effort of trying to get an heir can be quite wearying.'

Douglas clapped him on the shoulder, 'Come on, you need a fresh pasture. You've been concentrating all your efforts in one direction for far too long.' They didn't return to the boat until the next day. The following evening they decided to have a meal on the top deck, followed by a few drinks in Dieter's cabin. The food was wonderful as usual then they went down to the second deck. Douglas told Dieter to pour him a drink, he wouldn't be long; he was just going down to check things were alright downstairs. It was still quite early but Douglas was surprised to see that only the Head croupier and a few hardened card players were there.

'Where is everybody?' he enquired.

'I don't know sir; the staff are usually here before now.'

Douglas frowned, 'Well let me know when they turn up.'

'Yes sir.'

Douglas went back upstairs to join Dieter. He had a puzzled look on his face.

'Trouble?'

'I don't know, it's odd, only the Head croupier is there at the moment, perhaps there's a traffic hold up somewhere.' He took his glass from Dieter and sat down opposite him. He was just about to take a sip when there was a knock at the cabin door.

The head croupier opened it, his face was drip white. 'You have a visitor sir.' And before Douglas could respond he had disappeared. A small fat balding man walked straight in without waiting for an

78

invitation. Behind him were two large tough looking characters, they stayed out in the alleyway.

'And who might you be?' asked Douglas crossly. Dieter frowned at the intrusion.

'My name is Wim Henke.' Dieter thought the name sounded familiar.

'And what do you want with us Menheer Henke?'

'I have a proposition to put to you both.'

'Really!'

'Yes really, I take a dim view of the fact that you are operating on my territory.'

'What are you talking about?' Douglas rose to his feet. Dieter immediately put his hand out to restrain Douglas; he could see he was losing his temper.

'How is business tonight?'

'Have you got something to do with the fact our croupiers haven't shown up this evening?'

'I have offered them alternative employment. Most of them have had the common sense to accept.' There was a silence in the cabin.

It was Dieter who spoke next, 'And what is your proposal Menheer?'

'I believe you also have a sleeping partner, I suggest he comes along to our next meeting, shall we say, in three days time at ten o'clock sharp. I will put my proposal to you then.' He turned to leave, then said to Douglas, 'You have a lovely little boy Major Coulter, I believe his name is Jan, a good Dutch name.' Douglas went white. The man left with his heavies in tow. Douglas sat down with a thump.

'He knows Jan's name.' he looked at Dieter, 'he knows his name.'

'Go home Douglas, I'll stay here, go straight home and check everything is alright.'

Douglas left without another word. When he arrived at his apartment he found the door was locked. He put his key in the door, immediately Greta called out in a frightened voice, 'Who is it, I'll call the police.'

'It's me.' shouted Douglas.

Greta immediately unlocked the door. She had Jan by her side. 'There were two men here asking for you Douglas. I told them you weren't at home. One of them stroked Jan's head, he told me to tell you, you had a lovely son.' Greta was trembling. He put his arms around her. 'What does it mean Douglas? They frightened me.'

'It means Greta; that we are leaving here just as soon as I can arrange it.'

'You're not going back to 'The Lady Anne' tonight are you?'

'No, I'm not going back tonight.' He went into the apartment and bolted and locked his door.

Three days later, Leonard, Douglas and Dieter were in the owner's cabin awaiting the arrival of Wim Henke. Leonard had told his partners all he knew about him. He told them he was a gangster, a thug, who employed other thugs to do his bidding. He was into gambling, drug running and other unsavoury practises. Fortunately he had never interfered with the diamond trade: 'We have our own sharks to contend with.' he told them. Henke normally operated in the run down cafes and back streets of Amsterdam. 'I'm surprised he's interested in us, I would have thought we were far too upmarket to worry him. But on the other hand money interests him. He's a very dangerous man, don't underestimate him.' Douglas thought that this was serious if Leonard was scared, he was one tough cookie. Leonard was wrong about one thing, 'The Lady Anne' operation had harmed Henke's trade, not significantly but enough. There was a knock on the cabin door. Douglas got up to open it. Wim Henke walked into the cabin, his henchmen stayed outside.

'Good evening Gentleman,' he turned to Leonard, 'especially to you Menheer Warner, I believe that's what you now call yourself, we don't often see you out and about. I hope you're keeping well?' Even a question about his health sounded threatening to Leonard. Henke now turned specifically to Douglas, 'How has business held up these last three days Major Coulter?'

Douglas realized he knew he had been drummed out of the Army. 'It has been pathetic as I am sure you are well aware.'

'Yes, it seems to me you are not making the most of your opportunities here.'

'What do you mean?'

'I know this business inside out; your take is ten percent of wagers.' Douglas nodded. 'You need an angle to bend the odds in your favour.'

'You don't mean marked cards? Our clients are sophisticated people; they would spot that scam a mile off.'

'Not this one, shall we have a game of cards Major?' He sat down at the table opposite Douglas. He took a pack of cards out of his pocket; they were still wrapped in cellophane. He handed the pack to Douglas, 'You deal.' Douglas inspected the pack turning it this way and that, then he tore the cellophane away and took the pack out of the box. He shuffled them as only an expert card player can, feeling the edges as he did so. He dealt four cards face down to his opponent and four to himself. Wim Henke took one card and pushed the others away, 'Another three please.' Douglas complied, he didn't touch his cards. Wim pushed them all away and indicated he wanted more. Douglas dealt another three, this time Wim took two. Douglas put two more cards down. Wim took one, 'What's the odds of my holding four court cards do you think?'

'Slim.'

Wim Henke turned his cards over, they were all picture cards. Douglas slid them over to him and had a good look at them.

'I don't see anything.'

'How many court cards to you think you hold?' Douglas looked down at his hand. Wim Henke pulled one towards him and turned it over. It was a court card. This time Dieter had a good look at it, but shook his head at Douglas.

'How is it done?' asked Douglas, he looked mystified.

'Not so fast, I think we should discuss terms first. I want twenty five percent of profits.'

It was Leonard who exploded, 'Twenty five percent.' He was red in the face.

Dieter, who so far had remained silent, said, 'I wonder if you would allow my partners and myself to discuss this matter Menheer Henke.'

'Of course, I'm not an unreasonable man. I will go and inspect your casino and return in say, thirty minutes.' He got up and left, taking the cards with him.

'Twenty five percent with no capital outlay, that's monstrous. Can't we negotiate him down?' Leonard was still outraged.

'Make no mistake either of you.' said Dieter calmly, 'this man can close us down. Twenty five percent of nothing is nothing, so I don't think that's his intention.' There was a silence in the cabin while each of them digested what Dieter had said. 'Are we agreed? Shall we call him back?'

Leonard spread out his hands in an upwards gesture, 'As though we have a choice!' Douglas got up and went to find Wim Henke, he was sitting at the bar having a drink.

When he saw Douglas, he waved an arm to encompass the room. 'This is very classy Major Coulter. I wouldn't want to interfere with the running of this establishment. No, I would leave you in charge.'

'That's very generous of you.' grimaced Douglas, 'my partners and I are ready to discuss the operational details with you, and I should like to know how the card trick works.'

'Of course my friend.' Wim Henke followed Douglas back up to the owner's suite. He told them, 'If you follow my methods, I promise, you will not lose out. There'll be no welshing on bets, my colleagues will see to that. I will supply the croupiers and the trained personnel; I would also leave the day to day running of the venture in the capable hands of Major Coulter here.' He looked from one to the other of them, lingering longest on Leonard. 'Are you all in agreement?' They all nodded. 'And now, shall we play cards?' They all sat round the table. Wim Henke passed another pack still wrapped in cellophane to Dieter. Dieter repeated the actions Douglas had performed earlier. He didn't detect anything untoward with the cards either. He dealt out the hands face down in front of each player. Wim Henke chose various cards from each of them and theatrically turned them over. All but one was a picture card. 'You can't get it right every time.' he smiled. Douglas took the cards from him and turned them back over again. 'Do you see it now Major?'

'I'm not sure.' replied Douglas.

'It needs a trained eye.' agreed Henke.

Douglas tapped the top of a court card. It was ever so slightly bevelled.

'It's not sitting flush to the table.'

Henke smiled, 'You have a keen eye Major. Normally it takes hours of study and concentration to get it right. Of course you can't be sure what the card is, but it's enough to give the house a distinct advantage.'

'I still don't see how we benefit.' said Leonard.

'I have trained readers; they can guess the value of the other player's cards and bet accordingly. Of course you can't have obvious winners at the table, so they pass their chips to the croupier when they have the opportunity, undetected by the other players of course. The house wins and nobody is the wiser. The readers are interchangeable. It wouldn't do for them to be recognized.'

'Sweet!' Douglas was impressed.

'I have a very clever man who alters the cards ever so slightly, then they are repacked and distributed to where they're needed. It's as simple as that.'

Now that there were four partners, another account was set up in Zurich for the profits from 'The Lady Anne' after adequate provision for living expenses had been made and a fund for the running costs for the business. This account needed four signatories and the account number had been split into four, each partner memorizing his allocated numbers. This meant no two partners in collaboration could rip the others off. There was no such thing as honour between thieves. The possible exception was Douglas and Dieter, they had a deep understanding of each other and it was inconceivable they would ever let each other down.

CHAPTER 10

Douglas had relocated his family to London. He had had every intention of doing so anyway. The 'Wim Henke' episode just meant that he had implemented the change sooner than he had intended. Greta was apprehensive about the move, but Douglas was adamant. She didn't have the excuse of leaving family behind as there was only Aunt Bertha and Uncle Wilhelm. Douglas had never met them and he had no desire to do so. Nor could she say she couldn't speak the language as Douglas's insistence that English was always spoken in their apartment meant she and Jan were now fluent in the language. Douglas had bought a pretty House in Wimbledon, and now Douglas reversed his language strategy, only Dutch was to be spoken in the London House.

Jan was now of an age to attend school and Douglas had enrolled into him into one of the best prep schools in the area. It was his daddy who took Jan to school on his first day. The Major was a hit with the young female teachers and he flirted outrageously with them. Jan settled in with no apparent problems, he was an easy going child and his blond white hair and startling blue eyes made him a firm favourite with his classmates and teachers alike. Greta was somewhat isolated even though Douglas had bought her a little car and taught her to drive. She had never made friends easily. Douglas was back and forwards all the time between London and Amsterdam and Greta saw less and less of him. Unknown to her, Douglas had bought himself a little apartment in the heart of London's club land where he could entertain his lady friends, but one girl in particular that he had become very fond of, was the pretty corporal who had handed him his orders and met him outside the Cafe Royale all those years ago. They often went to the theatre and attended parties together and were living the high life. He had a Bentley for use in London and a Diamler-Benz in Amsterdam. Of course he also spent quite a lot of his time on 'The Lady Anne'. One thing Douglas was sure of, you couldn't afford to neglect your clientele. He had noticed one young man in particular. He showed all the symptoms of being a compulsive gambler. He held his cards with an intensity only seen in the addict, and he sweated profusely. Douglas asked the Head Croupier who he was. He told him he was Wim Henke's son and Henke was grooming him to one day take over his business.

'Does Henke know his son is here?'

'I don't think so,' replied the croupier, 'he has usually slipped his minders when he turns up here.'

'Well, keep your eye on him and make sure he doesn't lose too much money. The last thing we need is trouble with Henke.'

Jan was proving to be quite a scholar; he also excelled at field sports. If there was physical contact he never shied away, even if the result was a scraped knee and a bruised body. He was a popular boy and was often asked to stay at his friends' houses at weekends and during the holidays, which made Greta feel uncomfortable. She very rarely reciprocated and had to be badgered mercilessly by Jan to do so. This attitude made Douglas angry, he wanted to foster his son's budding friendships with his little school friends, especially if they were wealthy. Douglas made a point of attending the school open days and sports days, he became known to the young and impressionable female staff as the dashing major.

Greta had to concede she wasn't natural motherhood material, she was stiff and unbending with the boy, she didn't know how to show him affection or how to interact with him, but she was sure she loved him. Nor for that matter did she enjoy the physical side of married life, but of course she kept that well hidden from Douglas. She was totally dependant on him financially and she was quite prepared to overlook his dalliances as long as they didn't jeopardize her position. She knew of course his income wasn't gained by legitimate means, but this had never worried her, she was happier not knowing and never asked questions. Of late though she was becoming uneasy, Douglas stayed away for longer and longer periods without any explanation. He had never been brilliant in confiding what he was up to, or where he was going but he seemed even more evasive of late.

On one of his rare trips home Douglas said, 'Dieter has asked us to spend a couple of weeks at his estate. The house is finished at last and he and Christa are planning a big party to celebrate. But before the trip I have to go to London for a couple of days so can you be ready to go when I get back?'

Greta was excited at the thought of the trip to Bremen. Jan was on holiday from school, he had spent a few days with some of his friends, but now Greta was at a loss as to what to do with him.

Douglas arrived home driving his Bentley. Greta heard the car door slam as he entered the house; she came to the top of the stairs. 'I hope your both ready,' he called up to her, 'I want to leave early in the morning.' Greta's suitcase was standing by the door. Douglas heaved it onto the bed and checked the contents. It was important to Douglas what clothes she wore in Germany. He produced a box from his car bearing the logo of an expensive London store. He lifted an evening gown out of the nest of tissue paper. It was made of a deep blue velvet material with the hint of sequins contained in the folds of the dress. The colour was a perfect contrast for Greta's white blond hair and pale complexion. She wondered who had chosen it, but Douglas had marvellous taste so it was probably him. Jan burst into the room. 'I hope you're ready young man?'

'Yes Daddy, come and see.' He grabbed his father's hand and dragged him into his own bedroom. He had piled all his favourite toys into the middle of his bed.

'If I put all these toys into the car where are we all going to sit?' Jan's face fell.

'Tell you what, my car has a large boot, they might just fit in there.'

Next morning early the car was loaded and they set off in high spirits, they were heading for Amsterdam first as Douglas wanted to check out the arrangements on 'The Lady Anne'. They arrived at their apartment in the late afternoon. Greta was happy to be back in her own country, she hadn't been back since their hurried departure for London. She would have loved to have been able to walk around the City on her own, but Douglas was going straight to the boat. He wanted to talk to the head croupier who would be in charge in his absence. Douglas told Greta not to wait up for him as he wouldn't be back until the early hours of the morning. Greta walked around the quiet rooms looking at this and that, moving the cushions around, subconsciously she was looking for signs of female habitation. She didn't find any. She put Jan to bed early, he was tired from travelling all day and he was soon fast asleep. She decided to retire early herself; no doubt Douglas would want another early start. When Douglas returned, he let himself in, the apartment was in darkness but even through the gloom he could see that cushions had been moved. So Greta had been checking up on him, he knew she wouldn't have found anything incriminating, he had given the place a clean sweep. He opened the bedroom door to Jan's room; he could see the tousled hair on the pillow and hear his rhythmic breathing. He tiptoed back to the main bedroom; Greta was fast asleep as well. He climbed into the new monster double bed beside her, he had only recently bought it but he knew she wouldn't comment on it.

They set off for Bremen the following morning after a good breakfast. They made a quick stop for lunch as Douglas was concerned about Jan, but he needn't have been, he wasn't car sick, in fact he slept most of the way. They reached the entrance to the von Rheinhart estate in the early evening. The huge gates were swung open for them by the Gateman now living in the Gatehouse where Dieter had first made his home when he had returned to Bremen. They swept into the drive which wound through trees and shrubs; it was only when they reached the first bend that they caught sight of the house. It had crenellated walls of a pale coloured stone with towers at either end. Chimneys by the score soared over the red roofs; it looked just like a fairy castle. Both Greta and Jan let out a gasp, Douglas, of course, had seen it many times during its construction. 'Are there any wizards and dragons living there Daddy?' asked Jan in a subdued voice.

Douglas laughed, 'I don't think so, but we'll ask Uncle Dieter if we can look around it just to make sure.'

Dieter and Christa were standing waiting for them at the huge studded wooden doors; they had been alerted to their arrival by the Gatekeeper. They gave them an effusive welcome, a manservant came to take their cases and a chauffeur drove the car around to the garage block. The doors opened onto a large beautifully tiled hallway. There was antique furniture tastefully placed against the walls, but it was the magnificent return staircase which immediately drew the eye. Christa led Greta up to their rooms. A small bed had been placed into a dressing room for Jan. The main room had a large Chinese carpet, matching silk wallpaper and toning bed linen. The effect was very pleasing to the eye. 'When you are settled in, come down to my sitting room and we can have tea together.' Christa smiled closing the door. She was genuinely pleased to see Greta and was looking forward to her company.

Dieter and Douglas were ensconced in Dieter's study; they were catching up on their business interests. Dieter poured out two cognacs in crystal balloons, handing one to Douglas. 'Greta looks well.'

'Yes, but she's becoming suspicious of late.'

'You lead a very interesting and precarious life my friend.'

'You know the old saying Dieter, variety is the spice of life, and I have hot tastes.'

Dieter smiled ruefully, 'Yes, I remember. I am concentrating all my efforts in one direction at the moment, unfortunately all to no avail.'

Douglas raised his glass to him smiling. Dieter's virility was not in doubt. Dieter reciprocated with a chuckle.

'While I remember Dieter, do you mind if we three go on an expedition around the house looking for wizards and dragons, Jan thinks some of them might be hiding in dark corners.'

'Not at all, but I don't think we'll find any.'

'Good,' replied Douglas, 'because if we did, I think I would be more scared than Jan.'

Greta collected Jan and they made their way down the grand staircase. A maid directed them to Christa's sitting room. Christa was sitting in an antique brocaded armchair. On a table were plates of little sandwiches and cakes together with the silver tea service and a jug of cordial for Jan. 'Come and sit down beside me,' and she pointed to a little sofa, 'so we can have a little gossip together.' Christa was very interested in Jan's schooling, 'It's so different to our method,' she told Greta. 'Both Dieter and I had private tutors, but it can be very lonely.'

Just then Dieter came in to collect Jan, 'We have important business to see to ladies, and Jan is our leader.'

Jan let out a whoop of joy, 'Are we going dragon hunting Uncle Dieter?'

'Yes and if you spot a dragon's den you just let us know.'

Jan jumped up and ran towards Dieter. Suddenly he stopped and turned to his mother, 'May I leave the room mummy?' She nodded her head and he was gone. The hunt took a good hour and the house was declared dragon free. Douglas told Jan it was his bedtime and the child dutifully said goodnight to everyone, saving a beaming smile for his daddy and Dieter. Greta took Jan to their room and tucked him in. When she returned to the sitting room all three were there.

'You have such a lovely child Greta.' said Christa wistfully. 'We have decided to have a light supper in here this evening if that suits you both. Tomorrow is going to be a very busy day. We have guests arriving in the morning and the house will be full of florists and caterers.' She looked sternly at Dieter.

Next morning, both men were up early and made their way to the stables. Two of Dieter's hunters were already saddled waiting for them. They clattered out of the yard and rode across the parkland skirting the lake and eventually stopped on the crest of a hill. They turned their horses towards the house. 'This is my favourite view of the house.' Dieter stared across the valley. A white mist swirled about in the hollows and the house seemed to rise majestically through it.

Douglas shifted in his saddle, 'You've done a wonderful job with it Dieter; it looks the exact replica of the photograph you showed me all those years ago.'

'Yes, I've tried to stay faithful to the old building.' He paused, 'It's thanks to your intervention in my life my friend that I'm able to invite you here to my home.' They clasp hands, it was clear that a very strong bond existed between these two men. They both stared at the place a while longer, then turning to Douglas, Dieter said, 'But it's left me with empty pockets.' And as if to emphasis the point he turned both his pockets inside out. Wheeling his horse he shouted to Douglas, 'Race you to the copse over there.' And he was gone in a cloud of dust. The sound of hooves thundered over the ground and clods of earth were thrown up behind them, the race was on. Douglas won by a short head, he was a superb horseman. They drew in their mounts in a cloud of steam, their breath made halos of white in the early morning air. When they had recovered Dieter said, 'I suppose we must get back, the ladies will be requiring our company,' a naughty grin spread over Dieter's face, 'but I think we'll go back the long way.' And he trotted off away from the house. They arrived back at the house mid morning. Christa was standing outside on the steps. She gave Dieter a long meaningful look. Douglas decided Dieter had disobeyed his orders.

'Please change quickly Dieter, we have guests arriving imminently.' And to Douglas, 'Luncheon will be served promptly at one o'clock.'

Dieter slid off his horse and threw the reins to Douglas, 'Why don't you saddle up Smokey, the pony is just the right size for Jan and he's very docile.' He turned and sprinted into the house. Douglas walked the horses through to the stables where a groom was ready to rub them down. He asked if he would saddle up Smokey for him and told him he would be back in about ten minutes. He was as good as his word and was holding the hand of a very excited little boy, Greta trailed behind looking apprehensive. Father and son led the pony down to the paddock, Douglas put the little chap on Smokey's back, he stood quite docilely while Douglas instructed Jan what to do, how to hold the reins and where to put his feet. He led him around the paddock a few times while Greta watched from the rails, then he let him go on his own. Greta called out, 'Do you think that's wise Douglas?'

Douglas took a deep breath, 'Yes I do Greta. You mollycoddle the child too much. My father sat me on my first pony before I was Jan's age and it did me no harm.' Grim faced, Douglas walked slowly to join her at the fence. Meanwhile Jan was having the time of his life, he loved it. After a while Douglas pulled him up and lifted him out of the saddle. He struggled a little wanting to stay on board the little pony. 'That's enough for now, any longer and you'll have a sore bottom.' They led Smokey back to the stables and watched the groom brush him down for a little while.

'Can I have a pony when we get home daddy?'

'No Jan. I don't think your mother would be able to cope with a pony.'

Jan's face showed his disappointment. They left the stables and collected Greta on the way back to the house. Douglas had to change for lunch. People were scurrying around everywhere getting the house ready for the evening's entertainment. There were other guests in the dining room; they were also staying over the weekend. Some of them were Christa's relations, others, friends of Dieter's. The meal was a rather hurried affair, there was still much to do before evening.

Jan asked his mother, 'Can I stay up for a while tonight to watch you and daddy dancing?'

'No.' replied Greta, 'I want you in bed at your usual time.' Jan looked resigned to his fate.

Douglas had heard this exchange, 'Greta, why ever not? What harm can it do? He can get some rest this afternoon then he can watch from the balcony. I'm sure Christa won't mind if one of the maids looks after him.' Jan perked up at this exchange.

Greta said through gritted teeth, 'You always undermine me Douglas.'

'That's because you make stupid decisions.'

Greta went red in the face, turned and bumped straight into Dieter who had just entered the room but had overheard the conversation between man and wife. She fled upstairs. 'Women.'

exploded Douglas. Dieter tactfully left the room. Douglas took a stroll in the gardens to calm down, but before he did so he arranged for Jan to have an afternoon nap.

Activity in the house reached fever pitch, Dieter beckoned Douglas to his study for a snifter. 'Let's have a quick one before battle commences.' Douglas sat back, glass in hand, swirling the amber liquid round and round. 'Do you want to talk about it?'

Douglas looked up and grimaced, 'No, I don't think so.' They sat back in companionable silence. 'I'm going to have to do something about it, but I can't leave them.' Dieter said nothing. 'I don't want her to make Jan into some namby pamby child. I'll not stand for that.' Dieter just let him talk. 'I've been so looking forward to this break Dieter. Bugger! Bugger!' And he took a long pull at his drink.

'Sometimes I wish I had your problems, I've completed the house, now the future looks a little,' he paused, 'bleak.' They looked at each other and burst out laughing. These two, of seemingly complete opposite characters, had built up a comraderie that would withstand almost any shock.

It was time to get ready for the Ball, Douglas loped upstairs. Greta was sitting in front of the mirror tying her hair into a complicated chignon. Douglas checked his evening clothes and laid them on the bed, then went for a shower. Greta was used to seeing Douglas in evening wear, it was his habitual uniform for 'The Lady Anne', but tonight he was in white tie and tails and she had to admit, he looked the perfect English Gentleman. Douglas helped her into her gown and stood back to survey the effect. 'Perfect.' he said, and held out his arm for her. They descended the stairs. Christa and Dieter were standing together in the Grand Hall to welcome their guests. Dieter was resplendent in a uniform that Greta couldn't place. He kissed Greta on the cheek, 'You look stunning my dear; your dress is beautiful.'

'Douglas chose it,' she whispered to him.

'He has such good taste.' Then very quietly, 'Perhaps I could prevail upon him to choose a gown for my wife.'

Christa was festooned with her family's jewels. They had been sitting in a vault in Switzerland for the duration of the war, but had now been reunited with the family. She was wearing a tiara, a diamond necklace, matching bracelet, brooch and earrings which dangled and swayed as she turned her head. The colours were vibrant and sparkled

91

as the light caught them. Douglas assessed they were worth a king's fortune. Because of his activities in Amsterdam and Hatton Garden Douglas had learned a thing or two about jewellery. Unfortunately she had chosen to wear a style of gown totally unsuited to her figure and the colour was completely wrong for her. Dieter had confided more than once to Douglas that Christa was more at home in jodhpurs and an old sweater, but these things mattered to Douglas and he wrinkled his nose slightly. They turned away to be confronted by a waiter bearing crystal flutes containing the best vintage champagne on a silver salver. Douglas took two and handed one to Greta. He looked up to the balcony to see Jan's shiny little face looking through the balustrades at them. He lifted his glass to him in salute and twirled Greta on his arm so he could see her dress. The little boy was about to jump up and wave at them when he was abruptly pulled down again by the maid who was looking after him. Greta and Douglas moved on into the reception rooms. Beyond that was the ballroom where a full orchestra was playing softly. The walls were lined with delicate antique chairs and sofas where those disinclined to dance could take their ease. A sumptuous buffet was laid out in another room with tables covered in Smokey damask tablecloths and napery. The silver cutlery shone under the light from the chandeliers. Douglas guided Greta through into the ballroom. He just caught a glimpse of the maid leading Jan through to the balcony as he led Greta onto the floor for a sedate waltz. Christa and Dieter arrived, the chore of welcoming all their guests completed. They took to the floor for one of the rumbustious waltzes so beloved of the Germans. Douglas introduced Greta to the people he knew, most of the men were regulars of 'The Lady Anne'. Douglas proposed dancing with some of their wives, and Greta was led to the floor by their abandoned partners. They were joined later by Dieter and Christa, Dieter asked Greta to dance and Douglas reciprocated with Christa. Douglas was having a merry time, and Greta was certainly no wallflower. Douglas glanced towards the balcony and was surprised to see Jan still there. Douglas gave a sign to the maid by putting both hands to the side of his face, indicating it was time Jan was taken to bed. Supper was announced and Douglas led Greta to a table, he brought the delicacies he knew she favoured, he was a most attentive partner. More dancing followed into the early hours of the morning. Greta started to flag and many of the guests were taking their leave.

Douglas escorted Greta back to their room, but he didn't go in with her. 'Douglas, where are you going?'

'Sorry,' he smiled, 'I have to see some people about business.' And he disappeared. Greta was mortified. She should have known it was too good to last. She thought she could guess what sort of business he was about. She reluctantly peeled off her gown, hung it up carefully and climbed between the sheets. Next morning Douglas was fast asleep beside her, as usual he was in his birthday suit, his evening clothes had been carefully put away. Even though Douglas was in the habit of having a shower before he came to bed, she thought she caught a faint whiff of perfume on him. She bathed and dressed quietly, Jan's bed was empty with the bedclothes thrown back. She had better go and find him. She went down to the morning room and there was Jan and Dieter, blond heads together, Jan's a shade whiter and Dieter's altogether wirier. They looked up when she came in, both had startling blue eyes, they could easily be taken for father and son. They were doing a jigsaw puzzle together. Christa walked up quietly behind her, 'Dieter is so enjoying having Jan around. Of course we are trying for a child ourselves but nothing seems to be happening as yet. Come and have breakfast with me, they have already had theirs.' Before she turned away, Jan asked, 'Mummy can I ride Smokey again today? Uncle Dieter says I can if you agree.'

'You had better ask your father Jan when he appears.' She turned and left with Christa.

A shooting party had been organized for the menfolk who were staying over for the weekend, they were gathering at the front of the house. Some of the ladies were taking a turn in the garden. Greta saw Douglas join the party. Dieter put his hand on his shoulder telling him something. Douglas wheeled around and came out of the house holding Jan by the hand; they were making for the stables. Greta excused herself and ran after them. They were coming out of the stable yard heading for the paddock leading Smokey between them. A groom was following behind.

'Mummy, daddy says I can ride Smokey.' Greta followed them to the paddock. Douglas hoisted Jan onto Smokey's back, he settled him in the saddle and started to walk away.

'Douglas, aren't you going to stay with him?'

'No, I'm going hunting.'

'But Douglas----'

'The groom will look after him. If you're so concerned Greta, you stay and watch him.' he snapped back. And he marched off to join the others.

That evening it was a formal dinner in the Dining Hall. There were a dozen or so guests at the table. Greta noticed that one very attractive lady kept glancing at Douglas and he reciprocated. Later in the evening when she walked past Greta she left a trail of perfume behind her. Greta recognized it immediately; it was the same aroma she had noticed on Douglas that morning. Later that night when they were in their room Greta said, 'I want to go home Douglas.'

'You what?'

'You heard me, I want to go home.'

'But Greta we can't do that, I've told Dieter that we are staying for the full fortnight, it would be the height of bad manners to leave now. Why do you want to go home?'

'You know why Douglas.'

Douglas sighed and sat on the bed next to her. 'You know it means nothing Greta, it's just a bit of fun.'

'It's not fun for me.' she challenged him.

'O.K. Greta, I promise I'll behave myself. Now can we go to bed?'

Next morning after breakfast, all the other guests were leaving. Greta noticed the attractive brunette give Douglas a rueful smile. He didn't return it.

The few days that were left to them fell into a pattern. The men would go out for an early morning gallop then join the ladies for breakfast. Jan was given riding lessons on Smokey while Christa and Greta strolled around the gardens. Christa was full of her plans to restore them to their former glory. Lunch was a leisurely meal and sometimes they had a picnic in the grounds weather permitting. The last day of their stay was a glorious day so they planned a picnic by the lake. After they had eaten and drunk their fill, Jan asked his daddy if they could go boating on the lake.

'That's a wonderful idea Jan, why didn't I think of that.' said Dieter and he sprang up to get two skiffs out of the boathouse. The men were in one skiff and the ladies took the other. Dieter rowed for the male boat, Douglas sat with his arm around Jan. Christa took the oars for the females. It was a perfect day. After a while Jan asked his daddy if he could have a go at rowing. 'I don't see why not, but we will have to plan this properly. You stay in the middle.' Douglas plonked him the centre of the boat. 'Dieter will move over for me to sit next to him, and then he will come and sit next to you. Then Dieter will hand you to me. Have you got that?' Jan nodded. Douglas moved slowly to the front of the skiff, the boat started to wobble.

Greta looked across to see what they were up to. 'Be careful Douglas,' she shouted, 'I don't want Jan to fall in the water.'

'I don't want Jan to fall in the water either Greta.' He sat down next to Dieter who handed him the oars. When the boat was steady again Dieter moved down to sit next to Jan. It wobbled again. Dieter then handed Jan to Douglas. Douglas showed Jan how to hold the oars. 'You can't do it all by yourself, the boat is too heavy for you.' After a few practice strokes the boat moved forward, Jan was elated.

He shouted to his mother, 'Watch me mummy, I can row.' Showing off, Jan put all his strength into the next stroke and caught a crab. He tumbled over backwards. Both Douglas and Dieter simultaneously made a dive to grab him. The boat wobbled violently, Dieter lost his balance and fell into the water closely followed by the other two. Just before he went under the water Douglas heard Greta's scream. The two men surfaced immediately, they were both strong swimmers. They looked around for Jan. At first he couldn't be seen, but within seconds his little head popped up. Douglas grabbed him by the scruff of his neck, and towed him to shore. All three scrambled out soaking wet, but uninjured. Christa skilfully grounded her boat next to them and both Greta and Christa climbed onto the bank. Greta made a grab for Jan, but Douglas planted him firmly on his knee.

Greta shouted at him, 'You never listen to me Douglas, you never listen.' And she stalked away.

Douglas looked at his son, 'I think we're in a lot of trouble buddy.' And all three of them rolled about laughing. They strolled back to the house to get cleaned up. The evening meal was a little strained.

Next morning they were on the road early. Douglas was heading straight back to their house in London. They arrived late at night and went straight to bed. Jan was due back at his prep school the next day. He was none the worse for his adventures in Bremen. His daddy took him to school and immediately arranged for him to have swimming lessons which he thoroughly enjoyed. Douglas returned home, he was packing a suitcase when Greta appeared at the doorway. 'Do you have to go away so soon?'

'I've got urgent business in London.'

'Can't she wait-----'

'Greta, don't do this, don't be jealous, I have to go.' She sat down on the bed beside him, he took her hand. 'Greta, I'll never leave you, I'll always come back to you and Jan. I plucked you out of the canal, just as I plucked Dieter out of the prison camp. I feel responsible for you both, for good or ill all three of you are a permanent part of my life.' She started to cry. 'Don't cry Greta, you know I can't stand tears.' He paused, 'It's not as though you even enjoy sex.'

'But Douglas, I have never------'

'No Greta, you've never denied me, but you're,' he paused again, 'just compliant.' She looked at him, knowing he spoke the truth. 'Greta, you've no need to worry, I've set up an annuity in your name should my income be interrupted. I've set up a trust for Jan's education. Financially you'll have no cause for concern, and there's always Dieter, he's very fond of you both, if anything happens to me, he'll look after you. I must go. I'll be back in about a month. If you need me you can contact me via 'The Lady Anne'.' He grabbed his suitcase and went down the stairs, out of the door and got into his car. She heard him slam the door and drive away.

Douglas drove straight to Hatton Gardens, his relationship with the London diamond merchant hadn't improved. He often made snide remarks about Douglas's rapid change from one branch of the armed forces to another. But Douglas had been right; the customs men took one look at the uniform and generally waved him straight through. The diamond merchant had taken an urgent commission from a wealthy Middle Eastern client and only Leonard could supply the quality and cut of stones he required. It was an express job so Douglas told him it would cost him double his usual expenses as he would have to do a return flight. He will need two separate identities so as not to arouse suspicion. He decided to return as Lord Charlesworth, an identity he hadn't used before. He was surprised at the attention he received; it just goes to show what a little bit of blue blood can do for you. This was the part Douglas enjoyed the most. Impersonation and mimicry was all a game to Douglas. The more danger involved in the deception the more

96

the adrenalin flowed.

Back in Amsterdam Douglas needed to pay some attention to 'The Lady Anne', takings were down. The restaurant was doing fine. The head chef had a concession so it was in his own interest to keep up the standard there. He watched carefully on his first night back. Two of the girls had let their appearance slip, and they were too familiar with some of the regular clients. At the end of the night, he told them they were no longer required. There was no second chance with Douglas. Because of word of mouth there was no problem in getting replacements and Douglas set up interviews with six applicants. They all had good figures, but personality was of equal importance. He chose a German girl, a brunette, her name was Helga. She had an up front manner and showed plenty of confidence. She also spoke three languages which was always an asset in this business. The other girl that caught his eye was a Polish girl, a redhead. She had a quieter demeanour but knew bar work. He decided to give them both a month's trial.

The girls were well into their trial period, Helga was doing very well and was popular with the guests, Douglas wasn't sure about Irena, she was efficient and went about her work quietly, and that thought Douglas might be the problem, she was too quiet.

Dieter had informed him that he was coming down for a few days; he needed a rest from his exertions he told him. Douglas made sure the owner's cabin was ready. Dieter arrived while Douglas was still at his apartment. They arranged to have a meal in the restaurant. Douglas had set up a card game in the evening in the owner's cabin with a few favoured clients. The games there were always clean! The meal was definitely up to standard and they lingered over it, catching up on family matters. Back in the cabin Douglas poured them both a drink. 'Just the thing to set you up for a game.' he told Dieter.

Before they all gathered in the cabin, Douglas told Dieter he had to go down and check that all the staff had turned up. When all the card players were assembled Douglas poured them all a drink. They settled down to the game, Dieter was winning but not by much. There was plenty of banter flying about and they all appeared to be having a good time. Douglas got up to pour more drinks, always an aphrodisiac during a game. He had noticed that they were running out of Dieter's favourite cognac so he rang for Irena to come up to the cabin. There was a knock on the door, Douglas answered it and asked her to bring up two of the special bottles of cognac. She was back within a couple of minutes. She put one of the bottles in the drinks cabinet and deftly opened the other one. The light caught her hair giving it a burnished sheen as she moved around the cabin. Douglas saw one or two of his guests giving her an admiring glance. She poured out a drink for Douglas and moved over to fill Dieter's glass. He was studying his cards, he looked up briefly and their eyes locked for a moment. She blushed and he went pale. She was the first one to recover but she dribbled a few drops from the neck of the bottle onto the table. She quickly wiped them away and left the cabin with Dieter's bright blue eyes taking in every fluid movement.

'Dieter, Dieter, it's your turn.' He turned to the voice, recollected himself and played his hand. By the end of the night he was well down. Douglas was a winner.

When everyone had left, Dieter caught Douglas by the sleeve, 'Who's the girl, the redhead?'

'I've just taken her on, she's Polish. Her name is Irena, Irena Nowak. I'm not sure she's right for here though, she's rather quiet.'

Dieter blushed at his next question, 'She doesn't,' he paused, 'she doesn't----' he trailed off.

'She doesn't what Dieter?'

'Don't play games with me Douglas.'

'No, she doesn't.' Dieter looked relieved. But the mischief in Douglas exerted itself. 'I'm not sure of the other girl though, Helga. Shall I send for her?' One look at Dieter's face was enough to tell Douglas he had overstepped the mark. 'Oh dear, Oh dear!' he repeated and he punched Dieter lightly on the shoulder and went home.

The few days turned into two weeks. In the evening Dieter spent all his time down in the bar when Irena was on duty. He sat unobtrusively in a corner but his eyes followed her every movement. She kept looking to make sure he was still there, blushing frequently. It was obviously a mutual attraction. During the day Dieter simply was not to be found. One evening Dieter said to Douglas, 'When my brother was killed, I missed him terribly. I have always mourned him, but I mourn his passing more than ever now.' Douglas remembered the conversation he had had with Dieter before he married Christa. 'The second son could usually marry for love.' There was no doubt about it, Dieter was in love.

Dieter's visits to 'The Lady Anne' became more frequent and he stayed for longer each time. Douglas was quite aware of the reason for this change in Dieter's behaviour but the subject was delicate, he reasoned if Dieter wished to discuss the matter he would do so. It was however causing a little jealousy with the other hostesses. Whilst Douglas enjoyed the company of ladies, he had made a point of never mixing business with pleasure.

Four months went by and Dieter had spent more time in Amsterdam than he had at his estates in Bremen. One evening he collared Douglas and told him it would be an idea if he started looking for another hostess because Irena would soon be leaving. Douglas was not really surprised, in fact he was relieved, but he was shocked at what Dieter told him next. He was returning to Bremen to tell Christa their marriage was over, he knew she would be terribly hurt and it would cause a terrific scandal, but he couldn't go on living a lie. Douglas opened his mouth to speak but Dieter held up his hand. 'Don't try and persuade me otherwise Douglas, my mind is made up. Our friendship and partnership can go on as before, but I want Irena in my life.'

Douglas put his arm around Dieter's shoulders, 'I'm a little envious of you Dieter, I've never felt such intensity for a woman in my life,' he smiled at him, 'it must be a little uncomfortable though.'

Dieter laughed out loud, 'That's the understatement of the year Douglas; it's a bit more than uncomfortable.' Then he sobered up, 'Unfortunately it's going to be very painful for all of us.' Next morning Dieter had gone.

It was three weeks before a very chastened Dieter returned to the boat. Douglas joined him in the owner's cabin. A pale faced Irena was serving drinks in the bar. There was an empty glass in front of Dieter, he got up and poured a drink for Douglas and refilled his own glass and sat down with a sigh.

'What's happened?' inquired a concerned Douglas.

'Quite a lot really,' replied a morose Dieter. 'I seem to have hit a purple patch. When I got home, Christa told me her good news. She's pregnant, she's ecstatic. I just couldn't tell her.' He paused looking at Douglas, 'I was going to give it all up, the estate, the horses. Well, I might have kept my hunter,' he said with a wry smile, 'but I can't now. The child will be my legitimate heir.' He took a long pull at his drink. 'And just to compound matters Irena is pregnant as well.' Douglas whistled. 'What would you do Douglas?'

'Leave the country!' They both smiled.

Dieter stayed a week. His loyalties were obviously torn between Irena and his wife. His dream of forsaking all for love was over. He told Douglas he would make arrangements for Irena to move to Germany to be near him. He would buy her a house in the city of Bremen where she could have his child. At least he would be near them. He asked Douglas to take care of her until he could make the necessary arrangements. Two weeks later Dieter returned and he and Irena left for Bremen.

CHAPTER 11

Douglas was leading a busy life, he was still instrumental in the diamond smuggling business. This provided the danger element that was so necessary to his character. When in London he divided his time between his mistress and Greta. He tried to make sure he was on hand for important dates in Jan's life too. Sports days and the Christmas play being two important dates in his calendar. Jan was shooting up; he was a tall strong boy. His hair was still white blond which he wore quite long as was the fashion. His favourite subjects were languages and sport, which pleased his father. Douglas also spent time on 'The Lady Anne' as this was the mainstay of the wealth creation for the four partners. Wim Henke was an infrequent visitor to the boat, but the croupiers and 'watchers' were supplied by him so Douglas assumed he had eyes and ears everywhere. Strange he thought, that Henke had done nothing to dissuade his son from gambling on 'The Lady Anne', Douglas presumed as long as the son's losses were within limits, Henke put up with his son's addiction.

One of Douglas's pleasures was to go and stay with Dieter which he did as often as he could. Christa had given birth to a boy, which as Dieter saw it, was some compensation for his lost dreams. Irena obliged with a girl a few weeks later. Dieter spent as much time as he could with Irena and her little girl Katya, but he had onerous duties running his estate which had doubled in size since his marriage to Christa. Christa was a formidable business woman. She could account for every pfennig of income and outgoing connected with the business and never took her eyes away from the management of their estates which included numerous farms, woodland and of course the stables housing Dieter's beloved horses. Dieter didn't get much spare time to himself so he really looked forward to Douglas's visits which he vowed kept him sane. He always took advantage of Douglas's presence to spend time with Irena and Katya, so Douglas was involved with the young Katya from an early age. She was a delightful child, a redhead with green eyes like her mother. She knew both Dieter and Douglas as honorary uncles. Dieter knew he was on dangerous ground having Irena and Katya living so close to him so he was exceptionally careful that Katya didn't know of his paternity. Dieter's share of the illegal activities of the 'gang of four' paid for the upkeep of Dieter's second family. It would have been

101

suicidal to try to smuggle funds out of his and Christa's estates, she would have spotted any discrepancies in an instant.

His legitimate son Christian Ludwig von Rheinhart had his future mapped out in detail by his mother. Dieter agreed with most of these arrangements, they accorded with the way he and his brother had been brought up. Christian wasn't going to be a cosseted child. Loved by both parents yes, but cosseting wasn't in Christa's nature. He was to be schooled at home by various tutors as his parents had been. Dieter oversaw his son's outdoor activities and they both revelled in them. Dieter personally taught Christian to ride on the reliable old Smokey. A strong bond grew up between father and son which was cemented as the years passed.

On one of Douglas's visits to Dieter, they arranged to go on a picnic with Irena and Katya. It was Katya's fourth birthday. It was a lovely summer's day and they were sitting by the river side. A large rug was spread out before them with sandwiches, cakes and jellies, all the things little girls liked to eat. Katya was playing with a doll Douglas had given her for her birthday. She was sitting on her mother's knee and Douglas was taking photographs of them, making sure not to include Dieter in them of course. They had a lovely day, but all too soon for Dieter it was time to pack up and go home. Katya was quite tired by the excitement of the day and Dieter carried her in his arms to the car. Douglas was helping Irena with the picnic things when she suddenly turned quite pale and ran to the bushes. Douglas could hear her retching. He called to Dieter who quickly handed the now sleeping Katya to Douglas. Dieter ran to Irena who was recovering from the vomiting attack. She put her head on his shoulder and he helped her slowly to where Douglas was standing with Katya. Douglas looked enquiringly from one to the other of them. Dieter looked concerned but they were both smiling. 'Don't worry Douglas, there's nothing seriously wrong.' said Irena. 'I didn't suffer this with Katya, but this time sickness suddenly strikes out of the blue. I'm hoping it will go away in a few weeks.'

Douglas looked more closely at Irena. She was wearing a loose fitting summer dress and as the breeze blew the material against her, he could see the slight swelling of her abdomen. 'I take it congratulations are in order. Dieter, you old rogue, you never said.'

'No,' replied Dieter, hugging Irena to him, 'we're hoping for a

102

boy this time, but a little sister for Katya will be just as welcome.'

Douglas reflected on Dieter's domestic arrangements. They both looked so happy together, it was Dieter's timing that had been at fault, he had been so keen to get himself an heir. Christa was an admirable manager of their joint estates, on that front she couldn't be faulted, but she was a very domineering woman. Dieter himself was used to being in control and the constant battle for supremacy between them was always simmering away just below the surface. No, thought Douglas, this situation with Irena was a powder keg just waiting to blow up in his face. Douglas's thoughts turned to his own domestic arrangements. He led a bachelor's life in Amsterdam but in London, he too had two homes to maintain. Jan's arrival hadn't been in Douglas's plan either. He briefly wondered if Greta would still be on the scene if it wasn't for Jan, but what was the point of that. She was much more malleable than Christa, and much more pleasing to the eye to boot. His romantic gratification was well catered for by his mistress who fortunately showed no signs of broodiness. She was well aware of the existence of Greta and Jan and seemed quite content with the high stepping social life she engaged in with Douglas. Douglas silently congratulated himself on the management of his own domestic situation.

Douglas had completed two more successful diamond runs and spent some time with Greta and been to visit both Jan and his mistress when the bombshell exploded. He received an urgent and mystifying telephone call from Dieter, he was incoherent and garbled but the gist of it was; Douglas was needed at once. He left immediately for Bremen. When he arrived he was met by a very cross Christa. 'What is going on Douglas?' she demanded in a very strident voice. 'Dieter has been down to see you twice in as many weeks and now he has shut himself up in his study refusing to come out and speak to anyone but you. I demand to be told what is happening Douglas.'

'Sorry Christa, it's a confidential business matter.' he stammered. Christa stamped her foot in frustration. Douglas strode to Dieter's study closely followed by Christa. He knocked loudly on the door and shouted, 'It's me Dieter and Christa is just behind me.' At first there was no response; then they heard a shuffling noise followed by a crash as if a chair had been knocked over. Douglas turned to Christa, 'Go away Christa, let me deal with this.' Christa was about to argue but one look at Douglas's face made her change her mind. The key in the door grated in the lock, Douglas pushed against it and slid into the study firmly closing the door behind him. He was hit by the reek of brandy fumes. Dieter was leaning against his desk, his face was ashen. Douglas quickly covered the ground between them and took hold of Dieter's shoulders. He looked into his bleak eyes, 'What on earth has happened Dieter?'

Dieter just shook his head and opened his mouth as if to speak, but no words came out, only a strangled sob.

'It's to do with Irena isn't it?'

Dieter nodded his head and closed his eyes tightly as if to make the world disappear, 'I've lost her,' he croaked, 'she's gone.'

At first Douglas couldn't make head or tail of this other than it was very serious. He wondered if Dieter meant she had left him, but he immediately rejected that idea. The last time he had seen them together they had been very happy, looking forward to the birth of Irena's baby. Then the awful truth dawned on Douglas. 'Oh my God.' he murmured. He led Dieter to one of the arm chairs and sat him down. Dieter stretched out his hand towards the waiting brandy glass. Douglas tactfully removed it. He waited until Dieter had a grip of himself. He said softly, 'What happened Dieter?'

After a while Dieter responded, 'She kept being sick, I went as often as I could. She said she was fine. The midwife told her sickness sometimes continued right through a pregnancy and told her there was nothing to worry about. But I was worried Douglas. In the end I insisted she went to the hospital. I took her myself. The doctor told us he couldn't find anything really wrong but her blood pressure was a little high so he wanted to keep her in for a little while for observation.'

'What about Katya?' Douglas asked.

'I made arrangements with the neighbours to look after her. Irena has a sister living in The Hague, she is going to look after Katya until Irena recovers.'

Douglas sighed and thought thank heavens for that, the problem of Katya was solved for the time being, but the problem of Dieter remained. Douglas had noticed his use of the present tense.

'I went to see her every day,' he continued, 'she seemed fine.' Dieter stopped, his head bowed and his shoulders shook. Douglas didn't press him. 'She went into premature labour.' He stopped again, he held out his hand for his glass. This time Douglas gave it to him and poured one for himself. 'I got there as soon as I could, but I was too late.' His words were barely audible. 'They told me they had done everything possible but they hadn't been able to save them.' Dieter looked up sharply and stared into Douglas's face, 'Both Irena and my little boy are dead.' Tears were streaming down Dieter's face. Douglas had to swallow quickly to avoid the same fate.

Dieter slumped back into the chair. Douglas paced around the room, his mind racing. There were arrangements to be made and it was obvious to Douglas that Dieter was in no condition to make them.

'I can't face Christa Douglas, I just can't.'

'No, I can see that.' Douglas continued pacing. The first thing was to get Dieter away from Christa; in his present condition he would give the game away- no question. He needed space to grieve. The other pressing problem was what was to become of Katya. Douglas would have to go and see Irena's sister. Then of course arrangements would have to be made for the funerals of Irena and Dieter's child. He knew Dieter would insist on being there. Douglas took a long pull on his drink. First things first though, he must get Dieter to Amsterdam, then he would be able to tackle the other problems.

There was a loud knock on the study door. Dieter didn't seem to hear it. Christa's voice was loud and clear. 'What's going on in there? I want to come in.' Douglas strode over and opened the door. Christa tried to push her way in as she glanced quickly around the room, but Douglas blocked her. He left the study taking Christa firmly by the arm and led her away.

'Christa, we are in the middle of some very delicate business negotiations. You must trust me. If we get this wrong Dieter could very well lose the estate and I'm sure you don't want that to happen.'

Christa's eyes widened in shock, 'What have you two been up to?' she demanded. 'The estate finances are in perfect order, I oversee them myself.'

'I can't tell you that Christa, it's confidential. We have other business partners, but if we can pull this off we stand to make a lot of money. You must trust me Christa.' Douglas was an accomplished liar, his facial expressions exuded confidence. He was winning the battle with Christa.

She calmed down a little, 'Dieter has been behaving so secretive of late, I have tried to get him to confide in me, but he won't.'

'He's been under a lot of strain recently Christa, but don't worry, we can sort this out.'

'I know you and Dieter go back a long way Douglas, if I can help in any way, just let me know.' And she patted Douglas's arm.

'Well, you could organize some food for us Christa.'

She smiled, 'Of course, I'll send Helmut to the kitchen; he'll rustle something up for you.' Douglas gave her one of his most reassuring smiles and Christa left to go about her other duties.

Douglas returned to the study. Dieter was where Douglas had left him, but the glass was empty he noticed. 'Dieter!' Dieter looked at him with fuzzy eyes. Douglas took hold of Dieter's shoulders and shook him, 'Dieter, I'm going to take you to Amsterdam with me tonight when everyone has gone to bed. I'll leave a note for Christa to put her off the scent.' Dieter just nodded. Douglas decided he was best left alone just now, but as a precaution he locked the drinks cabinet and put the key in his pocket.

Douglas made his way to the stables. He asked the groom to saddle his usual mount for him. He rode out of the stable yard. The best place to think he decided was definitely on horseback with the sound of beating hooves in his ears. He rode to the wooded hillside which was a favourite place from which to view the house. He stopped and dismounted tying the reins around the branch of a tree but giving enough leeway for the horse to munch at the grass. The house was bathed in evening sunshine, the light striking the windows and reflecting back at him with dazzling brightness. Smoke was lazily curling upwards from one or two of the chimneys into the still blue sky. Cows were grazing in the meadows and a faint hum of a tractor reached his ears as it meandered its way homeward along the narrow lanes. The view was one of serenity belying the human misery hidden behind those dazzling windows. Douglas sighed and remounted his horse; he trotted slowly back the way he had come.

When Douglas returned to the house, he found a tray covered with a Smokey white cloth outside the study door. Douglas let himself in the study. Dieter was still in the armchair in a fitful sleep, his head on one side. Douglas decided to leave him. The sleep however unnatural would do him good. Douglas helped himself to the food provided by Helmut then stole up to Dieter's room. He packed a few things for him and stowed them in his car. He wrote a note to Christa and left it by

106

Dieter's bedside. Next he sought out Christa and told her they still had some business discussions to finalize so they wouldn't be joining the family for dinner that evening and he returned to the study. It was dark by now, Douglas turned on the table lamps and turned to look at Dieter. The movement woke Dieter. For a brief moment Dieter's eyes showed pleasure at seeing Douglas, then the awful realization of his loss engulfed him once more. Douglas told Dieter of his plan to leave for Amsterdam when the house was quiet. Dieter just nodded. 'I know it's hard to believe this at the moment Dieter, but you'll get through this.' Dieter stood up, walked to the fireplace and leaned against the mantel. Douglas stood next to him with his hand on his shoulder. Dieter turned to face him, slowly he put his forehead on Douglas's shoulder and his body shook with silent sobs. Douglas was at a loss as to how to comfort his friend.

The journey back to Amsterdam was a very silent one. Dieter just stared out of the window into the blackness. Douglas debated where to take Dieter; he decided the best place would be the owner's cabin on 'The Lady Anne'. Christa wouldn't be able to get hold of him there and they would have complete privacy. Next morning when Douglas awoke after a few hours of much needed sleep, Dieter was already pacing about the cabin. 'I need to go and claim them Douglas.'

Douglas put his hand on Dieter's arm, 'You can't Dieter, the hospital authorities won't release them to you. You're not their next of kin.'

Dieter's face registered shock, 'But Douglas, in reality Irena was my wife.'

'I know, but not in the eyes of the law.'

Dieter slumped down in the nearest chair, his head in his hands as the reality of the situation sank in.

'Tell me about the sister Dieter, how did they come to end up in Holland?'

Dieter was silent for a long time, 'I need a drink.'

'No you don't, you need to talk to me.'

A flicker of defiance showed in Dieter's eyes and then was gone. 'My Countrymen did some terrible things in the war. They killed Irena's parents for helping a Jewish family who lived near them. Irena and her sister went to the same school as the Jewish children, they were playmates.' He paused as if seeing the past being replayed before his eyes. 'They were smuggled out of Poland by an Uncle already living in Holland. She wouldn't talk about it very much, she found it very painful.' He paused again, then turned to look at Douglas with a slight smile of reminiscence on his face, 'she forgave me for being born a German.'

Douglas got up and made them some coffee, 'I think it would be a good idea if I went to see the sister.' Dieter half rose in protest but Douglas continued, 'Irena may have forgiven you for being a German, but has her sister? Let me go and see how the land lies. I can be your eyes and ears for the moment, Katya knows me.'

Dieter subsided into his chair, 'I know your right Douglas but I feel so helpless. Katya is my daughter.' he said despairingly.

'And the best thing you can do to help her now is to stay out of the picture. Don't forget Dieter, you also have a son! Christa would never accept your bastard daughter, you know that. I know it sounds brutal but it's true.'

Dieter's face was like thunder, 'She is not my bastard daughter.' he shouted and he thumped his fist on the table.

'You must accept reality Dieter, for your sake, for Katya's sake, for Christian's sake and even Christa's sake. If you don't, you stand to lose everything. Don't forget Dieter, in the eyes of the law you are the transgressor. Christa's no fool, she's a rich woman in her own right and she just might be able to stop you from seeing your own son.'

'I too have some standing, some influence-----'

Douglas cut him off, 'Against a wronged woman? Remember Dieter, hell hath no fury like that of a woman scorned.'

Dieter groaned.

'Give me the sister's address, I'll go this afternoon.'

Dieter wrote down the address and handed it to Douglas.

Douglas drove down the quiet suburban street in The Hague and located the house where the Van Heusen's lived. It was a small semi-detached house with blue paintwork and a neat little lawn in front. Irena's sister, Nina had married Peter Van Heusen when she was just eighteen, he was a school teacher and they had two children, a boy and a girl. Douglas sat in his car for a little while then made a concerted effort and strode purposefully up to the front door. Without a pause he knocked, he heard the noises of children playing from inside the house, and then adult footsteps. The door was opened by a woman in an apron;

108

she was drying her hands on it as she looked enquiringly at him. Douglas was a little taken aback. She was a slightly older version of Irena. Her hair not quite as red and a few more care lines around the face, but she had a pleasant face. 'Yes?' she enquired. Before Douglas could speak there was a squeal behind her and Katya ran forward trailing the doll Douglas had given her for her fourth birthday in her wake. 'Uncle Dougy Doug.'she called stretching out her arms to be picked up. Douglas crouched down to Katya's level. She thrust the doll into his face, 'Lily-it's Uncle Dougy Doug.'

'Hello Lily, Hello Katya.' He hugged both of them to him and looked up into Irena's sister's shocked face. 'I'm Douglas Coulter' he said to her, 'I was a friend of your sister's.'

'Your not------'she said, looking at Katya.

'No, I'm not.' he answered simply.

Nina Van Heusen leant heavily against the door, she recovered herself. 'No, of course your not, I think you had better come in.'

Douglas picked up Katya and followed Irena's sister into the kitchen.

'Where's Uncle Deety and Mummy?' asked Katya looking beyond Douglas.

'Uncle Deety couldn't come today.' said Douglas as Katy's little face crumpled. He didn't dare mention Mummy; he didn't know what Katya had been told.

Two other faces appeared at the kitchen door, Nina shooed all three children into the next room. 'All of you, go and play, nicely now.' she admonished. She turned her attention to Douglas, 'What is it you want Mr. Coulter?'

'First of all I want to say how sorry I am for your loss, Irena was a lovely girl. She used to work for me.'

'Ah, you're the English Major.' There was a suggestion of tears in the corner of Mrs Van Heusen's eyes, she straightened her shoulders as she said, 'I can't say I approved of Irena's behaviour, consorting with a German of all people. We have nothing to thank the Germans' for Major Coulter.'

'I understand that, but I haven't come to fight the war all over again Mrs Van Heusen. Believe it or not, there are some good Germans, just as there were some Polish collaborators.' Nina's eyes widened at this but she said nothing. 'Katya's father is a good man. He lost all his family in the war as well. The Allies killed his parents and his brother. We were on opposing sides during the war, but I have come to respect him and count him as my best friend.'

'He's a married man.' she spat out, 'Katya is his-----' she couldn't bring herself to use the word. The tears glistened more brightly.

'It's about Katya that I'm here.'

A tear escaped and ran down her cheek, 'I don't suppose he could spare the time to come himself?'

'And would you have let him in if he had?

'Of course not!'

'And yet he loved your sister, and Katya, and, make no mistake, they both loved him, so much so they planned to have a brother for Katya. Believe me Mrs Van Heusen, he's grieving every bit as much as you.'

This was too much for Irena's sister, she sat down and tears streamed down her face. Douglas decided tea would be a good idea, the English panacea for all occasions. He busied himself in putting the kettle on and finding cups and saucers in the various cupboards. He handed Nina Van Heusen a cup and she gradually recovered her composure. 'What does he want?'

'He wants to do the right thing by Katya.'

'It would be better if he forgot her and she him.'

'I can guarantee he'll never forget her, but I agree, it would be best for Katya if she forgot him.' Douglas sipped his tea, 'a relationship between them could spell disaster for all concerned. Katya has a half brother who's unaware of her existence. Believe me, if things had been different----'

'But they're not different Major Coulter.'

'No.'

'My husband and I have decided to bring Katya up as one of our own family. We will tell her the truth when she is old enough to understand.'

Douglas nodded, 'Katya will inherit a house in Bremen and there's a trust fund in place for her education.'

'We don't need any help from him.'

'The help isn't for you Mrs Van Heusen, it's for Katya from her father who loves her. She may just want to know that one day. Please don't put her at a disadvantage because of your own prejudice.'

A silence pervaded the kitchen. A door opened and Katya came into the kitchen. 'Lily wants to see you Uncle Dougy Doug, She wants to know where Uncle Deedy and Mummy are.'

Douglas stretched down and lifted Katya onto his knee, 'I hope you are being a good girl Lily.'

'Yes.'said Katya, thrusting the doll to the fore once more.

'I have to go now, but I'll come and see you again if I may.' Douglas looked at Irena's sister for her approval. She nodded her head. Nina got up to see Douglas to the door. He turned to her, 'About the funeral?'

'We don't want him there.'

'Please, it's his son as well.'

With a sigh, she relented and told him when and where, 'But we don't want to see him. Katya won't be there, she's too young.' And with that she closed the door.

It was very late in the evening by the time Douglas got back to 'The Lady Anne'. The restaurant was in full swing with lanterns hung out on the top deck. The sound of someone playing on the piano hung over the water mingled with the murmur of happy voices and laughter. Customers he knew greeted him but he didn't stop to converse. Douglas made his way straight to the owner's suite. A light was shining under the door. Douglas paused for a moment, then tapped gently and entered. Dieter turned round, to Douglas's relief he was sober. Douglas went to the bar and took a glass down for himself and gestured to Dieter.

'Yes.' he responded, 'I'll have one now your back.' Douglas handed him a drink. Dieter took it and held it up to the light, 'I've realized that Irena isn't going to be found at the bottom of a glass,' and he took a sip.

'Have you eaten?'

'No, I'm not hungry.'

Douglas shrugged, picked up the internal phone and ordered a light snack for two. He sat in an armchair opposite Dieter. 'Irena's sister is a very nice lady, Katya is in good hands.' Dieter fingered his glass. There was a tap at the door and the snacks were delivered. Douglas was hungry but Dieter just picked at the food. 'Katya was asking for you and her mummy, I don't know what she's been told, but she wasn't in distress. They have two children themselves, a girl about Katya's age and a boy who's a little older, so she has someone to play with.'

Dieter got up and paced around the room. 'Can I see her?' his back was to Douglas.

Douglas sighed, 'You're not going to like what I have to say next Dieter, I'd rather say it to your face.' Dieter turned around, his face had a stricken look. 'In my view your presence will only hinder Katya's welfare.'

Shock registered anew as though he had been hit in the face. 'I'm her father Douglas. I can't just abandon her to strangers. What kind of father do you think I am?'

'A caring and loving one! One who wants the best for Irena's child.'

'She's my child too.' he persisted, he turned away again.

There was silence in the room. Douglas stood up and walked towards Dieter but stopped short. He stroked his chin in deep thought. 'The only alternative I can think of is that I take her. That she comes to London and lives with Greta and Jan.' There was no response from Dieter. 'At least that way you will be able to visit her.' he concluded lamely.

Eventually Dieter responded, 'I appreciate what you're trying to do, but that won't work. Jan is away at boarding school, you flit between London and Amsterdam. And what would you tell Greta, that you found her under a gooseberry bush?' Dieter sat back down in the chair, head bowed. He took another pull at his drink and placed the glass on the table in front of him. 'Of course, you're right.' Dieter looked up at the ceiling then at Douglas, eyes burning. 'I must say goodbye Douglas, I must.'

'Nina told me when the funeral is to be, but she was emphatic that they didn't want to see you. Katya won't be there, Nina thinks she's too young. I'm sorry Dieter. I tried my best, but the best I can do is to drive you there, but you must promise to stay out of sight until the family have gone.'

Dieter nodded, his face set in stone. 'You know Douglas, I have faced bereavement and what I thought were unbearable losses before, but nothing like this.' He paused swallowing hard, 'I hope you never experience anything like it.'

Douglas patted him on the shoulder, 'I've never experienced your highs either.' said Douglas wistfully.

Dieter looked up sharply, then understood his meaning. After a while he asked, 'Has Christa been in contact?'

'No,' replied Douglas, 'I told her you were going to London with me, I'm afraid you'll have to fly there with me, then get a flight back. She'll want to meet you at the airport; if you just turn up out of the blue she'll smell a rat. Christian must be missing you?'

'Yes, yes, he's a good boy.' Dieter paused, 'I love him too you know.'

'I know.'

A couple of days later Douglas drove Dieter to The Hague, he parked a little way off the cemetery gates. He had timed it so they didn't have to wait long as Dieter's nerves were nearly at breaking point. He was in a dark suit, his blond head bowed down on his chest. Douglas stiffened as he saw the hearse and the funeral party approach. The funeral mass had been conducted in the nearby Catholic Church. The cars drove slowly through the gates. Thankfully the interment would be a short service. Dark clouds threatening rain were scudding across the sky and the mourners were wearing heavy coats against the cold wind. Douglas could see the caskets being removed from the hearse, both white, one pathetically small. He sensed movement next to him but didn't look in Dieter's direction. The coffins were lowered into the ground and the priest gave his benediction, his white robes fluttering in the strong breeze. The chief mourners threw soil into the yawning hole in the ground and after crossing themselves returned to the cars. Nina was the last one to leave. Douglas waited until the cars had disappeared around the corner before he got out and walked into the cemetery with Dieter. As they approached the grave side, the heavens opened and the rain came down in torrents. Douglas stood by Dieter's side then retreated to the shelter of a nearby tree giving Dieter time on his own to grieve. He stood there for a long time looking down, his bowed blond head uncovered, then he sank to his knees, hands clasped tightly in front of him. Douglas was suddenly aware of someone else watching from a few yards away. They couldn't see him as he was screened from view by the trees; he slowly turned to look and was surprised to see Nina. She was looking intently at the scene in front of her, he looked more closely, despite the rain it was obvious tears

113

were streaming down her face.

CHAPTER 12

Jan was excited, it was the school's swimming Gala and he was in a number of races including the relay. His mother and father were there with Uncle Dieter who had flown in unexpectedly with his father. Jan hadn't expected anyone to come and watch him, but his father had made it at the last minute. If he hadn't turned up he knew his mother wouldn't have made the effort. Jan had mixed fortunes, he won the freestyle, came second in the back stoke and a very close second in the breast stoke. His house, Forster, were level pegging on points with Cavendish. Everything depended on the relay. He was swimming the last leg, the freestyle leg. He looked across at his parents. His father was in earnest conversation with Uncle Dieter. His mother stood to one side looking a little uncomfortable and if he was honest, a little bored. The noise in the pool grew louder, the third leg was underway. Forster had been in front but now they were trailing. It would take a supreme effort on Jan's part, but freestyle was his best stroke. He glanced quickly at his parents, they had responded to the rise in the noise levels. His father gave him the thumb's up sign. Jan watched intently for his team mate to touch the side, it would be disastrous to make an error and be eliminated now. He had a couple of yards to make up in two lengths of the pool. He kicked hard with his legs, his lungs were bursting, heart pounding in his chest. He was up against the best swimmer Cavendish House could throw against him. He could hear the noise of the spectators as he came up for air. He had made ground on Cavendish but the pool side was rushing closer. He made one last concerted effort. It seemed that the two boys touched the side together. Both were breathless, their heads streaming with water as they looked towards the umpires. The decision was given to Cavendish. Jan was devastated but sportingly congratulated his opponent. When he was dressed and came out to meet his parents, it was Uncle Dieter who commiserated most. His father urged him to do better next time and told him unfortunately they wouldn't be able to stay for the prize giving as he had to drive Dieter to the airport and then he had business in London. His mother didn't look too pleased but she said nothing. Jan swallowed his disappointment as he had had to do on many occasions lately. He wasn't on his own in this, quite a few of the children here had absentee parents. Douglas told him that he would be down to see him before he went back to Amsterdam as he wanted to speak to the teachers about his future. Jan was due to sit the entrance exam for a prestigious public school in the near future and he knew how important it was to his father's future plans for him that he passed. He was a gifted scholar but he was nervous about the outcome, his father wasn't very forgiving about failure.

Back in Amsterdam Douglas made contact with Nina, Irena's sister. He asked how Katya was settling in. Nina told him they were making progress. There had been tantrums and tearful moments, but they were becoming more and more infrequent. Douglas then asked the big question – would Nina allow him to see Katya sometime?

Nina paused, 'Well – I don't think-----'

Douglas interrupted, 'I only mean twice a year, say birthdays and just before Christmas. She is used to seeing me you know; perhaps it's not such a good idea to cut her off from her past completely.'

There was a silence on the other end of the line. 'Well – I don't want her to forget her mother of course----'

'Perhaps I could be a conduit to her past, her mother did work for me remember.'

'I remember. If I do allow it, the visits must be restricted to no more than two a year, and I don't want any mention of her father. He's never going to be in a position to take parental responsibility for her.' There was another long pause. 'I know he visits the grave, he leaves behind two red roses when he has been. I have told Katya it's the angels who leave them.'

Douglas relayed this information to Dieter who was understandably upset that he wouldn't be allowed to visit his daughter, but relieved that at least he would get some reliable information about her progress.

In the next few days Jan received extensive coaching for the exam to come, but the school was aware that outside activities were important too. To this end, they had organized a cross country run for the boys. It was a blustery day but the boys were soon sweating due to their exertions. Jan was in the first half dozen boys who broke out of the woods on the far side of the huge playing fields. He thought he spotted his father's car parked on the other side and thought it strange, it was parked quite a long way from the visitor's car park. The car was a very distinctive one; it was unlikely that there were two Bentleys of

116

quite the same styling and colour in the vicinity. As he drew closer he could see there were two people in the front of the car. His father leant across and kissed the female passenger before he got out and strode towards the school. Jan was very puzzled; the passenger didn't look like his mother. He couldn't see the colour of her hair as she had a perky little hat on her head. She was also wearing a fur coat. He couldn't remember seeing his mother wearing one before. As he drew level with the car he looked in the side window just as the passenger turned her head to watch the runners. She smiled at him. She was pretty with curly brown hair and wearing plenty of makeup. She pulled the fur coat around her throat to keep her warm. Jan ran on to the changing rooms. He was disturbed by what he had inadvertently witnessed. A teacher came in and told him to hurry up and get dressed. His father had arrived and was waiting to see him with his form teacher.

When Jan entered the room, his father smiled at him, 'Good to see you boy, I'm sorry your mother couldn't make it but I'm all packed and ready to go to the airport from here, I can't stay long as I've got a taxi waiting.' Jan flushed at this blatant lie. 'Your form teacher tells me you're as prepared as you can be for the entrance exam,' he looked to the teacher for conformation, who nodded. 'I know you won't let me down Jan. Before you're due to start your new school, I want you and your mother to fly out to Amsterdam and we'll go see Uncle Dieter. He's setting up a new riding school, I'm sure you'll enjoy that.' Douglas put his hand in his pocket and withdrew a wad of notes; he peeled off a couple and handed them to Jan. 'Here, treat yourself and your friends. I've got to dash now.' He ruffled Jan's hair, turned and left. Jan hadn't uttered a word during the whole meeting.

The exams were over and school had broken up for the summer. There were many emotional leave takings amongst the older pupils who were going on to pastures new. One or two had places at the same public school, but the majority were being scattered far and wide. Most of the boarders were travelling overseas to join their parents who lived and worked abroad. Jan and his mother were due to travel to Amsterdam and then on to Bremen to spend the summer with Dieter, Christa and their son Christian. Douglas had warned his family that he would be there some of the time but not all of the time. Jan was secretly relieved. He couldn't get the image of the woman's face who had been in his father's car, out of his mind. He had long since realized his

117

parent's marriage was not an idyllic one but he had thought of it as a permanent fixture in his life. He had heard many a sob story from some of his former school friends whose parents had had acrimonious breakups and he was afraid his own parents might now be heading down that path.

Douglas was there to meet them at the airport in his Daimler. They went straight to his apartment in the City. They were to have dinner at the restaurant on 'The Lady Anne'. Douglas had one or two loose ends to tie up before they left for Germany he told them. The meal was superb and the atmosphere relaxed. When they had finished Douglas handed the car keys to Greta. He told her he would get a cab as he would probably be back late. Greta sighed and she and Jan drove back alone to the apartment. Jan tossed and turned in his bed and eventually he heard his father arrive home at about three in the morning. He knew he would want an early start and marvelled at his father's ability to be so active, to be able to do so much on such very little sleep.

They arrived at the von Rheinhart estate late in the afternoon. Dieter was there to meet them dressed in riding boots and breeches. He told Greta Christa had been delayed, but was looking forward to having afternoon tea with her in her sitting room. He ushered both Jan and Douglas to the stables with him, 'Christian is already down there.' he said to Jan, 'come on slow coach, I've got things to show you.' As they neared the stables Christian came out. He looked a younger edition of Jan, tall for his age, of slender build but with the same shock of blond, almost white hair.

He was delighted to see Jan, 'I'm so pleased you could come for the hols,' he said, 'I'll have someone to ride with now. Come and see the new ponies father has bought,' then in a low voice he added, 'one's a bit fiery, I think you'll like him.' These two boys had always got on well together, like their fathers, who watched as their sons raced away into the stables.

Dieter looked around cagily before he asked, 'Have you got any news?'

'No, I'm afraid not. Nina hasn't been in contact since I last spoke to you. At least she is agreeable to me keeping in touch, but only because Katya's mother worked for me. She wants Katya to integrate with her family. She has specifically asked that I don't mention you.

I'm sorry Dieter.' Just then a groom came around the corner and no more was said.

'Come on, I'll show you the new arena, I want to teach dressage and show jumping, but I'm getting ahead of myself.' Dieter steered Douglas towards the new barn like structure. There was clean sawdust on the floor but very little else to see. 'The dressage square will be at this end and the jumps over there at the other end.'

'It looks very impressive.'

Dieter shrugged, 'I need something to keep me busy. Christa approves of the venture and Christian is keen to get involved, but this is my project. I'm funding it personally and I control the purse strings.' He gave a wry smile, 'keeping Christa's financial nose out of it is a bit of a battle, as are most things involving Christa.' Dieter looked around, visualizing the future. 'When the Riding School becomes profitable, my intention is to sell my share in 'The Lady Anne'. I feel I owe it to my children to try and go legit.' He paused again, 'If I can,' he clapped Douglas on the back, 'trouble is, I have some very disreputable friends.' They both chuckled. 'Come on, we had better find the boys, they'll be itching to go for a ride.'

Douglas yanked Jan out of the stables and told him to change into riding gear, he tracked down Greta who was having tea with Christa and told her the men were all going riding.

'That's fine,' retorted Christa, 'Greta and I plan to take a stroll through the gardens and then take the dogs out for a walk.' Greta was always commandeered by Christa who had much the most dominant personality of the two. This suited Douglas who didn't have to worry about keeping his wife occupied. He was free to do his own thing.

The summer holiday was a carefree time for the boys, they helped assemble the jumps for the pony club. They went fishing and boating on the lake. Jan's German improved as did Christian's English and the days flew by. Douglas came and went, Greta relaxed in the sun and read her favourite novels, that is, when she wasn't being organized by Christa! And Dieter was busy implementing his plans for the Riding School. All too soon the holiday came to an end. The new school term loomed for Jan. He had passed the entrance exam for Dulwich College and his father was going to take him there. He needed quite a few things for the new school, including a new uniform and sporting equipment, the list was long. They were going to be busy when they returned to London.

Jan was to be a border at the new school. It was an all boys' school. There were no other boys from Jan's old prep school starting this term, although there were some older pupils that Jan vaguely remembered already there, but they were day boys. The first day at a new school was always a trauma for the new entrants and this was no exception. Douglas, always flamboyant, was very much in the foreground. He had parked his car very close to the main entrance to the school. It was one of many expensive cars ferrying the sons of eminent and wealthy families to the school. Douglas and Jan were shown around the school buildings by one of the sixth formers. There were quite a few parties being shown around and as they rounded one corner they came face to face with another family, the father was of obvious military bearing. The man took one look at Douglas and went red in the face, 'Coulter!' The word exploded out of his mouth. 'I certainly didn't expect to run across your type here.'

Jan glanced up at his father. His face had momentarily registered shock but he recovered in an instant. He ushered Jan ahead of him without uttering a word. Jan looked back and saw the military gentleman in conversation with his family. Jan just caught the words, 'standards slipping' and 'what is the world coming to.' before they were out of earshot.

'Who was that dad?'

'Don't call me dad, call me father.' Douglas snapped and strode off down the corridor.

That evening in the refectory, the new boys were allocated their places at table. Each table was headed by a prefect. Jan was sitting adjacent to where the other new boy sat, the one he and his father had bumped into earlier that day. He saw him whispering in the ear of the boy next to him. They both sniggered and glanced at him. Jan knew the conversation had something to do with his father but he didn't have a clue as to what it was all about. One thing was clear though, his father had been in a bad temper ever since the chance encounter. Jan turned his attention to the other boys at his table. His immediate neighbour was a timid young man, smaller than himself, who seemed completely overawed by his surroundings. He was dark haired, of slender build, wide dark eyes and a pale complexion. He was in complete contrast to Jan who, with his long white-blond hair, startling blue eyes, fringed

120

with long lashes, had started to fill out partly due to his love of the athletic life style. He had acquired quite a tan while he had been in Germany during the summer months and he looked the picture of health. The boy next to him nudged Jan and asked if he knew the other two. Jan told him he had never met either of them before to-day.

The boy, whose name turned out to be Jonathan, whispered, 'They seem to know you. The biggest one is Clive Thornton-Smythe, he was at my prep school. I was hoping he would flunk the entrance exam but he just scraped through unfortunately. I would give him a wide berth if I was you, he's a bully and he attracts other bullies around him. At least he did in our last school.'

'Why would he know me, his name means nothing to me?'

Jonathan responded, 'Has your father had anything to do with the military?'

'Yes, he was a Major in intelligence, my Dad's rather fond of his rank,' his face creased into a grin, 'he still uses the title even though he has been out of the army for years now.'

'That might explain it then, Clive's father is General Thornton-Smythe, he's some sort of bigwig in the Ministry of Defence.'

Their conversation was cut sort by a glare from the top of their table and they were told to pipe down.

The next few days were a period of settling into their new surroundings, of forging new alliances and assessing the strengths and weaknesses of your fellow pupils. Jonathan was a studious boy, not drawn to the athletic lifestyle of the school. His parents were quiet people, both academics, his mother a biologist and his father a geologist. He had been allocated a bed in the same dormitory as Jan which greatly contributed to his peace of mind. He told Jan of some of the tricks he had had to endure at the hands of Clive Thornton-Smythe at his previous school.

'Didn't you tell anyone?' asked an incredulous Jan.

'No, it's not the done thing,' replied a wide eyed Jonathan, 'it only makes matters worse in the long run.'

'What about the teachers? Didn't they notice anything?'

'Most turn a blind eye,' he paused, 'there were one or two good eggs who tried to put a stop to it, but they don't get much support from the others who consider it part of the process of growing up, a rite of passage they euphemistically call it.'

'I hope they don't try any of that on with me.' Jan was grim faced.

'They probably won't,' Jonathan grinned, 'you're a bit bigger than me.'

Jan settled into the new routine fairly easily, although he had a constant shadow in Jonathan. He was aware of the sniggering campaign being conducted against him by Clive Thornton-Smythe, who, as Jonathan had predicted, had gathered about him some of the more unsavoury characters at the school. Jan was stretched in the classroom but with a little coaching from Jonathan he got through. The language sessions however proved no problem to him and he gained the admiration of Jonathan and one or two others with his feats of horsemanship. Still, he was disconcerted by the odd glances he received from some of the older boys when they thought he wasn't looking. One of the other plusses at the school was that they had a very good rowing club, Jan joined in enthusiastically. It was also one sport Jonathan could participate in. Because of his size he became the coxswain with Jan as first stroke.

One afternoon, after a session on the river, Jan was walking back to the dormitory block. The corridor appeared to be deserted when, at the far end, Clive Thornton-Smythe and his cronies turned around the corner. They quickly came down the corridor towards Jan who had the distinct impression that they had been laying in wait for him. Jan knew this was going to be a showdown between them. He backed into a corner so that no-one could get behind him and waited.

Thornton Smythe swaggered up to him, leering into his face. 'Well, if it isn't little Jonathan's protector all alone. I wonder how good he is at protecting himself. He looks a bit girlie to me.' He looked around at his mates, 'He calls himself Jan,' he said. They were all smirking enjoying the encounter. Clive emphasized the English 'J', 'Jan's a girls name, and you know what we do to girls don't you Jan?' Clive started to giggle and the others joined in, taunting him with his name. Jan glanced up and down the corridor; there was no-one else in sight. He quickly sized up the situation, if these thugs got their way his life at this place would be ruined. Jan focused his attention on the ring leaders. He lunged at the biggest boy with the loudest mouth and hit him hard below the belt. The boy bent double, howling in pain. Another boy moved towards him in a very menacing manner. Jan didn't hesitate: he crashed his fist straight into the other boy's face breaking his nose. Blood spurted everywhere.

'Anyone else want to treat me like a girl?' Jan challenged.

The other boys hung back, unsure of what to do next. Jan had put two of the largest of their group out of action. Just then the Sports Master walked by at the head of the corridor and took in the scene at a glance. 'What's going on here? What are you boys up to?'

Jan kept quiet. The one with the broken nose accused Jan of making an unprovoked attack on them.

'What, on all of you, all at once?' the teacher asked with a decidedly sceptical look on his face. Some of the group started to melt away. No-one offered any other explanation. 'Come on,' said the master to the boy who was blubbing and holding a handkerchief to his nose. 'Let's get you to the matron's office, she'll sort you out.' Then to Jan, 'and what's your side of the story?'

'I haven't got one Sir.'

The Sports Master gave a long sigh, 'I'm afraid I'll have to report this incident to the Head Coulter. It will have to go down in the first aid book.' He gave Jan a long look, 'I suggest you think about some extenuating circumstances young man.'

Jan was duly hauled up before the Head Master. All those involved had been questioned. Clive Thornton Smythe and the boy with the broken nose held to their story that Jan had launched an unprovoked attack on them. The other boys said they hadn't seen or heard anything. Jan refused to say anything in his defence. In view of Jan's silence the Head had no alternative but to punish him, but the sentence was a lenient one. Both the Head and the Sports Master had their own ideas of the cause of the fracas and the Sport's Master determined to teach Jan Coulter the art of self defence and boxing. The unexpected result of the matter was that the sly glances in Jan's direction ceased. He had collected some kudos from the older boys and the rest of the term passed by without any further disruption. General Thornton-Smythe however, on hearing his son's version of the story, fired off a fiery letter to the Head Master insisting his son was being victimized and demanding that Jan should be expelled. The Head though, was skilled in diplomacy and defused the General's ire.

Douglas and his family spent another summer in Bremen at the von Rheinhart estate. Christian was becoming an accomplished rider in dressage and show jumping, responding to his father's expert tuition. Both father and son took part in competitions and gave exhibitions. Christian had won a number of first and second prizes in the junior events and was tipped to be an outstanding competitor in the years to come. Dieter's riding school was slowly gaining recognition and as a result was in danger of becoming a commercial success.

Douglas had kept his word to Dieter and visited Katya when he could. He took photographs of her as she grew, keeping them under lock and key in the privacy of the owner's cabin on 'The Lady Anne'. Katya was showing promise as a violinist and hoped to study music in Paris. Dieter still yearned to see her but felt he had to respect Nina's wishes to the contrary.

Jan and his mother returned to London without Douglas. Jan was due back at school and Douglas had business in Amsterdam. He, in fact, had a large consignment of diamonds to move to the London Merchant, smuggling was still a very profitable business. On this occasion he decided to wear the uniform of a Naval Officer. Douglas used different airlines and different airports for his trips; he wanted to avoid being recognized as a 'regular'. On this occasion the airport was crowded and there were long queues building up to go through customs. There was one officer who was doggedly searching through people's baggage. It sometimes happened if there was an alert on so Douglas wasn't overly concerned. When his turn arrived the officer indicated that he put his bags on the table top. He asked Douglas to unlock his cases. Douglas did so with a sigh. The customs man made sure he got a good look at Douglas's face despite the fact that he was wearing a peaked cap which shaded his features. He very carefully went through Douglas's luggage, gave him another good look, closed his suitcase and waved him on. Douglas heaved the case onto the floor and in doing so bumped into a naval rating who was rushing to join his shipmates. The rating immediately saluted him and Douglas, a little off balance, saluted him back.

The rating turned to his mates and said, 'That's funny, that officer over there, he gave me an army salute.' They all turned to look at Douglas. Unfortunately for Douglas the customs officer had also overheard the remark and without hesitation he called Douglas back. This time he searched Douglas's luggage very thoroughly and inspected the cases by tapping the sides. He found nothing. Douglas with a show of annoyance locked his cases and haughtily made his way to the gate watched by the customs man. The customs hall was brightly lit and Douglas was passing under the fluorescent lighting when the officer saw a bright flash on Douglas's shoulder emanating from his epaulettes. The man immediately gave a sign to his colleague on the gate and Douglas was stopped yet again. This time he was escorted to a private room where the diamonds were soon discovered sewn carefully under the gold braid. The game was up!

CHAPTER 13

The trial was high profile, conducted at The Old Bailey. Douglas had been remanded in custody for fear that he might disappear into another persona, given his previous history for impersonation. Greta had been able to see him and Douglas was able to tell her how to access the annuity he had set up for her and to tell her to contact Dieter. For some reason Douglas felt he wanted to protect Leonard Warner. They had never had what one could call a warm relationship, but Douglas, like many other service men in Germany just after the war, was aware of the tremendous suffering endured by the inmates of the concentration camps. He felt that if Leonard was incarcerated again it would break him. He told Greta to ask the German to move the Jew. The important bits of their conversations were conducted in Dutch, despite constant warnings to speak only in English.

Douglas had no qualms in offering up the Hatton Garden trader to the authorities, but he had no intentions of implicating Dieter in the smuggling rap. He had always been at arms length from it, the only link to him would be through Leonard. Douglas told Greta that Dieter mustn't attempt to communicate with him by visitation rights or by letter, only verbally through her.

The charges against Douglas were for smuggling stolen diamonds, using forged passports, and impersonating military personnel. The stolen diamond charge was a tricky one, he had been caught hands down on the smuggling charge, but diamond dealers were a close knit community and kept themselves very much to themselves. As a rule, they did not report stolen gems to the police. If they did, their insurance premiums would go through the roof, so they generally took the hit and moved on.

There was also talk of bringing charges of money laundering. Douglas's council advised him to turn Queen's evidence in the hope of a lighter sentence, they would do their best for him they said, but in their view, a guilty verdict followed by a lengthy custodial sentence was inevitable. Douglas decided however that the only sacrificial lamb he would give them was the London dealer and he smiled to himself at the thought of the police uniform being caught on the surveillance camera. Would the dealer think it was him in yet another disguise.

Greta stoically attended the trial throughout. The police had only interviewed her once, deciding early on, correctly, that she knew next to nothing about her husband's activities. She lived a modest lifestyle in the suburbs in a house she owned in her own name. The police had soon unearthed Douglas's other abode in London and exposed the glamorous lifestyle he lived with his lady friend.

The verdict was guilty as predicted, the sentence of twelve years a bit of a shock. The judge in his summary of Douglas's flamboyant and fraudulent life style, made much of the fact that Douglas had been dishonourably discharged from the army for black market activities, bribery and theft. He had been treated leniently on that occasion and had not been given a custodial sentence in recognition of his war record. He had, in effect, been given a second chance which he had blatantly abused. According to the evidence provided by custom and excise Douglas had been involved in illegal activities for some considerable time and an example must be made. Douglas was led from the court. He glanced briefly at Greta and then looked up into the gallery. Greta, ashen faced, followed his glance, just in time to see a young good looking woman leaving the court.

The arrest and subsequent trial of Jan's father couldn't be kept quiet for long. The news spread like wild fire through the school. Jan and his mother were both in shock and Greta was summonsed to a meeting with the Head Master. For days Jan's school mates had been avoiding him, the whispering campaign had started up again. Only Jonathan remained loyal. Jan and his mother sat outside the Head Master's study. A heated discussion was going on inside.

A loud voice proclaimed, 'I warned you Head Master, I warned you when my son was attacked. Bad blood, you overruled me on that occasion but I have the backing of all the Governors of the school behind me now. I'll not allow it to happen again, the boy must go, and today.' The door burst open and a very angry red faced General Thornton-Smythe stormed out of the room. He paused briefly to look at the two people waiting outside the study, growled and strode away down the corridor.

After a few minutes, the Head Master's secretary asked them inside. Greta was trembling, near to tears. The Head asked her to take a seat, he looked compassionately at her. 'I'm so sorry Mrs Coulter, I am afraid this is now out of my hands. There's no set rule to cover these particular circumstances, sometimes I am able to use my discretion, but the feeling of the Governors' is so strong-----' his voice faded away as tears rolled down Greta's cheeks. The Head got up and asked his secretary, who was in the next room, to make a cup of tea for Mrs Coulter. This gave Greta time to scrabble about in her handbag for a tissue to wipe her eyes and to try and compose herself. The Head continued, 'In Jan's own interests I feel it would be better if he left the school. It's a great shame, Jan was doing well here, he will be missed. He was a great asset in both the boxing ring and the rowing club, but if he continued here, his life would be made miserable. I'm sure you would agree?' Greta nodded. She left the cup of tea untouched. 'I have arranged for Jan's trunk to be packed and taken to the side entrance, the porter will take it to your car.'

Greta stumbled to her feet, head bowed. The Head Master rose and opened the door for her. Jan took his mother's elbow and escorted her out of the school to their car. She sat there for a few minutes, then started the engine and drove slowly to the side entrance of the school. The porter and Jonathan were both waiting for them. The porter loaded the trunk into the boot, he had only been asked to do this once before and on that occasion it had been good riddance to the young man concerned.

Jonathan was distraught, 'What am I going to do without you here?' he wailed, 'if you can't stay, I don't want to either.'

Jan put his arm around Jonathan's slim shoulders, 'You'll be fine,' he told him, 'what would the rowing eight do without you? You're the best coxswain they've ever had.'

Jonathan smiled thinly as Jan got into his mother's car and they drove away, Jonathan waving frantically as they disappeared from view.

Greta drove in silence all the way home, Jan couldn't think of anything to say. She turned into the drive to be confronted by a car already parked there. Dieter was sitting on the doorstep. The floodgates opened, Greta just sat there, seemingly glued to the wheel, tears streaming down her face.

Dieter came forward and eased her out of the car. 'Take your mother inside Jan,'

'They've sacked me Uncle Dieter.' Jan's face was bleak, 'my trunk is in the boot.'

'I'll see to your trunk Jan, you go inside and look after your mother. You're both coming to Bremen with me. Don't worry Jan, we'll sort something out.' Dieter told them he had found out that Douglas had been taken to Wandsworth Prison, 'He won't be allowed visitors for a while. In the meantime you both need a change of scenery.'

Christa was totally shocked about the revelations of Douglas's life, but she rose to the occasion and welcomed both Greta and Jan into her home. She had remembered Dieter's unexplained withdrawal into his study of a few years ago and Douglas's explanation. She suspected Dieter must have had some involvement with Douglas's nefarious activities and confronted him about it.

'Don't ask! You may not like the answer.' Was Dieter's abrupt response to her, 'I owe Douglas a great deal, it was chaos at the end of the war. I seem to recall you and your family were in Spain at the time. I did what I had to do to survive. Now leave it alone.'

One look at Dieter's face convinced Christa of his involvement in this murky business and she watched open mouthed as he stalked off to the stables. Greta and Jan stayed at the von Rheinhart's estate for a week. After a little initial shyness the two boys took up where they had left off. Christian showed Jan his newly found skills in the dressage ring, while Jan excelled in the jumping arena. Dieter had a couple of private sessions with Greta. He told her he had been able to pull a few strings on Jan's behalf and had secured him a place at H.M.S. Conway, a Merchant Navy Training School. He thought Douglas would approve of this arrangement. Greta was just grateful that Dieter had taken charge of Jan's future and when Jan was asked about his views on the subject, he was delighted and quite excited about his future prospects.

One evening just before Greta and Jan were due to return home, Dieter took Jan on one side. He put his arm around the boy's shoulders, 'I understand how shocked and disappointed you must be at what has happened Jan. Your father has always been a good friend to me.'

'But Uncle Dieter, you're a respected events trainer, people look up to you. My father's in jail.' His face looked stricken with shame.

'And who do you think I have to thank for this opportunity? If it wasn't for your father, I wouldn't be doing this now. Don't judge him too harshly Jan. We all have faults and secrets, secrets we hope will remain secret. Your mother owes her life to him, never forget that Jan.' Jan knew the story and bowed his head. 'Your father has shown me nothing but friendship and loyalty. I've had some very dark moments in my life Jan, and your father was there for me. I intend to be there for him when the time comes for his release. Now, off you go, those ponies need a good rub down.'

Jan joined Christian in the stables; they got on with the evening's chores.

'I'm sorry you're leaving so soon Jan. It's great having someone to help. I hope you'll be able to come back for the summer?'

'I don't know. Everything has changed. I don't know what mother has got planned for us.'

Christian put his hand on Jan's arm, 'My father won't hear a bad word said against Uncle Douglas.' Jan smiled at him and both boys set too with gusto.

CHAPTER 14

The first term at HMS Conway was a revelation to Jan. There were lessons in basic seamanship, boat handling and sailing, the principals of navigation and mathematics, and most importantly, a rowing and boxing club. Jan was in his element and forgot his troubles. His mother was a very infrequent visitor but Jan hardly noticed. He was having the time of his life. The summer term came to an end and Jan returned home. The contrast was enormous, life was very quiet. His mother seemed to have withdrawn into herself. He asked about his father. Greta told him she went to see him once a month, she was obviously reluctant to talk about it.

'Do you think I should visit him?'

'No! Your father has absolutely forbidden it.'

'Does Uncle Dieter go?'

'No, your father doesn't want Dieter on their radar.'

'Is he alright?'

'He seems to be coping. We've been invited to Bremen, but I've told Christa I don't want to go.'

Jan was horrified, 'But Mum, the change will do us good.'

'Well,' she retorted, 'you go if you must.'

'I want us both to go; you get on well with Aunt Christa.'

'Do I? I'm not sure I get on well with anyone any more.'

'Please mother, I've been looking forward to seeing Christian again.'

Greta turned round to look at her son. He was growing into a handsome youth. She realized how tedious it would be for him to spend the summer all alone with her, she relented. 'I'll think about.'

Jan let out a long sigh.

Dieter picked them up at the airport; he was genuinely pleased that Greta had changed her mind. He asked Jan how things were progressing at the Naval college and was glad to hear of Jan's enthusiasm. He didn't mention Douglas: he had his own ways of keeping up with the news from the prison. After a few days Greta relaxed, she enjoyed herself despite her initial reservations. Christian and Jan were hardly ever to be seen, they were out every day, riding, sailing and rowing.

Dieter had acted swiftly after Douglas's arrest and had managed to whisk Leonard Warner out of Amsterdam. When the Dutch police turned up at his apartment, the bird had flown. Leonard was now living in down town Tel Aviv, well out of harms way. Dieter had also cleared out the owner's cabin on 'The Lady Anne' of anything incriminating and had moved all Douglas's personal possessions, including the uniforms, passports and photos to a lock up he had rented. He intended to move everything to Douglas's apartment when the heat had died down. In the meantime he had rented the apartment out to a respectable family in an attempt to put the police of the scent. Things had changed radically for the partners in crime since Douglas's detention. The London merchant was in custody and there was a thorough on-going investigation under way of all his clients and dealings. There were some very irate individuals around who bore a grudge against Douglas Coulter.

Wim Henke had also seen his chance and taken advantage of the situation. As Douglas was no longer around to oversee the fortunes of 'The Lady Anne', Henke had moved his son into the vacant position. Henke couldn't believe his luck, Douglas was in prison, Leonard Warner had disappeared and Dieter von Rheinhart was now a respectable member of the equestrian world and was keen to disassociate himself from his previous dubious activities. Henke now had the field to himself and it had cost him nothing! He was still aggrieved that he couldn't lay his hands on the jackpot that languished in a bank vault in Switzerland. He had tried to persuade von Rheinhart to obtain the numbers of the account from the others, but he had told him he didn't know where Leonard had gone to ground. Henke didn't believe him for a moment, he realized he would just have to bide his time.

The other matter that troubled Dieter was that there was now no contact to be had with Katya. He had made discreet enquiries at the house he had bought for Irena. It was still in Katya's name and the rent was paid direct to a music school in Paris. He soon ascertained that Katya was enrolled there as a student studying the violin.

When Jan and his mother returned home to London, Jan was eager to start his second year at HMS Conway. He was delighted to find a new member of the rowing club was there. Jonathan had persuaded his parents than his overwhelming ambition was to go to sea. He, in fact was interested in, and excelled at navigation. The two boys prospered in this new environment. They enjoyed the sailing and rowing facilities on offer, they made friends with the other cadets and most importantly they passed their exams. Jan continued to go to Bremen during the summer with his mother. The riding school was a success and Christian was making his mark as an up and coming horseman. Dieter also entered competitions but his roll was more as a national trainer and horse breeder.

Jan hadn't seen his father since his conviction for smuggling. Greta religiously went to see him once a month. She had become resigned to living on her own and had made friends with one or two of the neighbours. When visiting Bremen she and Dieter occasionally went into a huddle, no doubt Douglas was the subject of their discussions. Dieter had respected Douglas's wish for him not to visit while he was serving his sentence, but Dieter had devised a way of communicating with him through a third party, they corresponded in various languages so Douglas was aware of developments in Germany and in Amsterdam.

Jan was now sixteen, crucially he had passed all his exams and he was looking for a cadetship. HMS Conway had supplied him with a list of major shipping companies, some of which had already visited the college looking for likely recruits. One company in particular, China Navigation and the lure of the Far East appealed to Jan. Both he and Jonathan applied, were interviewed and were accepted. For the boys, exciting prospects loomed ahead. The first task was to be kitted out in the company's livery. To this end Jonathan's parents took them to London to the major Naval and Military outfitters where they were measured, kitted out and provided with the various instruments and equipment they would require. This operation came to a tidy sum, unknown to Jan, Dieter funded his needs. The two boys were allowed home for a few days to make their final preparations. They would be away from home for a long time. Six cadets had been accepted by China Navigation and they were to be flown out en masse to Hong Kong where they would join their respective ships, two cadets to each vessel. The big day arrived and the families assembled at the airport. Each boy seemed to have a mountain of luggage. Excitement filled the air, the flight was called and final farewells were said. Most of the mothers had a tear or two in their eyes, but not Jan's mother. She had a resolute stoic look on her face. The boys, in contrast were chattering away with excitement, looking forward to their adventures at sea.

The flight from Heathrow to Hong Kong, including a short refuelling stop in Bombay, was long and tedious. It was a bedraggled group of cadets who trooped through the customs hall to be met by the company's agents. They were shepherded to a hotel for the night to recover from the flight. Next morning bright and early, a yellow minibus collected Jan and Jonathan. The others were destined to be ferried to different ships at different times intended for different destinations. The minibus drove into the bustling port. Even at this early hour, the noise, heat and humidity assailed the senses like a hammer blow. There was spilt packaging and cargo littering the cobbles

133

and the smell! There were ships of every size and nationality moored up, some working cargo, some not. The port was so busy that some of the ships were double banked. The two boys took in the scene with wide eyes, the minibus slewed to a halt and they got their first sight of the vessel that was to be their home for the next two years. She was called the 'Kweilin'. She had a black hull with white super structure with two separate blocks of accommodation. She was a general cargo ship bound for Australia via several other places en route. The crew were Hong Kong Chinese, the Officers mainly British with a sprinkling of Australian and New Zealanders. The second and third Mates were at the top of the gangway. Jan and Jonathan struggled up the gangway with their bags and books.

The first words spoken to them were, 'Are you sure about this lads, you've still got a chance to escape.'

Jan and Jonathan exchanged glances then looked into the weather beaten face which regarded them critically. They nodded in unison.

'Right then, let's see what the Captain makes of you.' And they were led through a maze of alleyways and up some stairs to a door which was open, but shrouded by a curtain. The second mate gave a loud knock.

A deep voice answered, 'Come.' And they were pushed through the open door. The Captain sat behind an old desk which was covered in papers, he was short, fat and grey haired. He gave them both a quick glance and without getting out of his chair he snapped in a grumpy voice, 'Keep your cabin clean or else.' And they were dismissed.

The second mate, who spoke with a slight Aussie twang, was waiting outside with a grin on his face. He took them back down to the accommodation block. 'You're to share this cabin.' Jan peeped inside, it looked like a cupboard! 'The one next door is where the other cadets live. The senior cadet will look after you,' he knocked on that door and shouted, 'The new cadets have arrived.' And he left.

A friendly freckled face topped by a mop of unruly red hair appeared around the door. 'Hi, my name's Tom, put your gear inside. I'll take you for breakfast first, then I'll show you around the old tub, afterwards I'll show you how to stow your gear.'

Both boys felt somewhat relieved. They followed Tom's jaunty walk, he took them to the dining saloon. There were two long tables with a Smokey damask table cloth on each, set with shiny cutlery. There was a menu card on each table. At the end of the room there were two smaller tables.

Tom pointed to the two long tables, 'The Captain and the senior officers sit there, the junior officers sit at the other one and we eat here.'

A Chinese steward in black trousers and a white coat appeared. 'Ah, customers at last, what would you like this morning? Scrambled eggs on toast or scrambled eggs on toast.'

'We'll have three scrambled eggs on toast please.'

'Coming up as fast as you like.'

The three boys slid into their seats. Jan picked up the menu.

Tom grinned, 'It sounds a lot better than it tastes.'

Another boy about their age rushed into the room and joined them. The steward popped his head round the corner and held up four fingers. Tom nodded. 'This is Bernard, now we're the four musketeers.'

'You're both from Conway aren't you?' without waiting for a response, Bernard continued, 'I'm from HMS Worcester same as Tom. It's nothing like you expect you know.'

The steward returned with four plates perfectly balanced.

'Let's eat quickly and scarper before the others come in, they'll only find us more work to do.'

Tom explained, 'The ship's working cargo so the rest of them will come in in dribs and drabs to snatch a bite when they can. Mealtimes are much more formal when we're at sea. The port authorities want us out of here by this evening.'

Just as he spoke a junior officer came in, 'Jones, I wondered where you'd got to. When you've finished see me on deck, there's a spot of tallying to do.'

Bernard groaned. Tom grinned.

After breakfast Tom took them around the ship, he showed them the crew's quarters at the aft end and the crew's recreation room. 'We don't go in there unless we're invited,' he explained, 'we have our own recreation room midships.' He showed them the crew's galley and mess and the laundry where the Chinese crew dealt with the ship's bedding and the officer's uniforms. He took them by an alleyway to midships. 'These are the heads: you won't want to linger in there!' Then up some stairs back to the accommodation block. 'We won't go out on deck while they're working cargo, we'll only get in the way. I'll show you the best way to stow your gear. Remember better down than up, things can fall out and hit you in heavy weather. When you've finished unpacking the Purser wants to see you both in the ship's office to sign articles. I'll be back for you in a couple of hours.'

The two new cadets had some idea of the layout of a ship having been on ship's visits before, but each ship was slightly different. They both drew a deep breath and got on with the task of stowing their worldly goods in the few spaces provided. True to his word Tom was back for them and whisked them to the ship's office.

The Purser was a New Zealander; he had the paperwork ready for them. 'If you sign these lads you're committing yourselves to slave labour for two years.' He slid the paperwork in front of each of them and pushed a pen within reach, then stood back. It was Jonathan who stepped forward first, he picked up the pen and signed without any hesitation, then handed the pen to Jan. Jan looked at the New Zealander's expressionless face and did likewise. The Purser scooped up the papers and shouted for Tom who came running at the double.

'They're all yours now Owens.'

Tom led then back up towards the Captain's cabin, 'You're in for a treat now,' he told them, 'the Old Man loves his lecture on morality. He'll tell you all about the evils of women and drink, but don't smell his breath!' and he chuckled, 'then the Chief will familiarize you with your duties and study hours. I'll take you for some grub before we sail. I'll be on the bridge when we let go, one of you will be down aft with the Second and the other forward with Bernard. Good luck!' He knocked on the Captain's cabin and was gone before they heard the Captain's growl.

All seemed bedlam, stations had been called, the agent had gone ashore and the pilot was on board. The gangway was being lifted and the tug was standing by waiting to pull the 'Kweilin' off her berth.

'There's only one way off now,' whispered Bernard to Jonathan, 'and that's to jump overboard.' Jonathan looked at Bernard's face to see if he was joking but couldn't tell in the shifting lights. There was a trembling from the ship as the engine responded to the clanging of the ship's telegraph and thick black smoke belched out of the single stack. The boys had been warned to stand well back as the ropes were let go and winched in. The 'Kweilin' was pulled sideways off the berth and then inched forward. The tug gave a loud hoot and let go the line, and with a roar of her powerful engine she returned to her base. The 'Kweilin' was on her own. Slowly she threaded her way through ships at anchor, junks and sampans and expertly dodged small fishing vessels returning with their catches. The lights of Hong Kong began to recede. The order to stand down had been given.

The Second took Jan forward to join the other cadets. 'You'll always remember your first time leaving Hong Kong,' he told them. 'You can stay up here for a while, but don't leave it too long before turning in, you'll be put on the shake at seven sharp in the morning and then your training begins in earnest.'

The ship gathered speed, water creaming away from her prow. A dim light was just visible on the bridge and they could see the outline of the lookout as he slowly moved about on the wing of the bridge. The lights from Hong Kong harbour were now just a smudge on the horizon and, in contrast, the stars shone much brighter in the sky. Jonathan gave a huge sigh of pure pleasure. Jan, on the other hand, decided it was time to go below. What Jonathan couldn't see was that Jan had gone just a tiny shade paler. They stumbled down the stairs to their tiny cabin and crammed themselves into the narrow bunks. The ship was just gently rolling from side to side. Jonathan turned to say something to Jan, but all he could make out was Jan's back turned towards him. Jonathan looked up at the bulk head and gently drifted off into a contented sleep.

Sharp at seven the next morning the Chinese watchman knocked loudly on their door. Jonathan and Jan quickly collected their things together and made for the heads. They had been warned of the early morning scramble. Jonathan was first out, Jan followed more slowly. They made for the saloon, Tom and Bernard were already there, anticipating the gong that denoted that breakfast was being served. The officer of the Watch had already been and gone. The rest of the ship's company were able to enjoy a more leisurely breakfast. As Tom had indicated, everyone knew their designated place at table. The cadet's table was virtually ignored, only the most junior officers who were not long out of their own cadetship acknowledged them. When their breakfasts were brought, Jan just toyed with his.

Tom smiled, 'It's best if you keep your belly full,' he said quietly, 'it'll pass in a day or two when you've got your sea legs.'

Jonathan looked at Jan open mouthed, it had never occurred to him than Jan was suffering from a bout of 'mal du mer.' Jan looked uncomfortably around him and blushed, a condition he was not prone to. The cadets were the first to leave the saloon. Tom told them to collect their equipment; they were to report to the Chief for their instructions. 'That's the First Officer,' he explained, 'he virtually runs the ship.'

The Chief Officer was a bluff Yorkshire man, no more than thirty years old. He told Tom and Bernard to report to the bosun who would give them their tasks for the day. He turned to Jan and Jonathan, 'You two are to report to the bridge, the Third is on watch. You can ask questions but make them pertinent, if you make a nuisance of yourselves, he'll throw you off. Don't touch anything unless you're told to. If you're stuck for a task, I like to see my reflection in the brass work.' And he dismissed them both. The Third was a pleasant chap, also from the north of England. He answered their questions with good humour. At the end of his watch he gave them the regulations for the rules of the road at sea. He told them to study them carefully that afternoon, because tomorrow, he would test them both to see how much Conway had taught them.

Next day they were due to dock at Kaohsiung. The 'Kweilin' was making twelve to thirteen knots and it had been impressed upon them how important it was to try keep to their schedule. To their disappointment they were not going to be allowed ashore in Taiwan. They were on deck duty, Jan with Tom and Jonathan with Bernard. Their job was security and to tally the cargo. They were told to make sure the dock workers didn't broach the cargo, 'They're a devious lot, so keep your eyes open.'

The ship sailed again the following day, this time they were in for a much longer sea passage to Brisbane. They now had ten to eleven days at sea moving southwards through the Pacific Ocean. They soon settled into the routine at sea. Jan suddenly realised he no longer felt any queasiness, he was starting to enjoy life once more. Jonathan was in his element, he loved every minute of it. The Pacific was famed for the beautiful sunrises and sunsets and it certainly lived up to its reputation. The sea was a deep blue, some days they were accompanied by large schools of dolphins which cavorted around the bow. They appeared to be trying to outdo each other in the most energetic display of acrobatics and then suddenly, as though someone had blown time on a whistle, they disappeared. Flying fish were everywhere to be seen and a whale was reported on the port bow by the lookout. As soon as the animal detected the sound of the ship's engine, it sounded. One heave of its gigantic body and one flip of its huge tail and it disappeared beneath the swell. As they passed to the west of Yap Island, they caught sight of the manta rays for which this area of the Pacific was famous. Their days were now spent in study, practising noon sights, chart work and basic seamanship. Part of their time was spent in chipping, scraping and painting under the watchful eye of the bosun, not forgetting the ever ongoing polishing of the brass work.

Jan and Jonathan became aware of strange activities and whisperings being conducted between the other two cadets, the third officer and the junior engineers. They both knew what was coming. They were due to cross the equator one day north of New Ireland. This ceremony had to be endured by all those that crossed the equator for the first time. They knew there was no point in trying to evade the inevitable. They would be hunted down, covered in the most foul and evil smelling gunk the engineers had been able to concoct and would eventually be hosed down with cold sea water before being presented with their crossing the line certificate. On passenger ships, they knew much was made of this ceremony. Some of the ship's company would be dressed up as creatures from the deep and it would be Neptune himself with his trident and a compliment of mermaids who would round up all the passengers crossing for the first time. Then after speeches and much play acting, they would be presented with the all important certificate, beautifully decorated and tied up with a blue ribbon. The best of these were highly valued by the passengers. But a ceremony along those lines was not for them; their crossing the line ceremony would be an endurance test!

Excitement mounted as they approached Brisbane, neither Jan nor Jonathan had been to Australia before and they had been promised some time ashore. The ship slowed down to take on the pilot and in no time the 'Kweilin' was tied up. The ship's agent who, most importantly had the crew mail, and the Port Authorities were waiting on the quay side. The first hour would be taken up with paperwork, and only then would the off duty members of the crew be allowed shore leave. Tom had promised to take both Jan and Jonathan to see the sights. The Purser distributed the mail to the crew, the boys soon realized how important this was, jubilant faces and crestfallen faces gave the game away. Jan had three letters waiting for him. He quickly looked at them, one from his mother and one each from Dieter and Christian. Nothing from his father! He stuffed them in his pocket; he would read them later in private. Jan had had no direct contact with his father since his arrest.

Brisbane was hot, humid and tropical. They were in port for three days so most of the crew had the opportunity for a run ashore. The dockers worked the ship from early morning when it was a little cooler, until five in the afternoon, then they evacuated en masse for what was termed the six o'clock swill.

The next port of call was Sydney. The approach to Sydney was in the early morning just as the sun was rising. Tom and the Aussie Second Officer had warned both Jonathan and Jan that this was an experience not to be missed so they were both on deck in plenty of time. The first sight of Sydney harbour was the sea crashing against the Heads. The bay opened up before them with the sun sparkling off the water almost blinding them. Even this early in the morning there were a few yachts with brightly coloured sails dotted around. After picking up the pilot, the ship turned to port and sun-bleached white buildings appeared to rise directly out of the blue water. In the distance the distinctive arch of Sydney Harbour Bridge, affectionately known as 'The Coat Hanger', was just visible. Tom pointed out the Governor's residence perched high on the headland overlooking Kiribilli Dolphins and Circular Quay where the very distinctive and controversial Sydney Opera House had recently been built. The 'Kweilin' swung slowly to port into Darling Harbour and tied up beneath the area known as 'The Rocks'. The new cadets were mesmerized, Tom and the Second had been right.

Sydney was a cosmopolitan city, much more sophisticated than Brisbane. The Aussie members of the crew were the first ones down the gangway. Jonathan had mail here but Jan hadn't. Even though he knew his mother wasn't the most diligent of communicators, he was surprised how disappointed he felt. The Chief Officer allowed the cadets a fair amount of time off to allow them to explore the city, but they had their duties to perform when the ship was being worked. Both Jan and Jonathan were enchanted with Sydney.

They left Sydney to make their way south following the coastline to Melbourne. At first the sea was benign, but gradually the boys were able to discern a change in the movement of the vessel. 'Look's like we're in for a bit of a blow.' was Bernard's assessment of the change in the movement of the clouds and the darkening colour of the sky. This was to be a baptism for the two young seamen, an initiation into the vagaries of the sea. The ship began to corkscrew in a quarterly swell and a rough following sea. The uncomfortable motion of the ship increased on entering the Bass Strait where the Tasman Sea met the Southern Ocean. They found moving around the ship more and more difficult, keeping upright was a feat in itself. Tom's advice about stowing low rather than high was vividly born out as anything not tied down was thrown about. At meal times it was advisable to hang onto your plate even with the storm boards raised in position at the tables. They were relieved to enter the relatively quiet waters of Port Philip Bay. Melbourne was now only two hours steaming away. Shortly after entering the Yarra River the vessel tied up. Work on her commenced within the hour. This was as far south as the 'Kweilin' was going on this voyage. Her return journey was to take her back to Hong Kong via Fiji. By the time she arrived there, the two young mariners felt completely immersed in their new life.

The next voyage took the 'Kweilin' to South Korea, Japan, the Philippines, Indonesia, Borneo, Singapore and Malaysia. Sometimes they were in port for quite long periods of time which enabled them to experience the diverse cultures and dress of the indigenous people of the countries they visited. Sometimes they were in and out without being able to set foot ashore. When the mood took him, the Captain lectured them on their behaviour and responsibilities when they had shore leave. Otherwise they relied upon the advice from the other Officers. If you weren't careful to adhere to the local customs, they were told, you could end up in a lot of trouble. The cadets weren't able to indulge themselves in the pleasures to be had ashore very much due to the lack of spending power. Wages for cadets were very low in the Merchant Navy. But Jonathan was keen to acquire some souvenirs from each place they visited for his mother. At every port Jonathan received a letter from his parents and he replied to them religiously, writing a little every day. Jan's mail was more spasmodic. He still received letters from Dieter and Christian, they were interesting and informative. The Riding School was doing very well and Christian particularly was interested in Jan's experiences and travels around the world. Of course he also received mail from his mother, but her letters tended to be short and brief, her routine didn't seem to vary very much. She never mentioned his father in them. In contrast Jan tried to make his letters to her as colourful as possible, he described in detail the different countries he visited and the sights he saw. He hoped she took pleasure from reading them.

CHAPTER 15

Excitement mounted as the 'Kweilin' approached her home port once more after two years roving around the southern oceans. The cadets had enjoyed shore leave but none of them had had any home leave during that time. For the two senior cadets it was even more poignant. It was the end of their cadetship. On returning home they would be sitting exams for their Second Mate's tickets which would involve them in four months of intensive study. Both Jan and Jonathan had a month's home leave to look forward to before they would be called back and assigned to different ships within the group. They would then be the senior cadets.

All four boys parted company at Heathrow Airport, vowing to keep in touch with each other. Jonathan's parents were very much to the fore when they cleared customs, it was a very tearful reunion. Jan looked around and he eventually spotted his mother at the back of the crowd. She waved in his direction. He made his way towards her. She gave him a hug and a peck on each cheek. When they were in the car she said she hoped he wouldn't find it too dull at home after all his foreign travel. 'Dieter and Christa have invited us to Germany for two weeks.' she informed him, 'I've accepted, I hope you don't mind?'

Jan was quietly relieved and pleased that his mother still visited the von Rheinharts. He looked forward to meeting up with Christian again. The two weeks sped by. Jan rode out with Christian and Dieter every morning, his show jumping skills were a little rusty but these horses had been well schooled and he managed to stay aboard. He noticed that his mother and Christa were quite relaxed with each other, the initial embarrassment of Douglas's conviction quite forgotten. Christian was travelling around Europe with his father on the show jumping circuit these days, but he was genuinely interested in Jan's escapades in the southern hemisphere and they spent long days in the stables swopping stories whilst grooming horses. Jan confided in Dieter that his mother never mentioned anything about his father in her letters, and he was loathe to bring up the subject with her. His father had been in jail for nearly six years now and in all that time Jan had never had any communication with him. Dieter felt really sorry for the boy, he put his arm around his shoulders and told him Douglas hadn't forgotten him. He wanted Jan to make a success of his career and had asked Dieter to watch over him on his behalf, something he was very happy to do. Douglas didn't want the slur of a jailbird father to blemish his future prospects, that's why he had cut all communication with him. He told Jan that his father, in all likelihood, would be moved to an open prison soon. He knew for a fact that Greta still visited Douglas religiously every month and that he and his father were still regularly in touch with each other.

Douglas, in fact, was on the verge of a move to an open prison in readiness for an early release from prison, he just had to keep his nose clean for the next year or two.

After the first shock of imprisonment, Douglas soon got his act together. He was a resilient character and he soon realized that the way to stay out of trouble with these hardened characters was to make himself indispensable to them. The majority of prisoners were uneducated, unable to read or write. Douglas undertook to look after their correspondence for them. He wrote love letters to wives and sweethearts and letters to lawyers about appeals and unjust treatment whilst in jail. He oversaw the distribution of magazines of dubious quality, much prized by men deprived of female company for months, even years on end. Cigarettes in jail were currency, as they had been in Berlin. His experience of the black market in Berlin stood him in good stead and he set up a gambling school. He understood that men deprived of their liberty would bet on anything, a fly crawling up a window, a spider making it across the cell floor, anything-anything at all. Of course gambling was strictly forbidden. Some of the warders were aware of Douglas's activities, but they turned a blind eye if it meant less trouble on their wing. Douglas had the knack of keeping these various schemes under control. Aggrieved punters were soon steered to another exciting prospect and Douglas made sure he kept everyone relatively content. The last thing anyone needed in here was enemies. Douglas even managed to smuggle out birthday and Christmas cards for Katya. He explained that as he now lived in England, it wasn't possible to visit her. He had promised Dieter he would keep in touch with her and he wasn't going to let the inconvenience of a prison sentence stop him from carrying out his promise. Dieter for his part, kept Douglas informed of Jan's progress in the Merchant Marine. Douglas was convinced he was doing the right thing in severing all contact with his son. He knew how the minds of the hierarchy worked, one sniff of scandal and Jan's career might go out of the window.

All too soon Jan's home leave came to an end. He had been to stay with Jonathan and his parents for a few days and they were travelling to Hong Kong together. They knew they would be split up when they arrived there. Jan was due to join the 'Kwantung' and Jonathan was to join the 'Kweichow'. They were now the senior cadets.

The two ships were on different routes, but occasionally they were in port together so they were able to see each other and swap experiences. In any event they kept up a lively correspondence with each other via the company's head office. Jan was amused, but sympathetic, to find that both the new cadets joining the 'Kwantung' suffered from sea sickness. He remembered vividly the discomfort he had felt on his first few days at sea. The Captain on the 'Kwantung' was a different breed to his previous Captain on the 'Kweilin'. He was younger and much more involved with his officers, the training of the cadets and the running of the ship. However, this didn't suit everyone, the Chief Officer thought he was an interfering so and so and a pain in the neck. The bosun was a huge man originating from the North of China, his name was Wong Kwai, but everyone called him George. His family had made it to Hong Kong years ago and now had a flourishing business in the fish market. He had taken a shine to Jan and he went out of his way to look after him. Jan learned a great deal from him and even experimented in talking to him in Chinese.

The next two years of Jan and Jonathan's cadetship flew by. They had long since decided to take their Second Mates ticket at the School of Navigation, Southampton, and after a little time with their families, that is where they met up again. Their friendship was undiminished. They shared accommodation and helped each other in their studies. Out of a class of twenty four, eighteen passed the exam. Jan and Jonathan were in the eighteen successful students. They decided not to return to China Navigation, other areas of the world and different experiences beckoned. They both applied to a large British registered shipping company.

Douglas, in the meantime, had indeed been transferred to an open prison. He found most of the prisoners in there had been convicted of white collar crime. There were accountants, bank managers, insurance agents all found guilty of frauds of various kinds, but naturally, all wrongly convicted. There were forgers, perjurers and the odd murderer who had committed family oriented crimes and were not deemed to be a threat to the general public. They were considered to be rehabilitated, reformed characters and were shortly due for release. Some inmates were allowed days out to familiarize themselves with society, usually they had a minder but if they were due for imminent release they were allowed out unescorted. Douglas struck up a friendship with one or two of his fellow inmates, all rogues of various degrees, but like minded villains nonetheless.

Greta found that visiting Douglas at the open prison a little less stressful. The families in the waiting room of these prisoners were, to put it bluntly, of a different social order and she didn't feel quite so intimidated. The day of Douglas's release was approaching fast and visiting was relaxed as a consequence. Greta received a new pass showing the revised dates when visiting was allowed. On the spur of the moment she decided to go on a day that wasn't usual for her. It was Douglas's birthday in a few days time and it was the nearest date to it that she could manage, she thought it would be a nice surprise for him.

She arrived in plenty of time and went through the usual security checks which were much more relaxed here. She sat down in the waiting room at the back and looked around her. There was an elderly couple seated a few rows in front of her, probably an inmates parents. A young woman in her early twenties, someone's daughter perhaps, and a sprinkling of middle aged ladies like herself. One woman who was sitting near the guard on the door was exchanging what appeared to be friendly banter with him. She was obviously a regular but Greta didn't remember seeing her before, but then she tended to keep herself to herself. These places weren't social clubs! Douglas would be informed that he had a visitor and then she would be called. She settled down to wait.

A warder came in and called for the visitors for prisoner Johnson. The elderly couple got up and went through to the visiting room. It was much more informal than the closed prison. The inmate sat opposite the visitor, a table between them but no other obstruction, and the warder on duty was much more discreet. Greta didn't feel anymore that everything she said was being listened to. The warder came back and asked for the visitor for prisoner Coulter to come forward. Greta bent down to pick up her handbag she had placed on the floor near her feet, but before she could retrieve it, the woman she had seen chatting to the guard near the entrance to the visitors' room got up, showed her pass to the warder and was escorted through. Greta went white! She hadn't taken too much notice of this woman, a woman of about her own age. She had assumed she was another prisoner's wife. Greta was stunned. She sat down again with a bump. She looked at her pass, Mrs Greta Coulter. Greta's mind was in a whirl, she knew of course that Douglas had had a girlfriend in London, but that was years ago. She never thought in all her wildest dreams that the affair would have survived his imprisonment. But evidently it had! Greta was in a total state of shock, she just sat there.

After about forty minutes, the woman came out. She smiled at the guard. Greta heard what he said to her, 'It won't be long now I hear, Douglas is full of the plans you have for him when he's released. You must be getting quite excited?'

'Yes,' the woman replied, 'we're planning a big celebration on

145

the day he comes out, than we might take a long holiday to the Caribbean. It will be like a second honeymoon. He's been in there long enough without any treats.' and she laughed. Greta couldn't believe her ears; she was rooted to her seat. As the woman walked past her, Greta got a good look at her. She was well dressed; her brown curly hair was expertly cut and styled. She had a pretty face, which was heavily made up. She glanced briefly in Greta's direction, then away. But she hesitated and quickly looked at her again. After a few minutes, Greta got up and followed her out, but there was no sign of her. Greta got into her little car, still undecided as to what to do when an open topped white sports car came around the corner. The woman was wearing a head scarf, but there was no doubt in Greta's mind, this was the same woman who had just visited her husband! For some reason, Greta noted the number plate, it was DC 11.

Greta drove slowly home and let herself into the house. How could he, she thought, how could he do this to her after all he had put her through. Shock gave way to a rising anger. Just then the telephone rang. It was Jan informing her he had just received the results of his examinations and he had passed. He was now the proud owner of a fully fledged Second Mate's ticket. He told her he and Jonathan were going out on the town that night to celebrate, it was a double celebration because he had also passed his driving test a few days earlier. He told her he would be home some time tomorrow. He wanted to know if she would be home. She told him, yes, she would be home all day, she sounded a little strained. Jan put the phone down; he had expected a little more animation from his mother at his news. He shrugged and turned his attention to the night's revelries.

Jan drove into the drive and parked his old banger behind his mother's car. The door opened before he had the chance to knock. Jan's ebullient mood was strangled as soon as he saw his mother's face. Her eyes were red and her cheeks puffy. He quickly went into the house, 'What on earth's the matter mother?' he asked her earnestly. She gave him one look and burst into floods of tears. Jan was really alarmed. His first thought was that someone must have had an accident or worse. It was unlikely to be his father; he was in one of the safest places in the country. His next thought was the von Rheinhart family, an accident with the horses perhaps? But when he asked about them she shook her head. 'Is it dad?' she nodded her head to a renewed bout of wailing. 'Is he alright? What's happened to him?'

Greta blew her nose into the handkerchief she was holding, 'Yes,' she shouted at him, 'Yes, he's alright, he's always alright.' And she collapsed onto a kitchen chair. When Jan had managed to calm her down, the whole sorry story came tumbling out. Jan remembered the woman in his father's car all those years ago. The description Greta gave Jan sounded like an older version of the same woman. 'You know he's due to be released soon don't you?' Jan nodded, 'Well, he needn't think he's coming home here. This is my house and I can do without all this upset and your father's constant lies. I've managed very well without him all this time.' She was clenching and unclenching her hands. 'How dare he humiliate me like this? I've never missed a visit to that horrible place, and all the time-----.' Her voice faltered and petered out. Jan was at a loss as to how to comfort his mother. 'She actually drove past me in an open top sports car, the number plate was DC11.' The anguish she felt was plain to see on her face. He thought it best to say as little as possible and let his mother's anger burn itself out. 'I want all his things out of here Jan, will you see to that for me? I'm going to play bridge tomorrow, will you do it then when I'm out of the house. I can't bear the thought of having his things here a moment longer.'

Jan was furious with his father, he had long since realized his father had had his peccadillos, but Greta was Douglas's wife and his mother! She deserved better than this. The awkward silence was interrupted by the shrill ringing of the telephone. Jan answered it, it was for him anyway.

Dieter's voice rang in his ears, 'Ah, your home, I rang your place in Southampton early this morning, they said you had left at the crack of dawn. Congratulations on passing your exams. I expect you're looking forward to some time off now to relax and enjoy yourself?'

'Thanks Dieter, I was---look Dieter, it's not such a good time right now. Can I ring you back?'

'What's the problem Jan?'

'Mother's a bit upset, Dieter, I can't really talk right now.' Jan turned round to find that his mother had already left the room.

'What's happened Jan? Your father was expecting your mother to visit him this week. She didn't turn up and there was no message from her. Is she alright? Not ill or anything? He's quite worried.'

Jan couldn't hold his anger in any longer, 'Is he? The old fraud, is he really!'

There was a silence at the other end of the line, eventually Dieter repeated softly, 'What happened Jan?'

'Mother took it into her head to surprise him. It was his birthday. But it was mother who got the surprise.'

Again there was an ominous silence at the other end of the line, 'I take it Douglas had another visitor?'

147

Jan drew in his breath, his anger mounted and he shouted down the phone accusingly, 'You knew Dieter, you knew all about it all the time.'

'Perhaps this isn't the right time to talk about it Jan, how about you and your mother coming over here for a few days. A change of scene may be just what Greta needs.'

By now Jan was furious, 'I don't think so Dieter, what mother needs is a change of husband.'

'Jan, we care about Greta and about you.'

'If you cared about her so much, why didn't you warn her Dieter? Why didn't you say something?'

Another pause, 'Sometimes it's hard to know what to say, sometimes it's best to say nothing.'

'How could you let her walk into something like that? I know dad's no saint, but you Dieter.'

'I'm no saint either Jan! Goodness! Who is?'

'Dieter, I don't mean to be rude but I don't see the point of this conversation.' And Jan put the phone down.

His mother walked back into the room. Jan was relieved that the tears had stopped and she looked more composed. 'Was that Dieter?' she asked.

'Yes.'

'What did he want?'

'He was ringing to congratulate me on passing my exams.'

Greta patted his arm, 'Is that all he wanted?'

'No, he knew you hadn't been to visit dad. He wanted to know if you were alright.'

'What did you tell him?'

Jan put his arms around his mother, 'I told him we were both fine mother.'

Greta smiled up at her son, he might favour her with his colouring, the white hair and the blue eyes so like hers, but he had inherited Douglas's quick mind and some of his fiery temper too. 'Is that all he wanted?'

Jan debated what to say, in the end he said, 'No, he wondered if you would like to go and stay with them for a day or two.'

To Jan's amazement his mother replied, 'That was nice of him, I'll give it some serious thought.'

Next morning Greta was up bright and early. She was busy in the kitchen when Jan appeared. He was relieved to see that all signs of yesterday's weeping had disappeared. She smiled at him, 'Would you like a full English breakfast?'

'Well, yes, but it seems a lot of trouble to go to, I'm fine with toast.'

'It's no trouble,' she turned to the stove, 'help yourself to coffee, it's freshly made.'

Jan poured himself a mug of steaming coffee; his mother had never lost the knack of making really good coffee. 'Do you want one as well?'

'Yes please,' she turned round to face him, 'you know Jan, I think I will go to Bremen for a few days, I haven't seen Christa for quite a while. It will be nice to catch up with things. Will you come with me?'

Jan choked on his coffee but covered up his surprise by complaining that it was a little hot. 'I don't think so mother, I've got things to do here. I've got to find myself a job for one thing. I've decided not to go back to China Shipping.'

'Oh, but you'll have time to do the little job I asked you about last night won't you?'

Jan looked at his mother searchingly, 'You haven't changed your mind then?'

'No, Jan, I haven't.' She sat down at the table opposite him, 'Don't worry about me Jan. Strangely enough I feel quite liberated this morning. It's the first day of the rest of my life.' She paused, 'It's almost as though I've been pulled out of the canal again. I don't feel that I owe your father anything anymore.' She gave a little smile, 'I feel free of him.'

Jan drove his mother to the airport, and then he returned to the little house in Wimbledon. He wasn't relishing the task ahead of him but decided the only way was to meet it head on. He collected a number of empty suitcases and went into the spare bedroom. He started on the wardrobes first, there were a number of Savill Row suits. They were classically cut, the material a little dated now, but had obviously been expensive. He checked out the pockets, they were empty. Next he emptied the chest of drawers; there were neat piles of socks, underwear and silk shirts. He conceded his father had good taste. It didn't take too long to clear that room, Jan found nothing incriminating in there. He made his way to what had been his parent's bedroom. His mother had told him about the secret compartment hidden behind her wardrobe and how to locate the spring which would activate the wooden panel at the back. He moved her clothes to one side and felt around for the knot of wood, then without warning the panel slid open. It made Jan jump. He peered into the dark interior and was met by a slight odour of mothballs. His eyes quickly adjusted to the dim light and he could discern a rail holding a number of uniforms. Jan pulled them out one by one. He was flabbergasted. There was at least one for every service showing the insignia of different ranks. There was even a police uniform! Jan knew what charges had been laid against his father, but the sheer boldness of his scams shocked him. His mother knew all about this and had said nothing. How complicit had she been he wondered. Dieter must have known about all this as well although he had never been implicated in his father's crimes. Jan knew the story of how they had met and they had been close friends ever since. Perhaps Dieter wasn't the shining knight he had thought him to be all these years. Jan knew Dieter was still in touch with his father, what secrets did they share he wondered?

Right at the back of the hidden compartment Jan spotted a briefcase. He pulled it out and tried to open it but it was locked. Jan sat back for a moment wondering if he should force the lock, then he decided to go through all the pockets of the uniforms. In the inside pocket of each uniform was a passport. Each identity coincided with the rank of the uniform. Jan put them into a pile on his mother's dressing table.

He checked the other pockets. Once or twice he pulled out notes written in his father's handwriting, times of trains, meeting places, details of flights etc. but in an air force uniform he pulled out a large envelope. Inside were some old photographs. Some were of little girl with red hair playing in a garden. On the back in his father's hand was inscribed Katya's 5th birthday, Katya's 6th birthday, Katya Christmas 1963 and so on. Others showed the same little girl with a woman who was obviously her mother, the same features, the same red hair and the same green coloured eyes. Jan turned one over; the inscription was Katya and Irena 1961. There was even one with his father, they were at a picnic, the little girl was sitting on Douglas's knee holding a doll with her mother in the background. Jan wondered who could have taken that photograph and who were these people? Irena and Katya, what were they to his father? He had never heard his mother talk about anyone of that name. In the police uniform, Jan came across a set of small keys, he thought they might be the ones for the brief case. He tried them and the lock gave a satisfying click. Jan looked inside but found nothing. Jan picked up the passports and the photographs and went down stairs to the kitchen. He made himself some lunch. He picked up the first passport; the rank was an Army Colonel in the name of Mason. Of course Jan didn't understand the irony behind the choice of name. His father's photograph stared out at him. The passport was now out of date. Jan flipped through the pages and turned it this way and that. It looked absolutely genuine. In fact it was, as were all the others. Douglas had bribed someone in the passport office in Berlin to supply him with genuine passports. The forger had done a good job with the rest of the information. Jan checked all the other passports, not all had yet lapsed. Then he turned his attention to the photographs. There was no indication as to where they had been taken, but the developer's mark on the photograph in which his father appeared was in Bremen. They were old photographs. He noticed that after the girl's fourth birthday, there were no more photographs of the woman he assumed must be her mother. After that date the photographs were only of the little girl Katya, usually by herself. They ended the year his father was arrested. Jan pondered the situation. His father had spent a lot of time in Bremen. Knowing his father's history Jan wondered if the girl in question was related to him. Jan decided to keep this information from his mother, she had suffered enough humiliation lately, revealing this to her wouldn't help and anyway, she had vowed to cut all ties to Douglas.

Jan scooped all the passports and photographs up and stuffed them into the briefcase and put it back into the hidden compartment right at the back way out of sight. He had to crawl into the space to hide it; he couldn't envisage his mother on her hands and knees searching the place. He fleetingly wondered if he should nail it up. Tomorrow he would take the packed suitcases to the open prison. The authorities could do what they wanted with his father's possessions. They wouldn't find out anything that they didn't already know.

Next morning he arrived early at the jail with the suitcases in tow. He presented himself to the reception area and showed his identification to the officer on duty. He was told it wasn't official visiting time but as Douglas was due for imminent release he would be allowed to see him. But to the Officer's surprise Jan told him he had only brought his father's belongings and he didn't care if he never saw the old bastard again. Jan turned on his heel and walked smartly away with the astonished prison guard gawping after him.

CHAPTER 16

Christa met Greta at the airport, she hugged her tightly. She told Greta that Dieter had told her a little of what had happened, he was busy coaching that afternoon but would join them later for dinner. Christian was away competing at a dressage event and wouldn't be back for a few days. They could have some quiet time together without any distractions. Greta was glad that only Christa and Dieter were at home, she didn't want to have to go over the story again and again. Strangely she felt quite at peace with her decision. She walked in the gardens with Christa and took some of the dogs out on her own or with Dieter. She was able to open up more with Dieter than Christa. She knew Dieter had been privy to Douglas's philandering for years, she even wondered if he had been party to it as well, it wouldn't have surprised her. As if reading her thoughts Dieter told her of the arrangements he had made for Douglas's apartment in Amsterdam. Douglas would have vacant possession of it at the end of the month.

Greta smiled, 'He won't be living in it with me Dieter, not any more.'

Dieter detected a tear in the corner of her eye. He slipped his arm around her shoulders. Dieter had always had a soft spot for Greta; she was an attractive woman with a placid temperament. 'We can't always be with the person we would like to live with Greta.'

Greta looked up into his face; he had a far away look in his eyes, he glanced down at her and gripped her shoulder. Greta had the distinct impression that the person Dieter would like to be with wasn't Christa. The few days came to an end and Dieter told Greta he would be travelling back to London with her as he had business there. Greta asked, 'It wouldn't be Douglas Coulter business would it? He's due for release in a few days.'

'I won't lie to you Greta, yes it is. Douglas saw me through some of the blackest days of my life and I won't abandon him now. I hope you understand Greta?'

'No, but it's O.K.'

They parted at the airport. Jan was there to meet his mother. He gave Dieter a curt nod. Dieter was disappointed but he couldn't blame the boy, in his shoes he might well have reacted in the same way. Dieter took a taxi to his hotel, he had an appointment to keep tomorrow and he felt strangely elated at the prospect.

Next morning Dieter hired a car and drove to a quiet pub near the open prison. He settled himself into an out of the way corner and ordered two coffees and two cognacs. He sipped his coffee and was

152

soon aware of a shadow looming over his shoulder. He looked up, and leapt to his feet. He laughed out loud and gave the leaner, fitter Douglas Coulter a bear hug, then held him at arms length, clapped him on the shoulder a couple of times then gave him another bear hug. 'My, it's good to see you Douglas. I have to admit I've missed you, yes,' he smiled, 'I've definitely missed you.'

To the onlookers, who were used to seeing the inmates of the local hostelry as the open prison was known, the sight of a well dressed foreigner and a no doubt soon to be released prisoner didn't excite too much attention. The two of them subsided into their corner, heads close together. They stayed this way for hours, reminiscing and talking about future plans. Dieter brought Douglas up to date with the events relating to 'The Lady Anne'. The restaurateur had long since moved out and she looked neglected and was now a seedy clip joint run by Henke's son. They still had their names on the title deeds but there wouldn't be much capital to come from that quarter, if any. Dieter told Douglas he still heard from Leonard occasionally, he appeared to be living a quiet life in Tel Aviv. He had even asked Dieter to pass on his regards to Douglas.

Douglas whistled at this piece of information. 'Is the old codger in his right mind?' he asked laughing.

Dieter became serious, 'Have you any plans Douglas? You know I will help in any way I can, money, a place to stay, anything, anything legal that is.'

'Am I welcome in Bremen?'

'Yes!'

'Will it cause trouble?'

'Yes!'

Douglas laughed and Dieter laughed with him.

'How's Greta?'

'She's fine, we came back together.'

'I told Greta I would never leave her you know.'

'I'm afraid the boots on the other foot now, my friend. She's adamant she won't have you back.'

'What about Jan?'

Dieter brought him up to date holding nothing back. Douglas sighed.

'He's young Douglas, he'll get over it.'

'No, he won't Dieter.' He looked down at his hands, then glanced up at Dieter, he had a mischievous look on his face, 'Don't you worry about my future, I have plans, meet the new me, The Honourable Bruno St Aubyn Charlesworth, it has quite a ring to it don't you think?

I did toy with the idea of Tarquin for a first name, but decided that was a little over the top.'

'That's quite a mouthful Douglas, who dreamt that up?'

'It's quite genuine I assure you, you can look me up in Debretts. I've met my future partner in crime over there and he's due for release shortly after me. Just promise me you won't buy any works of art without informing me first.' Douglas and Dieter went into a huddle and Douglas told him all about his future plans.

'Your incorrigible Douglas, you're bound to get caught eventually.'

'Probably, but it'll be fun don't you think?'

Dieter was serious for a moment, 'I can't get involved Douglas, I've got Christian to think of now. I've been clean for quite a while and I can't afford a scandal. The boy is doing well.'

'I know Dieter. Anyway, you must allow me to have one righteous friend. In any case, you'd blow the gaff!'

'I would not!' replied Dieter indignantly and they both laughed out loud.

Dieter booked into a local hotel. He met Douglas and Rodney March, Douglas's partner in his new venture, for the next two days. The third day was release day. Dieter had brought Douglas a couple of suits and shirts; he knew the emphasis Douglas put on looking smart. The uniforms had been confiscated by the authorities, but Douglas still had quite a lot of luggage when he at last appeared outside the gates. There were two cars waiting outside for him, Dieter was in one and the other was an open topped sports car, the number plate was DC11. Douglas lugged his cases to the sports car. The driver, a good looking woman with brown curly hair got out and embraced Douglas. They walked arm in arm over to Dieter's car. 'Dieter, I want you to meet Samantha. Samantha this is my best friend in the whole world.'

Dieter the perfect gentleman got out and shook hands. So this was the woman who had captivated Douglas's heart, or nearly.

'Sam's driving back to London, there's a lot to do.' Douglas winked at her and patted her bottom as she took her leave of them. 'Now, you and I are stuck here for a couple of days until Rodney is released, and we are going to enjoy ourselves. Let's set this little place alight and spend some money, I haven't got any so it will have to be yours. We desperately need to find some female companions.'

Dieter protested, 'I don't know about that Douglas, I'm out of practice.'

Douglas put his hand on Dieter's shoulder; he had a very serious expression on his face. He replied soberly, 'So am I my friend.'

The gates opened at exactly ten a.m. and Rodney Marsh walked out into the sunshine. He had one suitcase and a large artist's portfolio under his arm. He smiled and headed towards the waiting car which, with its occupants, sped off in the direction of London. The destination was one of the swankiest hotels in the city. Dieter had booked three rooms, one for Douglas and Samantha, one for Rodney and one for himself. That night they had a real hooley.

Next morning Dieter opened one eye, it was all he could manage, a thousand little hammers were drumming on the other one. He was aware of someone moving around the room. With difficulty, he lifted himself on one elbow. Douglas had brought him a cup of coffee and something else that looked disgusting in a glass. 'Get this down you, you'll feel better.'

Dieter grunted, 'It smells foul.'

'Don't be a baby, pinch your nose and get it down in one.'

'Have you had one?'

'No, I don't need one. I've not exactly been on the wagon for the last few years. The hooch in there prepares you for anything.'

'Well, I wish I had been,' replied Dieter with feeling. He felt as though he had lived a couple of years in just a couple of days.

Douglas laughed, 'I'll be back in a couple of hours. You've got a plane to catch. I'll drive you to the airport.' He left the room, slamming the door behind him.

The other passengers swarmed around the two men locked in an embrace.

'Take care Douglas!'

'You know where to come if you need some excitement.'

'And you know where to come if you're in need of any rest and recuperation.'

They patted each other on the back and the smartly dressed man with the short wiry almost white hair walked quickly away.

Dieter sipped a fruit juice that the air hostess had brought him. He realized just how much he had missed Douglas. He knew he would never regret knowing Douglas Coulter; such was the magnetism of the man. Those nearby looked across at the blond man who had a broad grin on his face, he appeared to be enjoying a private joke.

CHAPTER 17

Katya was scurrying to her next lesson with the professor. Her violin case was tucked under her arm, she was so lucky to have got hold of this instrument. The professor had come across it just at the right time and at just the right price. There was a steady drizzle falling and the cobbles under her feet were quite slippy, she hurried on, the professor hated his students to be late. Katya had almost completed her first two years at the academy. She was fortunate to have secured a place here, her uncle must have more clout than she supposed for a suburban school master. Her thoughts turned to her two cousins. They hadn't been as lucky as she had. Their further education had gone down the more conventional route, junior school, high school with the ultimate goal of a university education. She smiled at the thought of Stefan; he had always wanted to be an engine driver. Hannah wanted to design clothes and she probably would too, she was good at it. The lesson progressed well, with just a little tut tutting and foot tapping. She had only had to repeat two sections again after the promise that she would put in plenty of practise before she returned for her next lesson.

Back in her room Katya slumped down on her bed. She was thinking about the winter break her family had planned. They were all going skiing for a few days and Katya was particularly looking forward to it. She turned over on her side; the photograph of her mother looked back at her. She had two photos on the bedside table. This one of her mother on her own which she now picked up and another one of her and her mother at a picnic with the man she knew as Uncle Dougy Doug. She had a doll in her arms, Lucy, she turned to look at Lucy who was sitting over on the chair. She was a little worse for wear these days. Katya smiled, Lucy went everywhere with her. Katya couldn't really remember her mother, only from the photograph. But she must have done well for herself though because she had left Katya a house in Bremen and there was a modest trust fund that paid for her education. She knew her mother had at one time worked for Uncle Dougy Doug, who used to come and see her on her birthday and around Christmas time. He always turned up with a present for her and each of her cousins. However the visits stopped suddenly and all she received now were birthday and Christmas cards, but there was no return address. Katya often reflected on who her father might be. Her Aunt Nina had only told her he had been an Officer in one of the occupying armies. She couldn't even confirm what nationality he was. She supposed he must be dead like her mother, unless it was Uncle Dougy Doug, but her Aunt always denied it, she was adamant he was not the one. She was awakened from her reverie by a knock at her door.

A female voice called out, 'Phone for you Katya, I think it's your aunt.'

Katya scuttled down the stairs, the phone was hanging by the wire. Breathlessly she said. 'Hello Aunt Nina, is everything alright?'

'Yes, yes, I just wanted to be sure you have everything ready.'

'I've got just about everything on the list, I just need some gloves.'

'You'll be able to get a pair in Chamonix when we hire the skis. We'll pick you up mid morning on Saturday. We'll be making an early start so be ready - you know your uncle doesn't like to be kept waiting.'

The trip to the resort was slow and uncomfortable, five adults and all their baggage was crammed into the car. The roads were icy, there had been a fresh fall of snow overnight and the snow ploughs had been out early. The four wheel drive climbed effortlessly up the winding road, hampered only by the press of traffic making its way into and out of the resort. The chalet they had hired was just a little way out of the town. It had a lovely view of the slopes. Uncle Peter backed the car as near to the entrance as he could. They all got out and formed a chain to stow the gear into the chalet. This was a self catering holiday so there was a lot of food to unpack. Stefan got the stove going and pretty soon the place began to take on a warm cosy glow. Katya and Hannah were sharing a bedroom as were Uncle Peter and Aunt Nina. Lucky old Stefan had a bedroom to himself. Aunt Nina had had the foresight to precook their first evening's meal. Katya and Hannah laid the table and pretty soon there was a lovely aroma of one of Aunt Nina's casseroles emanating from the cooker. It was early to bed for them on the first night, everyone was tired from the journey. But early next morning, they were up bright and early at the hire shop, being fitted out for skis and anything else they had forgotten. Then they joined the queue for the ski lift which scooped them up to the start of the run. They all took it steady at first except Stefan who hurled himself headlong down the slope. He was waiting for them at the bottom. 'What kept you?' he wanted to know.

Katya and Hannah both had the same thought at the same moment and Stefan was bombarded with snowballs for his trouble. The first day was bright and sunny, but bitterly cold in the shade. They soon found their feet. Stefan and Uncle Peter were soon on a par with each other. Hannah was next quickest, followed by Katya and Aunt Nina. After an exhilarating first day, they made their way back to the chalet. They were all starving! After the evening meal, Aunt Nina and Uncle Peter settled down in front of the stove to watch television. The three younger members of the family were looking for excitement in the village, the delights of apres ski was calling. The revelry went on quite late into the night, but another day's skiing was on the agenda, so the trio reluctantly made their way homewards. The chalet was in darkness but still warm from the stove's glow. Stefan made them some hot chocolate while the girls discussed the merits of this male over another. Stefan declared he didn't fancy either of them. Chuckling they made their way to their respective beds.

The next few days were spent on the slopes during the day and, for the three younger members of the family, dancing, singing, eating and drinking in the evenings. The girls' skiing improved quite considerably over the next few days and Stefan had his work cut to maintain his superiority over them. On the last day the weather had deteriorated somewhat, it was a bit murky with the odd snowflake whirling around in the freshening wind. But the girls were determined to put Stefan in his place, he had been crowing all week about his prowess on the slopes. They lined up at the top of the run and Nina counted them away. Katya made a flying start and was in the lead closely followed by the two siblings. Nina watched as they sped down the mountain side. Katya's colourful hat was still in the lead, her red hair streaming out behind her. She had on a sky blue ski suit which suited her colouring and enhanced her figure. Hannah had chosen it for her. Hannah was wearing a bright red suit which accentuated her dark brown locks. Stefan had on a tight fitting white suit with colourful go faster stripes down the side and across the chest. It was wonderful to see all three getting on so well together, we ought to try and get together as a family more often she thought. As so often when Katya was around, Nina's thoughts turned to her sister Irena, Katya looked so much like her. Nina sighed and she turned away.

Katya was flying down the slope, but she could hear Stefan close behind her, he was whooping with exhilaration. She turned her head to see how close he was which meant she failed to see the slight uneveness in the piste ahead of her, she was unprepared for it and it threw her off balance. She immediately tried to correct but overcompensated. She wobbled for a second but there was no way back and she went down with a wallop, both arms thrown out in front of her in an effort to save herself. She slithered downhill in a shower of snow thrown up by her momentum. Stefan, who had been close behind, managed to stop himself within yards of her and was soon by her side. He crouched down next to her, his face showing concern. 'That was spectacular Katya, are you O.K?'

Katya wasn't sure, it had been such a shock to find herself on the ground, the fall had been so unexpected. She smiled up at Stefan, 'I think so.' And she tried to raise herself up. That's when she felt the searing pain in her right wrist and hand. She let out a groan and fell back.

'Don't move Katya,' advised Stefan, 'there's obviously something wrong. Let me check you out, where do you feel the pain?'

She winced again, 'My right hand and wrist.' she managed through clenched teeth.

'Can you move your fingers?' She tried and cried out in pain. By now Hannah and Uncle Peter were there. 'Stay with her,' yelled Stefan, 'I'll go and get help, the first aid post is just over there. Don't let her move and don't try to take her glove off.' And he sped away.

The first aid team were quickly on the spot. They expertly checked her over and declared her to be walking wounded, much to the relief of all concerned. They put the injured arm in a sling and secured it to avoid any further movement that might cause more damage and she was taken to the first aid post for further attention. They cut away the glove and quickly diagnosed a broken wrist and possibly a broken thumb. They administered a painkiller as the hand was badly swollen and throbbing viciously and then arranged for her to be transported to the local hospital. The accident and emergency department was specifically designed for the treatment of broken limbs, the most common injury sustained on the slopes. She was quickly taken through to the Xray department where they confirmed the diagnosis of a broken wrist and unfortunately also a broken thumb joint. She was plastered up in no time, given painkillers, copies of the Xrays, a letter for her own doctor and advised to go and see him or her as soon as possible. This really put a damper on the holiday. They went straight back to the chalet, packed everything up and drove back to The Hague with the patient wedged into a corner of the back seat.

Katya had been at home now for six weeks. The plaster caste had been changed once but was due to be removed on her next visit to the hospital. She was able to wiggle her fingers but the thumb was still immobilized. Katya had discovered doing anything without your thumb was next to impossible. When the caste came off, the doctor manipulated the thumb which caused Katya a certain amount of discomfort. He suggested she tried a course of physiotherapy - that should do the trick he told her. After two weeks Katya still had only limited movement in her thumb. True, she could do most things, but she was unable to hold the bow of her violin for any length of time. This could be catastrophic for her future ambitions to be a professional musician. She went back to see the doctor, he checked out the movement of the joint and ordered another Xray. When he turned around from studying the film, Katya could read the bad news in his face. 'You will get further movement,' he explained, 'but probably not much more and later in life there's the distinct possibility that arthritis may set in.' Katya was devastated. He asked her what her profession was. When she told him of her dreams for the future he was extremely sympathetic. 'The only alternative would be to break the joint again and try resetting it, but I really don't advise that course of action, it could make matters much worse. Of course you're entitled to a second opinion.' Unfortunately the second opinion re-enforced the first. Katya was forced to re-evaluate her plans for the future, but first she had to come to terms with her disappointment.

CHAPTER 18

For the next four years of their lives, both Jan and Jonathan sailed on passenger/mail ships with the Union Castle line. They secured positions as Junior Third Officers. As this was a mail run, the ships ran a regular service leaving Southampton every Thursday. The trip to Cape Town took eleven and a half days. The ships were named after English, Scottish and Welsh castles, plus a smattering of South African names. Their first ship was the Cape Town Castle.

Life onboard a passenger ship was a completely different experience to life with the China Navigation Line. The Deck officers' uniforms had to be spotless at all times. It was more relaxed for the Engine Room Officers, they were in boiler suits during their watch periods and weren't allowed on the passenger decks, but off duty the same standard of dress applied to them as well. Part of the duties of all Officers was to keep the passengers entertained, the more scrambled egg displayed on the shoulder, the more that Officer was in demand. Only the Senior Officers headed a dining table in the Saloon, the others ate at the staff table. After dinner, dancing partners were much in demand, this was the time to try and cry off. Study periods were the most common excuse used, but it was frowned upon if used too frequently. Of course, not all the passengers were middle aged ladies looking for a ship board romance, there were some younger female passengers looking for the same thing. Instead of the dance floor, there were deck sports to be enjoyed and the much smaller and more intimate atmosphere of the newly opened discotheque where most of the junior Officers gathered in their off duty hours. Jan and Jonathan had a great and carefree time, especially Jan who was blond, tall and good looking, but there were plenty of opportunities for all. They occasionally changed ships and Jan was promoted to Third Officer. This meant he headed a table in the Dining Saloon, a rather disconcerting experience for a young man, but he soon acquired the necessary skills of inoffensive small talk which kept his table happy.

After completing the requisite amount of sea time, Jan and Jonathan met up again in Southampton to sit for their First Mates ticket. Jan passed his exam first time around but Jonathan failed on signals and had to do a retake. Both were able to fleetingly catch up with their families before being recalled to their next ship. To Jan's relief, his mother was coping just fine. She had joined a few local societies with her widowed neighbour and still spent part of the summer in Bremen with the von Rheinharts. She told him they hoped he could make the trip with her sometime soon. Jan however cried off, he said he had little enough time at home anyway, certainly not enough time to go swanning off to Germany. 'Dieter tells me he hasn't heard from you for ages Jan.'

'You know what the post is like when you're at sea mother, some of Christian's letters have caught up with me and I replied to those, but Dieter's letters must be hanging around in an agent's office somewhere.' he added lamely. Greta knew there must be more to it than that but let the matter drop.

Jan was recalled to join the 'Edinburgh Castle' this time as Second Officer. Jonathan passed his retake, he got the 'Southampton Castle' there was a promotion for Jonathan as well to Third Officer. Both of them were on course to sit for their Master's Ticket after completing the relevant sea time. But by now there were rumblings of unease within the Merchant Navy, particularly within the Passenger Ship Companies. Some of the ships were sold, but for the moment both Jan and Jonathan had jobs and didn't take too much notice of the disquiet going on around them. The time soon arrived for them to sit for the ultimate goal. An intense period of study lay ahead of them and they buckled down to the task. This time Jonathan made no mistake. Out of twenty four who sat the exam, fourteen passed. Jan and Jonathan were among them. But unfortunately their celebrations were tempered by the unexpected news that the Union Castle line had gone out of business. Yes, they were both Master Mariners but they were also both unemployed! Jan confided to Jonathan that he had had enough of passenger ships anyway; he preferred a cargo that didn't talk back!

They weren't out of work for long, they were lucky enough to secure berths with World Wide Shipping based in Hong Kong. That company operated a variety of ships from tankers to freighters and hadn't been affected in the downturn in the shipping industry in the same way that the British fleet had been. Jan was taken on as the Chief Officer and Jonathan as the Second, the Navigating Officer. Jonathan was in his element. The Chief Engineer was British and hailed from Tyne Side, it took a little time to get accustomed to his accent and to his dry sense of humour but he was very good at his job. He just lived for engines. The crew were Hong Kong Chinese. The bosun was due to leave at the next port; he had been on the ship for over a year without any home leave. His replacement was from the north and a very hard man. Jan was delighted when the new bosun presented himself, he knew him immediately; it was Wong Kwai, known throughout the fleet as George. The freighter was called the 'Hope' known affectionately by its crew as the 'Hopeless.' It was a happy ship and tramped around the

Far East and Europe. Then one day when the 'Hope' was in Antwerp, the Captain returned to the ship after being taken ashore for a meal by the Agents, soon afterwards, he was clutching his stomach and retired to his cabin. Next morning, he was much worse and Jan called the agents who immediately summoned a doctor. Acute appendicitis was diagnosed and the poor man was carted off to hospital. The Company decided it was too far to send a replacement and Jan was promoted to Captain on the spot. Jonathan became Chief Officer and each Officer moved up one slot, the senior cadet finding himself as acting junior Third. The 'Hope' sailed on without a hitch with a new Captain at the helm. Jan relished his new position and his crew bonded to him. Not one of them applied for a transfer, this was indeed a happy ship.

Dieter was sorting through his morning's post when he spotted an English stamp. The envelope was small, buff coloured and made of expensive paper. He opened it and withdrew a stiff buff coloured invitation card with bold gold lettering in italics; the whole card was framed in gold. It was an invitation to attend the opening of a new gallery in London. The address was a very prestigious one in Mayfair and the opening was in week's time. Dieter smiled at the name printed on the bottom of the card and tried to read the illegible signature. It looked nothing like The Hon. Bruno St. Aubyn Charlesworth. Dieter looked at his diary; it was full for almost the whole week. He walked through to his secretary's office and asked her to make the necessary reservations for him to fly to London and to cancel all his engagements from the fourth for the whole of the following week. Dieter was anticipating the state he might be in when he returned. He still vividly remembered the rueful condition he had arrived home in from his last visit and the tongue lashing he had had to endure from Christa. His son, on the other hand, had wanted to know where the party was and could he please go with him next time.

The taxi deposited Dieter a few yards away from the gallery. The driver had told him it was his third trip to that address already that day, all the top knobs and posh folk were there he told him. Dieter had his invitation ready to show the doorman who was dressed in a green livery. He was ushered through to be met by Samantha, he hardly recognized the sophisticated lady who took him by the arm. Someone had done a wonderful makeover on the lady, she was pretty before but now she was beautifully groomed and looked wonderful.

'I'm so pleased you could make it Dieter, Bruno told me to take you straight to him when you arrived.' Dieter had trouble keeping a straight face; then he heard Douglas's voice behind him. He turned and found himself in a bear hug. Douglas was wearing a fine white linen suit, set off by a colourful cravat and a matching floppy handkerchief in his top pocket. His hair was longer than usual with just a streak of grey at the temples. Instead of his trademark pencil moustache, he now sported a small van dyke type beard. He looked very distinguished indeed. Douglas took two flutes of champagne from a waitress who, very professionally, weaved her way amongst the assembled guests. He handed a flute to Dieter who took a sip, he nodded in approval and looked around him.

'This is very impressive,' he paused, 'Bruno.'

Douglas winked at him.

There weren't too many people in the gallery so as to impede movement. Each painting had been given plenty of wall space and the lighting on each was superb. There were groups of admirers around each one. Douglas guided Dieter around giving him chapter and verse on each exhibit and introducing him to a dizzying array of titled people. Samantha glided around the gallery chatting to this group, then that, and now and then, discreetly placing a tiny sticker against a painting.

Dieter was particularly drawn to small canvas of a horse. 'Is that a Stubbs?'

Douglas laughed, and whispered, 'Don't stand too close, the paint is still wet.' Dieter spluttered into his glass. He looked about him, 'I don't see Rodney anywhere.'

'No, this isn't his scene; he's strictly a backroom boy. I hope he can keep up with demand, they appear to be selling like hot cakes.' smiled Douglas.

'How does all this work?' asked Dieter in a low voice.

'I'll tell you this evening, but for now, just mingle and enjoy yourself.' and he murmured in Dieter's ear, 'don't let Sam sell you anything.' Douglas raised his hand to someone in a nearby group and ambled off in their direction.

That evening in the plush apartment over the gallery, Douglas told Dieter how he had set up the scam. He had met Rodney in the open prison. He had been caught selling forgeries in a market, strictly small time stuff. Rodney showed Douglas some of the work he had done in prison. Douglas was very impressed and realised that if the right materials were used there was money to be made, but first of all they needed a stake. Douglas and Samantha attended the well known auction houses and got to know the backroom staff. Douglas knew there would be petty fiddles going on, and of course, there were. But Douglas wasn't interested in the small time stuff; Douglas had his eye on the larger horizon. Rodney had completed a canvas in the style of a well known collectable artist. It was a masterpiece in its own right and as long as it wasn't attributed to the artist, it wasn't a crime to sell it. But with the right provenance, the sky was the limit. Douglas provided the right provenance and, hey presto, they had the capital to set up the gallery. The trick, explained Douglas, is not to swamp the market, but to excite the collector, also to exhibit some genuine less expensive artists at the same time. When a viewing is in progress, I have told Sam to very discreetly put a sold sticker onto a couple of canvases; this stimulates the punters who think they may get pipped at the post and Bob's Your Uncle! You're in business.

'Now - I hope you're ready for a night out on the town?' and Douglas winked at him.

'I'm as ready as I'll ever be.'

'Good, you're going to need plenty of stamina for the night out I've got planned for you.'

'That sounds ominous, isn't Samantha coming with us?'

'No, Sam wouldn't appreciate where we're going; it's strictly a boy's paradise.'

Dieter groaned, 'I haven't fully recovered from the last one yet.' He was puzzled, 'Doesn't Sam object, well to put it politely, to your nocturnal activities?'

'You know me Dieter, one is never enough! Sam knows better than to keep me on a leash, she knows she's indispensable so I'm allowed a certain amount of freedom.'

'What about marriage? Most women in my experience want to tie the knot.'

'I'm already married! You don't want me to commit bigamy do you to add to all my other sins. No, I'm married to Greta and mean to stay married to her. Greta is doing alright without me around but she feels more comfortable being married – even to a man like me. Come on! The taxi's here.'

A few weeks later Douglas decided to return the visit, he had been burning the candle at both ends and felt like a change of scene. He rang Dieter to confirm he would be around, and then he caught the afternoon flight to Bremen. Douglas was welcomed wholeheartedly by both Dieter and Christian, but Christa was aloof and kept her distance. She was perfectly polite but the next day she found she had an important engagement elsewhere which would keep her away from home for the duration of Douglas's visit. Life for Dieter and Christian revolved around the stables and Douglas was happy to join them there. They rode out every morning providing they weren't travelling to an event.

Douglas informed them that his riding was somewhat rusty, 'There weren't many horses around where I've been lately.' a smile just touching the corners of his mouth. He walked along the row of stables looking at each horse with a practiced eye. He made his way towards a grey that had its head over the stable door, its eyes rolling as he walked towards it. The ears went back and it tossed its head. Christian was just about to warn Douglas that Snowflake, the pet name for the horse, was unpredictable and mean when Douglas grabbed it by one ear and rubbed its nose vigorously with his free hand. He let go of its ear and patted the horse's neck. To Christian's amazement Snowflake lowered his head over Douglas's shoulder, snickered and nuzzled him.

Dieter was standing at Christian's side, he told his son, 'Douglas was always a better horseman than I was, he really missed his way, he just didn't really have the opportunity to pursue it,' he paused laughing, 'or thinking about it, perhaps in Douglas's case, there were just too many other distractions.' Christian realized Douglas was a natural where horses were concerned. Douglas fitted into the routine with absolutely no problem, he tried his hand at jumping in the arena riding Snowflake, he handled him superbly. Snowflake knew who was in charge and he obviously trusted Douglas. He watched Christian work out in the dressage ring, but declined to have a go himself. When time allowed he and Dieter went on strenuous cross country rides across the estate, he rode Snowflake. Dieter stressed he mustn't take chances with him, he was a valuable animal, but it was obvious Douglas took no notice and he and Snowflake really enjoyed themselves.

On the last night Douglas asked, 'What do you do for fun around here?' Dieter groaned, 'Just joking, I came for rest and recuperation.' and he patted Dieter on the shoulder.

When Douglas had returned to London, Christian said to his father, 'Now I understand why you're in such a state when you've been to see Douglas. How does he do it? He drinks like a fish and smokes like a chimney and yet he's up early every morning ready to work out.' Christian moved a little away from his father before he jokingly continued, 'With men like him in the British Army, it's no wonder you lost dad.'

Dieter moved menacingly towards his son, 'You cheeky young pup!' But Christian was out of the door in a flash. Dieter could hear him chuckling as he went towards the stables.

Katya had returned to the Music School, and had been to see the professor a couple of times. The lessons were very distressing for her, she just couldn't hold onto her bow for any length of time. She had had

166

to face up to the fact that her future as a professional violinist was out of the question. She had even tried other instruments with the same result. She could play the piano but her right hand was just not flexible enough for the standard she wished to achieve. Her dream had been to play in one of the well known orchestras in the concert halls of Europe. That dream was now in tatters.

It was her professor who came up with the suggestion that she went to the finishing school in Switzerland. He knew the Head, the appreciation of Opera was a priority there and she would also get a fully rounded education. Who knew what opportunities might open up for her; after lengthy discussions with her aunt and uncle, it was decided that she would attend the school for a couple of years. Languages were another area the school specialized in, her French was not bad, but her English, Italian and German needed a lot of work. She still had no idea what she wanted to do with her life, other than it must have something to do with music.

Katya fitted in quite well with the other girls who were from various nationalities and backgrounds. Some of them, it soon became obvious, just wanted to find a rich husband. Others had ambitions of travel and making their mark in the world. Katya decided she would just go with the flow. The school arranged visits to go see operas performed by some of the best known touring companies around and later there were discussion groups about the set design, the costumes, the history of the various composers and many related matters to do with the productions. Some productions were very modern and performed without the benefit of any background sets or costumes. Some were sung in languages they hadn't been composed in. Katya decided she was a bit of a traditionalist. She also worked hard on her language skills. It helped having girls from different nationalities around; there was always someone to practise with. Dutch was Katya's first language so she found German the easiest to master, but the language of the opera was Italian. The school put on performances of many of the well known operas. It gave their pupils a chance to do choreography, set and costume design as well as performing. Katya was usually in the chorus, her voice was not strong enough, nor did she have the range to take on a leading role, or to be honest, even a small supporting role. But she enjoyed the experience.

Sports weren't neglected either, there were archery classes, swimming, rowing, tennis, running and even horse riding. Katya tried them all, but found her wrist too weak for the archery, tennis and rowing, she wasn't a great runner so she stuck to swimming and horse riding. Her friend Sophie, an English girl, was very keen on riding, or, as Katie suspected, keen on the Riding Master. Anyway, she was the one who dragged Katya along to the riding lessons. The Riding Master was a young Swiss nearing his thirties and most of the girls had a crush on him, so when it was announced that he was to take a break for a couple of weeks, there was a collective sigh from most of the girls. But the Head announced that the school had been very fortunate indeed. They had secured the services of a very well known and respected German trainer, Dieter von Rheinhart. It was quite a coup for the school. He was very much in demand and he had trained his son who rode in the German Equestrian team. This temporary appointment didn't seem to excite the girls as much as it had the Headmaster, as Sophie explained, he was ancient, he was over fifty! Katya didn't go to the first lesson with the new trainer as she was recovering from a severe throat infection but she heard everything first hand from Sophie. Sophie told her he wasn't as bad as she had feared. He was tall and strong, had short white hair and the most piercingly fierce blue eyes, and he spoke English with hardly any trace of an accent. Katya detected the beginnings of another crush developing despite the crippling age of the new Riding Master. The only drawback Sophie reported was that he insisted that each girl groomed and stabled her pony after the lesson and he was adamant that they also looked after their own tack. 'What a bore,' she said.

Katya's first encounter with Dieter was in the stables, he had his back to her. He was in tight white riding breeches, long highly polished black boots and had on a black riding jacket. He carried his whip and hat in his left hand and was gentling her pony with his right hand. He turned around as he heard her step behind him. Her first thought was, Sophie was right, he does have fierce blue eyes and he looks quite old, but that could be the effect of white hair over a weather-beaten face. He stared at her for what seemed an eternity until she began to feel uncomfortable. She started to fidget with her whip and changed her weight from one foot to the other. Suddenly he asked, 'Is this your pony?'

'Yes,' she replied, 'I call him Toby because he's a bit fat.'

He smiled at that but didn't take his eyes off her. 'Will you take him out into the yard so I can have a look at him?' She nodded and went towards the box, she had to brush past him and she felt those eyes upon her. She thought he was going to touch her at one point but he didn't. She led Toby out of the stable and only then did he step aside and make way for them both.

Out in the yard, he ran his hands all over the pony, 'Your right, he is fat, he would benefit from a spot of lungeing. How often do you take him out?'

'Well, Herr Becker sees to that.'

'You ride him don't you? If you ride him, you should be prepared to look after him.' Katya felt the sting of his rebuke, and for some reason she didn't understand, she wanted this man to think well of her.

When the rest of the girls joined them, Dieter asked who had been taught to lunge their horses. Only a couple of the girls held up their hands.

'The first part of today's lesson is going to be in the lungeing paddock. Please bring out your ponies and the lungeing ropes and tether your mounts to the hitching rail.' They all looked from one to the other but did as he instructed. 'Katya, please bring in Toby and stand by me.' Katya briefly wondered how he knew her name, but reasoned he must have a list of all the riders. Dieter deftly tied on the rope and started Toby in a clockwise direction. He held the rope in his right hand and the whip in his left. He expertly changed Toby's direction in one fluid movement. After a little while he indicated that Katya should take hold of the rope. He stood right behind her, his gloved hand over the top of hers. 'Feel his movement and rhythm,' he said to her, then he let go and stood back. He repeated this with each of his pupils and gave them a lecture on the care of their mounts. Then he instructed them to mount up, 'Use the mounting block or your neighbour can boot you up.' Dieter booted Katya into her saddle. He went down the line correcting each girl's posture, and if need be, showed them the correct way to hold the reins. Then he told them to walk on. After the lesson Dieter insisted that each girl watered, groomed and stabled her mount. There was a little grumbling but no real dissent.

Later Katya said to Sophie, 'I see what you mean, he's a bit of a tartar isn't he?' but the strange thing was that not one of them ever skipped one of his lessons.

Dieter went back to the school for two weeks each year during the time Katya was there. He was a stern task master but the girls learned more about the care and welfare of horses during those two weeks than at any time during the rest of the year.

Katya still had no idea about what she wanted do, but she was enjoying her time at the school. One day, one of her teacher's came to ask a favour of her. A friend of hers ran an opera and theatre agency. She provided guides who were specialists in their particular subject and they escorted her clients to the opera and theatres. They were expected to be able to answer any questions asked of them about the opera or play they had chosen to go and see and, to make sure that seat allocations and travel arrangements went smoothly. On this occasion she had been let down at the last minute. The teacher asked Katya if she would step into the breach. She was reluctant at first but the opera was one she knew well and loved. The clients were a diverse group of people united by their love of opera and Katya, to her amazement, thoroughly enjoyed the experience. She was also amazed at the size of the 'fee' she earned. The lady who ran the agency was delighted with the feed back she had from the visit and asked Katya if she could call on her again. Katya readily agreed and unknown to her, her future career was launched.

CHAPTER 19

This time around Jan didn't ignore the rumour mill: he listened intently to what was happening within the shipping industry. The 'Hope' had been sailing around the European Ports, picking up cargo here and there which were harder and harder to find. Containerization was the order of the day and the major ports were being adapted for that purpose. One of the rumours going around was that World Wide Shipping was going to divest themselves of all their freighters and concentrate on Bulk Carriers and Tankers. Neither of these options appealed to Jan, but on the other hand, it might be that that was exactly what it was, a rumour. Nothing concrete had come out of the office in Hong Kong.

The 'Hope' was bound for Amsterdam to unload a cargo of timber which she had picked up in Sweden. Jan hadn't been notified of an outward bound cargo from Amsterdam but he hoped the agents had something in mind for him. They sailed straight into a strike. On tying up, the agents informed Jan he could expect to be there for some days. Nothing was moving in or out of the port. His crew were ecstatic; this meant plenty of shore leave for them. The only constraint was security and a night watchman.

On the second morning in port, George the bosun was in a filthy mood. Jan asked him what the matter was, he knew it wouldn't be a hangover because George didn't drink, but he had other vices. He complained to Jan that really he should have known better, he had been to a clip joint the night before and had been fleeced of ever penny he had. Jan realized that could amount to quite a sum of money. George had no immediate family and he saved his money to have a binge ashore. The binge as Jan knew would involve ladies and cards.

The Chinese were inveterate gamblers and George was generally very lucky. Jan knew that because, as a cadet, he had been the holder of many a losing hand in George's company. The practise had been strictly frowned upon by the company, but Jan had realized t was impossible to stop them. The Chinese would always find a way to gamble. It turned out George hadn't been the only loser; there were other members of the crew who were very disgruntled. They had been ashore and gone to a floating clip joint, 'The Lady Anne', where the cheating had been blatant. When they showed their displeasure, they had been bundled ashore by heavies. George was all for organizing a reprisal that night and tearing the place apart. Jan gave him a severe talking to and told him, that that way, he would only end up in jail or worse. No, a more subtle approach was called for. He determined to go and have a look for himself with some of his officers. He gave George

171

the night duty shift to keep him out of trouble.

Jan and half a dozen of his men made their way to 'The Lady Anne'. He had told them to go there in dribs and drabs to avoid suspicion, although there would be plenty of seamen around the place anyway due to the strike. When Jan saw the boat, there was a slight flickering of memory but it was gone in an instant. When his father had been involved in 'The Lady Anne', she had been a first class restaurant, beautifully illuminated and alive with the cream of society. He had only been very young when they left Amsterdam for London. This couldn't possibly be the same boat. She had obviously been a working river boat at some time; she had nice lines but was very run down. The casino was on the bottom deck, it was very dimly lit. The other decks were given over to drinking and other pleasures of the flesh. Customers in various stages of inebriation lolled on the stairs and in dark corners. If trouble flared the heavies dealt with it in a fairly brutal fashion although no blood was spilt. Jan's men indulged in a little gaming and of course lost. It was obvious to the sober that blatant cheating was going on but there weren't that many customers who were sober. Jan had a drink in his hand; it was very expensive and tasted ghastly. He didn't fancy his chances of staying sober for long if he drank much more of that stuff. Wandering around he noticed one man, bald, red faced and fat sitting at a table playing cards. He was sweating profusely and had a continuous habit of tapping the cards. One or two of the 'security staff' spoke to him now and again. Jan decided he must be the main man. Jan moved around trying to be as inconspicuous as he could. He remained in the background but watched the fat man play. It was amazing how often he won. When he displayed his cards he always had a fistful of picture cards. Jan decided they must be marked in some way, but what was this constant tapping about, a nervous affliction? The way he sweated suggested that, but there was something suspicious about the action.

Jonathan came up to talk to him, he whispered, 'There's plenty of underhand dealing going on in here.'

Jan turned to him and muttered, 'Yes, and most of it's centred on this table.' A noise drew his attention back to the table. While he had been talking to Jonathan, something had happened. Jan didn't know what it was, but the croupier was picking himself up of the floor, his chair had been turned over and a very angry looking punter was being hauled away.

The man with the red face mumbled to one of his men, 'Get me another croupier.' The first croupier picked himself up and dusted himself down and threw a look of utter hatred towards the big man. Jan decided it was time to go. He walked round and nodded to each of his officers that it was time to leave. He put his drink on the bar; he had no intention of finishing it. He was the last one to climb the stairs and join the others on the quay side. He glanced back at 'The Lady Anne'. In the shadows he caught a glimpse of the croupier who had been knocked over. Another man was commiserating with him. He looked familiar. Jan looked again; it was his steward from the 'Hope'.

Back on board Jan held a powwow, they were all agreed: The crew had all been cheated out of their wages. The croupiers were bent, they had seen plenty of evidence of underhand dealing, but they couldn't agree as to how to deal with the situation. Go to the authorities, they were probably being paid off anyway. Let the crew smash the joint up? They would only end up in jail with smashed heads: No, there had to be another solution. Jan decided the best thing to do was to sleep on it and consider the problem again tomorrow. Jan had a sleepless night; images of 'The Lady Anne' kept encroaching on his thoughts.

Early the next morning the agent was waiting to see him, they went to his cabin. Jan wanted to know the state of play regarding the strike and had there been any news from Hong Kong regarding another cargo. The agent looked very glum. He told Jan that the reason the dockers were on strike was because of the plans to containerize the port. The fear was that most of them would lose their jobs. The other bad news he had was for Jan's ears only. The rumours that World Wide Shipping was going to sell off all their freighters had been confirmed. There wasn't another cargo for them. As soon as the present cargo of timber was discharged, they would all be out of a job. World Wide Shipping would of course repatriate any of the crew who requested it. Jan was devastated, it was no good appealing to the agents, they couldn't do anything; they were only the messengers.

'How long have we got?'

'Two or three days at the most, if the strike goes on any longer, the instructions are that you are to proceed to another port, but the outcome will be the same.' Jan digested this information, the agent shifted uncomfortably in his seat. As an afterthought Jan asked the agent what he knew about 'The Lady Anne'.

'Oh dear,' he said, 'have your crew been caught out there?'

'Unfortunately the answer is yes.'

The agent grimaced, 'I should've warned you I suppose, you'll get no redress from the police, rumour has it that Roger Henke pays them off handsomely. Mind you, he could be in trouble himself after his father was killed.'

Jan scowled, 'What happened?'

173

'Live by the sword, odds on you'll die by the sword. Henke's father had the gambling and waterside crime tied up. But there was a big falling out and one of Henke's own bodyguard knifed him. The son isn't a patch on his father, he's a compulsive gambler and afraid of his own shadow. He doesn't know who to trust these days, he won't survive for long. The wolves are circling already.' The agent stood up, 'I'm sorry about all this Jan, but I really must go.' He held out his hand to Jan who shook it firmly. Jan sat back in his chair, there was a timid knock on his door and the steward put his head around the curtain. Jan beckoned for him to come in.

'I've brought your morning coffee Sir.'

'Never mind about that now, what were you up to last night?' the poor man went bright red. 'Well!' demanded Jan.

'I was meeting a friend Sir.'

'Does this friend work on 'The Lady Anne' by any chance?'

The steward was wide eyed, 'Yes sir, but he's very unhappy there.'

Jan smiled. 'Is he really, I want you to tell me all about it.' A plan was forming in Jan's mind.

Jan convened a meeting of all the crew, including his officers and outlined his plan of action to them. He had learned a great deal from the unfortunate croupier who had been tipped up the previous night. He was originally from The States and had been employed on the big passenger ships sailing out of Miami. There had been some trouble on board and he and his boyfriend had jumped ship in Amsterdam. Unfortunately his boyfriend had found another 'friend' and moved on. The croupier now worked illegally for Henke. He told Jan that all the croupiers hated Henke and that everything was falling apart after Henke's father had been killed. And crucially, he told Jan how all the scams worked. He told him which of the bodyguards to watch out for; there were only a couple who were still totally loyal to Roger Henke. He felt sure the others would soon melt away if there was any real trouble. Later that day work started on unloading the 'Hope's' cargo. Jan knew he didn't have much time. They decided to put the plan into action the following night when Adam, the croupier, would be on duty.

The following day, the agent was again waiting to see Jan, this time he had all the paperwork relating to the sale of the 'Hope' and the redundancies for all the crew including the Captain. Possession of the vessel would take place the following day. The mission to seaman would provide accommodation for all those awaiting repatriation. Jan decided not to wait until tomorrow to tell his crew of their fate, it would add a certain amount of piquancy to tonight's action.

174

As before, they arrived at 'The Lady Anne' in small groups, each one knew their place. George was rubbing his hands in gleeful anticipation. Jan looked across, and gave him a warning look. The Chinese crew took their places at the gaming tables. They were steady winners but didn't push their luck too far and kept cashing in their chips. Jan was at a table near to the one where Roger Henke sat. Jan was a big winner. The cashier went up to Roger Henke and whispered something in his ear. He looked alarmed and glanced about him; he checked his men were where they were supposed to be. Reassured, he continued with his game. Soon there were only two tables still in operation, Roger Henke's table and Jan's table. Henke's men might be where they were supposed to be, but so were Jan's. Sensing something was very wrong Henke looked up. Jan scooped up all his chips and walked over to Henke's table. The other player's discreetly left. The croupier got up and left as well. Henke looked around him in panic and signalled for his men to come over to him. The ones Jan knew would respond started to move towards their boss, but George and Jan's Chinese crew had them covered. As sharp objects were pushed into their backs they hesitated and stopped.

Jan joined Henke at the card table and put all his chips down. 'One game: all or nothing Henke.'

Henke was now shedding sweat by the gallon. 'What's going on here?' he demanded.

'A card game: Mr. Henke.'

Adam joined them at the table; he produced a fresh deck of cards. He opened the pack and expertly shuffled and dealt them to the two men. Henke looked slightly reassured; he tapped his cards and rejected two. Jan picked his up and smiled across at Henke. Adam dealt two more to Henke, he looked as though he accidently tapped them again - a habit he had. But this time he shot a puzzled look at the croupier who looked back at him with a blank expression on his face. Henke broke out into another bout of profuse sweating. The game progressed: it was all very nerve wracking. Eventually Henke broke; he put his cards down on the table. He had a good hand, he was trembling. Jan smiled and shuffled his hand around. Then he put it down opposite Henke's cards. He smiled broadly, 'I win.'

'Impossible!' shouted Henke and grabbed Jan's cards, looked at them, and threw them across the room. One of the spectators calmly gathered them up and brought them back to the table. Henke was shaking like a leaf, 'I can't pay you - I'll have to give you an I.O.U.'

'I don't think so Mr. Henke.' Jan shoved some papers in front of him, 'Sign there,' Jan tapped the sheet with his finger, 'and we'll call it quits.'

Henke looked down at the papers and went white. 'No, I won't do it.' He looked around in desperation for his men.

'You lost Henke, now sign. I take all! You get nothing. That was the deal.'

Henke trembled from head to foot but eventually he signed in all the places indicated.

Jan got up, 'Now, get off my boat.'

Dieter found he was indeed in need of excitement every now and again. He was very busy with the riding school and travelled with Christian to the main show jumping festivals. But all work and no play wasn't good for anyone. Douglas would make sure he played a little. Dieter was also interested in how Douglas's new business venture was going. He must remember to call him Bruno when he was in the gallery he thought. He could afford to keep his friendship with Douglas in the open these days as he wasn't in anyway involved in Douglas's latest scam. He hadn't forgotten, and would never forget, that Douglas had taken the rap for both Leonard and himself. Douglas had never once mentioned or appeared to reproach him for keeping his head down.

Douglas was, in fact, delighted to see him. In the evening when the gallery was closed, they roamed through the various rooms. Douglas showed Dieter paintings by Monet, Picasso, Constable, Turner and many others. He told him, 'In this business the cover story is everything, hire the right premises in the right place, provide the right set of papers and of course, have a sophisticated receptionist with a plum in her mouth, and you're away.'

Dieter renewed his acquaintance with the artist himself, Rodney Marsh. The studio was behind the gallery, it was a large room with large windows and a skylight, natural light flooded in. Canvases were stacked against the walls, some were already framed, some awaiting frames. There was a pile of empty frames standing in one corner.

Douglas explained, 'We have to wait for the right frame to come along. It's most important that the frame compliments the painting in style and time. Sam usually sees to that side of things, she scours the auction rooms and if a suitable frame comes up, she bids for it, it doesn't matter about the painting itself. We can also get job lots from the back door, she knows the porters quite well, and of course they fancy their chances with her.'

Rodney looked every inch a maestro. He was wearing a pair of blue canvas trousers, topped by a white coverall that was splattered in paint of every hue, and a black beret. Rodney was contemplating a canvas on the easel in front of him, it looked half finished. A Gauguin he explained.

Dieter asked how long it took him to paint one of these-----, and he trailed off, searching for the right word.

Rodney smiled and stepped back examining his work, 'It depends on the artist, some are easier than others but I like to test myself, to give myself a challenge. You see, good artists copy, but great artists steal.' He left Dieter in no doubt as to which category he thought he belonged in.

Douglas chuckled, 'You know Dieter, it's like taking candy from a baby. Very few of these people who buy this stuff know anything about painting, but they're terrified someone will find them out so they bluff their way through. You ought to hear some of the guff they come out with.' He paused, 'Don't get me wrong, Rodney knows his stuff and he can fool the most expert of experts ninety nine percent of the time.'

'What about the one percent?'

'We'll face that when we come to it, after all, anyone can make a mistake, I'm not an expert: I'm just a gallery owner!'

When they were alone together Douglas wanted to know about events in Bremen. Douglas handed Dieter a glass of champagne and he lit up a small cigar. Dieter told him not much had changed since his last visit there. It was still the rest and recuperation centre whenever he chose to avail himself of it. Greta still visited in the summer he told him.

Douglas was quiet for a while, 'I miss her you know.' Douglas looked at Dieter's sceptical face, 'Oh, I know, I took her for granted, I treated her badly I suppose, but that was the point, she was always there.'

'What about Samantha?'

Douglas's face creased into a smile, 'That's the thing Dieter, I love 'em all.' Then he was serious for a moment, 'but it's cost me dear Dieter, it's cost me my son. I didn't want him to see me in that place, I thought I was doing the right thing but now Jan has cut me adrift completely.'

'And me, he never answers my letters, but he's still in touch with Christian.' Dieter pondered whether to continue but added, 'Jan was terribly cut up about his mother.' There was a silence between them, 'You know he's in command now don't you? Captain Coulter.'

'Yes, I knew, he's done well.' Dieter looked morose. 'What have you done Dieter, I know you. You've been up to something.'

He looked Douglas squarely in the eye; Douglas wasn't expecting the next sentence. 'I've seen Katya.'

'You've what?'

'She was at a finishing school in Switzerland and I wangled a fortnight here and there to teach riding. I knew she took lessons.' Douglas let him go on, he knew he wasn't finished. 'She had an accident skiing, which put paid to her musical career. I was worried, she's my daughter! And anyway she's a grown woman now. She might want to know who her father is.'

'Did you tell her?'

'No.'

'What about Christian?'

'I didn't think that far.'

'It's a dangerous game you're playing Dieter, but I can understand why you did it. What if Christian meets her accidently? Have you thought about that?'

'I've thought about it since, she's a lovely girl. I'm not sure -----'

'Dieter, when you're in a hole: stop digging!' Douglas drained his glass. He acknowledged the pain they were both feeling. They both had a child that was lost to them. After a moment Douglas slapped his thigh, 'Come on, get that down you, we're both in serious need of distraction.'

Katya had completed her two years at the finishing school. Her language skills were much improved and the lady from the Swiss agency had asked her to join her full time. Katya thought long and hard about it, she really enjoyed the work, she enjoyed meeting people. She was good at organization and wanted to specialize in the niche market of Opera and Theatre. She stayed with the Swiss agency for a couple of years to get experience and a feel for the market, and then she decided to take a crash course to get qualifications as a fully fledged guide within the travel industry. She landed a job with a large European travel company and they sent her all over Europe. She attended all the famous Opera Houses and Theatres in the main cities in those countries. She got to know the top people who put on the shows at the various venues and as a consequence was able to secure some of the best seats in the house for the popular performances. The clients warmed to her and she was much in demand.

Katya was in London, she had a group for the opera, 'Cosi Fan Tutte' that was being performed at Covent Garden Opera House. Her next group were scheduled to go and see 'The Magic Flute' but she had a few days to kill in between the two engagements. A friend at the company's head office was a keen fan of the local equestrian scene and she had a spare ticket for The London International Horse Show at Olympia for the last day. She asked Katya if she would go with her. Katya readily agreed. They had very good seats at the front of the arena right next to the entrance into the ring. The main event was the Show Jumping. There were riders from all over Europe vying for the ultimate trophy. It was a knockout completion and was very exciting. Britain was very strong in this event, their strength was in families. The most famous being the Whittakers and the Smiths. Both fathers were renowned international figures and their sons were very much up and coming competitors. There was great rivalry between them. Beth told Katya the other father and son team were from Germany, the von Rheinharts.

Katya picked up her ears at that, 'We had a Riding Master at our school in Switzerland called von Rheinhart.'

'Really! Well, I doubt it's this von Rheinhart, I can't see him teaching at an obscure girl's school. He trains the German team.'

'Less of the obscure,' laughed Katya, 'it's an unusual name though.' she commented.

'Yes, anyway the father has already been knocked out; his horse's hind leg took a brick out of the wall in the last jump. Only those with clear rounds are going forward. The son's still in contention though.' and they turned their attention to the events in the ring. The excitement mounted; there were still six riders left. The jumps had been increased in height and the first rider came into the ring. It was one of the Whittaker brothers and he scraped through, dislodging a brick in the final wall, but it didn't fall. The next two riders each had faults, the first, eight faults and the second four faults.

Beth nudged Katya, 'This is Christian von Rheinhart.' He was riding a superb grey horse, beautifully turned out. He was unhurried in the ring, he was intent in getting into the final and to do that, he needed a clear round, and he got one. The next rider was one of the Smith brothers - he also had a faultless round to much applause. Both the Whittaker's and the Smith families had plenty of supporters it seemed. The next rider from Ireland had a refusal mid way through, he tried again, but the horse stubbornly refused to oblige and the poor rider tumbled ignominiously over the horses head and landed on his feet on the other side of the jump.

There were three contenders left in the competition which would be ridden against the clock. To Katya, the first and last riders seemed to have the advantage. If the first rider had a clear round, that put pressure on the other two, the last, of course, knew exactly what he was up against. There was fever pitch in the practise ring behind the scenes whilst the jumps were hiked up another notch. The Whittaker brother rode out into the middle of the arena and acknowledged the crowd. His horse was jet black and gleamed under the lights. It was called Midnight Warrior and his rider took him to the first jump to let him have a good look at it, then, on hearing the bell, turned him around and went through the time barrier. There was absolute silence in the arena.

Michael Whittaker was no slouch! He didn't take too many risks by cutting corners. He had a clear round and posted a good time. He exited the ring to thunderous applause. Christian von Rheinhart trotted into the ring, the announcer told the audience he was riding Snowflake the Second, there was a bit of a titter at that but von Rheinhart took no notice and showed his horse the first jump. The bell sounded and he rode through the start. He couldn't afford to take his time; he had to go faster than Midnight Warrior. On the fourth obstacle he decided to take a short cut and that was his undoing. Snowflake clipped a post with his hind legs, it wobbled for seconds, and then it slowly fell to the floor. Von Rheinhart jumped the other obstacles perfectly and in a shorter timescale, but he had four faults. He slowly made his way towards the exit, applause rippled around the arena. Katya looked to her left and caught her breath. About four yards away from her, waiting to take Snowflake's reins, was Dieter von Rheinhart. He was still in his riding gear but wasn't wearing a hat.

'That's him,' said Katya to Beth, 'he's the one who took our lessons.' At that point Dieter turned round. Their eyes locked and Katya, with a broad smile on her face raised her hand in recognition. Dieter, on the other hand, seemed frozen to the spot. He had half raised his hand, but his face registered total shock. His son had by now reached the gate and expected his father to take the horse's reins and lead him away, but he didn't seem to notice him. Christian removed his riding hat. Katya looked from father to son, they were so alike, in colouring and in build, there was no mistaking their relationship. Christian followed his father's gaze. He was transfixed by a girl with long red hair. Christian smiled, she looked lovely, he didn't know her, but his father evidently did. His father suddenly turned away, took the reins and briskly led the horse and rider away to the dismounting area. Christian asked his father who the girl with the red hair was.

Dieter's face was set in stone, 'I don't know who you mean.'

'Come on dad, she obviously knew you.' Christian looked back, he could see the girl had turned and was still watching them. She had a really puzzled expression on her face.

'She's obviously mistaken me for someone else,' he snapped. 'Now see to this horse, I've taught you better than that, he needs a drink and a good rub down, now get on with it.' Dieter was badly shaken: Douglas's words reverberated in his brain. 'What if Christian should accidently meet her?' Christian looked at his father in surprise, what was the matter with him he wondered.

Katya was at first puzzled then angry. Dieter von Rheinhart had obviously recognized her and then very deliberately snubbed her.

The competition was soon concluded. Robert Smith had a clear round but couldn't beat the time set by Michael Whittaker. There only remained the presentation of the prizes. Christian was in third place and duly rode out on Snowflake to collect his prize. On returning to the enclosure, he made sure he got a good look at the girl with red hair. She stared back at him. He was intrigued by her and swivelled in his saddle to have another look, but she had disappeared. His father was nowhere to be seen either, he was preparing the horse box for a swift exit.

Douglas was checking the list of sales which Samantha supplied him with at the end of each week. It wasn't a long list, turnover wasn't huge, but it didn't need to be at these prices. One or two sales a week kept them all in clover. Douglas saw one name which really made him smile. General Thornton–Smythe had bought a Renoir for a small fortune. Douglas couldn't keep the smile off his face all day. Eventually Sam asked him why he was in such a good mood. 'Do you remember making this sale?' he asked her.

'Thornton–Smythe,' she pondered the name, 'Ah yes, he came in with his wife, but that didn't stop him from discreetly patting my bottom.' She smiled. 'He waffled on to his wife about investing in works of art. Can't lose he told her. I don't think she really wanted to, perhaps it's her money. Anyway he won her over. He was quite a teddy bear really.'

That made Douglas laugh out loud, 'I'm glad I wasn't around, the sale might have been a bit more difficult to pull off.'

'What do you mean?'

'Oh, it's a long story, but warn me if he comes in again and I'll make myself scarce.'

The General had hung his latest acquisition in pride of place in his drawing room. He often stood there admiring it; there was something about this particular painting that he really liked. He wasn't really an art connoisseur. He had been advised to invest in antiques and paintings by people who knew more about the market than he did. He also liked people to know that he could afford to do so.

The Thornton–Smythes were big on hospitality and often gave lavish parties. Some months after the purchase of the Renoir, the General had invited a number of his notable acquaintances to what his wife called a 'soiree'. Among them was a recognized reputable art expert. After supper the General proudly showed him the Renoir. The expert looked at it for a very long time which made the General uneasy. He realized he was being rude and moved away, but kept being drawn back to it. He looked at it surreptitiously from various angles and hung back until all the other guests had left. Then he asked the General if he could have another peek at the painting. Thinking the man was envious, the General readily agreed. The man took out a small magnifying glass which he always carried with him, from his suit pocket. He stepped up to the Renoir and examined various areas in great detail, and then he stood back and viewed it again from a distance. He asked the General if he could remove it from the wall so he could see it flat on a table.

The General was not at all enthusiastic at this suggestion. 'Good God man, why? You can see it perfectly well from here.'

'Where did you get it from?' the expert asked.

'From a very respectable Gallery if you must know, I have the papers to prove its provenance.' blustered the General.

'Ah yes, I've heard of the place. A fairly new establishment as far as the art world goes.' The attitude of the man was making the General a little bit jittery.

'Do you think there's a problem?'

The man deliberated before answering, 'I don't know, I just have an uneasy feeling about it.' Then he made up his mind and turned to the General, 'With your permission I would like to investigate further. There are tests than can be done, X rays and so forth. They won't harm the painting. The British Museum do it all the time to authenticate works of art. But while any doubt remains I wouldn't recommend you sell this on in the open market.'

The General was really alarmed now, 'Well of course, if you think it necessary-----'

'Good!' said the expert, 'I'll send my men around in a day or so to collect it, best to be sure General.' He held out his hand to the General and took his leave. The General stood looking at the painting for quite some time after he had gone, then he went into his library and looked up the name and qualifications of the art expert. He had a lot of letters after his name.

A couple of days later the painting was taken away. The General was told it would take a few weeks for the tests to be conclusive. He was advised that it was best to stay away from the Gallery until the matter was resolved. It was difficult advice to heed as the General regarded himself as a man of action.

A month later the art expert returned to the General's home, he had a sombre look on his face which didn't bode well for the authenticity of the Renoir. 'I'm very sorry General, but you've been duped. This is a fake, a very superior fake, but a fake.'

'But the provenance?'

'Forgeries I'm afraid, very well executed, they would fool most of my colleagues if it makes you feel any better.'

'Well it doesn't.' shouted the red faced General, 'who's responsible for this? Do you have any idea?'

'As a matter of fact I do. I've come across this man's work before which alerted me to this one. He was jailed some years ago but he's out now.'

'What's his name?' the General was incandescent with rage.

'It's Rodney Marsh, but he could well have changed his name now. The stupid thing is,' mused the expert, 'if he painted under his own name he could make a fortune. I rate him a maestro in his own right.'

But this was not what the General wanted to hear. 'What should I do now? I paid good money for this rubbish. I want redress.'

'Well, that's up to you General. You could hang this back on your wall and enjoy it, just don't claim it as a Renoir.'

'Don't be a fool man!'

The art expert understood the General's disappointment but after that outburst he was disinclined to help further. 'Go back to the Gallery where you bought it from, someone supplied the forged provenance. Go to the Police, it's up to you.' And the man turned on his heel and left.

When he had gone, the General immediately rang his solicitor and appraised him of the situation. The solicitor knew his client well and told him he would be with him in a couple of hours. The solicitor took down all the details and informed the police who had a special department dealing with art crime. The Gallery where the General had purchased his painting was owned by a man called the Honourable Bruno St. Aubyn Charlesworth they told him, he was mentioned in Debretts. They hadn't received a complaint about the place before, but then again it had only been in business a relatively short time, just a few years.

The best course of action they advised was the same as the art expert's. Return to the Gallery and ask for an explanation, the owner of the gallery might also be a victim of a fraud, best not to go in with all guns blazing. The General wasn't at all happy with this strategy, he had many influential contacts and he managed to secure the services of a plain clothes police officer for the visit. It was arranged to pay a visit to the gallery the following day, the General insisted that his solicitor should also be present.

The three of them marched into the Gallery at eleven o'clock the next morning. A couple of American's were strolling around with Sam in attendance. She turned to the newcomers and gave them one of her best beaming smiles, and then with a sinking heart, she recognized the

General. The American's were on the point of making a purchase, the wife wanted one particular painting, the husband another. They needed nudging towards the most expensive one. Sam excused herself momentarily and quickly told the General she would be at his disposal shortly. The two men with him smiled politely and Sam returned to seal the deal with the Americans. She took them into a private little alcove where they were shielded from the main Gallery and the transaction was completed.

The General's party strolled around looking at the exhibits. They heard voices and looked around. A door opened just a few yards away and three men walked out. One was saying to a rather flamboyant individual, 'Now Bruno, you mustn't keep these little treasures to yourself.' The one called Bruno turned around and came face to face with the General and his two companions. Bruno's disguise didn't fool the General for a second.

'You! It's you again Coulter.' And the General lunged at Douglas with murderous intent. He had to be restrained by his solicitor.

Douglas gave a big sigh, 'Bloody Hell, timing is everything.' He knew the game was up. Police were quickly swarming all over the place. They arrested Douglas, Rodney and Samantha. All the paintings and paperwork were taken away. The Americans tore up their cheque and watched proceedings from a safe distance, no doubt agreeing with Douglas, timing is everything!

At the trial, which was given great prominence in the press and on TV, Douglas pleaded guilty, as did Rodney who was actually basking in his notoriety. Samantha pleaded not guilty. She claimed to have been under the malign influence of Douglas, who, she agreed was her lover. She told the jury, he had never discussed business with her and she genuinely believed him to be a member of the British peerage. Under cross examination, Douglas agreed that Samantha was only an employee who did as he asked. Sam got away with a suspended sentence. Douglas and Rodney weren't so lucky. The judge in his summing up said they were unreformed, unrepentant villains and deserved custodial sentences. The sentence, when it came, wasn't as punitive as might have been expected. They got six years each, each being equally culpable. Later, Douglas's solicitor offered the opinion that the judge was secretly amused, he thought that General Thornton–Smythe was a puffed up buffoon and deserved all he got.

When the dust had died down a little, Samantha visited Douglas in jail. She had become a minor celebrity due to all the publicity. Her picture had been in the newspapers and on TV and she had been asked to give a few interviews for which she had been paid. She told Douglas she had received several proposals of marriage, one from a Lord.

Douglas smiled at her, 'What are you going to do Sam?'

She twisted her figures in her lap and said quietly, 'Time waits for no-one Douglas'

'No,' he answered, 'growing old is compulsory, but growing up is optional.' he grinned.

'This might be my best opportunity.' She couldn't look him in the face.

He leant forward, 'Sam, I completely understand. You must go for it.' he paused, 'but promise me one thing.'

She looked up at him then, 'What?'

'Make sure he's a real Lord.'

Sam had tears in her eyes. 'It was great fun Douglas.'

Even before the last of the footsteps were heard leaving 'The Lady Anne' the Chief Engineer Tom Ryder was down in the engine room. Fortunately the engines weren't in too bad a state. As the Chief said, a condition of 'The lady Anne' being permanently moored alongside in a canal was probably that the engines had to be maintained and turned over ever now and again. He worked solidly down there all night along side his Second and Third, the evidence was clear for all to hear, a banging and clattering that echoed and resonated throughout the boat. Just before daybreak an oil stained figure in what had once been white overalls appeared on the bridge. His face was grease stained and beads of sweat were running down his forehead. Jan could see the whites of his eyes and then his white false teeth as he broke into a big grin. 'They'll do.' he said simply.

The deck side hadn't been idle either, they had been through the boat from stem to stern assessing her and stacking all the now redundant furniture out of the way so they were able to move around more freely. The crew had already checked the moorings so they were able to slip the ropes at a moments notice. The Chief asked, 'What if the river police stop us?'

Jan had his story ready, more plausible because he spoke fluent Dutch. 'We're a relief crew taking her to a yard for urgent repairs. Let's get her fired up Chief.' The engines started first time with a bit of a rattle and vibration. Clouds of black smoke were emitted from the exhausts which gradually cleared to a murky grey colour. Jan gave the order to cast off and 'The Lady Anne' gently nosed away from the quay side pushing the accumulated detritus to either side of her as she slowly made her way into the middle of the canal. The engines gradually subsided to a muted throbbing and everyone breathed a collective sigh of relief.

Daybreak found them moving slowly down the canal leaving the centre of Amsterdam way behind them. Jan had already done his homework and knew were he was taking her. With the help of the agent he had identified an obscure yard down a secondary canal that was capable of doing the work he required. Of course, his own men were capable of doing quite a lot of the internal renovations needed. The Chippie was an excellent carpenter, after all merchant seamen when out at sea, had to be a self reliant bunch. You couldn't call a plumber out when you were in the middle of the ocean!

After two days they reached their destination without further mishap or being stopped. The hard work for Jan now started. First he must see that any necessary licences and certification required for sailing on the canals was obtained. The next priority was the funding of the renovations! Jan's vision of what he wanted from 'The Lady Anne' was becoming clearer in his mind. He wanted to be his own boss. No more taking orders from invisible people in an office miles away in another country, but he knew he couldn't achieve this on his own.

He convened a meeting with his crew. He laid before them his idea of what 'The Lady Anne' could become. If they stayed with him, he asked for total commitment to the project. There was a slight shuffling among the men. Jan said he was sympathetic to anyone who felt they couldn't make this commitment especially the Chinese who had families to think of back home. Two of them stepped forward. Then a few moments later, so did Jan's steward. Jan had a word with the Chinese; he gave them their redundancy pay and told them not to gamble it away. The agents in Amsterdam would see that World Wide Shipping honoured their obligation to repatriate them and he thanked them for their loyalty. His steward falteringly told him that he and his new friend were heading to the States where his friend had the promise of work for them both with a large cruise line sailing out of the Caribbean. Jan put his hand on his shoulder and wished them both well. Jan then distributed the rest of the redundancy money owed to his men. He was surprised and quite overwhelmed when some of them told him they wished to put a percentage of their redundancy into the pot to get the ball rolling, plus they were willing to put their considerable skills to work in an effort to reduce costs. He felt quite humbled by their loyalty and faith in him. The rest of the money needed for the project, Jan was confidant he could raise with a marine mortgage.

Work started in earnest on 'The Lady Anne', Jan delegated the day to day supervision to Tom Ryder, his Chief Engineer. Jan and Jonathan had other priorities. A boat the size of 'The Lady Anne' didn't need a large number of able seamen to run her, but if she was to be a successful Hotel Boat, she needed housekeeping and catering staff. Some of the remaining Chinese crew were very happy to retrain and change into smart looking waiters. One of their number turned out to be a really good chef, he found he thoroughly enjoyed it and had an aptitude for the work.

Jan went to see the agent in Amsterdam who had tipped him off about the sale of the 'Hope'. He told Jan the disappearance of 'The Lady Anne' had created a great deal of speculation for a day or two, but no-one was looking for her. Roger Henke had disappeared into the back streets of Amsterdam and good riddance to him. He was extremely sympathetic to Jan's plans for the boat and promised any help he could give him.

'Well, I was rather hoping you would agree to be my agents in the Netherlands.'

The agent beamed, 'It's quite a change from our usual type business, but as you're painfully aware, the shipping industry is undergoing a major revolution and business is very quiet at the moment, let me talk to my partners and see what we can come up with.' Jan was delighted at what they came up with. The agency set up a separate department headed by his friend to promote hotel boats on the canals of Europe. They saw it as an opportunity, an up and coming trend. Jan was closeted with the agent for hours at a time while they worked out routes, berthing rights and schedules. The agent undertook to do some promotional work. Jan had to negotiate very hard and skilfully, he didn't want to surrender his new found freedom so soon or so readily. His friend understood this and kept the contract to a minimum time scale. They both had to find their feet in a new market. The agents initially undertook to fill a certain percentage of cabins; Jan had control over the rest. They were in business!

While Jan was busy in Amsterdam, Jonathan had gone back to England. His brief was the same as Jan's. They needed paying passengers. He went to see his parents who were delighted to be reunited with their son. He explained the situation to them and asked if they had any ideas. They had. They were well known in the academic world and members of various groups were always on the look out for new venues to hold lectures and meetings for their different interests. Jonathan's father was a geologist, how interesting to get a group of like minded people together and do a trip through the waterways and gorges of Europe. They would have ample opportunities for field trips and to study the terrain. He felt sure he could interest enough people to make it worthwhile. His mother had an interest in photography and she did the same thing with her group. By the end of his stay he had amassed a decent number of firm bookings for 'The Lady Anne'.

Next stop for Jonathan was London, he was more a fish out of water here, but he persevered, calling on various travel companies trying to drum up some interest in River Cruising. He had some successes but few firm bookings. One large company expressed an interest in becoming sole agents in Britain for the boat, but they wanted to see how the maiden voyage went first before committing themselves.

The big day arrived for 'The Lady Anne' to be handed over to them. Tom Ryder had expressed his satisfaction and given her the thumbs up. Jan was extremely pleased with the internal refurbishment of the boat. She could take ninety passengers in total. All the cabins had ensuite facilities, even the crew quarters. A duel system of air conditioning and heating had been installed in all cabins, an essential requirement in the summer on the rivers in Europe and in the cooler months. The season was expected to last from April to the New Year. It took a crew of nineteen to operate 'The Lady Anne' efficiently and they had all undergone extensive training. The maiden voyage was a steep learning curve for everyone, only Jan and Jonathan had previous experience on passenger ships to call on. Jan decided they must continually have training sessions to thrash out any difficulties they came across on the way. They had taken on a guide who knew the history of the rivers and Jan made recordings of his broadcasts to be played back to his staff. He wanted them steeped in local knowledge. Any complaints from passengers made to his crew Jan had asked them to pass on to him so he could iron out any niggles. Operating the boat proved to be the easy part, making sure both passengers and crew were happy was much more difficult!

The first season was quite a revelation to all concerned. Many important lessons had been learned and there hadn't been any major disasters. Many of the passengers declared they would like to come again and would tell their friends about the boat. Jan had decided that the crew should participate in a profit sharing scheme which meant every one had an incentive to give of their best. When the figures were checked they had made a small operating profit and the crew where quietly optimistic about the success of the venture. They were now due some well earned rest.

During the next couple of years, the business slowly picked up, mostly by word of mouth. There was very little turnover of crew and their experience grew and their confidence was boosted. 'The Lady Anne' was one of the very few owner operated Hotel boats in Europe and it was reflected in her management. She certainly had style combined with five star comfort and it wasn't that long before she was sailing with a full compliment of passengers in the peak season.

One afternoon on a very hot day when most of the passengers were out on the sundeck and Jonathan had relieved him on the bridge, Jan walked through to the Lounge bar and ordered himself a beer. One of the passengers recently arrived from England had left his paper behind. Jan picked it up. It was open at the sports page, he looked at the date, it was yesterday's paper, a treat indeed. The papers were usually a week old by the time they got to him. He quickly scanned the sport's pages and then turned to the front page. He went white! There staring out at him was his father's face. The headlines screamed out: 'Six years for the bogus Lord'. Oh God, thought Jan, what has he been up to now! He hadn't heard a word from his mother about any impending scandal. He quickly read through the article. So that was it, he had been selling fake paintings, apparently very successfully too. He detected a whiff of admiration in the way the article had been written. Just then the owner of the paper appeared. 'Sorry,' he said, 'I left it behind by mistake.' He saw the article Jan had been reading. 'Quite a character that one, it's all over the papers and the TV back home. He's ruffled quite a few feathers in the art world, serves 'em right, stuffy old duffers.' he paused, 'come to think of it, he has the same surname as you, any relation by any chance?' It was said as a joke. Jan smiled weakly. The man continued, 'His girlfriend has done well out of it though, I hear she's going to marry a real Lord!' He took his paper, and then turned back to Jan, 'You can have it after I've finished with it if you like.' Jan managed a thank you and turned back to his beer then, much to the surprise of the barman, he burst out laughing.

Jan had recently negotiated a deal with a travel company in London for the off seasons. They had initially wanted sole British rights but eventually they agreed to a lot less. They had groups of opera lovers who wanted to combine a river trip and at the same time go to some of the prestigious opera houses to be found in the larger cities which 'The Lady Anne' visited. Cologne, Koblenz, Mainz, Frankfurt and Strasbourg were all on their list.

The company retained the services of a young lady who would arrange the bookings and pick up the passengers from the boat. The first group had joined in October. They had stayed overnight in a Hotel in Cologne for the first night's performance of 'La Traviata'. They joined 'The Lady Anne' the following morning for the ten day trip from Cologne to Basel and they were paying handsomely for the privilege as each stop necessitated an overnight stay. The coach arrived and the baggage was brought on to the boat. Jan and his crew were there to welcome them on board. The courier had remained with the coach to check all the bags had been accounted for, and then she walked to the gangway to wave off her charges. Jan had just caught a glimpse of her, she was tall and slender but the most striking thing about her was her long bright red hair which was blowing freely in the fairly strong wind. The crew who had been handling the baggage transfer told Jan and Jonathan she was a real corker and they whistled after her when she left. Jan frowned at them but she turned and cheerily waved back.

The new passengers were absolutely no trouble and a pleasure to have on board. They were discussing the previous night's performance and were looking forward to the next venue in eager anticipation. They were due to see a production of 'La Boheme' in Koblenz where the coach would pick them up. The evening meal had been served and 'The Lady Anne' arrived in plenty of time for the evening's entertainment ashore. The coach was waiting for them as was the courier. She came to meet her group at the top of the gangway when it was secured. Jan, who was still on the bridge, got a much better look at her this time. She was indeed 'a corker'.

The party arrived back at the boat quite late. They made for the bar where they animatedly discussed the individual performances of the singers before retiring to their cabins. Jan heard the name of Katy mentioned quite frequently in the conversation and decided that must be the name of the courier. He thought that at the next stop, which was Mainz, he would make the effort to meet her. He smiled in anticipation; he was looking forward to meeting her.

They arrived in Mainz with time to spare. The locks on the river had been favourable to them so they were comfortably tied up with the gangway down when the coach arrived for the opera party. Jan walked ashore just as Katy alighted. She was the first one to speak. 'Hello, I'm Katy, I've come to collect my charges from you.' She thrust out her hand, 'You must be Captain Coulter?' She shot a quick glance at his shoulder confirming his position. She had a very engaging smile, white teeth, a fresh complexion, compelling green eyes and the crowning glory of fiery red hair. Jan took her hand, she had a firm handshake.

'Yes, Jan Coulter. We're a little early. Perhaps you'd like to come aboard and wait there?'

'Yes, thank you, I would.' Jan had used the Dutch pronunciation of his name. 'You're Dutch?'

He smiled at her, 'Well, I'm a hybrid really. My father is English but my mother is Dutch.'

Then she said in perfect Dutch, 'Really, I was brought up in Holland, but now I seem to live wherever the job takes me.' She reverted to English, 'I'd love to see around your boat, I've heard a lot about it.' She turned to the driver and told him they wouldn't be long, then she preceded Jan onto 'The Lady Anne'.

'Careful!' he said, 'the headroom is rather low just as you enter. You can give yourself a nasty knock on the head. Steel is very unforgiving.' She half turned, smiled briefly and ducked her head as she went on board. Jan was very intrigued by her. She was nearly as tall as he was, but he noticed she was wearing stylish high heeled shoes, not really suitable for a boat. Her coat was camel coloured and of the wrap-a-round type. He escorted her through to the lounge bar and asked her if she would like a drink.

She declined politely, 'Better not, but thank you. I do allow myself a glass of champagne during the intervals,' she grinned, 'I find it helps my concentration.' And she laughed. She looked around her. In front of the bar area, there was a small dance floor and in the corner a piano and seats for other musicians. She turned to him enquiringly.

'My passengers quite enjoy dancing of an evening; we try to provide a variety of music for them.' he said in explanation. She walked over to the piano and expertly played a few bars of something classical which Jan vaguely recognized. He realized she was an accomplished musician. He was more intrigued than ever by her. Beyond the dance floor were tables and very comfortable looking chairs arranged in small intimate groupings. The windows were panoramic to allow maximum views of the wonderful scenery they passed through. They were immaculately clean. There were already a few passengers sitting around quietly chatting. Some had drinks in front of them, some were playing cards or board games and others quietly reading. Others had already gone ashore.

'It's charming.' She said. Just then she was interrupted by a passenger announcement asking the group who were going to the opera to assemble by the gangway. 'My call I think, I would love to see one of the cabins when I have more time. Would that be possible? I mean, I don't want to be a nuisance.'

'Of course! And you wouldn't be a nuisance.' And he meant it from the heart. She turned to go and Jan caught sight of a classically cut green cocktail dress underneath the coat, the green of the dress exactly matched her eyes. She was beautifully dressed; they were going for an evening at the opera after all. Jan stood at the gangway and helped his passengers disembark. He watched and waved as the coach drew away.

Jonathan was standing by Jan's side, he had a knowing smile on his face, 'Interested?'

Jan turned to watch the coach as it disappeared along the road. 'Mildly.' he answered. Both Jan and Jonathan knew that wasn't true.

Back in his cabin, Jan calculated that there were three more venues to go, three more chances to see Katy. He wondered what her surname was, he knew he had seen it but he couldn't remember it. He dug out the paperwork relating to the opera party, yes, there it was. Katy Novak. She had told him she had been brought up in Holland, but that wasn't a Dutch surname, and yet her Dutch had been fluent! He read on, but really, there wasn't that much more to be gleaned about Katy Novak. She had been retained by the company for a number of years. She was a qualified guide and had worked all over Europe and in Britain. And, yes, there it was, she had been a student at a well known school of music in Paris. Jan was puzzled; it was a strange choice of profession for a musician to make. He was awakened from his reverie by a knock at his door. It was Jonathan with a sheaf of paperwork in his hand. Jan groaned. Nonetheless, he had better buckle down and get on with it, he needed to get an early night. It was an early start in the morning.

The opera in Mainz was a production of 'Die Fledermaus'. Katy had seen the opera many times before but always enjoyed it and was captivated by the music, but on this occasion, she found her attention wandering more than once. Her thoughts strayed to the good looking Captain of 'The Lady Anne'. Katy was used to admiring glances from the opposite sex, but on this occasion she was quite gratified to notice him covertly watching her. She tried to assess his age, but it was difficult. He had obviously spent quite a lot of time in the tropics as his skin was tanned and weather-beaten. She decided he was probably younger than he looked. His almost white hair didn't help in the age assessment process, but the eyes were alert and bright blue suggesting her first assumption was right. She suddenly thought about Dieter von Rheinhart and his son. They were of a similar build and colouring. She wondered if there was a family connection there, but she dismissed the idea. He had told her his father was English and his mother Dutch. The von Rheinharts were German through and through.

At the end of the performance, Katy herded her people onto the coach for the return journey to 'The Lady Anne'. She secretly hoped she would see Captain Coulter again, but she was to be disappointed. The public lounges were lit up and she could hear the sounds of people enjoying themselves, but there was no sign of her Captain. Katy sighed; it was back to a lonely hotel bedroom for her. The next stop along the river was Frankfurt and the opera was 'Der Rosenkavalier', not one of her favourite operas, then the stop after that was Strasbourg and the opera there was 'Faust', which was.

Frankfurt was a large university city on the river Main. A walking tour of the city had been organized for the fit and healthy types, a small coach to tour the city was provided for those with walking difficulties so most of the passengers were ashore during the afternoon. Both Jan and Jonathan had been on the go for hours and as Jan would have to make another early start the next morning he left the second in charge of 'The Lady Anne'. He left strict instructions that he wasn't to be disturbed unless it was a dire emergency. He and Jonathan were going to get some much needed sleep. At the back of Jan's mind was the thought that Katy Novak was due to pick up her group in the evening and he wanted to be fresh when she arrived.

194

Unknown to Jan, Katy was already in Frankfurt and she had decided to walk down to the river to see if 'The Lady Anne' had already berthed. And there she was; looking spic and span in the weak autumn sun shine. She walked along the path at the side of the boat. She could see a few people sitting on the top deck. Some of them were from her party who had decided to have a restful afternoon on board. They recognized her, waved and called out for her to come on board. This alerted the Second Officer who also recognized her immediately. Normally, anyone who wasn't sailing on the boat wasn't allowed on board, but the Second thought this should be an exception to the rule and he asked her if she would like to see around the boat. He explained that most people were ashore and it would be an ideal time to look around. Katy said she would love to, but first she would go and say hello to her group.

She spent half an hour or so chatting to them and then joined the Second for a tour of the boat. He showed her the restaurant which was deserted at that time of the afternoon, but was already set up for the evening meal. She noticed how well it had been done, plenty of spaces between the tables, so no jostling to get to your seat. The cutlery gleamed and the table napery was as white as snow. Definitely five star standard providing the food was of a similar quality. He let her have a brief glimpse into the galley, but he wasn't as sure of his ground here. The Captain was very particular about who was allowed into the food preparation areas. Next he showed her a couple of the cabins that weren't occupied on this trip. There were three price ranges he told her, bottom deck, middle deck and top deck. Each price range had a little bit more floor space and storage space for the extra money. The decor and cleanliness of the cabins Katy saw was excellent. The Second explained he couldn't show her any on the top deck because they were all occupied, mainly by her own group. They were always the first ones to be booked up. He took her back to the Lounge Bar; the temperature in there was just right for the time of year she noticed. He asked if she would like a drink, she replied that she would, she would like a dry white wine with ice and soda. Katy was secretly disappointed that again there was no sign of 'The Lady Anne's' Captain, she nonchalantly asked where he was. The Second guilelessly told her the Captain was getting his beauty sleep and had left strict instructions that he wasn't to be disturbed for anything or anybody, only if the boat was sinking were they allowed to wake him. Katy chatted on about the trip and the wonderful scenery the boat passed through, she told him she was getting very good feed back from her passengers and felt sure her company would want to repeat the exercise. Then she drained her glass and said she really must go and get ready for the evening. She said to say hello to the Captain for her but she needed a cat nap herself before the evening's excursion.

Jan appeared in the Lounge Bar shortly before the evening meal was due to be served. He liked to be seen to eat with his passengers so they could see he wasn't getting preferential treatment. He and his staff were eating the same food they were. He ordered himself a beer, the Second came in and Jan asked if everything was alright. The Second reported that there hadn't been any problems, in fact he had had a very pleasant afternoon.

Jan replied, 'Good! That's what I like to hear, no problems and my staff enjoying themselves. What have you been up to?' he said chuckling.

'Nothing much, I hope you don't mind, but I let the opera lady on board, she asked if she could look round the boat.'

Jan stopped chuckling, his glass was half way to his mouth, 'Why didn't you wake me?' he snapped.

The Second was completely off guard and taken by surprise, 'I'm sorry Sir, you gave strict instructions not to be woken up, and I didn't think you would mind. After all she's been on board before and I heard you ask her if she would like to see around the boat.'

Jan was immediately contrite and coloured up slightly, he was relieved when Jonathan ambled into the bar. The Second took his cue and left.

Jonathan noticed the strained atmosphere, 'What was that all about? he asked.

'Nothing, nothing really, I must have got out of the wrong side of the bed that's all.' Jonathan looked surprised but said nothing. Later he asked the Second what the altercation had been about.

'Don't ask me, all I did was show the opera guide around the boat. There was no need to bite my head off.' Jonathan smiled, now he understood.

Katy arrived on time and Jan was waiting at the top of the gangway as she alighted from the coach.

'I'm sorry I wasn't about to show you around the boat this afternoon, I----'

Katy cut him short, 'Oh, that's quite alright, I understand you were getting your beauty sleep,' she said light heartedly, 'your Officer gave me a complete tour, he was a perfect gentleman and I am very impressed with 'The Lady Anne'. My report will be very favourable I assure you.'

Jan was a little taken aback by her business like approach after

196

her earlier friendliness, 'Thank you, I hope the evening is a success.' And Jan turned on his heel and returned to 'The Lady Anne'. Katy could have bitten her tongue out, she hadn't meant to sound so severe, it emphasised how nervous she was about him. Her eyes followed him as he strode back on board. It was a long evening for Katy, but she smiled and answered people's questions. At the end of the night, she was glad to get back to her hotel room.

Katy had had a restless night, but in the cold light of morning she pulled herself together. This is ridiculous she thought, I've got a job to do and so has he, I mustn't let my personal feelings interfere with it. Strasbourg and the opera 'Faust' were next on the itinerary. Strasbourg was a lovely old town, particularly the 'Petite France' area and the opera to be shown that evening was one of her favourites. She determined to enjoy herself, so that afternoon she became a tourist and meandered around the narrow cobbled streets.

For the time of year the weather was quite benign and the summer crowds had thinned out, so it was easier to get around and appreciate the architecture of the place. The houses were higgledy-piggledy and painted in a variety of colours, each different to its next door neighbour, many half timbered with gargoyles looking down on the streets below. It was difficult not to get a crick in the neck as you wandered around the place. Katy decided a coffee was in order. Many of the street cafes had closed down for the winter, so she wandered around looking for a suitable place. As she rounded a corner, she bumped straight into Jan Coulter. Surprise registered on her face, as it did on his. At first he looked delighted to see her, and then doubt clouded his face. A sombre look entered his eyes. 'I'm so sorry. I wasn't looking where I was going.' he said as he stood aside to let her pass.

'No, really, it was my fault.' They stood awkwardly, each making room for the other to pass. Then Katy said, 'I was looking for somewhere to have a coffee, will you join me?' she faltered, 'that is, if you have time.'

His face softened immediately, 'Yes, I would be delighted to. I've just passed a place that's still open. Shall we try there?' She gave him a dazzling smile and nodded. Jan ushered her to a small table in a quiet corner by the window looking onto the street. He pulled the chair aside for her to sit down then sat opposite her. There was a strained silence between them then they both started to speak at once and stopped. Katy giggled nervously, fortunately the waitress appeared at Jan's shoulder, pad and pencil poised. Jan ordered two coffees, he enquired if she preferred black or white.

'I'd like a cafe crème please.'

'And I take mine black.' added Jan. The waitress disappeared and returned in a few minutes with the coffees. They sat sipping their coffee's, both a little tongue-tied.

'I see you're out of uniform.' Katy immediately regretted such an obvious remark.

He replied, 'Yes, sometimes it's a little claustrophobic on board. I thought I'd take some time out to relax a little.'

'Me too,' she added lamely. Jan drank some more of his coffee; those green eyes of hers unnerved him. Katy sat there stirring her cup, thinking desperately of something clever to say, she felt like a gauche young girl.

He leaned forward slightly and said softly, 'Shall we start again?' that broke the tension between them and they both laughed. They chatted about this and that, much more at ease with each other. They talked about what a lovely place Strasbourg was, about the opera that Katy was to attend that evening. He owned up to not knowing much about classical music.

Reluctantly Jan looked at his watch, 'I'm afraid I have to get back to 'The Lady Anne', I'm afraid she's a very demanding mistress, but I'm glad I bumped into you this afternoon.'

'Quite literally.' added Katy. Jan leaned across the table, put his hand on top of hers and gave a little squeeze. He stood up and left. He had reached the end of the street when he realized he had forgotten to pay the bill.

'Oh hell,' he whispered under his breath, but he hadn't got time to remedy the situation now, still, he walked briskly back to his boat with a much lighter step.

Basel was the last stop on the itinerary. Everyone was leaving the boat here. Those that were going to the opera were transferring to a hotel for the last night. The other passengers were being ferried to the airport for their flight home. The last day was always a real workup for the crew, and everyone had to join in, including the Captain. All the cabins had to be stripped and thoroughly cleaned. The boat had to be resupplied, refuelled and water taken on. There were a million and one things to think about as a new quota of passengers were joining that evening. But one thing Jan always insisted on was that he and his Officers were lined up on the gangway to say goodbye to the passengers as they left.

The coaches were on the quayside, people were milling about exchanging addresses and telephone numbers. Most, soon to be discarded as memories faded and normal life took hold once more.

Suitcases were loaded up and everyone embarked on the coaches for their onward journey. Jan entered each coach in turn to thank his passengers and to say he hoped to see them again sometime soon. When he boarded Katy's coach she was just settling into the front seat, he bent down and whispered into her ear. 'Thank you for my coffee in Strasbourg, perhaps you'll let me return the favour sometime soon.'

She gave a tinkling little laugh, 'My pleasure Captain.'

CHAPTER 22

The very last voyage of the season was the New Year trip which ended in Koblenz with a superb display of fireworks on New Year's Eve. The previous year had been the best ever and bookings looked good for the following season. Jan was delighted that the opera group had rebooked for trips in the spring and autumn seasons. He looked forward to renewing his acquaintance with Katy, he was very much hoping it would blossom into something a lot more serious than just a working relationship between them. But before that he had to take 'The Lady Anne' back to the boatyard for her annual overhaul. He must also make a trip home to see his mother. She knew all about Douglas's latest 'difficulties' as she delicately put it, but she didn't go and visit him this time. His mother never rebuked Jan for his lack of attention to her; she just got on with her life and seemed quite content. Jan would have liked to have made a visit to Bremen as well, but he had snubbed Dieter for years now, an action he now regretted. His mother still went there every year in the summer and he was pleased she still kept in contact with them. He was still in touch with Christian who was becoming a power to be reckoned with in the equestrian world. Christian had made tentative invitations to Jan over the years, but Jan felt too awkward to accept.

The next season was soon upon them and the crew had renewed enthusiasm after the winter break. Many of their passengers were repeat bookings so acquaintances were renewed. The very first voyages of the year were from Amsterdam to view the bulb fields and the Keukenhof Gardens. These early voyages didn't last very long and allowed any problems to be ironed out. 'The Lady Anne' then ventured further afield to the Rhine and the Moselle rivers. Katy was due to bring her first party to 'The Lady Anne' in early May and Jan was looking forward to seeing her again.

Katy had also been busy during the winter months. She had had engagements in London, Paris, Berlin and Prague. She had also been home to spend Christmas and the New Year with her family in The Hague. Both of her cousins had also made it home for the festive season. Hannah was doing very well in the fashion business. She told Katya tales of what went on behind the scenes. Katya's eyes widened at some of her stories, it sounded a very cut throat and unfriendly business to be in to her. Katya however did benefit from her cousin's talents, it was Hannah who designed and made most of the dresses Katya needed for her visits to the opera. She couldn't just turn up in any old thing.

Stefan, who had initially been training to become a teacher like his father had, at the last minute, swopped courses and was now training to be a doctor. Quite a change from wanting to be an engine driver mused Katya. Still she thought, her path in life hadn't gone smoothly either, she had made one or two detours herself. At home everyone called her Katya, she had only responded to the anglicized version of her name due to someone mishearing it on her very first engagement in London. It was easier to go along with the flow than to keep correcting her charges.

Katya was also looking forward to her first opera-river trip. The feedback from the first year had been very good. The passengers said it was a very relaxing way to travel from one opera venue to the next. 'The Lady Anne' was very comfortable and the food had been excellent, the staff cheerful and helpful. The only criticism that one or two of them made was that there weren't enough opera lovers on board!

Her first party were due to join the boat in Bonn. As before, they had travelled there independently and stayed in a hotel for the first night after seeing 'The Magic Flute'. The coach drove down through the city and there berthed on the Rhine was 'The Lady Anne'. Katy felt a quickening of her pulse at the sight of it. It was a dull day and the rain was falling steadily, 'The Lady Anne's' Captain and crew were sheltering on board but came out to welcome them as the coach drew alongside. Jan, who was bare headed, strode up the gangway closely followed by the crew whose job it was to transfer the luggage on board. Katy's heart lurched at the sight of him. She was the first to alight from the coach. Jan was standing by the door and offered his hand to help her down. 'Welcome back.' he whispered to her.

Her first words to him were, 'You can buy me the coffee you owe me now.' He squeezed her hand and smiled. Then he was all business, organizing the transfer of the luggage and welcoming each set of passengers and making sure they were shown to their allocated cabins. When everyone was on board Jan asked her if she would like to join him for a quick welcome drink in the bar.

'What, at this time in the morning?' she said, surprised.

'Yes, at this time in the morning.' he repeated, 'Jonathan is taking first stint on the bridge and I wanted to hear all about what you've been up to since I last saw you. We'll have to be quick though as we're casting off in thirty minutes.'

She followed him through into the Lounge Bar, they weren't on their own though, the weather was such that the place was full of passengers. In muted voices they told each other what they had been doing over the winter. It was Jan's off season until the middle of

March, but that didn't mean he had been idle. He told her he had spent time with his mother for a large part of January. He mentioned that she lived alone in London, but he was deliberately vague about the details surrounding his family. Then he had returned to the boat yard near Amsterdam for 'The Lady Anne's' annual steam clean as he put it. Katy told him she had been in Holland as well during the winter at her family's home in The Hague, she also skirted around her family's background. She had been in London and then travelled as far as Prague.

'It sounds as if we've been chasing each other around. Perhaps next year we just might manage to bump into each other.'

'Perhaps we will.' she answered brightly. At that point one of the A.Bs came to tell Jan they were ready to lift the gangway and caste off. Katy collected her things and Jan went with her to see her away.

He gave her a gentle peck on the cheek and said, 'See you in Koblenz.'

Katy watched from the quayside as 'The Lady Anne' gently pulled away. Her hair was soaking, the rain now coming down in torrents. He was still where she had parted from him, she waved and he waved back. As she turned away to climb back on the coach, she touched her cheek and smiled.

That night Katy had a very disturbed night, her throat felt like razor blades and her bedclothes damp to the touch. Her hair was plastered to her skull and she groaned as she got up to look in the mirror. She had bright red patches on both cheeks and a thundering headache. She just made it to the bathroom before she was sick. She knew she wasn't going to Koblenz. The Hotel Manager called a doctor. He took her temperature and looked down her throat and shook his head. A severe case of tonsillitis was the verdict. He left a prescription for painkillers and told her to stay in bed; he would call again in a couple of days.

The hotel management were not pleased, neither were the agency in London. They had to scramble a relief guide to meet 'The Lady Anne' in Koblenz. Finding someone with knowledge of classical music to fill Katy's shoes wasn't easy. Things didn't get any better for Katy, in fact they got worse. The doctor became quite concerned, 'If you don't improve by tomorrow, I'm afraid you'll have to go to hospital, those tonsils will need whipping out.' Katy was dismayed, but hospital it was. She was operated on within twenty four hours. It was nearly a month later before she was fit enough to resume her schedule. She had missed the river boat bookings; the next one wasn't until the autumn. Her summer bookings were mainly in London, Paris and Prague.

Jan was only given a couple of hours notification that a relief guide was coming for the opera party. He was just told that Katy was unavailable. He was nonplussed. The relief guide didn't seem any the wiser either. He had only been given the briefest details about the make-up and requirements of the group he was taking responsibility for. When Jan asked about Katy at the London agency, they refused to give out any details about the personnel they retained. It would be a breach of their privacy he was told, all they would tell him was that she was still booked to take the autumn group. Jan was disappointed but he still had a business to run. Time went very quickly, groups of passengers came and went; new faces and familiar faces amongst them. Luggage was lifted on board and lifted off again. The boat needed refuelling, topping up with water and provisioning. Laundry was another constant headache, but it was all in the day's work of a Hotel Boat.

October arrived, the days were shorter but the weather was settled. 'The Lady Anne' was in Cologne. The last set of passengers had just left and the new ones were due to join at around six o'clock that evening. The boat was a hive of activity when one of Jan's staff told him a young woman was on the quay side asking to see him. Jan raced down hoping the young woman had red hair. She had.

Jan took her hand, 'I didn't think I'd see you until tomorrow. How are you? I couldn't find out what had happened to you in Koblenz. The agency would only say you were unavailable.'

'Well, that was true. I'm fine now but minus my tonsils. I know they aren't allowed to give out any personal information about us but I did write to explain via the agency. I take it you didn't get the message?'

'No, I didn't, and I still owe you a coffee.'

She gave a lovely tinkling laugh at that. 'I can't stay and take you up on that right now, I have to get back.'

'I'm not that easily deterred.'

'Good!' she replied, 'I'm going to see a performance of 'Carmen' this evening, but I'll be bringing my lot down here before lunch to-morrow.'

'I hope so. We're due to sail before lunch.'

'It sounds as though that cup of coffee will have to wait a little longer then, doesn't it?'

'We'll be docking in Mainz in the afternoon, how about then?'

'It's a date!' She squeezed his hand and quickly walked away. Jan returned to his boat, he felt as though he was walking on air.

It was quite late when 'The Lady Anne' finally docked in Mainz

203

but Katy was there to meet it. She was wearing a pair of grey lightweight wool slacks, a lilac cashmere polo sweater and a warm winter jacket. Jan was the first one up the gangway when it was secured.

'The coffee is cancelled again I take it?'

Jan laughed, 'I'm afraid so, but I've got a better idea. Your party isn't due to leave until after dinner so why don't you join us?'

'Would that be allowed?'

'Of course it would, I'm the Captain!'

'In that case I'd be delighted Captain, but I'll have to scoot back to my hotel first, I need to change, I can't go to the opera dressed like this. I won't be long.' And within three quarters of an hour she was back.

Jan ushered her onto the boat in front of him and took her to the Lounge Bar. He took her coat. Underneath she was wearing a silk dress with a cowl neckline. It had a white background with lilac and purple swirls on it which complimented the colour of her hair. She looked fabulous. He ordered drinks for them both then whispered something to the barman. He quickly served them then disappeared but was soon back. It was always busy just before dinner in the bar. Most people enjoyed a drink before they sat down to the evening meal. Just before the announcement that dinner was to be served, Jan took her down to the restaurant. He sat her at his table, and Jonathan and the Second Officer joined them. The dinner was excellent and conversation flowed easily. After coffee was served, the announcement was made for the theatre party to gather in the foyer as the coach was waiting for them. Katy reluctantly joined them. She turned to Jan to thank him for a lovely dinner, so much nicer than eating alone in her hotel she told him.

Jan was surprised he hadn't thought of it before, 'In that case why don't you join us again?'

'Really! I would love to, thank you.'

'See you in Strasbourg then.'

She turned and waved. Unfortunately there were only two more opera stops on this trip, but Jan intended to make the most of them. The two of them spent as much time together as they could, but there wasn't much room for privacy on a hotel boat full of passengers and crew. She had her duties to perform and he had his.

This time when they reached Basel, Jan made sure Katy had the agents telephone number and address in Amsterdam, she also gave him a point of contact, at least now they will be able to keep in touch with each other. Jan told her that he would rather not chase her around Europe this winter, he would much rather catch her. Of course his season didn't end until the New Year but he would be in London to see his mother for most of January, then he would be in Amsterdam. Perhaps they could meet up in either or both places.

Katy pulled a wry face, 'I'm going to be in Holland for Christmas and the New Year, and then I'm going on a skiing holiday with my family to Canada. We've had it booked for ages; it's the only time we can all get together.'

Jan's face fell, 'What about February?'

'I'm booked solid, London, Edinburgh, Paris. Then I'm with you in April, a guide's life is a busy one.'

He shrugged, 'Yes, I know. One of my regular guides is retiring at the end of the season. I'm having trouble finding a replacement for the few weeks he fills in for me.'

Katy smiled, 'I'm a guide.'

'But you just told me, you're fully booked.' He looked incredulously at her.

'I'm also self-employed. I have a certain amount of manoeuvrability. I can manage other things besides opera you know, I'm fully qualified. I speak Dutch, English, German and French. If you're interested-----'

He grabbed both her hands and drew them to his lips, 'If I'm interested---I'm in dire need of being guided.' She laughed and tousled his long blond hair. 'You're hired, when can you start?'

Just then the coach driver blew his horn, his passengers were getting impatient. Katy turned round, 'I must go, I'll get in touch with your agent.'

Jan caught her arm, 'You're not going anywhere until I say goodbye.' And he turned her out of sight of the coach and took her in his arms, he looked into those green eyes, he knew he was losing control. She reached up and put her arms around his neck and he kissed her long and deeply.

They didn't manage to bump into each other over the winter months but they kept in touch. Katy signed a contract with Jan's agents in Amsterdam. She was booked to do three weeks in total, two in the spring and one in the autumn. She couldn't manage more due to other commitments, but Jan was determined she would be with him permanently next season, and unknown to him, so was she.

He looked forward eagerly to the start in the New Year. Jan had allocated a cabin for Katy as near to his own as he could without raising too many eyebrows but he wasn't fooling any of his staff, especially Jonathan. Katy joined the staff on 'The Lady Anne' in late April. Jan raised his eyebrows when he saw the amount of luggage she had with her.

'I still have operas to attend.' she said in self defence. Katy had prepared well for the journey on the river. Her memory was excellent and her local knowledge couldn't be faulted. Her dialogues to the passengers were interesting and informative. Jan was never far away from her. Even the passengers noticed the glances they kept exchanging and the quick unnecessary touches as they passed each other. They spent as much time together as possible, mostly off the boat, if they could manage it. Her first two weeks sped by in a flash and they said a long and lingering goodbye.

'See you in October,' said Katy in a husky voice.

'You've got our itinerary, if you're within a hundred miles of us, I want to know and I want to see you. No excuses, you haven't got any tonsils to lose now.' he watched her go with a heavy heart.

Jan's summer season had been one of his most successful yet, he had paid back the start up loans made by his original officers. Some had moved on but most were still with him. He had even made inroads into the bank loan, another couple of seasons like this and 'The Lady Anne' would be his.

Katy had rejoined a couple of days ago, his feelings for her hadn't waned, in fact they had intensified. As far as she was concerned absence had also made the heart grow fonder. Jan had asked if she would consider being his permanent guide. Light heartedly, she told him most of her next season was free and she would consider it. He was delighted; he was looking forward to his next season more than ever now.

At the end of the voyage the changeover was in Cologne, they had to clear, clean and re-provision the boat before the new influx of passengers arrived in the evening. Katy helped, working alongside Jan. She was staying until the new people arrived, but after dinner, she was catching a train to Mannheim. When the coaches arrived Katy disappeared into her cabin. She had to pack for her journey. She heard all the noise of the new arrivals but was ready to join them when dinner was called. Most people were already seated and serving was well underway when she joined Jan and Jonathan at his table. The food, as she had come to expect, was delicious. People were starting to return to their cabins to claim their baggage and to unpack as their table still lingered over their coffee.

A male passenger suddenly stopped at Katy's side, he said in a booming voice, 'Katya, I thought it was you, there's no mistaking that hair of yours.' He spoke in Dutch, 'I was with your uncle just a couple of weeks ago, he told me you'd had a wonderful trip to Canada. What are you doing here?'

She replied in Dutch, 'I was the guide here until a few hours ago but unfortunately I'm leaving this trip. Someone else will be looking after you.'

'Ah! What a shame! Give my regards to your Uncle Peter when you see him.'

'I will.' she said raising her eyebrows to the others.

Jan was looking at her strangely, he also spoke in Dutch, 'That man called you Katya.'

'Yes.' she replied, 'that's my given name, I only anglicized it for the English passengers, my real name is Katya Nowak, I changed it to Katy Novak. My mother was Polish you see, we lived in Bremen, but she died when I was very young. I was brought up in The Hague by my aunt and uncle.'

'I thought you were Dutch,' there was a long pause before he asked quietly, 'what was your mother's name?'

Katya smiled, seeing her mother's face from the photograph floating in front of her eyes, 'Her name was Irena, I don't really remember her but I have her photograph, I always carry it with me.'

'What about your father?'

'Oh, I'm probably an orphan. I don't know who my father was. My aunt told me he was an Officer in the army. My only memories though are of an English man who used to come to see me. My mother worked for him. He gave me a doll for my birthday, I call her Lucy, she comes everywhere with me as well.'

Jan's face had drained of all colour. In front of him was the photograph of his father with a little red haired girl on his knee, she was holding a doll in her hand. He remembered vividly the inscription on the back of the photo, Katya and Irena, 4th birthday. He suddenly got up and left the table. Everyone looked at his retreating figure, astonished at his abrupt exit. Jonathan looked in surprise at Katya, he of course, hadn't understood their conversation. He didn't speak Dutch, and it wasn't like Jan to speak in Dutch in front of him. Jonathan knew he had done it on purpose to exclude him from the conversation. Jonathan asked if Katy would excuse him, he went straight to Jan's cabin. The door was closed but Jonathan didn't let that stop him, he went straight in. Jan was standing by the window, his back to him. Before Jonathan could open his mouth Jan barked, 'Leave it Jonathan.'

Jonathan slowly closed the door behind him as he left.

Katya was waiting outside, her face white with shock. 'What's happening Jonathan? What did I do? I don't understand.'

'Neither do I Katy.' He put his arm around her trembling

shoulders and took her back to her cabin. 'What did you say to him?'

'Only that I was an orphan.' She had tears in her eyes as she added, 'and probably a bastard.' The dam burst.

Jonathan cradled her head on his shoulder, 'I've known him since school, that wouldn't upset him. It must have been something else.'

She looked up into his face, misery etched in every one of her features. 'There was nothing else, I don't know anything else.' He sat with her holding her hand.

'What time does your train leave Katy?'

She looked at her watch, 'In half an hour, I'd better go.'

'I'll take you.' he said, 'wait here a moment. I'll get someone to collect your luggage.'

Jonathan went straight back to Jan's cabin, the door was locked, but as Jonathan was the Chief Officer he had a master key. He didn't hesitate. He unlocked the door and walked in. Jan was still standing where he had left him. 'Katy's leaving now,' he told him. There was no response. 'She's very upset.' he added forcefully.

'I told you to leave it Jonathan.'

'What's wrong?' he asked in exasperation.

'It's none of your business, now leave it!'

After a lengthy pause, Jonathan said, 'I don't know about Katy being a bastard, you're the one who's behaving like one.'

Jan swung round, his fists clenched, the look on his face made Jonathan gasp. Jan struggled for composure and turned back towards the window. Jonathan left quietly. He took a very subdued Katy to the station, he touched her tear stained face as she got into her carriage and watched as the train pulled away.

For the following few days of the next trip, Jonathan was acting Captain. Jan didn't appear in the restaurant, he had his meals in his cabin. When he eventually emerged his face was strained. His crew gave him a wide berth. Jonathan was very worried. On one occasion, when discussing a mistake made by the guide, Jonathan, without thinking, mentioned Katy's name. Jan immediately stiffened and turned away.

'I wish you'd tell me what's wrong, we've been friends since we were children.'

Jan's shoulders heaved, 'I think I've made love to my sister.'

'What! What are you talking about? You haven't got a sister.'

'I'm talking about Katya, I think she's my sister.'

'Oh my God! You can't be serious!' Jonathan couldn't take this in, but he knew quite a lot about Jan's father. He knew about his illicit affairs. He knew about his criminal activities. He had to concede, it was credible. He put his hand on Jan's shoulder, but didn't utter another word.

'Don't you understand Jonathan. I love her. I've loved her in the carnal sense, and what's worse is I still love her and I still want her.'

Jonathan bowed his head. He didn't know what to say.

CHAPTER 23

Within months of being sentenced Douglas had been transferred to an open prison, he wasn't considered to be a risk to society, well, perhaps only to high society. He had very few visitors this time. Samantha came very occasionally, she was now Lady Corby. When she came she always wore flat shoes, a head scarf and dark glasses. She was still fond of Douglas.

Greta didn't visit at all. Dieter came regularly once a month. As before, Douglas made himself indispensible to the more vulnerable prisoners. The warders, on the whole, quite liked him. He entertained them with stories of his scams and about the people who had fallen for them. They often wondered about Douglas's relationship with his German visitor, it was generally known he was of the old German aristocracy but Douglas never ever talked about him.

Douglas had kept his nose clean in prison and was soon to be considered for parole. He knew how to play the game. He had to convince the parole board that he was a reformed character and show the right amount of remorse for his previous unacceptable behaviour. Attitudes in society had changed since his first incarceration. There were a lot more reformers and bleeding hearts about now, Douglas didn't think he would have any trouble with them. It was his pending parole he was discussing with Dieter.

'Where are you going to go Douglas? Where will you live?'

Douglas was suddenly affected by a paroxysm of coughing; it was happening more and more frequently these days. He had always suffered from what he called his 'morning spasm'. He took out a cigarette and lit up, dragging the smoke deep into his lungs.

'It's about time you gave up that bad habit Douglas, Christian made me stop years ago.'

'It's obvious you haven't spent much time behind bars Dieter, there's not much else to do in here.' Dieter immediately felt guilty. Douglas smiled, he knew he would, but that hadn't really been his intention. He added softly, 'It wouldn't have helped if we'd both been banged up Dieter. At least you had the opportunity to go straight. I never would have made it. There was always too much excitement in getting one over on the establishment. I could never have resisted the temptation. And as for where I'm going to go, well, my options are limited. I can't go to Sam's place and I haven't seen Greta in years. Mind you, I've got quite a fan mail out there, one or two proposals of marriage from some very sad women. But I expect the parole board will dictate where I live for a little while. I wonder if my Parole Officer will be a man or a woman.'

'Be serious Douglas!'

'I am serious.' And he was overcome by another bout of coughing.

'What about your apartment in Amsterdam, I can arrange for it to be free for you.'

'The board won't let me travel abroad, at least not for the moment, but it's a thought.' he paused, 'I need money Dieter, they took everything.'

'What about selling the apartment then, I can do that for you.'

'I mean real money, I've never lived without it and I don't want to start now!'

'What can I do to help? How much do you need?'

'I don't need your money Dieter, I need my own, I've got plenty of it in Zurich remember. I suppose the diamond account was cleaned out?'

'Long ago. You know Leonard died?'

'No, I didn't, they don't post death lists in here.' He took another drag on his cigarette, 'Is this your way of telling me his gambling account numbers died with him?'

'Leonard was a wily old bird, his solicitors sent me a copy of the New Testament, apparently it was a stipulation in his will.' He paused before asking, 'Did you know what Leonard did with his share of our profits?'

'No! but your going to tell me.'

Dieter smiled, 'All his money went to Jewish charities, every penny.'

Douglas absorbed this information, and then laughed out loud, which brought on another bout of coughing. 'You mean to tell me I was risking my neck for charity!'

'I'm afraid so.' Dieter looked into Douglas's face before he added, 'I expect that's where he would like his share of the Zurich money to go.'

'You know the numbers!'

'I don't know that for sure, Leonard could be having a joke from beyond the grave. He'd torn out two pages and put one in the front of the book and one in the back. There are only four numbers in each block, there are two sides to each page; did he mean the front of the first page and the reverse of the second? I don't know. Anyway it's academic, your forgetting about Wim Henke, he's dead too.'

'But his son isn't.'

'You're grasping at straws Douglas.'

'Straws are all I have left.'

Douglas was granted parole, and he was right. The parole board dictated where he had to live, at least for the first few weeks anyway. To Douglas's disgust, his parole officer was a man, no point in mounting a charm offensive there.

Dieter met him at the gates and as before he had clothes for him. They went to a nearby pub for lunch, no swanky night out this time. Douglas had to abide by a curfew. Dieter pressed some money into Douglas's hand, but he refused. Dieter persisted, 'Think of it as cans of food in a cupboard.' A slow smile spread over Douglas's face, the two men embraced, each remembering the past.

Douglas gained the trust of his parole officer who turned in good reports about his progress. After a few weeks the restrictions were lifted. Douglas also gained his support in getting his passport back. He told him if he could get to Amsterdam he could get work there as a translator and he had somewhere lined up to live. Dieter was as good as his word, the Amsterdam apartment was ready for him to move into. Douglas wasn't as good as his word though; he had no intentions of getting work as a translator. He was intent on finding Wim Henke's son, Roger. It didn't take him long; Douglas knew all the right places to look. Roger Henke was in a worse condition than Douglas, he was bloated and an alcoholic. Douglas soon got the story of 'The Lady Anne' out of him, so there was no hope of any money from that quarter. Lost in a game of cards, typical! Douglas questioned him closely about his father.

Drunk as Roger Henke was, he detected an ulterior motive behind the questions. 'Why all this interest in my Dad?' and he asked with sudden insight, 'are you after his money?' So, thought Douglas, he does know something. Douglas was going to have to become his confidant and friend, quite a challenge.

He spent days softening up Henke, but Douglas had been around much harder men then Henke, he knew their weak spots, and with Henke it was drink and cards and lack of money. Douglas became the crutch for Henke to lean on, everything would be fine if only they could lay there hands on some easy money.

One night when Roger was in his cups and in a maudlin mood, he confessed to Douglas that his father was always talking about a stash of money in Zurich. He had been frustrated because for some reason, he couldn't get his hands on it.

'What do you mean?' asked Douglas, pretending to be just as drunk as Henke.

'It was something to do with numbers, something to do with a

212

German Count, I can't really remember.'

'Shame,' commiserated Douglas, 'we could do with some of that money now.'

Henke suddenly sobered up, 'What do you mean, we? That's my old man's money and he would have intended it for me.'

'You'd need help to get it though, wouldn't you?' Douglas thought he had better tread carefully here, the last thing he needed was to antagonize Henke.

Henke subsided again, 'Yeah, I suppose I would, I've only got one set of the numbers.' Douglas couldn't believe his luck, all he had to do now was wheedle the numbers out of Henke. Henke suddenly screwed up his eyes, 'You know something about this don't you? No-one's talked about that money in years. Everyone thought it was a figment of my old man's imagination.'

'No, I don't, only what you've told me.' protested Douglas.

'I've seen you somewhere before. I'm going home.' And he got up and lurched out into the street.

'Bugger!' said Douglas under his breath. He had underestimated Henke, underneath the drunkenness and general debauchery, there remained a certain amount of animal cunning. Douglas decided to go back to his apartment and get cleaned up. He needed a clear head to think through his options. Between them, Dieter and he had three sets of numbers, providing of course that Leonard wasn't playing some massive practical joke on them. Roger Henke had the other set. He didn't want to tip his hand to Henke.

Douglas didn't see Henke for days; he wasn't to be found in any of his usual haunts. Then, to his surprise, Henke turned up on his doorstep. 'I knew I'd seen you before, you ran the casino on 'The Lady Anne' with that German bloke.' Douglas stared in dismay at Henke. 'You thought you could get the numbers out of me just like that.' And he snapped his fingers in Douglas's face. 'Think again!'

'Alright, alright, you're right.' There was nothing to be gained by subterfuge now. 'But you still need my help. You'd better come in.' Henke waddled in and sat down. 'Drink?'

'No!'

Douglas poured one for himself anyway, he noticed Henke looking longingly at it. It could still be a weapon thought Douglas. 'So, what's on your mind?'

'What do you mean, what's on my mind?'

'You turned up on my doorstep remember, what's on your mind?'

'The money's on my mind you creep.' he sneered.

'What do you suggest?'

'That we go and get it. What do you suggest?'

'What about the numbers?'

'What about them, I've got one set, you must have got the other three lots. Otherwise, why have you tracked me down?' He looked longingly at Douglas's drink but he didn't ask for one, 'Don't try and pull the wool over my eyes Major Coulter, my old man was obsessed with trying to track down those numbers. He knew you were in jail and he knew the Jew was in Israel. He couldn't put the squeeze on the German, he was too high profile, but if he hadn't been killed, he would have found a way though believe me.'

'Come back tomorrow, I've got a phone call to make. We'll talk then.'

'O.K. but no funny business mind, I won't have the numbers on me.'

'I didn't think you would.' mumbled Douglas. Henke got up and left. Douglas gave him a few minutes start, then he followed him. Henke went straight into the first bar he came to.

Douglas rang Dieter and told him everything that had transpired.

'I don't like it Douglas.'

'I know Dieter, but I need that money. I spent years in jail for that money.'

There was a silence at the other end of the line, 'I know Douglas, why don't you let me give you some, I can afford it.'

'No Dieter, that's my money, I earned, we earned it, the three of us, Henke muscled in remember.'

'Alright, I understand that you want to go and get it, but why don't I just give you the two sets of numbers I have, then you and Henke can access the account.'

'No Dieter, I don't trust Henke, I need insurance and so do you. He knows all about you. Can you get down here by tomorrow morning?'

'Yes, I suppose so, Christian is more than capable of running things here. We've no major tournaments on at the moment.'

Dieter arrived the next morning, they worked out their strategy. They would all make their separate ways to Zurich and meet outside the bank. Henke couldn't track both of them.

'But we could track him,' said Douglas.

'Don't even think about it Douglas, let's just get this over with. I want you to agree on one thing though. Leonard's share goes to his charities.'

'I agree, the old curmudgeon, he's entitled to do what he wants with his own share.' Douglas made them some coffee, 'When we've settled matters with Henke this evening, how about a night out on the town for old-time's sake?'

Dieter laughed, 'You'll never change Douglas, yes let's.' A night out with Douglas was always fun.

Arrangements were made with Henke to meet in Zurich the following week. He made no further stipulations, his voice was slurred and he smelt of drink. But Douglas knew drunks, he knew he wouldn't forget.

The two of them then set out on their own night of pleasure. They returned to Douglas's apartment in the early hours, arms round each other singing German army songs. Next morning Dieter lay in bed, nursing another headache. He could hear Douglas in the kitchen coughing away. Next moment Douglas came in with freshly brewed coffee. Dieter hoisted himself up in bed, 'That's the last time I'm going out with you, I can't take it anymore.'

'You say that every time you go out with me.'

'I know, but this time I mean it.'

'You always say that as well.'

'I know, but this time I mean it.'

'Oh no you don't you old grump!'

They both laughed, Douglas handed Dieter his coffee. 'Do you need a pick-me-up?'

'No, the last time you gave me one, you nearly poisoned me.'

'It worked though didn't it?'

'Funnily enough, it did. But seriously I have to get back to Bremen. Why don't you come with me?'

'No, I'll see you in Zurich next week, but after that, when I'm a wealthy man, I'll come.'

The following week Douglas made his way to Zurich by train. He didn't know how the others were getting there. The arrangement was that they were to meet outside the bank at twelve o'clock. It was a miserable day, the rain was sheeting down. Douglas was wearing a brown trilby and a sleuth type raincoat. He arrived with five minutes to spare. He looked around, he couldn't see Dieter but he spotted Henke. They nodded to each other and started to make their way towards the bank's entrance.

'Where's your buddy?' asked Henke, 'he'd better turn up.'

'He'll be here, in fact there he is.' Douglas had seen Dieter getting off a tram on the other side of the road. Dieter raised his hand and started across towards them. Next moment, out of no-where, came a terrific roar of an engine and a high powered motorbike came round

215

the corner and skidded out of control on the wet cobbles in a shower of sparks. The rider parted company with his bike and slid across the cobbles. The bike was on its side in the road, the engine still going at full throttle.

Everything then, seemed to Douglas, to go into slow motion. Someone screamed. The rider picked himself up and went to retrieve his bike. He manhandled it upright and looked down on the road. His face seen through the visor, registered the shock he obviously felt. He got straight back on his bike and rode off leaving the prostrate figure of a man lying in the road. Douglas set off at a run; it seemed to take him hours to get there. He knelt down next to Dieter whose head was turned on one side, his eyes closed. Douglas could hear himself shouting Dieter's name. Dieter's hand fluttered, Douglas grabbed hold of it. Dieter turned his head towards Douglas, his eyes opened. They were bright blue and showed surprise. His other hand grabbed Douglas's shoulder, Douglas lifted his head. Dieter smiled and looked straight into his eyes, a flow of blood trickled out of the corner of his mouth. Then Dieter's eyes focused just to the left over Douglas's shoulder, he very faintly said something. Then the eyes glazed over and Douglas felt the body go limp. Douglas's tears were streaming onto Dieter's face, diluting the flow of blood from his mouth.

Henke was next to him, shaking him, 'What did he say? Did he give you the numbers?' Douglas couldn't at first make out what he meant. Henke kept repeating it, 'did he give you the numbers?' Henke bent down to get closer to Dieter.

Douglas suddenly grabbed him, 'Don't you touch him. Don't you dare touch him.' he shouted. Other people were starting to gather around them. Douglas tenderly pulled Dieter towards him and cradled him in his arms. Henke slowly sidled away, a policeman was asking for witnesses to the hit and run. Douglas had his head buried in Dieter's chest sobbing. He had heard what Dieter had said, just the one word. 'Irena.'

Back in Amsterdam Douglas had hit the bottle in a big way. He had given a fictitious name to the police in Zurich. He reasoned all he could do now was to try and protect Dieter's reputation. The police had found Dieter's car parked streets away. It had been established beyond doubt, that moments before the accident, he had alighted from a tram. No-one from his family had a clue why he was in Zurich, he hadn't told anyone he was going there. They understood he had gone to look at some horses. It was a complete mystery. It was also a mystery why he was carrying a copy of the New Testament, he wasn't a particularly religious man.

Dieter's body had been taken back to Bremen. He was to be buried next to his parents on the family estate. It was to be a private family funeral with only the closest family and friends in attendance, the Coulter family among them. Later in the year, there would be a memorial service. Douglas sobered up for the funeral. Greta was also among the mourners but Jan had sent his condolences and his apologies. He couldn't get away in time, he was in Basel.

Greta hadn't seen Douglas for many years and she was quite disturbed at his appearance. He looked gaunt in the face, his features had a chiselled look about them but the remnants of the handsome face were still there to be discerned. He had also lost a lot of weight. He had a persistent cough, not helped by the fact that he appeared to be chain smoking.

The ceremony itself was quite brief but dignified. Christian seemed to be the most affected. Christa conducted herself in a very controlled manner. It was difficult to judge what people were thinking or feeling. The manner of Dieter's death was such a shock to them all. After the ceremony Christa asked Douglas if she could have a word with him. Douglas was nervous, but agreed.

She asked him outright, 'Do you know why Dieter was in Zurich?'

Douglas had anticipated these questions and had his answers ready, 'No, I don't.'

'So it had nothing to do with you?'

'No.'

She paused, struggling for words, 'Was he seeing a woman?' she asked quietly, she couldn't pluck up the courage to look Douglas in the face, frightened about what she might see there.

'No Christa, he wasn't. What makes you think that?'

She looked up then, her eyes slightly moist, 'Because after

Christian was born, Dieter never touched me again.' She saw the sympathy in Douglas's eyes and became all businesslike again. 'So you have no idea why he was there?'

'Perhaps he needed to raise some money? Zurich is the banking capital of Switzerland after all.'

'But why?'

'I don't know, you know Dieter, he was very proud, if something had gone wrong, he wouldn't want to burden you with it. Perhaps he'd seen a horse he wanted to buy. There could be any number of reasons.'

She sighed, 'You're right, I don't suppose we'll ever know.'

When she had gone Douglas breathed deeply with relief. Strangely he felt some sympathy for Christa. She was such a formidable, severe woman, she would frighten any man away, but Dieter had stayed with her, often escaping, but he had stayed.

However Douglas's trials weren't over by any means. Later in the day Christian collared him, 'You know father left a will don't you?'

'Well, I didn't know, but that's not surprising is it? Dieter was a wealthy man! Naturally he would want to leave his affairs in order.'

'The fact that he left a will is not surprising I grant you, but what's in it, is.'

Douglas became very wary, 'The contents of your father's will, is a matter for the family Christian. It's nothing to do with me.'

'The way he made his money seems very much to do with you.'

Douglas was alarmed, 'What do you mean?'

'Oh, it might have been legal on paper, but knowing your history Douglas, I doubt in fact that it was.' Douglas kept quiet, Dieter wouldn't have been stupid enough to put anything incriminating in writing. 'How can anyone make that much money from honest gambling?'

'Luck!' said Douglas hopefully.

'Cheating!' Christian shot back.

'Well, maybe, just a little.'

'Maybe quite a lot!'

'Well, I suppose you had to be there, they were strange times.'

'That's not the only shock Douglas. Mother isn't aware of this yet, but I bet you are.'

'Oh no,' groaned Douglas, 'what now.'

'Dad has left quite a substantial sum of money to a young lady called Katya Nowak, he had also set up a trust in her name a few years ago for her education.'

'Did he?' said Douglas innocently.

'Stop the pretence Douglas, I know who she is and so do you.'

218

Douglas gave in with good grace, 'Yes, I know.'

'I'm absolutely furious with him, and with you Douglas. You knew all about it and kept it quiet all this time.'

Douglas shot back, 'And what would you have had me do Christian, sneak round to your mother and tell her all about it. That would have made her very happy I'm sure.' Douglas was angry now, 'Dieter was my best friend, we looked out for each other, we trusted each other. And yes, we made a lot of money in some shady deals, but as I said, you had to be there.' Surprisingly Christian started to laugh. Douglas looked up, 'That's exactly what Dieter would have done.' he said.

'I know, I could hear him.'

'At least Dieter put his share to good use, I spent mine,' Douglas smiled, 'but I thoroughly enjoyed it. I miss him Christian.'

'So do I Douglas, so do I.'

Douglas returned to Amsterdam, he started drinking again and the cough got worse. He thought a great deal about the past, but he knew if he had his time again, he wouldn't do anything any differently. He was becoming desperately short of money. Debt collectors were starting to harass him. The Zurich account was now a closed book, his legendary charm was fading. He remembered Henke's story about 'The Lady Anne'. He reasoned he should be due a share of her value. He had been surprised to learn that his own son was the new owner. He felt a slight resentment stirring towards Jan, not helped by the amount of alcohol that was coursing around his system. He had paid good money for his education. He was the one who had made it possible for Jan to succeed. And his reward? Jan had turned his back on him. He completely blanked the fact that he was the one who had refused to see his son. The more he drank, the more the resentment grew. Well, he could afford to let his father have some of that investment back now. Douglas knew he would never ask Jan for money, but he could take it and he knew how.

Jan had been shocked to read about Dieter's death which was widely reported in the Swiss papers. In one of the local papers, buried in the small print, was a report about a grief stricken witness who had given a false name. There was no mention of it in the national press. Jan had a good idea who this witness might be.

Jan genuinely had been unable to get to the funeral. Jonathan's parents were doing a trip with them and he had given Jonathan a couple of days off. He was accompanying them on a field trip to the Alps and that left Jan as the only certificated Officer on the boat, he had to stay.

He had read there was going to be a memorial service later in the year; he would make sure he went to that to pay his respects. He had fond memories of Uncle Dieter from when he was a boy. He knew he had been impetuous in blaming Dieter for his mother's distress. He deeply regretted it now. Dieter had persevered in corresponding with him but he had been too stubborn and too proud to reply.

He had a long letter from Christian in his hand right now: he had read it and reread it. In it Christian talked a lot about the past, about the good times they had had in the summer holidays in Bremen. He also told Jan about the shock he felt at discovering his father's criminal past. He and Douglas had been involved in all sorts of shady financial deals after the war. Gambling and smuggling being only two of them. He wrote it was a wonder his father had escaped jail. He suspected that Douglas had shielded his father and taken the blame upon himself. When Douglas was caught he had never pointed the finger at Dieter, but there was no doubt that he had been deeply involved. The other shock the family had to come to terms with was that Dieter had had a brief affair which had resulted in Christian finding out that he had a half sibling. His mother, he wrote, was still coming to terms with it so he had decided not to investigate the situation at the moment, perhaps in the future when his mother was calmer. He ended his letter though by saying that despite his faults, he loved his father and the last line read 'if I could have chosen who was to be my dad, I would have chosen him.' Jan was deeply affected by this letter and found he had a lot of soul searching to do. He also wondered how many other half siblings were waiting to be discovered. The difference between Christian and himself was that he was in love with his half sister.

It was time to take 'The Lady Anne' back to her winter quarters, Jan had had another good year financially, but on the emotional front it had been turbulent in the extreme. 'The Lady Anne' needed some expensive refitting this time. Jan had put funds aside in the bank in anticipation, so he wasn't too worried about the cost of it. He ordered the work to be done and left for London.

His mother was quite distressed at the news from Bremen. She was deeply upset about Dieter's death, but who would have thought that Dieter had a love child. 'If it had been your father I would have been half expecting it,' she said, 'it wouldn't have been quite the shock for me that it has been for Christa.'

Jan hoped his mother wouldn't take it into her head to investigate the secret compartment behind her wardrobe. 'How was dad?' asked Jan.

Greta was surprised at the question, Jan usually skirted around anything to do with his father. 'I'm sorry to say he doesn't look at all well. He's been neglecting himself, probably drinking too much and definitely smoking too much.'

'Where is he now? Dieter's death must have hit him hard.'

'I think he's living in our old apartment in Amsterdam, but I'm not sure. You know your father, he could be up to anything. But there's one thing for sure, what ever it is, it won't be legal!'

A few days later Jan had an urgent phone call from the yard where 'The Lady Anne' was undergoing repairs. He was told all work on her had been stopped.

'Why?' he asked, 'what's the problem?'

'The bank is the problem, you didn't tell us you had taken out another mortgage on her. The bank is threatening to foreclose.'

'What!' shouted Jan, 'there has to be some mistake. I haven't taken out a mortgage.'

'Well,' said the owner of the yard, 'I suggest you get here just as soon as you can and sort this little lot out because they say you have.'

Jan was on the first available flight out. The boatyard owner was sympathetic but said he had been instructed by the bank not to do any further work on the boat as the owner was in arrears with his payments. Jan made an urgent appointment with the manager for the following day. He had a sleepless night. He couldn't understand what was going on.

When he arrived at the bank, he was shown straight through to the manager's office. The manager had a file of papers in front of him. He was quite affable, 'Please sit down Captain Coulter, I'm sure we can sort this unpleasant business out.'

Jan's pulse was racing, 'What's all this nonsense about a new mortgage, I haven't requested one, I don't understand.'

The manager looked slightly alarmed, 'It was all done by post Captain Coulter. I assure you everything is in order. We were happy to grant it because of your past history. Previously you had always made the payments on the due date, but on this occasion, the account is in default.'

'I repeat, I have not applied for a new mortgage.'

The manager looked at him severely over his glasses. He shuffled the papers in front of him. 'This is the application for the loan,' he said, pulling out a folder. He opened it, 'and this is your signature, here and here and here.' He pointed to the appropriate places and turned the folder around for Jan to see. Jan looked at the signatures in disbelief. It was indeed his name and they looked for all-the-world like his signature. He pulled the papers closer and studied them closely.

221

'I've never seen this document before and I certainly haven't signed them.'

'Are you telling me that these are not your signatures?'

'Yes, that's just what I'm telling you.'

'But Captain Coulter, we have your original mortgage papers here.' The manager drew out another file, 'look at the comparison, they are the same.'

Jan studied them both, 'They look the same I agree, but what I'm telling you is that I signed that one, the original, but I didn't sign that one.'

'Then who did Captain Coulter? Tell me that.'

A horrible thought had just occurred to Jan. 'I can't tell you that because I don't know, but what I can tell you is that these signatures are forgeries, I did not sign them.' The bank manager was exasperated. He looked at the signatures again.

Jan asked, 'You said this mortgage was done by post. Tell me, did you ever speak to me about it on the telephone.'

'No, there was no need. Everything was in order, the application filled out correctly.'

'Where did you send the money?'

'To your bank in Amsterdam, your personal account, we followed your instructions to the letter.' The manager sat back in his chair, 'Captain Coulter, these are very serious allegations you're making. We have a department that investigates such matters, I intend calling them in. Do you have any objections to that course of action being taken?'

'No, the sooner the better, my boat needs repairs before her next voyage and---'

'Captain Coulter, your boat isn't going anywhere until this matter is sorted out.' The manager got up and showed Jan to the door, his parting words were, 'We'll be in touch.'

Jan went back to his hotel room. He sat on his bed, head bowed, he ran his hands through his hair. He hoped against hope that his suspicions were unfounded, but he had a good idea who was responsible for this fraud. He certainly possessed the expertise to pull it off. But even now, Jan couldn't believe that he would actually stoop so low as to do it. He made up his mind. There was only one way to find out for sure, he would have to beard the lion in his den. He set off for his father's apartment.

Jan got there in the middle of the afternoon. He hesitated outside the door. He noticed the paint was peeling and the place had a neglected feel about it. He plucked up his courage, this had to be done.

He rang the bell. There was no sign of any movement inside. He rang it again, still nothing. It had rung; he had heard the echo inside the hallway. He tried knocking, there was still no response. He tried again, louder this time. He was just about to turn away in despair when a neighbour opened a window. He shouted down, 'If you're looking for Major Coulter he's not in, and I'm fed up of you lot calling, if you come again I'll call the police.'

'I'm his son.' Jan shouted back.

'Well, in that case, I'm surprised you don't know where he is. The poor bugger collapsed on his doorstep last week. He's in the General Hospital.' and the window was banged closed.

Jan walked slowly away, Oh Christ, he thought, his next thought was that he had better ring his mother and tell her. He quickened his pace and went straight back to the hotel. His first phone call was to the hospital, he told them he was Douglas Coulter's son but they wouldn't tell him anything other than that he was poorly but comfortable. The next of kin according to their records was a Greta Coulter, they had been trying to contact her.

'That's my mother,' he told them,' I'll get in touch with her.'

His mother didn't sound too surprised when he told her Douglas was in hospital, 'He looked ill at Dieter's funeral, I know it hit him hard.' She told Jan she would come straight over. Could he pick her up at the airport? Fortunately she still had a key for the Amsterdam apartment so they could stay there until they discovered what was happening. Jan tried to put his other worries behind him whilst they concentrated on the current crisis, but his mother insisted that he told her why work had stopped on 'The Lady Anne'. The whole sorry story came tumbling out. 'You suspect your father of this don't you?'

'Yes mother, I'm afraid I do.'

She sighed, 'Well, I can't tell you that he's not capable of it, because I'm afraid he is. I know this is hard on you son, but if he is behind this, I don't want you to bring fraud charges against him. I don't want your father to die behind bars.' Jan said nothing. His feelings were in complete turmoil. 'You can take me to the hospital this afternoon Jan, but I'll go and see him on my own.'

When Greta came out of the hospital she was grim faced. She tried to put on a light hearted tone, 'Well, he looks better than the last time I saw him. They've tidied him up and he's eating well.'

'What's the matter with him mother?'

'They're still doing tests, perhaps we'll know more in a day or two.' She looked steadfastly at her son, 'He asked to see you Jan. I think he has things he wants to say to you.'

He groaned, 'I don't know whether I can face him right now.'

'Best to get it over with don't you think, he is your father!'

'Did he do it?'

She nodded. Jan sat there for ages. Greta put her hand on his knee and squeezed. 'For me?'

He closed his eyes for a minute, took a deep breath, then got out of the car and marched up the steps to the hospital. When he got to the ward, a pretty little nurse pointed out his father's bed, it was shrouded in curtains. Jan hadn't seen his father in the flesh since he was thirteen years old, then he was in the prime of his life, confidant, flamboyant and fully aware of his power over women. He didn't know what he expected after all these years, but he certainly didn't expect this frail looking man with sallow cheeks who lay propped up in this hospital bed. He was only just over sixty but looked older. He was bluish around the mouth but the intelligent eyes were still bright and alive absorbing every detail around him. As Jan pulled the curtain aside his father looked towards him. Jan saw the emotions charging across his face, for a moment Jan thought his father was going to cry, but he didn't. Jan walked closer to the bed but he didn't speak, he didn't know what to say. His father was the one who broke the silence, 'It's good to see you boy, I wasn't sure you would come.' He started coughing but controlled the spasm. Jan looked away, he still couldn't speak. 'I'm sorry son, I was desperate, I was being badgered from all sides.' Jan looked at him, anger welling up inside him, he swallowed to control it. 'Can you save the boat? I haven't spent all of it.'

'I don't know.' That was all Jan could manage, he really wanted to scream at him, to tell him what a selfish old man he was. He stood there clenching and unclenching his hands.

Douglas was watching him all this time, 'Will you forgive me son?'

Jan turned to look at him, 'It's not me you need to forgive you father, you need to forgive yourself.' He turned on his heels and walked out.

In the following few days Jan tried all the avenues he could think of to secure finance to cover the second mortgage. True enough his father hadn't spent all of the money but he had made sufficient inroads into it to make life very difficult for Jan. The bulk of the money had gone in paying off debts Douglas had run up since he had left prison. Douglas had always been a prolific spender, cars, clothes, expensive restaurants, all very necessary to Douglas's lifestyle. Jan hadn't heard from the bank, he didn't know what stage or conclusions the 'in house' investigation had reached if any, but he knew he wouldn't go ahead and bring fraud charges against his father.

CHAPTER 25

Dieter's memorial service was being held in Bremen the following week. Jan was to attend with his mother, his father was too ill to go. Most of the German show jumping world would be there. The service was to be held in the Cathedral and the front rows of pews were reserved for the family. When Jan and Greta arrived the family were already seated. The ushers showed Jan and Greta to their places about half way down the aisle. Christian had been in touch with Jan earlier and asked if he and Greta would go back to the estate after the service was over.

The music chosen for the service were rousing German songs. There were speakers from the Equine community praising Dieter's horsemanship and his ability to pick out the best blood lines. There were jokes wondering if this ability extended to the human species, especially the female variety, which must have made Christa feel most uncomfortable. Obviously Dieter's earlier misdemeanour was not common knowledge. The last speaker was Christian who gave a most moving speech. He glossed over Dieter's activities just after the war years, but praised his father's dedication to restoring the family estates. He was one of the best show jumping trainers in the business and Christian himself owed his success to his father's ability and to the fact that Dieter got him out of bed very early each morning which caused a ripple of laughter. Finally with a catch in his voice, he praised him as a loving and caring parent. Jan thought of his own father laid in a hospital bed in Amsterdam and the difference between the two men. And yet, they had been the best and firmest of friends for just over forty years. Jan couldn't imagine what invisible bonds held the two of them together, but they were very obviously there.

Christian walked his mother down the aisle and out into the cold blustery wind of winter. They got into a black limousine which purred away down the drive. People milled around outside chatting in groups but not for long because it was very cold in the searching wind. Jan didn't feel like going back to the von Rheinharts place, but Christian had been insistent and extracted a firm promise from Jan.

They drove to the estate in almost complete silence, each busy with their recollections of the past. Then his mother suddenly said, 'I want to take Douglas back to London with me Jan.' Jan was flabbergasted, 'The doctors have stabilized his condition but he's in a long decline. The cancer is inoperable and the best that can be done for him is to make his last months comfortable and pain free.'

'Are you sure mother? It's a big commitment to make.'

'Whatever you think of your father Jan, he made a big commitment to us. He made sure you had a good education and he made sure I was always financially secure whatever happened to him. And there's also one other very important thing Jan, he's my husband!' Jan quickly looked across at his mother, her face was set. He put his hand over hers and squeezed it. He saw a thin smile flicker across her face.

They reached the von Rheinhart's massive front door. There were only two cars parked outside, the black limousine and a red Opel. The door opened as if by magic and the maid took their coats. To Greta she said, 'Madame is waiting for you in her drawing room, she asks if you will take tea with her?' To Jan she said, 'Master Christian is in the library and he would like you to join him there.'

Jan made his way to the library, the door was slightly ajar and Jan could hear muted voices. One was Christian's, the other, belonged to a woman. Jan pushed the door open. Christian was standing by the fire with his arm around the shoulders of a young woman. Jan was struck by how much Christian reminded him of Dieter in his younger days. The same tilt of the head, the same bearing. Christian was as tall as his father and had the same colouring, the almost white crinkly hair and the same searching blue eyes. The young woman was dressed in a sombre but well cut suit in a rich brown and she was still wearing a hat with a low brim. Jan couldn't see her face.

Christian turned to him, 'Jan! I'm so pleased you could make it,' he walked towards him and took his arm. 'There's someone I want you to meet.' He guided Jan towards the fireplace, 'I want you to meet my sister.' The young woman turned slowly towards Jan and at the same time she removed her hat. Cascades of red hair fell onto her shoulders. Jan stopped in his tracks, he grabbed for the back of a chair feeling slightly unsteady. He couldn't believe his eyes; they must be playing a trick on him. A smile slowly spread across the girl's face.

'Katya!'

Christian asked facetiously, 'Do you two know each other?'

'Katya, I don't understand.' Jan looked from one to the other, he was completely bewildered.

'You always try and claim the best for yourself don't you Coulter. Well this time I win, Katya is my sister!'

Jan sat down with a thump.

'I think we'd better get the man a drink, don't you sis?'

When all three were seated with a drink in front of them, Christian filled Jan in about the search he had made for his sister. 'It wasn't too difficult,' he said. 'Dad had left clues. It was easy to trace

227

Katya to her finishing school in Switzerland, and then onto the travel company in London. They were obstructive so I had to use subterfuge. I went through a third party telling them I needed a guide, and look who turned up!' Jan's eyes kept returning to Katya's face. Christian was quite enjoying his friend's embarrassment.

Katya told them both how her Aunt Nina had eventually opened up and told her all she knew. 'I'm not sure I really do remember those early days but Aunt Nina says I used to talk about Uncle Deety. I do remember your father though, I called him Uncle Dougy Doug and he gave me Lucy for my birthday.' Katya shyly stole a look at Christian, 'I don't really feel abandoned by my father. Aunt Nina, I'm sure from the best of intentions, didn't want any communications between us. That's where Uncle Dougy Doug came in, he was the go-between.' She paused in her story and took a sip of her drink, she kept looking from one to the other then continued, 'My aunt hasn't much time for the German race generally, but that's another story. But my father kept tabs on me and we did meet. He came to the school and took us for riding lessons.' She looked to Christian, 'I liked him.' she said simply.

'And I couldn't be happier for you Christian.'

Christian had to laugh at that statement from Jan. Later when Katya was out of hearing Jan asked how Christa was taking it.

'My mother is not quite as forgiving, but she's slowly coming round. After all, it's not Katya's fault. People fall in love don't they Jan?' Jan coloured up immediately and looked away, much to Christian's amusement.

CHAPTER 26

Back in Amsterdam, arrangements for Douglas's repatriation were underway. Jan had put Katya in the picture regarding the situation with 'The Lady Anne.' He told her wryly that he wouldn't be in a position to offer her employment in the coming season after all. But, at some point he was determined to get his boat back. Katya was extremely sympathetic. She knew how much 'The Lady Anne' meant to him and had witnessed the hard work he had put in to make the business the success it had become. She had more sense though than to offer him financial assistance.

Jan had discussed the situation with his mother. He had told her he had no intentions of implicating his father in the fraud. The bank had finally reported its conclusions into its investigations. They admitted that there had been 'some impropriety' in dealing with the mortgage application by them, but they concluded that there was nothing more they could add without concrete proof that fraud had been committed, and as Jan was unable to provide that proof, the foreclosure threat remained unless Jan could redeem the second mortgage or take on the additional payments. The negotiations were at a stalemate.

It was Greta who came up with a partial solution. She was taking Douglas home. She told Jan that there would be no need for her to keep on the apartment in Amsterdam. Perhaps the proceeds from its sale would in some way alleviate Jan's financial problems.

'But mother, won't you need the money yourself? Looking after dad won't come cheaply.'

'I'm fine Jan, I have sufficient for both of us. It was your father who got you into this mess, as I see it, it's simply paying off some of his debts. Believe me Jan, he won't be running up any more!'

For the first time in weeks Jan saw a chink of light, but would the bank go for it? There was only one way to find out. Jan made the appointment to see the bank's senior manager. He was quaking in his shoes as he was shown through to the inner office. To his amazement it was a woman, he hid his surprise well. He most definitely couldn't afford to antagonize anyone at this stage. Then Jan relaxed, he thought of his father, if he had been in his shoes right now, this would be a piece of cake. He smiled, the woman smiled back. She was no pushover though, she had a very keen mind, but it was a good start.

After intensive scrutiny of Jan's financial position and incisive probing into his future prospects, the manager leaned back in her chair. 'Captain Coulter, we're not in the business of wrecking businesses unnecessarily.' Jan closed his eyes waiting for the blow. When he opened them again she was smiling. 'And on this occasion I think your business can be saved. I'm recommending the lifting of the foreclosure notice.' Jan let out his breath with a whoosh. He hadn't even realized he had been holding it. 'There are stringent conditions however.' And she went through each clause of the agreement in great detail. She wouldn't move on until Jan fully understood the implications of what she was telling him. Eventually the document was signed, sealed, and delivered. Jan rushed straight round to the boatyard. He showed them the agreement. It was verified by the manager who had taken the trouble to ring the boatyard beforehand. The repairs could go ahead.

Jan and his mother were at the hospital, the ambulance was standing outside with a nurse in attendance waiting to transfer Douglas to the airport. Jan had had a quick private conversation with his father.

Douglas told him, 'I've lived my life regretting nothing,' he paused, 'perhaps just an odd thing here and there.' He added with a wry smile, he looked into his son's eyes, 'I can't change things now, but I hope everything works out for you son.'

'Strangely enough father, I think they might.'

Jan helped his mother settle Douglas into the back of the ambulance, she turned to Jan and embraced him, 'Don't leave it too long before you come home son.'

He kissed her on the forehead, 'No I won't mother, I promise.' She squeezed his hand and got into the back of the ambulance to join Douglas. The nurse closed the doors and the ambulance drove away. Jan watched it until it disappeared. Darkness was falling quickly and drifts of drizzle were blowing into his face. Jan turned away and made his way down the cold empty street. Pools of water were lying in the road which reflected the sodium lights of the street lamps which were just coming on. The cobbles were wet and slippy and as he walked towards the corner. Jan caught sight of a woman standing under one of the street lamps. She was wrapped up in a long cream coloured military style raincoat with the collar turned up. Her red hair was caught by the breeze. Jan quickened his step.

THE END

www.ingramcontent.com/pod-product-compliance
Lightning Source LLC
Chambersburg PA
CBHW020655030726
47498CB00002B/518